Acclaim for *The Law of Falling Bodies*

I read *The Law of Falling Bodies* late into the night, cover to cover, all the house lights on, the real "unreal" of where this novel took me refusing, still, all these weeks later, to let loose of me. This is a powerful, bracingly gutsy page-turner about war and innocence, and about the ways in which untamable human desires—and their attendant fantasies—render us both vulnerable and sometimes agonizingly alone. The writing is high-wire-Faulkner gone Fargo—and it is as deeply moving as it is disturbing, as daring and captivating as it is humane, and virtually bursting to life on every page. A triumph!
> —Jack Driscoll, author of *The World of a Few Minutes Ago*

Some of Brenna's scenes are as delicately detailed as Monet paintings, others so powerfully sensual you may experience olfactory hallucinations. Early on, one of his characters says, "Everything adds up to one big true." The one big true materializes as Virgil Foggy comes of age in a maelstrom of awakening urges, family brutalities and mysteries, his big brother's gut-wrenching letters from Vietnam, and the rigors of farm life during the sixties.
> —Robert Gover, author of *The One Hundred Dollar Misunderstanding*

The prose is sweet and rich and sounds like life itself. Virgil Foggy and his family are of the earth, human stalks bracing the weather of existence, discovering truths that are at times too much for the heart to bear. The writing is hypnotic narrative magic, Brenna at his best.
> —Greg Herriges, author of *JD: A Memoir of a Time and a Journey*

The Law of Falling Bodies demonstrates what we already knew about its author: Brenna not only entertains and keeps you on the edge of your chair—he is an artist of the highest order.
> —Thomas E. Kennedy, author of *The Copenhagen Quartet*

Duff Brenna's *The Law of Falling Bodies* is an astounding achievement both in language and insight into the medley of human character. What muscle in his prose! Brenna seems to exhale on every page. And yet his characters are never over the top; always unflinchingly believable. This is the kind of novel that has needed to be written, but had to wait until someone with Brenna's inventiveness and power could pull it off. A bravura performance by one of America's best talents.
> —Michael Lee, Literary Editor of the *Cape Cod Voice* and a member of the National Book Critics Circle.

On the spectrum between Faulkner's *As I Lay Dying* and Cormac McCarthy's *The Road* lies Duff Brenna's *The Law of Falling Bodies*. This comic novel uses a deep irony and a fine sense of the grotesque to show the home-front casualties caused when old men send young men off to war. It reminds us that Vietnam wasn't

an anomaly in our nation's history, and it reminds us that recovering from war requires loving the unlovable, doing the unthinkable, and seeing the world with clear and courageous eyes.
—John Rember, author of *Sudden Death, Overtime*

Duff Brenna's *The Law of Falling Bodies* echos with the sensibility of Faulkner. Set in the dirt and guts of contemporary American ruralism, Brenna's descriptive prose is hauntingly organic and gritty. Brenna's ear is so fine-tuned to the smallest details of his characters' lives and chatter, that you begin listening differently to the seemingly insignificant things you too say in your day. Brilliantly, at the edges of his story lurks the political reality of a powerful nation that sacrifices its humans like farm animals. The America in Brenna's fiction is one that urgently needs to be revealed
—David Applefield, author of *On a Flying Fish* and
publisher of the Paris-based literary journal *Frank*

Acclaim for the Work of Duff Brenna

NEW YORK TIMES [Brenna's prose] is "unfaltering, unflinching, piercing."
LOS ANGELES TIMES "Brenna is a master at capturing the helplessness of humans, particularly humans with "tough written all over them."
WALL STREET JOURNAL "Duff Brenna displays a spectacular talent for crafting complex, believable characters."
WASHINGTON POST BOOK WORLD "Crystal-clear writing . . . Brenna sees with an unflinching eye, but also with measures of love."
PUBLISHERS WEEKLY " . . . vivid characters, rich dialogue and spellbinding narrative."
MILWAUKEE JOURNAL SENTINEL "The sheer energy and humanity of [his story] leaves the reader eagerly awaiting Brenna's next act."
CHARLESTON POST & COURIER "… funny, disgusting, poignant, … Duff Brenna has done it again."
SAN DIEGO UNION "Finely crafted prose coupled with a powerful story makes this beautiful book a page turner."
AUSTIN AMERICAN-STATESMAN "… will fascinate and surprise but also will resonate with its readers' most basic desires."
WEST COAST REVIEW OF BOOKS "Brenna's prose, polished in its sophisticated simplicity, provides poignant discourse on the burdens involved in finding the heart's path in a mundane world."
WILLAMETTE WEEK "… the cumulative small revelations Brenna affords will have the reader wondering at the mystery and beauty of life."
OJAI VALLEY NEWS "… all the gusto and verve with which Saroyan infused his characters … easily, moving the reader from incredulity to laughter to tears … Wondrous and remarkable. Gusto, exuberance, … pathos, empathy, and a great deal of love. It's got everything."

The Law of Falling Bodies

Duff Brenna

A Nine Lives
Edition

SERVING HOUSE BOOKS

The Law of Falling Bodies

ISBN: 978-0-9858495-0-4

Cover image: National Archives

Author photo: David Memmott

Serving House Books logo by Barry Lereng Wilmont

A Nine Lives Edition
Published by Serving House Books
Copenhagen, Denmark and Florham Park, NJ

www.servinghousebooks.com

Originally published by Hopewell Publications 2007

First Serving House Books Edition 2012

To R.A. Rycraft

and

In Memory of

Leon Abbott

Drowned Dead, Age 20, Oahu, Hawaii

Books by Duff Brenna

Fiction
Minnesota Memoirs
The Law of Falling Bodies
The Willow Man
The Altar of the Body
Too Cool
The Holy Book of the Beard
The Book of Mamie

Nonfiction
Winter Tales: Men Write about Aging (co-editor: Thomas E. Kennedy)
Murdering the Mom: A Memoir

Part One: Every Morning the War Arrives

Virgil Francis Foggy

Chop . . .
    chop . . .
        chop . . .
You hold him by the legs.
You place his head on the chopping block, setting it there in blood and wedged feathers.
Eye rigid, leathery lid blinks.
Eye glistens.
Eye a target, yellow, alive, stunned.
Eye says - *What!*
Says, *Mercy, Virgil, mercy!*
But you are fourteen and fourteen knows no mercy.
Ax falls—*chop!*
The body makes you think of a pillow on legs. The pillow runs into the fence. It bounces off. It quivers in the dust of the killing yard. On the chopping block, the head in profile is flat, triangular. Resembles a bright red leaf, needle-tongued silence.
The beak curving like a toy banana.
There are two galvanized tubs side by side on short, metal sawhorses. A small, round charcoal stove beneath the first tub keeps the water hot inside. Wet feathers and humid flesh and steam float in front of your mother and grandmother as they dip the limp bodies into the hot water and tear the feathers from the prickly skin. The tearing sounds like sandpaper. Into the cold-water the naked bodies go. Tilted decoys floating.
Ginger reaches inside the cage and grabs another bird. Hands it to you. Using the blade of the ax, you brush the head off the block. You put the new, living thing down, senses alive, heart pumping, lungs panting, feathers feathering. Senseless blood and oxygen coursing through

pulsing veins. On the block, no mercy, head down. Plump chicken by the legs blinking. One eye gaping at the ax. At the boy who came for eggs this morning. Whose hand ran softly over the silken back. Whose throat clucked quietly in the haze hanging in the coop at sunrise. The birds stirring awake in a world of peace without end.

- *We'll live forever, won't we?*

Is this the same boy, then? The eyes are not the same. The simian brow. The pitiless lips. This boy shows teeth. He mimics the growl of a dog.

—*Mercy, Virgil! Mercy!*

Fall the ax—*chop!*

The scarlet heads pile up. Candy for cats snaking through the yard, snatching this head and that. You promise the cats you will chop off their heads too. But they come anyway, one by one dashing from under the milkhouse, dashing past the bloody ax. Tricky swift slinky. Snapping heads in their pin fangs. You kick dirt at the cats. You whirl the blade overhead.

"Will sure kill you cats! Gimmee nother hen! Gimmee that one there!"

Chop!

"Watch it with that ax!" shouts Dick.

He is sitting on the patio in front of the house, slouching on his neck, his long legs stretching out, crossing at the ankles. His fingers play with his hair, pulling at the thinning strands, stringing them back like shoelaces over his balding pate. Dick and Pappy in the shade of the live oak, drinking iced tea, watching the work twenty yards away in the killing yard.

The windmill tucked between the tool shed and chicken coop, whirs in the breeze, its piston slipping up and down the platform guides—*tick-slip-tick-slip-tick-slip*. You smell the organs, the wet feathers, sweet blood, dusty droppings piling up. Faint whiffs now and then of Gramma's potent White Owl cigar. She rips more feathers. Rips them as if she hates them.

Forty yards away on the other side of the road, the Crow River makes the same sound as the wind through the trees. The blue sky observes your skill with the ax. The deft, murderous Virgil Foggy—ax-killer.

You salute Dick with the blade.

"It's not a toy!" he growls. "Take care of business, boy!" He lights a cigar, jabs it at you like an angry finger.

You lower the ax and reach for another panting bird. The cold, scaly legs rasp against your callused palm. The wings flap weakly. They go limp, defeated. Its target eye is fixed with wonder.

- *Mercy, Virgil, mercy.*

Chop!

The two women cut the bodies open. They ladle the guts. Stomach and bowels, soft pink eggs, broken eggs, eggs half-formed litter the bottom of a cardboard box. The bottom rim of the box oozes. Livers and hearts and gizzards and kidneys are saved in a pan of water. When the killing is over, you will start a fire inside the oil drum and burn the guts and the feathers and the membrane eggs and the open-eyed heads. Burn them to ashes. Ashes for the garden. You will work the ashes into the dirt with the shovel, the hoe. The ashes will add nutrients and aerate the soil.

You watch the women dip the bodies. The stove beneath the tub has a rim of gray ash around its mouth. The charcoal inside the bowl is as white as Pappy's bristling chin. Stripped of feathers, their skin steaming, the bodies bob in the tub. The cold water tightens the skin. Baubles of fat harden along the seams of gaping bellies.

"Make it clean!" orders Dick, fingering his glass, long fingers draping like tarantula legs over the rim. "Make it clean! Don't shame yourself like that dumb bastard in the paper!" Dick chuckles and says something to Pappy, who cups his hand behind his ear as he says, "Omm?"

You recall the story of the farmer who didn't make it clean. Who chopped the chicken's face off, but didn't kill it. Saw it strutting around afterwards and felt sorry for causing the chicken such suffering. So the farmer kept it alive by dripping Cream of Wheat down its throat. And the farmer bragged about his headless phenomenon. And made bets that it was not a trick, the faceless chicken was truly alive. And people came to see what seemed impossible. They paid a dollar to look. The impossible chicken got famous and was put in a carnival and the farmer made money from sensation seekers lining up. The grotesque bird in a cage, scratching the floor, dipping its neck as if pecking at grain. The chicken with no face lived several months like that. It got written up in the newspaper, a professor explaining the autonomic nervous system, how it was all the chicken really needed for its organs and muscles to function. A human being could live that way too, faceless and fed with a tube.

Dick read the article to the family and took it to Lando Lakes Tavern, where he read it to Alma Lando and her father Big Al. Big Al tacked it to the corkboard for others to read. The article is there every time you go in with Dick and sit on a stool, eating hamburgers and drinking Coke and waiting for Dick to get wobbly and need to be driven home. He doesn't dare get stopped again and lose his license again and have his car insurance go up again. The cops won't bother you, fourteen-year-old Virgil driving the car. The cops are used to farmboys going back and forth in pickups from the farms to the mill.

"I been makin it clean!" you answer. "I'm a pro! Nerves of steel, Uncle Dick!"

Dick turns his head and says something more to Pappy. Dick grinning goatish. Pappy cups his ear, "Ey?" Dick wears a sleeveless T-shirt and blue jeans, the top button open, hairy belly button exposed, waistband curling back like insolent lips. On his left biceps, a fading tattoo of an eagle strangling a snake and the fading blue words SEMPER FI. You hear Dick saying, "—half-wit parading a blind bird and both of em fall in a ditch." Throwing his head back, his laughter barks.

Pale-yellow Pappy smiles. His reedy voice saying, "None so blind will not see."

"Yeah, I know, I know," says Dick, left side of his upper lip sneering.

You watch their eyes swing round on you. Judging your manhood. But you handle your job flawlessly. No more severing a chicken comb or nicking a throat. No chopping off a prayerful wing. That was when you were little and learning, but years of practice has honed your skills, made you an efficient executioner.

Chop!

"Nother massa*cud* Dick," you whisper.

Ginger frowns. She says, "Let *him* hear you say that, smarty-pants." Her thighs and shorts and the backs of her hands and forearms are freckled with blood. You can see blood on your hands and jeans and shirt. Fresh drops of bright blood mix with old drops on your boots. You take your cap off, check it for blood. Your cap is black. The WHO logo on the rim is silver shiny. You wipe your forehead with the inside of your wrist. Resettle your cap so the brim shades your eyes and no one can guess what you're thinking. Your hand shoots out. Your hand fists reptilian legs. This particular chicken is braver than most and tries to peck you.

"Do what!" you say. "*You* fighting *me*!"

You bully the bird onto the block. Pin-feathers wedged in wood shiver in the wind.

Fall the ax—*chop!*

At last Gramma Nez counts the chickens and says it's enough. Virgil has killed thirty and she wants to stop because thirty is an even number. Must never be an odd number or the dead will call for a companion. "Ask the Asians. They writ the *I Ching*. They know numbers and hexagrams tell your fortune." Her voice is bossy. "Read the inscrutables," she says. "You'll see." She has books she's been reading ever since Vernon was sent to Vietnam—*The Mysteries of the Orient, Book of Changes, Bhagava Gita*. She says, "The Orients are strange but no stranger than Europeans. No stranger than Americans dealin with Satan's politics and the Beyond. All em dealin with death the same way—prayers and icons, sacred rituals and magic numbers. Holy stones and medals blessed in holy water, charms full of heaven, thunder, water, mountain. Superstitions, you bet. Don't kid me. Earth, wind, fire, water, all things yin yang. Hey, Regina?"

"Hey," says Regina. Her ball belly leads the way as she turns a crate to sit on.

Virgil tells Grandma Nez that thirty isn't lucky for them. He points at the floating bodies and grins.

"Be respectful of them dead," she says. "Even if they're only chickens, God sees you," she says. She rolls her eyes upward to see if God is watching. "You make fun of the dead and God marks days off your life," she says. "You'll remember that and weep when your time comes and you're thinkin how many more days you could'a had if you showed respect."

Regina clasps her big belly and sighs. Self-pityingly she tells them, "Lord, I'm weary today. This kid weighs a ton." She gives her tummy a tug.

Gramma Nez is chewing her unlit cigar. "Tell the boy, Regina," she says. "Tell him what he needs to know." She adjusts her glasses and her steely gaze pierces him.

"Is that true?" he asks.

There is a chill around his heart, the chilling power of the occult that his mother and grandmother know. It has been a long time, but he can't rid his memory of the mirror his father accidently broke, his mother and grandmother bemoaning seven years bad luck. And at the end, someone dead, they said.

In fact, it happened that way. A few months short of the deadline, his father died. Surrounded by curious Holsteins moaning at him, he grew

11

cold in the pasture before anyone missed him. A massive heart attack was the coroner's verdict, overwork.

"You see what comes of workin so goddamn hard," Dick had told Virgil at the funeral. It killed my stupid-ass brother."

"You killed him," Virgil murmurs in retrospect.

"What?" says his mother.

"Weren't makin fun of dead chickens. It's just fact, I'm sayin. These leftovers is the luckys." He points to the three Rhode Island Reds in the holding cage. Unchosen others prance in front of the coop, scratching, pecking, mumbling—*spwaaak, spawaak, humans are crazy*.

"They'll have their day," says Ginger. Her mouth sneers in a way similar to Dick's upward curve of the lip showing a vampire tooth.

Wearily, Virgil's mother tells him, "Just understand what I'm sayin, honey. These poor chickens gave their all for you. You need to be grateful." She is dressed for killing. Her raven hair wrapped in a red scarf. The butcher apron smeared with blood and pinfeathers clinging, shivering.

"Yes, ma'am," Virgil answers. He rubs his Holy Mother medal hanging from his neck. No broken mirrors for Virgil Francis Foggy.

The women sit on the crates, backs resting against the tubs, the box of guts and the box of feathers at their feet. Regina lights a cigarette. Gramma Nez relights her cigar. They have been discussing bad luck with men, how so many of them have died in the past five years—uncles, brothers, cousins, grandfathers—but the women keep living the way women generally do. Most of them, anyway. Except for Ginger's grandmother dying so young. But then again, she had bats loose in her belfry.

"Women gotta be tougher than men. It's nature's way," says Gramma Nez. "We got to bear the burden. Birth em and bury em." Elbow on knee, she holds the cigar between her first two fingers and moves her hawkish profile to it. Her hair fits her head like a bowl. No fuss, she cuts it that way. Thumb flicking the slick cigar butt, she adds ashes to the ashes and guts near her boots.

"Jim was the best," Regina says. "Though more vulnerable than I knew, God love him, a prince among men. It was that damn mirror. That curs*ed* mirror, Inez."

"Cuss*ed* mirror," grumbles Gramma Nez. Her wrinkled mouth twisting with disdain, she spits. Her spit is speckled yellowish.

"I tole him, but he just laughs," says Regina. "He calls me silly girl.

12

But who looks silly now? Hmm? Huh?"

Her voice is rich with insight. What she knows, she knows. She knows things Virgil can't even guess at. Knows who is good and who is bad and how everyone should live and even what the rotten government should do. He doesn't know anyone smarter than his mother. She has an entire wall in the living room filled with books. She has vowed to finish reading every one—one of these days. She and Jim got halfway through them. Up to *Finnegans Wake* before he died. She will read the books in memory of him, because he would want her to continue improving her mind. "An impossible book, *Finnegans Wake*," she told Virgil and Ginger. "So far I don't understand nuthin. Except there is a sacred river running to a sea, the Irish Sea I think, and a man named Finnegan has fallen down a ladder and died. But he's not really dead. No one is ever really dead. Resurrection, I'm sayin. Christ risen. Christ blessed guaran-damn-tee-ya."

Virgil's father told him that Regina was special. She was like a high-strung filly. She has a nervous, impulsive nature and needs to be handled with care, he said. She should have stayed in college, he said. Done more with her mind—it's how he put it. That's when she was young and mischievous. That's when she was slim and pretty. She's gotten fat now. Double-chinned. She blames it on the baby. The baby makes her eat for two, that's the thing.

"Jim was too damn good for this world," says Gramma Nez. "The good die young. It's true. Never an unkind word from that man. No farmer I know ever worked harder, not even Pappy."

Since he's been dead, nothing bad is ever said about Jim. He was the salt of the earth, a saint in farmeralls and dirty work boots. Earth is a poorer planet without Jim Foggy. Both women cross themselves and kiss their thumbs. They stare at the sky. The smoke from their mouths mingling.

"Yep, too good for this world," Gramma Nez insists. The straight line of her glasses hides her brows. The thick lenses magnify her eyes. Virgil has seen pictures of her when she was young and sexy, a babe in hip-huggers and pearls. Monkey business in her eyes. Lips that say *come kiss me*. Her lips are thin now, lots of vertical lines. There are age spots on her forehead. Veins roving the backs of her hands. In hot weather the blue veins swell. In cold they become thin purple threads.

"Dick is a good man mostly. But he's goddamn lazy. Sure not what this farm needs," says Regina. "Hardly at all like his brother, I'm sayin."

"Handsome bastard trading on his face," Gramma Nez says. "Really, though, he's just a damn kid. Will be till the day he dies. Some men are like that, yes they are." She sighs and her sigh says she's tired of doing with men like her son Dick.

"Some men never grow up," concurs Regina.

"Most men don't, that's what I say." Inez glances over the rim of the tub at Pappy. "There's a war inside every man: good and evil an endless battle. Took him gettin sick to knock nonsense out of him," she says. "Slowed down overnight. Got old in a flash. But truth be told, I'd give ten years of my life to have a strong Pappy back. Except this one damn sure nicer than t'other. I have to give his illness credit for that. This version don't yell at me. This version needs me now. But he's not strong and how do you get used to a man not being strong when all your life he was such a bull? A weak Pappy, it scares me. I'm used to him runnin things. I never thought I'd live to see . . ."

"I still can't go there," says Regina. "Let's don't talk about it, Inez."

"But give him credit, he gets up ever day and gets to the barn and milks them cows with me and Virgil."

"He don't complain," adds Regina.

"But he's turned inward now. There's the thing, you see. I don't know how to handle the silence. I'd rather he cussed and fussed like he used to. He's how men get when they're givin up, preparin to die."

"I know, honey, I know. Let's don't talk about it no more."

"The other day he said he was a short-timer. That's what Dick used to say when he was gettin out of the Marines. I don't know what I'll do when that old bastard dies. How could I go on livin after forty years of him in my bed? Short-timer. We're all short-timers. All time is short-time." She clicks her fingers.

"Let's not think about dyin, honey. This is your home. This is where you'll be. You'll be with us and we'll be doin whatever we need to do. Life goes on. If anybody knows that, I certainly do, after what I've suffered. Next year when it's time to cull chickens and fill the freezer again and slaughter a lamb and a steer again and harvest corn again and the haying again, you'll be recyclin beside me. *To everything there is a season.*"

"*A time to be born and a time to die,*" returns Gramma Nez.

Their eyes glance upward like fingers pointing, as if the bringer of pain is picking on them. They etch crosses on their bones. Kiss their thumbs. Gramma Nez puffs her cigar, smoke signals rising making God aware of her.

"After winter comes spring. That's what you gotta keep in mind," says Regina. She's looking across the killing yard at Pappy dozing.

Gramma Nez says, "Another baby in the house before then. A baby to take care of. Think of that. That'll liven things up."

"A reason to live." Regina looks at her belly. "It's amazin. I mean, who would'a thought three years after Jim passed, I'd be havin his brother's baby?" She shakes her head, the gesture saying she can't fathom the mystery of life.

"Once a Foggy, always a Foggy," says Gramma Nez. "Who else should you have married? I know Jim would be glad of it. They were close, they were bosom brothers those two."

"Vernon will never forgive me."

"Stop that now. Vernon's just a boy who don't know a goddamn thing. The Army will teach him, you'll see, he'll come back a man knowin the ways of the world. And besides, it's your life, not Vernon's. He needs to give you a break. Ornery cuss."

"I'm gonna have Father Hess say a mass for him."

"I already took care of that," says Gramma Nez

"We could do a Rosary."

"I've prayed for him every night. That boy will be fine. I've run the hexagrams. Yin is balanced with yang just right. You hear what I'm sayin? Metal cuts wood, fire melts metal, water puts out fire, earth conquers water, wood conquers earth. All are saved in the blood of the lamb." She pauses. Lays a finger on her lips cryptically. "He'll be fine, I tell you."

"I know he will."

Ginger and Virgil lean side by side against the cage. He takes a nervous hen in his arms and pets her. The women flick ashes over the guts in the box. Ashes to ashes, Virgil reminds himself. Dust to dust.

"Vernon don't like the Army," he says. "He says he can't stand orders from stupid sergeants."

"Well, he's always been smarter than anyone. Just ask him, he'll tell you." Regina turns to Gramma Nez. "See, there's another thing. He'll write to his brother, but not to me. If it wasn't for Virgil, I wouldn't know what's going on. Is that a way to treat your mother?"

"He'll come back a man, you mark my words." Gramma Nez tosses the stub of her cigar into the box. The ember sizzles briefly. "He'll come back to us with knowledge of the world, a wiser man than the boy who left. Mark my words. No atheists in foxholes."

"I don't think Vernon meant that, do you? He was just mad. He was just sayin stuff to hurt me. How could a son of mine be an atheist?"

"Impossible."

"A few masses for him, a few Rosaries."

"That's right. Fire melts medal."

A black cat slips toward the box, its belly dragging. Gramma Nez kicks dirt at it. "No black cat cross my path! Scat, you ferlie, you bad luck devil!" The cat hurls toward the milkhouse. Slips under the warped footing. Turns back and glares with vengeful eyes.

Gramma Nez winks at Virgil. She adjusts her glasses, looking at him over the rim. "Did I ever tell you why Mr. Cat is such an ungrateful rascal?" she says. Without waiting for an answer she says, "Because Mr. Cat was given nine pennies by the Lord and told to spend the money wisely and he could buy whatever he needed. So Mr. Cat said, 'I'll give you three pennies if you'll let me see in the dark.' 'Done!' said the Lord. 'And I'll give you three more pennies if you give me nine lives.' 'Done!' said the Lord. 'For the last three pennies I'll have a plate of milk ever day.' 'Done!' said the Lord. And that's why, what with his seein in the dark, his nine lives and plate of milk, no gratitude can be expected from Mr. Cat, no matter what you do for him, because he figures he's paid his nine pennies and owes you nuthin. People are like that, you know. If they could make a bargain with the Lord, they'd dismiss you with a wave of their tail. They'd be just as ungrateful and arrogant as damn cats."

"Is that true?" Virgil asks. "Did Mr. Cat get nine pennies from the Lord?" He kicks at the chopping block, feeling a pleasant vibration in his toes. Snuggling the chicken under his chin, he kisses her rubbery comb. She smells of dirt and straw. She smells of droppings.

"Everything adds up to one Big True," says Grandma Nez. "The longer you live the more you know there is one Big True."

The two women bow their heads. Standing up, they brush their backsides.

Ginger leans over and says mockingly to her cousin, "Is that true? Did Mr. Cat get nine pennies from the Lord? Jesus Christ, Virgil, how lame can you be?"

"Shut up," he tells her.

"You're such a dope," she says. "Fourteen going on four."

He tries to spank her, but she scoots to the other side of the crates. The hen is asleep in his arms and the jostling startles her. She starts thrashing and squawking as if she's having a nightmare. *This is it!* she seems to be saying. He throws her in the air and she flaps heavily to the ground. Stands amazed for a few seconds before joining the others in front of the coop. They all strut warily, looking left-right-up-down. They talk among themselves and throw distrustful glances at Virgil. They scratch the dirt, stabbing at bugs, bits of grain, tiny rocks for their craws.

Can they smell the blood? Virgil wonders.

"What you women gabbin about?" yells Dick.

"Shit and shinola," says his wife.

"Pig shit and pepper," says his mother.

Dick's long mouth smirks. "Smart-ass broads," he says.

Pappy scratches his whiskers thoughtfully. He gets up slowly and wanders towards the door. Looking back over his shoulder at his wife he says, "I need my hat, Inez. Sun's comin round." He walks into the wall—*thunk!*

Gramma Nez yells, "Watch where the fuck you're goin, Daddy! Sit down! Sit down, I'll get your goddamn hat!"

"Sweetheart, burn this stuff," Virgil's mother tells him.

The two women go through the gate. They cross the patio, peeling off their aprons as they enter the house. A minute later they come back with wine and glasses, crackers with cheese. There is more iced tea for Pappy, who isn't supposed to drink alcohol. Gramma Nez has Pappy's floppy hat. She arranges it for him, the brim shielding his eyes.

Virgil gets matches and lighter fluid from the tool shed. He rolls the barrel over and hoists the guts in, followed by the feathers and some lighter fluid. He flicks a match with his thumbnail, throws the match into the barrel and hears a *whoosh.* Heat waves dancing above the rim.

"Pull that stove out and dump the charcoal in," yells Dick.

Virgil dumps the spent charcoal in the barrel.

"Feed it straw," yells Dick. "You too, Ginger. Get goin."

Under her breath she whispers, "You feed it straw, lazy bastard."

They go to the barn for straw. Pile it near the barrel, twist it and feed it to the fire. Accidentally Virgil touches the barrel and gets a burn. He sucks his finger and thinks how painful Hell must be. Making the sign of the cross, he murmurs, "Father, Son, Holy Ghost."

In a hushed voice Ginger says, "Her baby is low and that means a boy. She carried you low and Gramma Nez put a knife under the mattress to cut the pain and make sure you'd be a boy. Do you believe that shit? These are our relatives." Her lips look like limber strips of bubble gum.

"What she want a damn boy for?" he asks. "Why any damn baby at all? Wish she wouldn't."

"Me too."

"Babies," he says and spits in the dirt. He sits on one of the crates, leaning his arms on the rim of the cold-water tub, while he pokes at the bodies, pushing them under, watching them rise over and over. "I wish Vernon would come back," he says. "That's what I wish. Pappy can't handle it, and your dad's not worth piss."

She glances at Dick. "I hate him."

"Pappy needs him to help now. Pappy's gonna die, you know, from kidneys."

"Don't tell me about it."

"Vernon hates your dad too, you know."

"Everybody knows that."

"Why'd my mom marry him anywho? What you think, Gin?"

"I think you should keep your voice down. Big-ears hears everything. Who knows why she married him? She's crazy that's why. Bats in her belfry like my granny." Ginger pauses. Then adds, "Married him cuz he looks like Uncle Jim, that's why."

"Daddy had more hair. Daddy never sat around with his pants unbuttoned, showing his belly. He's a slob. His feet always stink."

"It's incest," says Ginger.

"Incest?"

"Her and him. Grandma and Grandpa comin back here. All us livin this way. Incest."

He tries with hands and elbows to push all the bodies underwater at the same time, but they pop up too fast. "When Jesus comes, that's what'll happen," he says. "Pop up out your grave like these guys. Resurrection. Sail to Heaven."

"What if you been cremated or fell in a vat of acid or got eaten by an anaconda and there's no body, no grave, no nuthin? Huh? What then?"

"Jesus makes you a new body."

"You don't know nuthin," she whispers. "There's only this body and it's flesh and bone and mostly water. Like them." She points to the chickens. "Bodies are full of corruption waitin to happen. Bodies end up like guts in a barrel." She scowls at the barrel. "My body ain't nuthin. It don't matter what happens to it, cuz it's all corruption." Her whisper has risen several decibels, but is still a whisper.

"Geez Gin, don't have a cow. You should hear yourself. That's a bad way to think about your body. Bodies are temples. You defile your body, you defile God. Ask my mom."

"She should know."

"Should know what?"

"Forget it."

Her eyebrows knit, bubble gum lips curling, she breathes and breathes until her breathing is calm again. She calls herself hardboiled. When she's not putting hardness on, she looks nubile, a word Virgil heard his mother use to describe Ginger. She plays with her hair now, releasing the ponytail and pulling it forward over her eyes. He watches her face disappear behind her hair and her blood-dotted hands and he feels suddenly tired and sad. Virgil misses his father. He hasn't felt safe since the day his father died. He misses his big brother too. He misses the way Pappy used to be so strong. He wants to go back to when it was just them. No Dick or Ginger in the house. No Gramma Nez and Pappy in the Airstream under the live oak. He can hear the grownups yakking, the women mostly. Regina Perpetua most of all saying, "You know me and you can just guess how I lit into her for that! Who do you think you're talkin to? That's what I said. And she—"

Italian temper. She loves having an emotional Italian temper.

Looking south past the barn and the pasture to the corn, he spots the Allis-Chalmers B at the edge of the field, its cultivator blades resting on the earth. The corn is too high to cultivate now, or he would go get the B and drive down the rows and find some peace. He would go to the back of the field by the woods and shoot pigeons with the twelve-gauge. Eyes heavy, he rests his cheek on the tub. Feels the heat of the crackling barrel on the side of his face. The water on his fingers is cool. The water is calm. The calm chickens floating calmly along.

Ginger strolls away. He turns and watches her bottom jerking. She wears one of her father's old work shirts. It is knotted at the waist. She's as tall as Virgil who is tall for his age. The sun flicks through her hair. The sight of her reminds him of the drawings on the walls in her room— wispy, naked women sketched in pencil. Women with flat bellies, no eyes, no hands, no feet. Bodies long and slim. Bodies wavy as water. Basically, they look like helpless fairies, he thinks.

Going to the sheep pen, he climbs over the fence and tries to get Rachel to give him a ride. Hands gripping her wool, knees bent, toes dragging the ground he yells, "Giddy up, go!" She bucks and he exaggerates a fall off her back. He is grateful to hear Ginger giggling, to see Ginger smiling.

"You're way too big for that," she says. "Won't you ever grow up?"

"Tryin not to," he tells her.

He chases Rachel's stubby tail. When he looks to see Ginger's reaction, she isn't watching. She has taken a rabbit from the hutch, cradling it. Beyond her is the pasture and beyond the pasture is the fence and the cornfield. The mottled Holsteins lie on the mottled green. Their jaws masticating cud. Moses ambling toward the barnyard, his head bobbing like some cool colored man pimping along.

"Hey, let's see if we can ride Moses."

Ginger shakes her head. "No fun," she says.

The steer strolls out of the pasture and goes to the tank in the barnyard, dips his head and—

"Moses! Moses, here!" Virgil yells.

Eyes suspicious the steer says - *Whatcha want?*

"Ride'um cowboy!" Moses shakes his head and trots back to pasture. "Moses is a fraidy cat!" the boy sings.

Virgil turns round and round, searching for something. Every year is the same. The same boring things over and over. There will be chicken packing later and cleaning up the tubs, putting them away. Ashes need to be spread in the garden. At evening the cows will have to be milked as always. He wonders what it would be like to join the Army and go to Vietnam. And kill gooks. Win the Medal of Honor. The President of the United States hangs the medal round his neck. Shakes his hand. Calls him an American treasure, a hero. Virgil is humble. He limps off the stage using a cane. He hears someone saying, "That boy is a wonder."

Scuffing the dirt, he kicks up dust and ponders his future. Will he really take over the farm like Pappy says and Vernon wants? Will he be a farmer like Pappy and Jim? Uncle Dick has told him he is too stupid for school anyway, so he might as well be a farmer. Dick doubts Virgil can learn anything more than machinery and cows. Virgil's hands know what to do with machines. There's no shame in having a mechanical aptitude.

Makes you useful. Lots of people with brains aren't useful, that's what Regina said. She's been to college and knows.

Being stupid about math has made him afraid of school. Last year he tried so hard to understand story problems it gave him acid. He had to take chalky pills. He quit trying to learn math, gave up on everything. When summer is over, he's not going back. To hell with it.

Walking to the willow, he breaks off a thin branch, skinning the leaves. He stings the air with the whip. Spanks the chopping block. The blood on the block is purple. It will be black by nightfall. He remembers the cats coming for the heads and what he promised them. Looking around he doesn't spot any cats, but the dog has come over and is sniffing the dirt, licking aromas of the dead.

"Get out of there, you stupid!" Virgil yells, cutting the whip across the dog's back. The dog darts away. Then turns facing the whip, moving sideways, showing fangs.

"That old bastard will bite you," says Ginger.

Virgil slashes at the dog again and again, forcing him to give ground. "I don't care. I don't give a damn," Virgil says. "We killed a lamb yesterday with the two-pound sledge right here on this spot and he's in there roasting and Pappy will eat the eyes. Get out of here, Husky! We'll sledge you too! We'll eat your eyes! Roast you and eat your eyes!" Laughing he chases the dog, slashing at him with the whip and crying "Eyes! Eyes!" The whip sizzles.

"Stupid Husky," Virgil says, turning back.

Ginger says, "I can't stand when Pappy eats the eyes." She has her face buried in rabbit fur. The rabbit keeps looking at Virgil and the whip.

"I like to watch him eat the eyes," Virgil says. "I suck raw eggs and get a dime for each one. It comes out the shell like a glob of snot."

"Grow up."

"Egg snot is what makes me strong." He giggles.

"Grow up, I said."

"Pure protein. Look at my muscles!"

She laughs as he cocks his arms. "They look like little eggs all right," she says.

Pleased that he has made her laugh, he thrusts out his chest. "I'm Hercules Unchained!"

"You're a scream," she says. "You look like a stork," she says. "You look like a monkey stork! You're a monkey stork!" she says, shimmying with laughter. Then abruptly stops and puts the rabbit away and repeats, "Grow up."

"See what I got here, woman?" he says shaking the whip at her. "It's to beat yo butt!"

"Don't you dare, Virgil," she says.

He likes spanking her, making her dance and scream. Once he chased her with the B-B gun, shooting at her feet to make her dance and he hit her in the foot, giving it a welt, and she cried and made him kiss it. And then she got to shoot him in the foot for revenge. It felt like fire and as he hopped around yelling, she laughed so hard she peed her pants. Running to the outhouse now, she hides inside and says through the door, "Don't hurt me, Virgil. I'm your sister now. You're supposed to protect me."

"I have to pee," he tells her.

She lets him inside. "Me too," she says.

They take down their pants and sit side-by-side peeing over the lime. He ekes out a meager fart to entertain her. She lifts her thigh and farts commandingly.

"Show off," he says.

They turn pages in the SEARS catalog. She shows him what clothes she wants.

There is a page of sexy women wearing brassieres. He points at their breasts and says in Dick's velvety voice, "How'd you like a acre of those to walk on in your bare feet?"

"Don't be stupid, don't be *him*," she says.

Virgil sings to her, "Oh she burped and she farted and she started for the door and that's when I knew she was a goddamn whore!" He breaks into howling laughter. Looks toward the ceiling, spider webs shaking in corners. There are Black Widows up there.

"That's not funny," Ginger says. "What's funny about it? Him and his dirty jokes, his mind in the gutter all the time. Perverted bastard." Her eyes look as hard as ballpeen hammers. It always amazes Virgil that someone so pretty could look so instantly tough and dangerous. She turns the page and stares at a pair of sexy shoes. "Those are stilettos. I want those," she says, putting her finger on heels six-inches high, thin as ice picks. "And some black-knit stockings and garters," she says. "You can take my picture if you want to. I could be a model, you know."

He peeks at her crotch wedged in the wooden hole. Hairs reddish blond. His hairs are dark brown, like the hair on his head. He has round, brown eyes same as his mother. Ginger has the blue eyes of her parents. But she looks mostly like her mother, an Irish Swede. She looks like the girl in the shaving commercial who says, "Take it off. Take it all off."

Leaning toward a crack in the door, he sees the chopping block and the tub of chickens, the willow tree, the windmill *tick-slip-tick-slip*, the tool shed, the coop, the barn. Grownups at the patio table, munching wafers with cheese. The oak tree shadow is stunted. It looks like a gnarled dwarf climbing Pappy's legs. Pulling a sack of Bull Durham and Zigzags from his pocket Virgil rolls a cigarette. Lights it. Shares it with Ginger. He continues glancing through the crack in the outhouse door, keeping Uncle Dick in view.

Thirty yards to the right of the house is the house trailer shaped like a potato bug, Airstream Limited, where his grandparents have lived since after Jim died and they moved back to help run the farm. An electric line runs from the house to the trailer. On the line walks a tightrope walker using nothing but hands and footskill for balance. Fearless and laughing at danger high in the air, he stops and stands on one leg. Does a backflip. Frontflip. Stands on his head. The crowd below him gasps in awe. Pretty girls scream and faint. It's him, it's Fearless Foggy, look at him go! Come down and I'll give you a kiss, a blond beauty says. I'm a Foggy legend, he tells her. He is sixth generation Foggy farming the land. Other Foggys run the mill in town. Others live as farmers in northern Wisconsin, others live in Mankato. Golden Valley itself was settled by Virgil's forefathers in 1851. Fergus Foggy, a widower, came to the Minnesota Territory, with his two sons and a grinding wheel. He made a living sharpening knives, axes, tomahawks and distilling potato and corn liquor called splow.

"I wonder if old Fergus ever sat on this pot and took a dump," Virgil says.

"His place was over by the graveyard," she replies. "This was his son's farm."

"I know that, but maybe this is the same outhouse."

"Not a chance. C'mon, Virgil, be real."

"Well."

Ginger hands back the roll-your-own.

"Ever hear from your mom?" he asks.

She bites her bottom lip. "She writes, but he burns her letters. So I don't know where she is exactly. Last time she called all we did was bawl at each other till he grabbed the phone and hung up."

"I liked her. She was nice."

"She's a whore. We're both whores."

"She always smelled good."

"He drove her to it. Her and that guy, what's-his-name? Earl."

"And Wild Bill," he says.

"I think that one's a lie. Bill's a bragger. Peter says he brags all the time and you can't believe him." Ginger is quiet a moment. She clears her throat. "It's clinical. We're nymphomaniacs. Maybe there's a pill for it."

"Who cares?"

"That's what your mother calls her. I heard her say it to my dad. She said it's clinical nymphomania and she needs psychiatry."

"How does a woman get like that? What's it mean? It means she's got to have it, right? Like a drug addict, she's got to have it. She can't help herself."

"Look it up in the dictionary. Ever heard of a dictionary?"

"You're sayin that 'cause you don't know."

"Everyone knows, stupid. Except you."

He finishes the cigarette, drops the butt in the hole between his legs. Looks through the crack again.

Dick is looking at the outhouse.

"Oh, oh, he's lookin, Gin."

She leans forward. They're cheek to cheek. "He's drinkin," she says. He feels her hair brushing the side of his face. Peach-like lightly fuzzy he wants to tickle his lips over it. He loves her. He thinks of them in the bedroom in the bunkbeds. Him in the bottom one with his head poking out. Ginger taking mouthfuls of water from a bottle. Aiming at his open mouth below. Spitting water into his mouth. Hitting his eyes and nose. Laughing.

"You remember when we were little and you spit water into my mouth from off the bed?"

"Don't remind me," she says.

"It was fun. People kissin, they swap spit all the time like that."

She thinks about it. "You're right, that is what they do."

"You and Peter swap spit."

"Grow up," she tells him.

"He's a jerk, you know. He wants you to think he's cool, but he's a jerk with bushy hair and bell-bottoms and love beads. I don't know how

24

you stand him. He's phony like his dad, like Wild Bill."

"Is not. Shut up, none of your business. Grow up."

"How can you kiss a guy with one eyebrow, Gin? The whole family has one eyebrow. Peter's the worst. Fuzzy caterpillar between his eyes that's what it looks like. Blech!"

She laughs and gives Virgil a shove. She says, "I pluck it for him with tweezers."

"When you kiss him, do you ever think about his eyebrow crawling onto you? Grabbing hold right there."

"Don't," she says.

"Yes, by golly, I see hairs comin in. Look out, its planted babies and they're hatching. Oh my god, Gin, Pete's infected you."

"You're sure interested in my love life, Virgil. You jealous? Is that what?"

"What?"

"You're into me and Peter. You want to see what we do."

"What do I care what you do?"

She changes the subject. She wants to know what Dick is up to now.

"Still lookin," says Virgil.

"Maybe he heard you singin his filthy song," she says.

"I sang it soft. His ears ain't *that* good."

"I bet he heard you. He hears everything."

From far off, Virgil sees Dick's lips moving. He shouts, "What're you kids doin in there?"

"Tell him somethin," Ginger whispers.

"What?"

"Tell him we're lookin at the pictures."

Swinging the door open at arm's length, he yells that they are looking at pictures in Sears.

"Sittin in the stink, them two," Dick says.

"He says we're sittin in the stink," Virgil whispers.

"I heard him," she says.

Faintly, Regina's voice reaches them. "Ought to tear it down and fill in the hole, Pappy."

"What for? It's handy. No use fixin what ain't broke."

"Nobody uses it."

"I use it sometimes. What if the well runs dry one day and you

25

got to go? There's your backup, right there. She'll never let you down."

"The well run dry? That'll be the day."

"It could happen. A well's no guaranty, Regina."

"In Minnesota?"

"Wells run dry in Minnesota too, don't think they don't." Pappy rubs his bristly chin as he contemplates the outhouse. Regina says something to Gramma Nez. Dick continues to stare, shielding his eyes from the sun.

"He's still lookin," Virgil tells Ginger. "Staring real hard. What's he thinkin?"

"He's jealous," she says.

When she goes out with Peter, she sets Dick off by parting her hair down the middle and wearing love beads and false eyelashes and painting her eyelids blue. She wears tight skirts like her mother wore. Regina says that Ginger is just trying to look pretty and Dick should trust her, leave her alone. It depends on his mood. If he's drunk, he'll mess with her and sometimes not let her leave. If he's sober he'll warn her that she better not come home knocked up. There are some nights when she'll be gone before he gets there and Regina will say she had permission to go. And Dick will wait up for her. He'll sit in the kitchen and drink beer and wait for her to sashay in.

"Why is he jealous?" says Virgil.

"Because of you. You're a male in here alone with me and he can't see what we're doin. God knows what we're doin. Could be nasty. Some sex thing in the toilet like he would do, old pervert."

"Like what? What sort of sex thing?"

"Stupid becomes you," she says.

"I don't know what you mean. What's wrong with this? What's to be jealous of? We used to take baths together, Vernon and Albert and us. All four of us are in that picture in the bathroom."

"We were little kids then, dumbbell. You're just a baby in that picture and I was a toddler."

"I remember bathin with you when I was eight. I remember it. We washed each other's backs."

"That's true too."

"Jealous of nuthin," Virgil mutters.

"That's what drove her away. She said jealousy can kill your spirit and she wasn't going to let it kill hers. He accuses people cuz he's got a dirty mind. Won't trust others because he don't trust himself. You don't want to know the things he thinks, Virge. You don't want to know what he's done."

"I know more than you think I do."

"Yeah, yeah." She stares out the crack, her eyes resentful. "You ever hear him and your mother in there bangin the wall when they're boozin? God, come on, you're not that deef. And you're not so innocent as you like people to believe. I see how you look at me."

"You look at me too."

"Oh yhah, big deal."

He doesn't say anything, but he wants to tell her what he saw. The two of them in the loft, he saw them. She on her knees, bare breasts and milky blue belly in the gray light. Navel poking out like the tip of a thumb. His hands moving in her hair, her hands clutching his thighs. Virgil has seen cows get horny and lick each other that way. And there's more. Lots more.

Moses comes into view, wanders past the pen and stops. Virgil reaches through the crack with the willow whip and flicks the steer's nose. He jumps, turns to the whip. Sniffs it.

"Nyaa, nyaa, Moses," Virgil taunts.

The steer is blinking his eyes. Thinking slow. Slower. Sss.

"Wake up, stupid," Virgil says. "Duh, ah duh, what was that? Duh, gee, I don't know. Duh."

Moses snorts and shakes his head so hard his ears flap like wooden clappers. His tail twitches. He puts his head down and bumps the outhouse. Ginger squeals. Moses thinks about it.

Then bumps the outhouse again.

Both kids squeal. The steer starts scratching his neck on a corner. The outhouse rocks and the kids squeal louder. Virgil keeps flicking Moses with the whip. The steer gives them a carnival ride, The Rocking Barrel, The Tottering Bridge.

"Don't whip him, don't whip him!" says Ginger, but she is shrieking with laughter.

Then it's over. They can hear Dick cussing. The door flies open and Virgil sees Moses high-tailing it, his hind hooves kicking. Dick's dark face looms. He catches Virgil by the throat, lifts him off the hole.

"You stupid little bastard," he says. "You tryin to knock this shithouse in the shithole? You tryin to drown in caca, you dumb ass?"

27

Virgil can't breathe. His eyes fasten to the tattoo on Dick's arm, Semper Fi, Sempter Fi. Virgil pounding the tattoo with his fist.

"Daddy don't!" shouts Ginger. "You're choking him, Daddy! Stop it goddamnit, Daddy!"

Dick lets go. Air rushes into Virgil's lungs. He starts coughing. Hurriedly he pulls up his pants.

"What? What did you say? What did you call me?" says Dick.

"I was coughing," whines Virgil. He cinches his belt and tries to go around Dick but is grabbed by the hair and put in a hammerlock. Dick steps on his foot, all in one motion, pinning him, grinding his toes. Virgil can't do anything about it. He goes limp.

"C'mon, hit me. Why don't you hit me, Virge? What's the matter, ey?"

Virgil's muscles are dead.

"When I'm eighty years old I will still be able to kick your ass!" Dick puts more pressure on the back-slung arm. It feels like the shoulder is twisting off.

Ginger is pushing against Dick's back, pushing and pounding. "Let him go, you fuckin bully!"

The kamikaze arrow backflashes through Virgil's mind. The arrow coming from the sky only inches from his head and sticking a foot from his foot in the snow. And Dick standing there grinning. The bow in his hand. Dick shouting, Happy Birthday! Good to go another year!

The old man is lumbering towards them, his body swaying like a balloon on a string. The patio is empty. The women have gone inside. Dick wouldn't have gotten away with anything if Regina had seen him.

"Quit hurtin the boy," Pappy says. "Get your foot off the boy! I see what you doin!"

Dick gives the arm another twist. Let's go. Stands back. Virgil rubs his shoulder and tries not to cry.

"Gonna cry, little baby?" says Dick. "Is the baby gonna cry? Boohoo."

Virgil's eyes are leaking. He wipes them angrily.

"See what you make me do?" says Dick. "See how mad you make me? Why you do that, Virge?"

Pappy steps in front and nudges Dick away. "What's the matter with you? Keep your hands to yourself!"

"Listen to you," says Dick. "Mister Big Hands himself."

"What did this boy do to you?"

"Nuthin. Not a goddamn thing."

"Then what's your point?"

"Nuthin. He's stupid, that's my point."

"This is your brother's boy. You don't call your brother's boy stupid. You listen me?"

"Sure. Whatever."

"Your brother is up there lookin down. He sees what you do."

"Not that again. Gimmee a break, Pappy."

"You hear me?"

"I hear you, Pappy. Sure, sure, Jim is lookin down. Jim is an angel and he's watchin over his boys and I better watch out because he will get me. Ooh, I'm scared!" Dick walks around, hands on hips. "Jesus, why'd you have to go soft? Man, this ain't *you*. Since when did you believe in all that shit? I mean, you fucked up your kidneys and now you *ba*leeve, help me, Jesus, save me, Lord! And Jim is a angel now? Not the hard-drinkin, fist-fightin Jim I knew in this bloody bitch of a world. Sonofabitch, Pappy, gimmee a break!" Dick's nose is wrinkling as if smelling something bad. "Too much for me," he says. "I need a drink."

He steps around Pappy and heads toward the house. Turns back, says, "Hey stupid, hey shit-for-brains, if that steer had had its way, you'd be suffocating in caca! Maybe I'm a little rough, yeah, but that's what it takes. Ask Pappy about discipline. He used to dish it out, by god. Old tyrant."

"Go on, go on," says Pappy. "Go drink your wine. Maybe if we're lucky you'll fall asleep."

"Stupid little shit-for-brains," says Dick, walking off, grumbling. They hear him grumbling all the way to the house. The screendoor slams, drifts open and hangs at an angle. The wind plays with it, fanning it open and banging it shut, open and bang-shut, open and bang.

Ginger makes a circle with her thumb and forefinger, gesturing toward her father. Virgil makes the same sign and mouths the word, "Asshole."

Pappy takes him by the hand and says, "They're gettin dinner, c'mon." Virgil limps to show how bad he is hurt. Ginger stomps toward the patio, anger in motion. Moses peeks from the corner of the barn, watching Virgil limping. Moses snickering, toothless upper gum displayed as he says - *Got you good, hee-hee.*

"Big fat coward," Virgil tells him. "I'll snap your tail, you coward."

29

Moses claps his ears. He winks. Cleans out his nostrils with his long, gray tongue. Virgil draws out Minnesota vowels, "Yhah, you look tough but you're noht! If I whas big as yew, I'd knock him to the moooon!"

- If you whas big as me, uh-huh, says the steer. *Yup . . . yup. Sure, Virge, sure, hee-hee.*

From under the New Holland spreader, the dog is watching. The dog grinning like a werewolf. The hens and Aaron the rooster limp like they are imitating the boy. The arrogant cats glare. Rachel puts her head down and bumps a post and looks at him with vengeful eyes. She sticks out her tongue and Virgil sticks out his. She does a little jig, happy that the brat who led her kid to slaughter got his ass kicked. The rabbits stay hidden in their hutches. Rabbits are bigger chickens than chickens.

"Pappy, remember when the goat knocked you down and wouldn't let you up?" asks Virgil. "Remember him? His name was Samson? Member him?"

Pappy nods. "Never bend your can to a goat," he says.

"He come runnin and hit you right on the can," Virgil says. "Yhah, and you went headfirst in the dirt, and the goat backed up and give you another when you tried to get up. Right on the can, pow! Funny! Mom and me was fallin down and did you ever cuss, Pappy. I never heard such cussin. It was grand!"

Virgil is chuckling with every word. For the moment he has forgotten the twisted shoulder, the bruised neck, the mashed toes. He starts prancing beside Pappy, nervously happy for no reason and wanting an excuse to laugh. "Boy, I wish we had got a picture of that. Your can hanging out like a punching bag. You could tell Samson was havin fun."

"I got the last laugh," says Pappy. "We ate that fella."

"You ate his eyes."

"I ate his eyes. They were tough eating. You gotta roast eyes just right or they turn into fiber."

Pappy holds the gate open. Virgil walks through. "Pappy," he says, "why does Uncle Dick say you never believed in God? You believed in God, didn't you? Mom says you got to believe in God. It's a mortal sin not to."

Pappy points a finger toward the sky. "God is up, lookin down," he says.

"When I was little I still believed in Santa Claus, and I got in a fight with Danny Raven because he said there wasn't none. And I said he was talkin mortal sin to say there wasn't Santa Claus and if he didn't take it back, I would clean his clock. And he wouldn't take it back, so I made him fight me. I fought for Santa and got whipped. Wild Bill got in Danny's corner, helping out, tellin Danny to uppercut me. He made my mouth bleed. Knocked out some baby teeth. It hurt like hell. But . . . but I got dirt in my eyes, you see? And had to quit because I couldn't see. I wouldn't have quit for the teeth and the blood, but I couldn't see with the dirt in my eyes. So I got whipped for Santa."

"I remember you gettin your baby teeth knocked out," says Pappy. "I didn't know you lost em for Santa Claus, though." The old man chuckles. He stops on the patio, puts a hand on the table to steady himself. The tree's shadow cuts diagonally across his body. Half-shadowed he still holds Virgil's hand, thumbing the back of it.

Virgil says to him, "I said to Mama - I said, 'Mama, Danny says there ain't no Santy Claus. Is that true?' And she sighs fifty yards long and she says, 'Okay, you're old enough to know.' And just then it flashed through my mind there weren't no God neither and I said to her, 'Does that mean there's no God neither?' And, man, she come unglued! She yells not to ever say that or think it. I tell you what, she looked like she wanted to knock more of my teeth out. I learned not to question about God. Don't question God. Nope. No way."

Pappy lets go of Virgil's hand, turns a patio chair and sits down. He pushes his hat back and soothes his eyes with his thumb and forefinger. Then he says, "You know, son, I had the same thought when I found out about no Santa. My mind jumped just like yours to God. We're born doubters. It's in the blood. But you get my age, you just don't want to doubt no more. It's dangerous to doubt when you're my age, son."

"Because you got sick and nearly died," the boy whispers, remembering his grandfather collapsing, the acid smell radiating from him, the cold sweat covering his face. And then the ambulance and red lights, the dispatcher's voice squawking the whole time the medics were wrapping Pappy up. Gramma Nez so unsteady she could hardly walk. It had been worse than when Jim was found dead and brought home on a stretcher. He had been dead awhile. With him there had been nothing to do. But with Pappy, a person had time to appeal for mercy. Say a Rosary. Light a candle. Walk on your knees till they bled. Lay hands on and assert your will.

He touches his grandfather's shoulder. "The ambulance had to come get you."

"It was close," says Pappy. "And it's still no fun. Having to get diluted every five days. Hope it don't happen to you, my boy. Hope it's not genetic."

Pappy gazes far-eyed at the pasture. The hills roll. Grass clipped close. The cows chewing cud or sleeping. "But it makes a fella think," says Pappy. "Makes a fella take stock of his life and what he's done with it. What if there is life after death? And everything the priest been sayin, what if it's true? I always said before there's no proof. Gimmee proof. And all these questions about the universe, how could it be here and the world and life itself, how could it get here? Those questions didn't bother me when I was strong. But when I nearly croaked, that's different. Then I wanted to know. And I saw that I had been piling up a list of sins that would go to the moon if you put them end-to-end. I shudder to think of the sins of my life laid out before a judge. Back when I was strong enough to lift an eight-cylinder engine and put it in the back of the truck . . . back then I thought I was up to arguin with the judge, you see? I was so strong once upon a time that I didn't see who could whip me. Not even God. You know, I've been lucky with my health. Hardly a cold or nuthin. Nuthin to keep me from the barn or the fields since I was a boy like you. Till these kidneys. It happened fast. That's what I can't get over. Things turned on me so fast, I can't believe it. And that's when I reached out. I knew there wasn't nuthin else but His hand that could keep me from fallin. I'm no coward, but I'll tell you, I was more scared than I ever thought possible. I want you to promise to be a good boy and say your prayers every night. Pray to your father and pray for the farm and yourself and your brother at war. Will you do that?"

"Yessir."

Virgil is in awe. He is riveted by what his grandfather says. Virgil hasn't ever heard anything like it. Pappy has been very quiet since he came home from the hospital and no one knows for sure what he's thinking, and he has started going to church and saying grace at the table and saying, "God is up, lookin down." His tone is softer. His eyes are often puzzled and a little alarmed. Who is this Pappy? Where'd the other one go?

Virgil smells roast lamb, the onions and garlic. Wonders if it was right to bring up the subject of Santa Claus and God. Pappy most definitely doesn't sound like Pappy when he talks about dying and meeting the judge. Pappy had been the rock and the force that kept the farm going until he retired. And then returned when Jim died and kept it going again. Till now. Mostly Virgil keeps it going now. But he remembers the Chrysler engine Pappy hoisted from the ground to the pickup bed all by himself. Betting Dick and Jim he could do it. This Pappy here, the one talking about kidneys and fear and prayer, is a shrunken version of the other. This Pappy has deep thoughts and talks deep and doesn't seem scary the way the old Pappy did. The old Pappy had a look that could paralyze your lungs. His brows gouging together like chisels. The jaw muscles grinding. The threatening hands that he never used on the boy, but which the boy feared more than anything. If that Pappy had ever hit him, Virgil would have shattered in a zillion pieces.

"Want to go eat?" Virgil gestures toward the house. "Smell the roast?"

The old man's eyes have turned toward the tank in the killing yard, thirty bodies in the galvanized tub.

"We'll wrap them chickens later," Virgil tells him. "I'll clean the tubs, you won't have to. We'll go eat and you can rest and have a cigar. Me and Gramma Nez can milk the cows."

Pappy's eyes are looking elsewhere.

"What you seein, Pappy?"

On top of the coop, Aaron stretches his neck and crows. The hens stop pecking and stand at attention, waiting for orders. Aaron sounds like a straining piccolo leaking high notes.

"What's he doing that for this time a day?" says Virgil. "Hey, Aaron!" he shouts, "what's into you?"

"Callin for his wives," says Pappy. "Maybe he thinks they're hidin." Thirty bodies float in the tub. Guts burn in the barrel.

The War According to V –

Little V,

The flight was 20 hours because we had to make stops in Hawaii and Wake Island and Okinawa. I was ready to face a battalion of VC all by myself just so I could get off that fucking plane. I met a guy at processing who was rotating out. He called the plane his Freedom Bird. He said he would shoot a toe off before he would ever come back here. He said the worse thing is not the little man in black pajamas sniping at you, it's the booby traps, the toe poppers, the bouncing bettys. He told me I will see soon enough what he is saying. He didnt hate anybody when he got here 12 months ago, he said, but he hates everything now including our goverment. His attitude started changing the first time he saw a buddy blown apart by a mine. He described how the guy was draped all over a tree like grotesque Christmas ornaments. Him and that guy went through AIT together. He was one of his best friends he said and from then on he wanted nothing so much as to kill the enemy. He wanted revenge. It's what a lot of guys fight for over here. Not for home and country and Mom's apple pie and bullshit like that, but for REVENGE. Or simple self-preservation. The enemy isnt seen as human by some of these guys. He is a gook or a dink or slope. I am going to remind myself everyday that these people are human. Just a different culture, but basically we all want the same thing. Food, shelter, a hot bath and now and then a warm piece of ass.

10,000 miles from home and believe me it feels like it. It definitely another world. It is nothing like Minnesota except for the wet heat and lots of trees. Mostly it is dusty and dirty and smelly or wet and sticky and smelly smelly. Lots of rotting vegetation and waste of all kinds laced with rubber trees and something sweet, like fruits of some kind rotting in alleys and fields and dumps at the edge of town, all them odors carried on the wind right up your nose. No wonder we all smoke like chimneys. Smoking cuts the stench and calms your nerves and holds mosquitoes at bay. Well sometimes. Add the stink of motor scooters, jeeps, trucks and planes with their long streaks of exhaust fouling the air. And garlic, lots of garlic, people here eating it like candy. I kid you not kiddo. Like candy. You can smell it on their breath and in their sweat. Every body sweats like a pig.

And there are ants like you aint ever seen. Some of them gigantic mothers big as crickets. They eat the sweating furniture like termites do, the wood parts, no kidding, and anything eatable that isnt nailed down they carry off to their tunnels. Dead dogs and dead birds, all the dead everywhere, things like that, the ants take care of them. But they love wood best and rotting fruits. People ride around on motor scooters and bicycles and carts drawn by oxen. Unreal. Jesus where am I what century is this? The oxen have horns that would put our Moses to shame, like Texas Longhorns but not quite that wide. Is Moses still alive by the way? I am thinking you guys might have slaughtered him by now and packed him in the freezer. That is one job I dont miss, that and killing chickens or rabbits. People over here kill without batting an eye. They eat dogs I kid you not. Pet them one minute, hang them from a tree the next. The natives wont look at you unless you are buying something. Then they smile and show fingers for prices and talk English if they know any, Vehwee good plice. Vehwee chep dis. You hear a lot of that. Sometimes they write the price in the dirt with a stick and you erase it and write a lower price. Back and forth it goes. They expect you to bargain, but I hate it. I bought a can of sardines from one trader, old and dusty can. Canned in Norway King Olaf Sardines in Mustard Sauce it said. I do not know why I bought it. I started thinking it might be poisoned. Maybe it was canned in Hanoi and a false label put on it and smuggled to Saigon where the unsuspecting grunt would buy it and die of ptomaine. It is biological warfare that we introduced, so why shouldnt they try to poison us back? I threw the sardines away. Hey, you can not help but be paranoid in a paranoid place. You wonder all the time who is enemy and who is not and you feel surrounded when you are on the streets. Christ, they all look alike Virgil. If I had to pick a Cong out of a lineup I couldnt do it. Sure like to be elsewhere right now. Like to be back in school, playing on the Elks team and hitting a homerun and listening to the cheers. I feel so far away and empty. I guess I am pretty darn homesick. I did not think I would be this homesick, but I am. I miss my little Bro, and I miss the farm, the cows, the haying and harvesting and Gramma Nez bitchy mouth and Pappy grumbling and our cousin Gingers beautiful legs. I miss all that. Dont miss Mom much though and dam sure not miss that prick Uncle Dick. Keep in touch. There it is.

Big V.

Rolling Thunder

You can kill ten of my men for every one I kill of yours,
but even at those odds, you will
lose and I will win. **(Ho Chi Minh)**

You have a row of dominoes set up; you knock over the first one, and what will
happen to the last one is that it will go over very quickly. **(President Dwight D. Eisenhower)**

Should I become President . . . I will not risk American lives . . . by permitting any
other nation to drag us into the wrong war at the wrong place at the wrong time.
(President John F. Kennedy)

We could pave the whole country and put parking strips on it,
and still be home by Christmas. **(Governor Ronald Reagan)**

It became necessary to destroy the town to save it. **(U. S. Army Major Not Identified)**

We want nothing for ourselves—only that the people . . .
be allowed to guide their own country in their own way.
We will do everything necessary to reach that objective.
We do this in order to slow down aggression.
We will not be defeated.
We will not grow tired.
We will not withdraw. **(President Lyndon B. Johnson)**

The war . . . is only the ghastliest manifestation of what . . . afflicts America's whole
culture - aware only of its own history, insensible to everything which isn't part of the
local atmosphere. **(Stephen Vizinczey)**

What the hell's Vietnam worth to me?
What is it worth to the country? **(Johnson)**

Virgil Francis Foggy

The radio on the counter is playing bluegrass, Flatts and Scruggs: "The Soldier's Return."

My love was lost . . . in a foreign bat-tle . . .

"Grace before glutton," says Dick. His long lips smiling. His dimples deep. The wine polishing his eyes.

"Thirty-six going on six," Gramma Nez says, giving him a look. Pappy's eyes are saying *tired, so tired.*

With both his parents staring him down, Dick bows his head, his smirk hidden in his hands, while Pappy says, "Bless us, O Lord and these thy gifts . . ."

Across the sea in a distant land . . .

The plates are piled in front of Pappy. When he's done praying, he starts carving the lamb and passing the plates down amid clatter and music.

The woman in "The Soldier's Return" doesn't recognize her sweetheart because his face is changed by battle scars. Which makes Virgil think of Vernon in harm's way fighting for his country, a patriot. A hero. What's a hero? What might happen to his face? He could come back like the faceless chicken living because of its autonomic nervous system. Vernon might have a face no one would know. Or he could be getting killed today (right this second) and the family wouldn't have a clue until the telegram came: *Your son, Vernon Joseph Foggy died in action at the battle of—* Or something like that. If that's how it goes. Maybe no telegram, maybe they phone you instead, or drop by in uniform and say, *We regret to . . .*

Vernon's letters often have funny parts in them, funny things that happen on patrol or at a base or in some bar. He says he is no longer amazed at how goofy soldiers can be, how they might make bets on who gets the most leeches while crossing some stream. Or how they watch a leech suck blood, until it's stuffed like a manicotti. And then they'll smash the thing with a fist, burst it like a water balloon and laugh about the blood splattering. At base, he says they sometimes put on music and dance inside the hooch, drinking and smoking pot and dancing and stripping down naked and playing Knights on Horseback. At which, he says, he and Melvin Paine haven't been beaten, when Melvin is the horse and he's the Knight knocking other Knights off their horses. Sometimes getting pissed and fighting for real, fists and feet. Which is strange that you would fight each other with charlie gook in the woods laying traps and waiting to cut your throat. You do whatever you can to forget about the war, he says, forget about gooks and leeches and mosquitoes big as your fist and scorpions that crawl under your poncho and sting you and no matter how you smash them they won't die. They're like punchdrunk boxers, he says, who keep coming back for more. You go to the bars and drink yourself silly and get yourself laid, and for an hour you put the war in some walled off part of your mind. Sometimes pot and booze and pussy are the only things that can make you feel like there is still some fun in life. Like life is more than grieving and terror and boredom and homesickness and longing for love.

He's got to go all the way till August 1970 until he's done his year and will get rotated. Unless he volunteers for more. Like hell he will. He pretty much has had it with everything except his buddies and banging slantways beaver, he says. Lots of Vietnamese girls are really beautiful, he says. He says some are so beautiful they don't look real. They are like little dolls you can hold in the palm of your hand, he says. And you can bang them for fifteen dolla and pak cigarette, he says. He says it's the war that's done it, the war has made them whores, the easy money and the war and the will to survive and always everywhere, too, is the greed you can count on. The war has taught him that communists and capitalists are the same people, he says. Basically no difference in what they say or do. Both are trying to save the world from each other, he says. He says that when people in the cities need what you have, they'll do whatever has to be done to get it—kill you or fuck you, he says. He says we would be that way too if the war were in America. Best country in the world, he says, but move the war there and you would have desperate women in alleys on their knees and men jumping out of garbage cans to stab a soldier in the back, he says. Not because they're patriots. But because they want to steal your money and buy some rice, he says.

He says Nam makes you sweat worse than Minnesota in August. Everything gets moldy, he says. Even your rifle perspires, he says. He saw beads of sweat dripping from a M-67 recoilless rifle like it was alive, like it was getting sunstroke. But when you go into the mountains it gets so cold at night you freeze your ass off, he says. The choppers carry you everywhere, even into Cambodia, even into Laos. Everything there is made of extremes, he says, and you become extreme yourself. You do things you never thought you would do. You think things you never thought you would think. See parts of yourself you didn't know were there. He says he is always surprising himself. He says he has gotten to know himself better, but he hasn't reached the end of who he is and he isn't sure he wants to go there to find out. He says that one thing he wondered about was if he had the courage to be a good soldier and now he knows he has. He says he knows it because he is terrified when the shooting starts but he goes forward anyway. Which is what courage is, he says. If you're not scared, then you don't have courage, you're just a robot running on chemistry. Combat is confusion and fear and anger, he says, but he puts one foot in front of the other and does his duty. Fear doesn't paralyze him like it does some guys. He is glad to know that about himself, he says. *There it is*, he writes at the end. There what is, Virgil's not sure.

"Turn that radio off," says Dick. "Who told them they could sing? They ought to stick to their banjos."

Virgil turns the music off, but the tune is catchy and he continues to hum it in his head.

Pappy dips into the pot, bringing up chunks of potato and carrots and peas, diced onions and chopped garlic, all swished in gravy together and smelling like home and security. The refrigerator motor kicks in. Its faint rattle keeps time with the song in Virgil's head—*face is changed by battle scars*. He can't imagine Vernon's face being so changed that no one would know him. But sure it can happen. Scars can go so deep they change a fellow forever. Make him someone else outside and inside.

Virgil looks round the kitchen and sees changes. But it's all little things. The refrigerator has yellowed with age and is the shade of Pappy's skin now. The long counter, with its many drawers below and cupboards above covering the entire wall, has been painted white again. Above the sink the window is full of lines, like a drunken spider spun them. There are greenish tints between the double panes. On the counter are new black and white stair-step canisters going nowhere. A plastic tray filled with bottles of vitamins runs the length of the counter. It didn't used to be there before Regina started reading *Reader's Digest* and went on a vitamin kick. Regina wants the cupboard knobs replaced with ones she saw in a catalog. Gothic knobs with fancy initials (YOUR FAMILY INITIALS HERE!) in the center. Gothic F's. Gothic, Regina has said, symbolizes royalty. When Virgil asked her what Gothic actually meant, she said it was French for castle. "Safe in our castle," she said. "Our sanctuary from gonna-getcha."

Pappy passes the meat to Dick.

Alive and kicking yesterday. Cute and playful that lamb. Pappy hit it with the two-pounder and it flopped down dead. No pain, no understanding of what had happened. Not like the army guys getting gut-shot and knowing full well. *Am I dying! Don't let me die!* Rachel has been pretty upset ever since her baby bought the farm, but she'll get over it. Animals have short memories, else how could they stand it? Humans have long memories, but God has given them animals to kill and they don't have to mourn because God said so. In fact, humans are going against the will of God if they mourn the animals. That's what Father Hess has said. Humans are showing they haven't got faith in God's system and not having faith makes them candidates for Hell. Virgil looks at his burnt finger. A blister there that he'll pop later with a pin. Heat drifts from the stove. It's done its job and can rest now. Virgil's bedroom is directly above. Hot up there when the stove is on. But the panes will ice over from condensation in January when the coal-fired heater in the basement is banked at night. He breaks ice from the panes and sucks it if he gets thirsty.

"When I grow up, I'm going to live in Arizona and never be cold again." Without realizing it, Virgil has said this thought out loud.

Everyone looks at him baking in Arizona. Virgil the color of coffee. He has a masculine body in Arizona and bikini girls love stroking his chest. They are all strawberry blondes like Ginger but with boobs and wind-blown dresses like Marilyn Monroe.

"What's in Arizona?" says Ginger.

"Average daytime temperature in July is eighty-nine degrees," Virgil says.

"Fry what little brains you have," says Ginger.

"Heat will kill you quicker than cold," says Regina. "Especially Arizona heat. It literally boils your blood. That's what heatstroke does. Boils your blood. Boils it right out of your pores. My father died that way. He was only forty-seven. He worked all day in the sun laying bricks and the heat murdered him."

"Boils your blood," Virgil repeats. He decides not to live in Arizona. He looks at the radio and remembers the song. On the other side of the window, poplar leaves rubbing the glass make sounds like an untuned violin. In the center of the window hangs the sampler on silver chains. Gramma Nez made it after Jim dropped dead in the pasture. It says:

NEVER LET ANYTHING SO FILL YOU WITH SORROW
THAT YOU FORGET THE JOY OF CHRIST RISEN

Gramma Nez came across the quote from Mother Theresa
in *Catholic Times.* She claimed the quote was a sign of her son's spirit
hovering. He had guided her to it. "There are more things in heaven and
earth than are dreamed of," she said. "A proverb sent by Jimmy to comfort
my brokenheart, my bitterness. The Lord can be mean, he can be vicious.
Indeed, indeed. He hurts you and you don't know why. There's no way to
tell what the old boy's thinkin. There's no way to know why he does what
He does. He's a puzzle. A bigger puzzle than the *I Ching.* At least with it
what matters is how the coins fall and feelin your way to the message. But
what can you do with a God remote? He's got everything his way. Prayin
might help you, but talkin stern can work as well. At least that's been my
experience. Remember that Jacob wrestled with God and won respect. No
namby-pambies, no whiners, God hates em."

Always she is cussing those secret plans he won't tell. Like the
goddamn war. It's part of some cosmic plan she doesn't approve of. Not
when it touches her kin. He can be a Bastard, she admits, and the only way
to handle him is not to give in. If you give in and grovel he knows you're
defeated and he sneers at you. Forget about singing psalms and offering
to kiss sacred toes. She's good at shaking her fist at the heavens when her
arthritis is bothering her. Or when Pappy is walking into walls. Or the next
crisis has come to the farm (dead calf, down cow, machinery failure), things
occurring when she's too tired to cope. She's good at saying prayers, going
to mass and demanding attention. It's the squeaky wheel that gets greased.
You need to try everything in your arsenal. You never can tell what will
work, so you need to do everything to reach your objective. That's why she
studies the sixty-four hexagrams of the *I Ching* and the sayings of Krishna
in the *Bhagava Gita* and such. Let the Old Boy know—you're not the only
game in town.

She stitched the proverb to a piece of ivory batting. Above it she
embroidered white daisies with green stems and curling leaves. Tiny blue
bells tumbling at the borders. Regina looked at the bells and said, "*For
Whom the Bells Tolls.* Poor Jimmy, poor Jim." And she started weeping, and
Gramma Nez said, "Oh come on, Regina, enough is enough. Show some
backbone, girl."

Virgil saw the *Bells* title on the bookshelves and found it was a quote from a sermon by a preacher named John Donne. Virgil copied some words down and memorized them and said them every night as his evening prayer: *No man is an island entire of it self; any man's death diminishes me, because I am involved in man kind; and therefore never send to know for whom the bell tolls; it tolls for thee.* It is comforting to say the words. For the length of saying them, he doesn't feel isolated or unwanted or unloved. For those few seconds he knows that he is exactly what it says, not totally alone, no matter how scared he feels since his father died and Vernon went to war. Virgil believes that the sermon was written in the language of God. If God wrote in English, He would write the same way. If Virgil empties his mind and asks Jesus about Donne, Jesus whispers, "When I breathed voices into men, Donne's English is what I had in my mind."

Gramma Nez crocheted the bells and finished the sampler off with a walnut frame. It has been hanging in the window for nearly three years. When she and Pappy come over for dinner, she sits where she can see it and read the words. Virgil prays to his dad and feels he is there— *My Father who art in Heaven*—and asks him for strength and courage and protection from Dick. And make Pappy well and watch over Vernon on the battlefield.

"You gonna eat?" says Dick. "Or stare out the windur?"

"Earth to Virgil," says Ginger.

"There he goes," says Regina. "Where you been, sweetheart?"

"Bout Daddy. Bout Gramma Nez makin that." He points at the sampler. "And never send for whom the bell tolls," he says. "John Donne."

"That's right." She looks at her son, her round eyes shiny with pleasure. "See, you got a brain if you'll just use it for somethin besides namin stupid cars. He can tell every car by its grill. What's the good of that, I'd like to know?"

"Better than algebra," says Dick.

"Oh, hush up."

"Christ risen," says Gramma Nez. "The knowledge of the Resurrection taketh away the sorrows of the world," she says. "The trick is to get him to listen!" She shakes her fist at the ceiling. "Sometimes the Old Boy deaf as a doorknob!"

"Inspiration is all I ask," Regina says. "Breath of God."

"Inspiration, but don't forget to pass the ammunition," says Gramma Nez.

Ginger studies the sampler, her eyes mournful as if she wants comfort. Maybe it reminds her of sad things. Her Uncle Jim's death, perhaps. His death changed her life from town girl to farm girl, from cousin to sister, from Daddy's girl to the stepdaughter of an overweight, moody Italian step-mom who used to be her aunt. Ginger's mother was honey-blond, willowy, a walking advertisement for beauty and grace. Ginger is shaping up just like her. Not a farm girl, not used to the farm or the marriage, even after two and a half years. The smells of the farm make her sick, she says. She says the smell gets into her hair. She showers every morning and every night before bed. Dick calls it hygienic overkill. He says she should allow herself to smell like a real woman once in a while. He says people who over-bathe have a fetish. They are not comfortable in their own skin. And she tells him that people who don't bathe enough stink like dirty feet. He does have a foot odor problem, he admits. He says his shoes don't breathe and the sweat glands in his feet have always been over-active.

Dick sops gravy with a piece of bread. Pops it bird-quick into his mouth. Washes it down with wine. Dick's teeth are very strong. A goat would be lucky to have such teeth. They look like they could chew glass, or maybe even tin. He looks at the platter and forks another slice of lamb. Dick can put a handball inside his mouth. Virgil has seen him do it.

"S'good, Ma," Dick says. "Yom, yom." He shows his dimples.

"Eat," Gramma Nez orders, "you mother's blight." She squints one-eyed Popeye-style at him.

Dick guffaws. "A mother's look of love," he says.

"Pappy will whip you," she says. "You don't straighten up."

"That'll be the eff'n day!"

Balanced on Pappy's fork is a dented eye. He lifts it, sucks it in, squishing it in his back teeth. He lifts the second eye and does the same thing.

The eyes make Virgil think of oysters. One bite, then swallow. People who eat the eyes will never go blind. This is gospel according to Gramma Nez. She has second sight and can divine the future by using the *The Book of Changes*. Or the Bible. She says that her prayers and Vernon's holy medal will keep him alive and he'll come back a man of the world. The medal round Virgil's neck was blessed with holy water. No harm can come to him either. As long as he wears it and says three Hail Marys and *No Man is an Island* before going to bed. The Virgin has told Gramma Nez that the baby coming will renew the promise between Regina and Dick as

43

long as the baby gets baptized right away in the Church.

Gramma says . . . Gramma says-says.

To distract himself from the chatter, Virgil carves a piece of potato into a tiny ball and glazes it with gravy. Lifting it, he shows it to Ginger.

"Eye for an eye," he whispers, hoping she'll smile.

"Don't act up," she warns.

"An eye for an eye, a tooth for a—"

"You're not cute," says his mother. "Don't play with your food. Kids in China are starving."

"Name some," says Dick.

"Ching Chong and Wong Dong and Yu P. Yu," she says.

The War According to V –

Little V,

I am told the NVA have a 200 mile tunnel all the way from their border to about a third of the way into South Nam. I don't know what to think of an enemy who would build a 200 mile tunnel Virge. I wonder if it true. If so, it seems like one of the wonders of the world. Think of IT. 200 miles underground. All of it dug by hand. Shovels and picks I mean. How amazing would that be? Course he has had 30 years of war to build it and thousands of other tunnels that run like underground highways through mountains and flatlands and jungles, you name it. These asian fellas are master miners and no one is better at gorilla warfare. They wrote the book. They know ten times as much about it as we do about hit and run wars. If they would fight in the open, Army to Army, man to man they would be wiped out in a week and we could all go home. But they know what they doing Virge. They aint stupid. They beat the French that way and now, frankly, everyone says they are beating us. I am going to keep my head down and put in my time and get out as soon as I can. But that is a long from now. Some guys get to rotate back sooner if they apply for OCS, Officer Candidate School, and become a Second Loony of which there is a shortage. I do not have any intention of re-uping so there isnt any point in my taking the exam, though my company commander has ordered everyone to just in case. Duty calls. Hump the boonies lil Bro. Ambush time. Search and destroy and all that shit. CO says we need to pour on the steel. West of me napalm was shattering the horizon. Fablous horrible flame looking like the god of war. There it is.

Big V.

Rolling Thunder

Tell them they've got to draw in their horns or we're going to bomb them back into the Stone age. **(Gen. Curtis LeMay)**

We still seek no wider war.
This is not a jungle war,
but a struggle for freedom on every front.
It will require patience as well as bravery,
the will to endure
as well as the will to resist.
I wish it were possible to convince others with words
of what we now find it necessary to say with guns and planes:
Armed hostility is futile. **(Johnson)**

We are at war with the most dangerous enemy
that has ever faced mankind
in his long climb
from the swamp to the stars. **(Reagan)**

The yella bastards do all their shootin from hidin, don't they?
(John Wayne)

Virgil Francis Foggy

Virgil puts the potato in his mouth, smashes it and shows the mess to Ginger.

Dick says, "Got a deathwish, boy?" Reaching over he flicks Virgil's ear. Everyday he does something like that, flicks Virgil's ear or twists it, or tweaks his hair, gets him in hammerlocks or headlocks, gives him Indian burns. He is quick to slap. Quick to punch. One time Virgil came into the kitchen and Dick punched him in the eye, knocked him right on his can. Gave him a shiner that sealed the lids together and made the eye blind for a while. Dick pulled the bill of Virgil's cap over the eye to hide the damage. He didn't tell Virgil what wrong he had done, and to this day and for the rest of his life the boy will never know. Kids don't forget things like that, of course. Virgil knows that when he grows up, he will kick Dick's ass or maybe kill him. In the three years since Dick married Regina Perpetua, Virgil has had at least one black eye or bruised cheek or swollen lip a month. He tells his mother that he got it playing football or in a fight at school. She thinks he is a fighter, a rough and tumble kid. All *boy*, she says. She says she hopes he's not a bully, but if some boy gets tough, she wants Virgil to fight back and fight hard. She says never be a coward. Gramma Nez says to smack the bastard with a stick, hit him with a rock.

Regina pushes her plate back and makes a face.

"Nausea again?" asks Gramma Nez.

Regina nods and says, "I can't digest anything the way this baby is crowdin my guts."

"Don't," Virgil tells Dick, rubbing the stinging ear.

"Don't tell me *don't*, boy. I'll don't your ass to the moon."

Virgil looks at his mother. When she is around, Dick usually won't hit him. Dick pours more wine from the jug and repeats, "Your ass to the moon."

"Knock it off, you two," Regina says. Turning to Gramma Nez she says, "Did you see that story in the paper about the mother who let her boyfriend sleep with her daughter?" Regina gets up, grabs the *Minneapolis Star* and opens it. "Only thirteen. Now what the hell wrong with that woman, Inez?"

Virgil laughs.

"It's not funny!" says Regina. "You got a warped sense of humor,

47

Virgil. All teenage boys have sick minds." She looks at Gramma Nez. "You just have to get them past that stage, you know what I mean?"

"Men ain't worth much til they're thirty," says Gramma Nez. "There's 'bout a fifteen year span when they're all insane."

"Some women too, obviously," says Regina, tapping the paper.

Gramma Nez warms to the subject of the bad mother giving her daughter to the bad man. "Whore of Babylon. Whore of—"

"Jezebel," interjects Regina.

"I tell you this," says Gramma Nez, "she gives all women a bad name. One woman actin like that taints us like shit on a shoe. Men see it and they say we're all like that under our skins. Whores, whores, whores. But what they don't see is, there's a man behind it. A man will take up with that type and prey on her weakness, you see."

"Women need to get smart about men."

"Listen to the experts," says Dick.

"Experience with guys like you makes us experts," says Regina.

"Yhah, he made her do it—yhaah-yhaah. She don't got a mind of her own. Oh, such a brute, your honor. He gets me drunk and brainwashes me and makes me do awful things in bed. I can't stand it. Poor helpless me. Fut! She'd be doing them if a fairy lived under her roof. There's no accounting for what's in the blood. Blood of *some* women, I mean. Present company excepted, of course."

"No accountin for what's in men's blood neither," says Regina.

"That's right, men neither. One drop in the blood can corrupt the whole. I mean w-h-o-l-e, not h-o-l-e."

"Oh, shut up, will you? You disgustin thing."

Check out Ginger. She has raked her hair over her face again. Tips of gold touching her plate, sweeping an inch above the gravy. Virgil watches happily, waiting for the moment when the hair gets wet. Her hair is everything to her. She plays with it for hours, trying on styles, modeling in the mirror. She will do a high-pile job, like a society lady. Or a part down the middle, broomstick sides like a hippie. Or sweep it back like a boy. Or a French braid. Or a rope braid. Or pigtails. She often goes round the house and asks opinions. Truth is, she looks good in everything, but Virgil likes the bouncy waves to the shoulders best. Dick likes the French braid. He likes to weave it for her when she'll let him. He makes a very tight braid that pulls her ears back and makes her forehead smooth, like its been ironed that way. Gramma Nez wants the loose bun low on the neck with

48

curls falling in front of the ears. Regina likes the arched sides parting from the middle and framing the face, feathery tails down her neck and back. Which is how Regina styles her own hair.

"*Vanity, vanity,*" Pappy has been telling Ginger lately. He used to like her fashion shows. But that changed when he got sick.

"Watch your hair," says Dick. "It's in your plate."

Look at her sad face, the sad expression contradicted by the curl in her lip, the ever-ready sneer. "Thirty dead chickens in a tub," she says. She fixes her gaze on Virgil. "For whom the bells tolls. Maybe the bell tolls for Vernon. Or you, you murderous brat."

"Bite your tongue!" says Gramma Nez. "Why do you always say such things?"

"I was thinkin about that song on the radio," says Ginger. "He gets wounded and comes back and his sweetheart don't know him. It's sad. But it's happenin all over this stupid country." She bursts into tears. Her hands over her face.

"She's nuts," says Dick. "Look at her."

"Now-now, Ginger," says Gramma Nez. "Regina, this girl has no self-control. What are you raising?" She is glaring at Dick. "Raising a nervous breakdown."

"Hormones," says Regina.

"She's her mother's daughter," Dick says. "Cry if you look at her cross-eyed."

Ginger has told Virgil several times how she dreams of Vernon dead. She will cry when she hears certain songs and thinks he's been killed or maimed. Virgil has told her she should write Vernon, he wants her to, but she won't. It's too painful. The less she thinks of where he is the better off she'll be, she says.

"Think how many thousands have died already," Ginger continues, words blubbering. "Think how many thousands are wounded and in wheelchairs and blind. What if it happens to Vernon?" The tears roll. "It's thirty thousand dead so far."

"We lost more in Korea," says Dick. "It's always Vernon with you. Like there ain't half a million guys over there goin through the same thing. Like I didn't go through it myself in Korea. My forgotten patch of hell at the thirty-eighth parallel. Who wept for me? Who wept for a war fought to stem the rising red tide, the war to end all wars? We stopped communism dead in its tracks."

"The main subject has always got to be *you*," says Regina.

"Like you're not Miss Narcissi herself."

"No worse sin in the world than the deliberate destruction of a child's innocence," says Gramma Nez. She has read the article and is folding the newspaper.

"None worse," Regina agrees.

"As great a crime as murder." Gramma Nez pauses. Then adds: "In fact, it is murder. The murder of innocence. Herod murdered them."

"Dogs treat their pups better than some women treat their kids," Regina declares.

"Signs of Apocalypse," says Gramma Nez. Her chin juts like she dares them to deny the apocalypse. "Mark my words, Regina. Remember this day I said it. Mark it on the calendar. Signs this country be dyin."

"An absolute cryin shame. Nothing to do but shoot a mother like that. Shoot her like you'd shoot a mad dog. It's the only way to stop child abuse. You got to make the penalties so severe people just won't dare."

"Hang, draw and quarter them," says Dick.

Ginger raises her slobbering face. "What's everybody talkin 'bout?" she whimpers. "Virgil, quit grinnin! Don't you know who's sad around here?"

"They're back to the girl whose mom give her to a guy to—"

"But I'm talkin thousands and thousands!" says Ginger.

"You want to know where it will end?" says Gramma Nez. "They'll be rapin babies next."

"What will happen to us, I wonder?" says Regina, eyes baggy, a quiver in her double chin, her thick neck that used to be so thin. "What's the world comin to? What kind of world have we made? War everywhere. Terror in the streets. Hatred in our hearts. We'll self-destruct. It's happenin right now. Look what's on TV. Nuthin but trash, riots, protests. Read the papers. Read *Reader's Digest*. Did you see this, by the way? Look at this." She grabs the paper, holds it up. The headlines: SHARON TATE, FOUR OTHERS MURDERED!

"A *Valley of the Dolls* star gettin murdered in her own home? I mean, if home isn't safe, what is?" She shuffles the paper, shows a picture of a smiling blond whose hair curves softly around her neck.

"Signs of the Apocalypse."

"This country fallin apart."

"She's so pretty," says Ginger, wiping her eyes.

50

"What happened to her?" says Gramma Nez.

"*Film star Sharon Tate, another woman and three men were found slain Saturday, their bodies scattered around a Benedict Canyon estate in what police said resembled a ritualistic mass murder. The victims were shot, stabbed or throttled. On the front door of the home, written in blood, was one word:Pig. Miss Tate was 26, and the wife of Roman Polanski, director of Rosemary's Baby. She was eight months pregnant. He is in England.*"

Regina gives the names and ages of the others slain: "Abigail Folger, 26. Jay Sebring, 35. Voityck Frokowski, 37. Steven Parent, 18."

She shakes her head sorrowfully. Then she adds—"*In the living room, dressed in underwear—bikini panties and a brassiere—was Miss Tate. A bloodied nylon cord was around her neck.*"

"They would say that," says Dick. "Titillate us with '*underwear-bikini panties*,' sick bastards." He laughs contemptuously. His eyes fix on Ginger. She has curtained her hair again, hiding herself.

Gramma Nez says, "Poor thing, eight months gone."

Regina puts her hand on her belly. "What can you say about a thing like that? There's what burrows in the blood, Dick. You can bet it's the work of some dope fiends! They catch those bastards, they should shoot them on the spot. Execute them just like they did her. No trial, just kill them. No mercy. No damn mercy."

"Terrorists in America," says Gramma Nez. "They're comin for us. They're bringin the war here, you mark my words."

"Twenty-six years old," murmurs Pappy. "I'm forty years older than her."

"This Parent kid was only eighteen," says Regina.

"God is up, lookin down," says Dick mockingly. He is looking at Pappy.

"Wipe your face, you slob," says Regina, pointing to grease on Dick's chin.

Pappy gestures with his hands toward the ceiling, asking the question, "Where's God in this?"

"There is no end to it," says Gramma Nez. "Anyone kill a woman eight months pregnant is not human, I don't care what anyone says. They might walk around with two arms and two legs and a head. They might look human, but they're not. They're something else. They don't belong on this planet. Not human. Nuh-uh. I bet they link it to Vietcongs."

"That's the trouble," says Dick, "they do belong on this planet.

51

They're just the tip of the iceberg, Ma. What we love best is to kill one another. Just give us an excuse. Any excuse will do."

"Here is hell," says Regina solemnly. "Right here on God's green earth. People like thems makin a hell of what could have been paradise. Before the age of sin cometh."

"In Adam's fall we fell all," says Gramma Nez.

Echoing in Virgil's ears are the words, *bikini panties and a brassiere . . . a bloodied nylon cord was around her neck.* He looks at his mother's hand resting on her six-months belly. It has happened to women just like her. Virgil had heard them talk about it when she and Jim were into the books on war, the things they would discuss. Atrocities. Soldiers bayoneting unborn babies was nothing new. Huns. Mongols. Goths. Vandals. Emperor Caligula did it to his wife. She also happened to be his sister. Is incest sexy? Sisters and brothers used to marry all the time. *Bikini panties . . . a bloodied nylon cord.* If he lived in another time and place, Virgil could marry Ginger. He wishes they were still little kids and could take baths together and wash each other.

The phone in Ginger's bedroom faintly calls. She starts to rise.

"Sit still," says Dick. "No phones at dinnertime. You tell him that."

She leans back. Crosses her legs. Curly-cues her hair with her middle finger. A clear thread of snot runs over her lips.

"Blow your nose," says Dick.

Virgil has heard them on the phone, Peter and Ginger. Sometimes she tells him she's doing things to herself. But Virgil doesn't know if she really does them or maybe she's saying it because that's what Peter wants to hear. Virgil could kneel and look through the keyhole, but he won't do it. He wants to, but he would have to confess to the priest. Like when he saw Dick and Regina in the loft, he's held that one back so far. And what if Ginger is just teasing? He wouldn't want to know if she is teasing.

"The family. The family is unrave*ling.*" Gramma Nez shakes her head. "Signs of Apocalypse, I say. Mark my words. No yang without yin. Vicey versey."

"Going to hell in a handbasket," adds Regina.

"Like a bucket down a well," says Gramma Nez.

"*That's one small step for man, one giant leap for mankind,*" Virgil says. "We landed on the moon."

They all turn. They all blink.

52

"Just thinkin," he says. "Last month Neil Armstrong landed on the moon, him and Buzz Aldren."

"And?"

"Well . . . it's . . . I don't know, it just pop into my head."

"A schizophrenic nation," says Pappy, "that's what the boy means. We can go to the moon and yet we make war. Nuthin makes sense that's what he means."

"Schizophrenic everything," says Dick. "I saw it in Korea."

Gramma Nez says, "Jesus, it makes me tired."

Regina is staring at Virgil. "What's that on your neck?" she says.

He touches a sore spot. Glances at Dick. Dick is eating off the serving platter, scarfing the last of the lamb.

"The way he bruises, you know, I wonder if it's his blood, if somethin is wrong with his blood. I should get him a physical," says Regina. "He bruises too easy for a boy his age. He probably needs vitamin K."

She and Gramma Nez keep talking. They switch back to the whore who lets her boyfriend sleep with her daughter and how in her own way she is as bad as those who killed Sharon Tate.

Virgil giggles.

"This is not a funny subject," says his mother. "Why do you keep laughin?"

"It's nerves," says Gramma Nez.

He giggles again.

"What?" she says.

He points to Ginger.

Ginger has braided her hair. Long and fat, she has roped it around her neck like a noose.

"Ginger, stop that," Regina says.

"What?" says Ginger. She lets the braid drop. "Jesus, can't do nuthin 'round here."

"Kids," says Regina, her eyes disgusted at how insensitive and stupid children are.

Round-shouldered in his chair, Pappy folds his hands at the table edge. Closes his eyes, a gnomish figure praying. Is he praying for the slaughtered sheep in Benedict Canyon? Sharon Tate and her unborn baby? Or Vernon dodging bullets? Or an eye for an eye, tooth for a tooth? Or love yee one another, turn the other cheek? Or God please spare me an ugly death?

Or maybe none of those? Shh, says his breath. His mouth hanging open. Worn out Pappy has fallen asleep.

The War According to V –

Little V,

Sho nuff should no writ to me lil bro drunk as skunk but what the fuzz? Virge baby bro In Country piece of cake dam sure if you stay on the night side of love. Oh I am so fugger smash. Hey kid, what happenin? Daddy Dick kicking your ass? Kick him back Virge. In the balls. Don't take shit off that mothafucka prick in his pants.

hey guess what? PFC Vernon Foggy in love. Stop laffing. Vernon means loving her up baby woo! name is Candy Chien Hoi. Pretty name hey? What can I say? Dam these exotic girls drive me crazy bro. best thing in my life. So kind and sweet so ALL FEM and glad to be so and yummy just like her name. She took me home to meet Mama San and she honor me by killing rooster and making some dish that very hot, wow, with tiny red peppers and garlic and god knows what else, but very delishus, I mean delicius. Mama San likee me vurry much and give big approve of me as boyfriend. I go buy lots of grocery and carton of cigarette and some furniture they need and bring to them and they make fuss and love me up coochee coochee. Good soldier man, good soldier Vernon. Such fine people here Virge. So friendly these people. And Candy is just like her name. The sweetest kisser I ever kissed and great in bed. I cant even tell you all she does cuz you would be hiding in the bathroom doing you know what. Back off those bones kid. You go blind! Ha, ha, ha, but if there is anything she don't know about giving pleasure I cant imagine what it could be. Whew, I learned a lot.

Little bro, I have fallen in the manure and come up smelling like a whore. Never thought I so lucky as to meet Candy and her family. Hope I dont sound stupid but she stole my heart and even thinking of marry her and bring her back with me to Minn. She says she love farms and she love America. My buddies say I want to marry her is because I am lonely but will get over it they say. No think so. I feel this way about one other girl and you know her but I am not going to tell you who she is. Big secret! I write this on Candy kitchen table which I bought and the chairs too. I mail to you in minute. Then we going to hit some bars and dance and fun. Candy says I am the most fun guy she ever met. I was fun cuz I met her. God I cant keep my eyes off her she is so gorge, such beautiful dark eyes, such silky skin, and she smells like flowers. Heavy sigh. Tell Vernon not in love if you can. Just try. Write soon. There it is.

Big V.

Rolling Thunder

We are also there to strengthen world order.
[These] are people whose well-being rests in part on the belief that they can count
on us if they are attacked.
To leave would shake the confidence of all these people in the value of an
American commitment and in the value of America's word.
Let no one think for a minute that retreat . . . would bring an end to the conflict.
The battle would be renewed in one country and then another.
The appetite of aggression is never satisfied.
In the words of the Bible: Hitherto shalt thou come, but no further. **(Johnson)**

I see light at the end of the tunnel. **(Walt Rostow)**

You know, perhaps one day history will record that we goofed. **(Reagan)**

HELL NO WE WONT GO!
LBJ HOW MANY KIDS DID YOU KILL TODAY?
(Protest Sign)

Virgil Francis Foggy

Virgil thinks about the slaughter 10,000 miles away that his brother and the papers write about. And the slaughter of Sharon Tate, her fetus and friends. The Kennedy brothers are dead. Martin Luther King Jr. is dead. Riots on campuses, riots in Washington in the cities. Half the country trying to kill the other half. He feels in his bones the End is near. Apocalypse soon.

He takes his plate to the sink and looks at the sampler—NEVER FORGET THE JOY—and feels a sliver of hope. Maybe it's all as Gramma Nez says it is. All a part of God's cosmic plan. Virgil's heart lifts as he goes outside to fetch the cows to the barn. Behind him the main door closes with a weighty *chunk*. The screendoor hangs cockeyed, the hinges jiggling. Voices fade as he strolls away talking to himself, reminding himself never to forget the joy of Christ popping out of the tomb and showing his wounds to doubting Thomas. Virgil knows that if he could just see those signs every fear would vanish.

As he crosses the patio, he sees Husky sitting on Pappy's chair licking wine stains on the table. The sun has dropped to tree level west. The woods and the sky are shades of reddish orange. Some of the cows are clipping grass. A few are lined up at the back of the barn, looking in the Dutch door, waiting for Virgil to open it. They want their cornmeal. They want alfalfa. Virgil tells Husky to fetch the cows. "Go get them, boy! Good dog!" The dog's purple tongue slips back inside his mouth. He eyes the boy as if sizing him up. Virgil whistles to show him they are friends again, no more playing with willow whips, just some fun was all that was. Be a sport. "Good boy, get them cows, Husky!" Virgil whistles and points at the cows in the pasture.

The dog's ears lower. His shoulder fur ruffles like a lion's mane.

"Aw, come on!" Virgil tells him. "Get over it. Knock off the bullshit, man. Let's get the cows. Go get em, go get em!" Turning his head toward the pasture Virgil hollers, "Cooom boss! Cooom bossies, coooom!" He glances over his shoulder at the dog. "Come on, Husky. What's the matter, hey? Like how many times have we fetched the cows, huh? Here, boy, here! Good boy."

Nothing doing. Husky refuses to move. His upper lip trembles. But Virgil has known the dog all his life and is not afraid of him. "Get your ass in gear!" he orders, marching up to the dog, reaching out to jerk him off the chair.

The instant fingers touch fur, the dog leaps for your throat. There is a roar and a flash of fangs, a blur of purple tongue. The teeth stabbing here and there. You know you are being killed, but it doesn't hurt like you thought being killed would hurt. The killing of Sharon Tate zips through your head and you wonder if it was painful to be choked to death like that. Your lower lip is ripped open; it spanks your chin. Twisting and turning, you try to get away. Teeth are everywhere whirring, catching a chunk of ribs, biting your left leg, the hamstring. Your chore-hardened muscles won't let you fall. Falling means dying. Down means out. Throat ripped open means bleeding to death. The dog hangs onto your left leg, while your right leg works to drag you to the house. You pull the dog inch by inch toward the hanging screen.

At some point Husky realizes you won't be hamstrung, won't go down and make the job easy, so he lets go of the leg and races to block the path to the door, seizing now on your right arm, biting just below the elbow, canines locking. Head shaking, jerking, tugging at the arm as though it is a rag the two of you are playing with.

Are you screaming? You think you are screaming, but you're not sure the screams are leaving your mouth. There is a power in you that moves you on somehow, a power that drags the dog across the bloody patio. Your eyes fix on the cockeyed screen, the worn knob of the heavy door. Ox-like you move, pulling the plow that is Husky, until at last your hand grabs the screen and gives you leverage—jerks you forward, your hand clutching the knob, the door flying open. Your wail reaching those in the house. They come rushing to save you.

"Oh, my God!" shrieks your mother.

"The boy! The boy!" cries Pappy.

In your mother's hand is a broom, which she uses as a stick. Pappy is kicking the dog's sides. The dog lets go and you sink into Ginger's arms. You watch Husky tumbling backwards under the blows. Dick fills his hands with fur and lifts him. Whirls him overhead. Hammers him onto the concrete patio. He lies there leaking blood from his mouth, one leg pawing, trying to run. Your mother wraps a towel around your gushing leg. Ginger takes her shirt off and ties it around your gushing arm, above the gushing hole, trying to make a tourniquet. Ginger is blubbering and saying ,"Poor baby, poor baby." Gramma Nez keeps trying to put your lip

59

back in place. Pappy is biting his fist helplessly.

Well, it is a fuss all right, much more than any of the other times you have been hurt on the farm. You try to tell your mother it isn't your fault. You look for Husky and see him limping towards the pasture. Too late to herd the cows now. Why did he go crazy? What happened in his head? Dogs go crazy like people go crazy and kill eight-months-pregnant ladies. When Husky was a puppy, a ball of reddish fuzz, the two of you played with a sailor doll. Husky chasing it, bringing it back as you threw it again and again and said, "Fetch, Husky, fetch!" The two of you tumbling, Husky biting playfully. Not for real, not killing. This day in August 1969 when he attacks, he means it.

"He . . . he tried to kill me," you say, feeling your mouth splattering blood with the words, lowering your eyes, seeing the blood fall. "Like that," you say. "Like cherries."

"Goddammit do some*thing*!" commands Gramma Nez.

Your pregnant mother tries to carry you to the car. Dick takes over. He hoists you into his arms, rushing you to the car. Your mother jumps to the door, opens it and sits down. Dick places you in her lap. He runs around to the other side. There are seconds of panic when the car won't start and your mother yells, "Get us to the fucking hospital! Get us to the fucking hospital!" The engine roars, the tires spray gravel as the hind-end flails side to side.

The ride to the hospital makes you think of the time after Dick married your mother and you all moved him and Ginger from town to the farm. He had rented a trailer and drove it over the lawn, right to the apartment door, and everyone helped load it. When the trailer was full and Dick was tying things down, the landlady showed up. She was standing like a Sumo wrestler, surly hands on surly wide hips ready to take Dick and Regina on. "I never want to see you Foggys again," she said. "I want you to know, I've watched this man carrying on with his foul mouth and drunken ways, and you better believe that this little girl will grow up one day and won't forgive her father carrying on like that in front of her. You watch and see how she'll make you pay for what you done, Richard Foggy. Children have long memories, you fool. They don't forget nuthin."

"Shut up, you old cow!" Dick told her. "For I put my fist in your face!"

"Just try it, buddy!"

There had been a lamp in Regina's hands. "That's my husband

60

you're talkin to!" she said.

"Up your kazoo!" said the landlady.

Regina threw the lamp at the landlady, hitting her shielding elbow. The lamp bounced off, fell to the walk and shattered.

"Goddamn you!" the landlady cried, hopping around, rubbing her elbow. "Assault, I'll get you for assault! Goddamn! Jesus Christ!"

Ginger and you were pushed inside the car. Doors slammed. Dick started backing the car and trailer off the lawn. But he wasn't good at it and the trailer kept jackknifing. Neighbors were watching. Forward, reverse, forward, reverse as Dick worked the shift lever and his face flamed and his mouth spewed every cuss word he knew. He ordered you to move out of the way, you were blocking his rear view, and when you didn't move fast enough, he slapped your ear and broke your eardrum. But you didn't know it was broken until later when you complained of feeling like a needle was in there and your mother took you to the doctor and he said, "Ruptured eardrum." You've been slightly deaf in that ear ever since.

The neighbors pointed and grinned at the flailing car. Dick kept cussing and your mother shouting, "Do some*thing!*"

He slammed the car into gear, tires buzzing, hitting the sidewalk and leaping forward, grooving the grass for twenty yards to the playground, kids scattering, sand catching the tires and spewing backwards like buckshot. Dick gunned the car into the juniper bushes that bordered the street. The car tore through and leaped over the curb. The muffler broke loose and skittered. A noise like an open-throated tractor filled the air. Dick plowed on, making a hard left onto the street, tires crying, trailer fishtailing over the pavement. Pounding the steering wheel, Dick yelling, "Shit-cunt-fuck! Shit-cunt-fuck! Sonofabitch! The fucking muffler! The fucking muffler! Jesus Christ, the motherfucking muff-diving muffler! Cocksucking old bitch, cornhole ass-licking pig twat from hell!"

And your mother said, "That's enough of that cussin, Dick Foggy! There's kids in here!"

Helpless with laughter, Ginger and you kicked your legs and pounded your fists into the seat cushions, and Dick said, "What's so funny back there? What's so goddamn, fuckin funny?" You tried to smother your giggles and you were holding your ear and your ear felt like a firecracker had blown up inside but you couldn't stop laughing.

Bloodsoaked now—blood flowing all over your mother—you feel the car vibrating with speed, and you see Dick's fuming face, the hot pink bald spot that whips into view when he glances at the side mirror. You keep giggling about something. You don't really know what.

"Don't worry, sweetheart," soothes your mother. "Mommy's here, Mommy's got you."

Your palm rests on her belly. You feel the baby kicking. "Don't be in a hurry," you whisper.

"What?" sweetheart?" says your mother. "Mommy's here. Don't be scared."

You try to tell her you aren't scared, but the words are garbled in blood.

The War According to V–

Little V,

I learn couple things over here. First what I learn is that fear kills hope and when that happens you are done for. Hope burns out but fear not burns out and fear can destroy your hope and your will to live. You have to watch it. You have to know. And have to allow yourself to be afraid. You have to face up to the fact that only death will take your fear away. You want to live? You have to be able to LIVE with that fact. Because once a guy gets it in his head that he would rather be dead than live round the clock in fear he is already dead. We got walking zombies over here. The living dead. I see them. Macho guys who start out Gungho Gungadin and end up walking by you with eyes that don't see you, eyes like open wounds because they can not believe they seen what they seen. You do not see those guys on TV. You see John Wayne wannabes the heros, not the guys who are basket cases. Guys who had no idea they could be so totally fucked by fear and war. Guys who bleed out their assholes. I am not kidding, no joke man. If you can not get a grip, your backbone collapses. Everywhere I look I see backbones collapsing, I see eyes full of cancer. Where is John Wayne when you need him? Ha! Not here, you can bet! War is not the old father figure teaching his platoon how to kill and how to survive and then dying himself heroically on the sands of Iwo Jima. That movie is pure Hollywood bullshit Virge. Did you know that bastard was never a Marine? True. He never even got out of Hollywood during World War II. They showed us his movie about the Green Berets last night. What a phony fuck that thing was. We were laughing our asses off at it, so full of cliche it makes you want to puke. Yeah you wont believe this but in the last scene they have the sun setting in the East and he is spose to be walking west into the setting sun. I shit you not little Bro. Film makers think we are to stupid to catch such things. They can not get their act together any better than the idiots giving the world this war. I am thinking lately none of this is necessary. I didnt know that before but I damn sure think it now. Jesus what a mess. But what are you going to do? You fight for yourself and each other that is what you do. Was Nixon or Johnson ever in a real war? I bet not. Johnson should not have been so quick to pull the trigger over here. I think he knows that now. And as for Nixon, not one man in my outfit believes he will get us out of here. We laugh when we talk about his promises. Him and Green Beret John Wayne make us laugh till we cry. Lots of phony, arrogant fuckers in charge of things and all they are good for is to get more men killed on both sides. Any wonder we smoke so much dope? You got to be a dope to be here. When we go out on patrol we can hardly wait to get back and get blasted. Melvin and me and Rice are usually together on patrol and we watch each others backs, but you are so alone in yourself on patrol and you feel the enemy out there and you feel him tracking you with his gunsight. Rice, me and Melvin all carry thick paperbacks in our left shirt pockets to sheild our hearts when we go out. Melvins book is a little black Bible. He reads it whenever we stop and he quotes things. Like today he said, We are members one of another. And he said, For to live is Christ and to die is gain. And he looks at me like its real significant and I feel better now with Christ on my side. I pad my heart with a book called Sweets of Sin and on top of that is my pack strap and for good measure I try to carry my rifle over my chest too, but that gets very tiring. My M16 weighs 8.2 pounds fully loaded 20 rounds in the magazine and eventually my arms cramp and I have to lower my weapon and expose my chest to the bullet with my name on it. I figure I can survive anything but a heart or headshot, which is stupid because not many guys survive gut shots from a Bouncing Betty or a Toe Popper and quite a few die from being shot in the legs in the big artery and they bleed to death that way. You can not believe how fast the blood pumps out, a fountain keeping time with the pounding of your heart. The paperback Charles Rice is protecting his heart with is another hot porn. This one is called Fanny Hill Meets Candys Fanny. It pretty sexy if you like lesbo stuff and threesomes and group bangs. Best thing about it is having Rice read it and so consuming its like booze or grass it takes us out of this armpit a while until some fucking mortar rounds come in or some grunt who is off taking a crap steps on a mine. Let me tell you something little Bro, FEAR is more your enemy than charlie slope or NVA. Some guys get bloody trots and shit themselves into the hospital from the fear raking their intestines. Honest it is true. Bloody colitis caused by fear and it can dehydrate you and kill you if you dont get a I. V. in your arm putting fluids back in. It wears a soldier out and some end up so miserable they go round not giving a dam what happens and some shoot themselves and are relieved to die no doubt. Guys like that are a minority, but there are boo koo enough that they have their own category. Xin Loi, we call them, which means something like sorry about that. I am grateful to whatever combination of Mom and Dad that made me who I am that I am no Xin Loi. Mostly I can control myself and not let it eat my bowels and give me bloody colitis. Every day I survive is a surprise. I wake up and say to myself, I say, Whoa Vernon you are still in this freaked out war! And I tell you the truth, there are days it seems like a bad break badder than death, so I understand what a Xin Loi feels. The difference is that I dont live with it round the clock like him. When I'm not able to be with Candy, which has been quite a lot lately, I get high or I sleep as much as I can, because when I sleep I am not here where people I have nothing against are trying to kill me. But sometimes I dream about them and sleep dont help nothing. I walk round exhausted breathing this air that chokes you because it is so hot and damp and full of bugs. Everybody breathes through their mouth like panting dogs that can not get enough oxygen and they spit flies and mosquitoes and other shit I cant name. Pretty soon you do not get much excited about anything because your to damn tired, unless you are getting shot at, then you get a rush, but each time it is not as much as the time before because your so Goddam TIRED and can not react at the same level as you did when things were new. I am saying that I go numb at the edges. My brain gets numb I am saying. Soldiers that you know do not come back from patrols and at first it was pretty bad, but next thing it is not so bad because you can not be always thinking about them or you wont make it. FNGs, Fucking New Guys, come in with fresh faces and some go out in zipper bags the next day and you dare not think much about them because you better not or you will go crazy and shoot yourself which, like I said, happens more than you think. Some guys get so crazy they shoot their hand or foot so they can get out of here. Some who have lost the will to endure shoot their head permanent. Some pick a fight with an officer and get thrown in LBJ doing time so they can get out of combat for a while. There it is. Boy I am in a piss off mood this night. Sorry, but why should you know this shit? I wish everybody back there, the whole fucking country all those armchair warriors especially knew this shit that is what I fucking wish. There it is.

Big V.

PS – sorry to be so fucked up but I dug down to where there are no heroics and everything smells bad. Take a whiff, little Bro. Breathe deep and weep.

Rolling Thunder

We will not be defeated.
                              We will not grow tired.
We will . . . grow tired.
                              not . . . **(Johnson)**

Well . . . I think all of us are agreed that war is probably man's greatest stupidity
and . . . peace is the dream that lives in the heart of everyone,
but . . . it doesn't take two to make a war.   It only takes one . . .
every person is born with the right to life, liberty and the pursuit of happiness.
But my pursuit of happiness, if it comes from swinging my arm,
I must stop swinging my arm just short of the end of your nose. **(Reagan)**

Virgil Francis Foggy

At the hospital he is light-headed, dreamy, semi-awake. Cradled in his uncle's arms, smelling blood and sweaty hair, sweaty neck. Virgil is so important that he goes past all the people waiting in the waiting room. All eyes following him. "Look at that bloody boy," someone says. A woman with yellow hair fastens her gaze on his wiggling lip. The lip is waving to her. Touching her own lower lip, she says, "Poor thing." An old lady claps her hand to her cheek and says, "Bleeding-buckets!" Another woman says, "I'm gonna be sick!" Virgil hears a little girl's voice piping enthusiastically, "Was he shotted, Mommy? Was the boy shotted?" Others in the waiting room are silent. He wishes they would shout. Make horror gestures because he frightens them. He likes the term "bleeding buckets." He likes the word "shotted."

Bloodspots twinkle on the floor behind him reminding him of cherries again, cherries splattering. Pain is waking in his arms and legs. Something gnawing at his left hamstring. A ripping pain runs across the right half of his ribs. His torn lip burns. Both arms bleed over Dick's back. Wounded everywhere Virgil is content that there is nothing to do but ride along and watch. He is content to look shotted, helpless, awful sick. Sicker than any of the people waiting for treatment. A dying boy, a poor, shotted child, a battle-scarred, bucket-bleeding, bloody-dying boy. Is he scared? Does he need Jesus saying, *For to live is Christ and to die is gain?* Not Virgil. Virgil doesn't need it because Virgil feels no fear at all. But what if he put his finger on the verse saying the snares of death encompassed me? That would be scary all right. Fear defeats you, Vernon told him. Fear warns you of impending death. He wishes he had some kind of book over his heart to protect it the way Vernon protects his heart from charlie-gook. What would he put there? He tries to remember some titles but he can't. Any book will do. *No Man is an Island?* It's a sermon, not a book. A few pages not even as thick as your skin. Not thick enough to protect your heart from a bullet.

And then pops up the book Vernon is using, *Sweets of Sin*. Virgil wishes he knew where to find it. Maybe Vernon will send it to him if he asks for it. He adds it to the storm in his head, the storm whispering naughty prayers—life of Christ in a threesome thing with Ginger and Alma Lando, the bartender at Lando Lakes who is always flirting with him. He has been halfway in love with Alma ever since she said, "Jesus, I'd sure like to plank you." *Sweets of Sin. Sweets of*— What about Hail Mary full of Grace making love to a Dove? Was that possible? The Bible says so. You gonna argue with the Bible? And what about that story in the *Book of Myths*, Leda and the Swan? And what about yin and yang doing 69. Yang is the man, says Gramma Nez. Yang is light. Yang is warm. Yin is the girl. Yin is earth. Yin is dark. Yin is moist. *Feel*, do not think your way to yang and yin. And once upon a time there were Giants in the Earth who made love to the daughters of men. Who were those guys? Were they gods? Oh, great Father. Oh, communion of saints. Oh, forgiveness of sins. Oh, my God I am heartily sorry for . . . for the *Sweets of Sin.*

He watches the blood dripping on the floor, dot after dot trailing behind him and he thinks about how being the wounded brother gives him an edge on Vernon. Bite wounds and bullet wounds are both very bad, but maybe the bites are worse in some ways. Deeply chewed, ragged holes, not clean holes like bullets would make. At least the wounds he has seen in movies *seem* clean. The place to get shot is in the shoulder. Those guys are up and around in no time. Virgil Foggy would get the Purple Heart for his wounds if he were in Vietnam now. *A Purple Heart.*

"A casualty of war," he whispers.

"What?" says Dick.

"I didn't cry."

"You're a big boy," says Dick, his velvet voice droning like sweets of sin.

Virgil's body is strong from farm work, but he is not big in the way he wants to be. A certain type of bigness that buys a boy respect. A bigness that swallows bullets and comes back to fight again. Our hero. That boy is a wonder. Give him a Purple Heart. Give him the Silver Star. He must be John Wayne's son. Vernon is big that way. Wide back, thick-armed, heavy-chest, slim waist. Rockhard belly. Virgil wants very much to have a body like Vernon's, a manly body that impresses people. A body that magnetizes girls. Virgil is five foot nine, still growing. Dick is six feet. So was Jim and so is Pappy. Virgil feels the strength in his uncle's arms and his six-footer legs moving easily down the hall, following a bustling nurse in a red sweater who has beckoned him with her finger and is now half-running to stay ahead.

When they enter an exam room, the boy is laid on a table. His mother bends over him, kisses his forehead, strokes his hair. She is weeping. He can see panting pores in her skin, red nostrils and her nose running, smearing her mouth, smearing her chin. All those tears are for him. Weep for Virgil. Weep for Vernon too. Weep for Pappy and thirty hens floating in a coldwater tub and a baby lamb baaing for its mommy. Give them Purple Hearts. It is the least you can do.

Dick's face is ashen. His upper lip trembles. Which impresses Virgil more than anything else. Dick pale-trembling-ashen. Even looking like he might cry. Unheard of. Amazing.

"I didn't fall, I didn't cry," Virgil tells him. The torn lip flutters and stings when he talks. "Husky couldn't bring me down."

Dick nods. "A real man you are," he says. His voice is tender, a choking sort of whisper now. Virgil loves him for that. Virgil loves Dick Foggy and is glad to have the wounds that make Dick call him a real man.

The nurse tells him to smell her perfume. She folds a handkerchief over his nose and he takes a whiff and the perfume cooks the insides of his nostrils. He blows the hanky away. "Smells ick," he says. She chuckles. Her eyes admire him.

"Tough monkey," she says. The grownups look at each other smiling painfully.

He is amusing them. He tries to think of what else to say that will entertain them. "Stinks," he offers. "Poo."

Dick rubs a thumb over Virgil's ear, bends close and whispers, "You're goin to be okay, son. Don't worry about a thing. Daddy's here. Daddy will get you fixed." Virgil is a car needing repair, a broken tractor, a gasping combine, the clicking haybine that has hit a rock.

Dick watches the nurse, his eyes traveling. She has righteous breasts, a thick pair of parted lips. Take-charge eyes that say she knows everything there is to know about Dick. His brows pinch inwardly asking for sympathy. "Don't worry," she says, "he's in good hands." The long line of Dick's mouth smiles bravely. The fond father role. The sympathetic nurse. Virgil has noticed it before—good-looking women like to look at good-looking Dick.

Virgil repeats the alien word: "Daddy," he says. "Dad-dy."

"What?" says Dick. His smile saying, *My son's calling for me.*

Daddy-Dick's breath is bathing Virgil's eyes, tickling the lashes. Smelling of wine and underdone lamb. A fine man. Six-feet-tall. Macho man from top to toe. Bloody shirt, bloody arms, bloody pants, like he's been in a battle. All wickedness drained from his warrior face. Give him a Purple Heart too. This noble face is not the face that insists on playing Russian roulette with arrows. A birthday arrow went straight up, like a Roman candle—s*wishing past the vanishing point.*

Stannn still, you Virgil! The birthday arrow chinking, not quivering in the snow beside the boy's boot. *Good to go nother year, boyo!*

"Yeah, I didn't cry," Virgil repeats.

"Proud of you, you're my brave man," says Dick.

Dick's birthday is next April and Virgil gets to shoot the arrow for him. He won't flinch. He'll smoke a cigarette and look indifferent, like the Russian poet Regina told about: "He ate from a bag of cherries during this duel and his opponent got so unnerved he couldn't shoot straight. When it was over, the poet shot his gun into the dirt and walked away. That's what they call having icewater in your veins. What a man! The iceman cometh. It's havin savoir-faire. Be cool like that, son. Don't let em see you sweat." "You're our biggest boy," she says now, dabbing her eyes, pinching her reddened nostrils with tissues. Her dress is slathered with blood. She leans weakly on Dick's shoulder, one hand holding her swollen belly. His arm goes around her. He pats her hip, kisses the top of her head while winking at the nurse. Who smiles gloriously, a smile that says she is proud of her pearly teeth—see how clean-kissable my mouth is? She is clean all over, Virgil is sure. The smell of clean vanishes when the nurse's hanky covers his nose and mouth again. She holds it firmly this time, her hand an eagle's claw that dares him to try shaking her off. He is forced to breathe her perfume to keep from dying. When the hanky is lifted the boy can feel himself smirking at Dick and Regina, no pain, hoo-hoo. He wants to tell them something entertaining. He wants to make contact again. Touch me. Let me know how you love me. Love me for my war wounds. Give me a Purple Heart.

"Look at his eyes," Dick says from a distance. "He's in dreamland now."

A man in a white coat and black tie appears. Balding head, thick glasses. Stethoscope round his neck. Hand holds a long needle, which he shoots into Virgil's arm. And everything flushes warmly. Virgil knows he is safe for sure. *Fear kills hope and when that happens you are done for.* Not him, no way. Full of hope is Virgil. This is how it feels: drifting, fading, fearless, painless, sweets of sin and . . .

Now we got the murderous bastard!

Where's Daddy? he says, looking around at . . . is this Heaven? Where's God?

70

Surrounding the boy are . . . are chickens! Thousands of chickens. White
ones, red ones, black ones, pepper and salt ones. Beaks curving like wicked hay hooks.
Needle-tongues waiting to stab him.
How's it feel!
 Feather boy, where's your bloody ax now?
 Head on the block!
 Lips open, panting, head full of horror. This can't be happening.
 Drown him in the tub. Let's see how he likes it.
Fixed yellow eye helpless-hopeless.
 Eye, circle, target, pupil black.
One blink away from. . .
 Mercy! Mercy!
 No mercy for fourteen-year-old merciless boys.
 Ax falls—chop!

The War According to V–

Little V,

Melvin cracked. He was crying and shaking and would not, could not stop. I never seen such tears and trembling. Only maybe Regina cried that hard when Daddy died. Those kind of sobs that wrench the gut and choke you half to death. We lost 4 men to a mine. Melvin was number 5 in back of them and got knocked on his ass. He didn't breakdown right then. It was later that night in his foxhole I could hear him sobbing. I crawled over there and got in his hole with him and held him. What else could I do? He finally settled down and said he had a premonition that he was next. He showed me verses in his Bible. He had opened it with his eyes closed and his finger lit on a line that said snares of death confronted me. So he tried it again. Flipped the pages and stabbed and this one said almost the same thing. The snares of death encompassed me, the pangs of Sheol laid hold on me. I will tell you something Bro it give me creeps. I told Paine it was a coincidence and did not meant anything concerning him. But I dont think he buys it and I am not sure I do either. His nerves are shot. He needs to get out of combat for a while. We all do. I have seen guys predict their own deaths before. Some have uncanny accuracy. They give their stuff away and tell you what person and address to send it to and they go out and get their head blowed off. I cant explain how they know but they do. It is more than Gramma Nez doing the bones or flipping the coins of that I Ching thing, those hexagrams and shit. It is something deep inside a fellow that knows the future even if he do not want to. Melvin is okay for now. He is trucking along on patrol and still saying I am watching your back Vernie. When he goes on point I tell him I am watching his back not to worry. But he does not look good. He has that look in his eyes. That hollow glossy death look like he sees it coming from far away coming closer. I wish they would send him to Japan for some R & R. We all need to have a wild drunk and get laid. Get back in touch with life. I am watching the platoon lining up for chow just now. I look at them and I see lots of walking wounded. Including me. Including even Charles Rice, though he never show it. It is a mask. We all got masks on. Except Melvin mask fell off. There it is.

Big V.

Rolling Thunder

We believe that peace is at hand. (**Henry Kissenger**)

This war has already stretched the generation gap so wide that it threatens to pull the country apart. (**Sen. Frank Church**)

If the Americans do not want to support us anymore, let them go, get out!
(**President Nguyen Van Thieu**)

We will not grow tired.
We will not withdraw, either openly or under the cloak of a meaningless agreement.
We hope that peace will come swiftly.
But that is in the hands of others besides ourselves.
We must be prepared for a long continued conflict.
Our objective . . . has been to bring about a recognition . . that [the enemy's] objective . . .
could not be achieved
We will not be defeated.
We will not grow tired.
We will not be defeated.
We will not grow tired.
(**Johnson**)

Virgil Francis Foggy

Aaron commands and the sun rises. A moment later, Dick's thirteens are drumming down the hall. He enters the bathroom. He coughs and spits and blows his nose and pees loudly. The toilet flushes. Virgil turns over. Since he is recovering, he doesn't have to get up for chores.

Minutes later, Dick goes past the door, descends the stairs to the kitchen. Coffeepot is filled and put on the stove. Regina gets up and showers. Sounds of water lull the boy to sleep again. He wakes when he hears her high-heels clicking.

Ginger stays in bed. She will not get up until someone yells at her. Next week she starts school again. Then there will be no more lollygagging. The smell of coffee and cigarettes drift under Virgil's door. He hears Ginger's phone ringing. Getting out of bed he hobbles to the bathroom and cleans his teeth and rubs antibiotic ointment into his wounds. The stitches are out, the scars look angry. The scar trailing from the corner of his mouth to his chin makes a lazy S. It looks like a thin red worm. He runs a finger lightly along it. It is bumpy but not painful. The scars on his leg and arms and side still hurt a lot. Pain to the bone. The color of the skin shades reddish to yellow green to violet black and blue.

Going back to the room, he pulls on a T-shirt that says:

PREVENT PINKEYE

On the back it says:

ANCHOR ANIMAL HEALTH

He slips on jeans and boots and a denim shirt. Puts his WHO cap on, squaring it above his ears just so. Grabbing the .22 off the rack on the wall, he limps out of the room to the stairway. Pauses by Ginger's door to listen to her and Peter on the phone.

"Just my nightie," she says.

Then, "All right it's off."

Then, "Prick, cock, cunt, suck."

Then, "They're in."

Then, "Two."

Then, "Did you hear it?"

Then, "Only for you. Are you jealous?"

He descends the stairs one at a time, guarding his leg. In the kitchen Dick and Regina are drinking coffee. Dick saying, "Gimmee a break, woman, it's still morning. Take Mom with you to those goddamn classes."

"It's your baby too," she answers.

"That's no place for a man," he says. "It's all brainwashin, all this sensitivity shit and going in the delivery room to see your wife turn inside out. Ugh."

"Selfish, asshole," she says. "Always thinkin of yourself."

"Fuck you," he says.

"You already did," she says. "This is your fault. Our fault. And who wants it?"

Virgil eases out the door. He hobbles to the barn thinking: *When does it happen that married people start cussing like that at each other? All lovey-dovey at first and then something happens and they turn on each other and nothing is the same.* In the milkhouse, Pappy is pouring milk through the filtered funnel into the tank. The paddle inside stirs the milk. Virgil hears it sloshing—a cherished sound that means money, a monthly milkcheck. The electric motor grinds. He looks into the parlor and sees Gramma Nez slipping inflations on a cow. A row of Holstein rumps stretch the length of the barn. Tails swat at pestering flies. The exhaust fans are going full blast, but the sour stench of manure still wafts through the air. Virgil breathes deeply. He is glad to be home. All he wanted in the hospital was to go home. The air compressor chugs. Radio playing country:

Cra-zy arms . . . that reach to hold sommm body new . . .

There is a five-gallon pail sitting in the aisle. He grabs the pail and drags it to the tank. The weight tugs at his wounds. He gives the pail to Pappy and Pappy pours the milk through the filter. He tells Virgil not to be lifting such heavy things. "You might tear somethin and have a setback." He takes Virgil's cup from the hook on the wall and fills it with milk from the tank. Then he gets an egg from the cooler and puts a pinhole in one end and a slightly larger hole in the other end. Virgil sucks the egg dry. He drinks the milk.

"Best thing for you," says Pappy.

"Snot," the boy says, grinning, feeling tightness at the corner of his mouth.

Pappy reminds him that the egg is nature's perfect food. The grinding motor makes the lip scar tingle. The paddle turns and the milk

75

sloshes and Virgil knows by the sound that the tank is nearly full.

Pappy's voice is slow and phlegmy as he clears his throat and says, "Seen a coyote in the brome. He was weavin back and forth lookin for mice and birds. He stopped and stood like a birddog, one leg up. Hell of a sight. Never seen em do that afore."

Pappy clears his throat, coughs. Spits a gob in the drain.

"Yeah, this guy was funny. He would throw all four legs in the air and pounce. We should quit shootin em. They keep the fields clean. They got a right to be there."

He pauses, breathing deeply. He looks at the drain in the cement floor, clears his throat, clears his throat, clears his throat. "I never thought about them havin the right, but they do."

"Uncle Dick says shoot them."

"I say no. Not unless they get close to the yard."

The old man's face is sweaty-yellow, gray around the lips. He has coin-purse pouches beneath his eyes. His shoulders are high. Like they are guarding his ears. His mouth is melancholy. He has shaved the bristling silver beard, exposing red veins embedded in his jaws. As he talks about the animals his voice whispers.

"We'll need to get another guard dog, so the coyotes don't get cheeky. A good dog keeps em off."

"What kind of dog?"

"A German Shepherd. They're smart."

Coughs. Punches his heart. Coughs really hard. Spits.

"They pick things up right away. We had them when I was a kid and they were no trouble to train. Next to poodles, they're the smartest dogs in the world. Coyote and fox won't mess with em."

"They look mean," Virgil tells him. "Look like wolves."

The motor grinds. The exhaust fans suck warmth out of the air. The coolness in the milkhouse tightens the wounds. "Don't be afraid. The dog will be yours to raise. You'll be the alpha dog. He won't bite you, you're his master."

Pappy clears his throat over and over. *What's in there?* Virgil wonders. *Spit it out, old man.*

"A once in a lifetime thing what happened. It won't happen again. Husky was old and cranky and had those bad hips and you could tell sometimes that his teeth ached too. Probably pain drove him crazy, who knows?" Pappy pushes a fist into his kidney and grimaces. He takes a deep breath. "Pain can do that, you know."

Virgil doesn't want to talk about dogs. He wants to go to the woods and shoot something.

He leaves the milkhouse and sees Dick and Regina walking to the garage, the car, Dick in his tan work shirt and pants, she in her waitress uniform, black purse hanging from her shoulder. The weight of her tummy makes her waddle. High-heels ridiculous. Dick looks curiously across the car roof at Virgil in the killing yard, but he doesn't say anything. Doors slam, the engine fires. The old Cadillac backs out of the garage and goes down the driveway, turns onto the main road and Dick punches it, tires flinging the gravel. Virgil sees silhouettes rigid as cardboard inside the car. To the left, the Crow River is a bright morning ribbon. Beyond the river are acres of very old trees. Live oaks mostly. White birch too.

Through the upstairs window he sees Ginger in her bathrobe. Now she will have the house to herself. She will smoke and watch the soaps and Peter Raven will come and they'll go for a ride. School will put a stop to her lazy ways. When he told his mother he had quit for good, she said he was breaking her heart. She wants him to finish high school and go to college. She wants him to be a doctor or a lawyer. Sometimes she says stupid things like that. As if he is smart enough, as if he could actually do it. And then other times she admits he's not too bright and he should just be practical. He is mechanical, good with animals. It's something anyway. At least he's useful.

He makes his way over the pasture toward the woods. The dew on the grass wets his boots and cuffs making them heavy, accentuating his limp. Fog fills holsters in the earth. The sun shooting through the haze makes the air look ghostly. Moses lifts his head, watches as if expecting trouble. Virgil enters the woods. The woods are cool, full of shadows and undergrowth, trees dripping noiselessly. His muscles are warmed up now and he feels less pain. He stops and loads the .22 and takes a shot at a leaf that looks like a three-fingered hand. Squirrels skitter out of sight. It hurts to hurry the rifle, so he's not quick enough for the squirrels.

But who wants stringy squirrel, anyway? Some quail would be good. Or maybe a wild turkey. Wild turkey would surprise everyone. They would believe he is quite a hunter if he brought home wild turkey. Turkeys used to be common as pigeons, Pappy has said, but now they're rare. Or maybe extinct, at least in Minnesota. The game is going north, hiding in Canada from American hunters roaming the woods with AR 15's and those things called UZIs.

Midway in his journey he comes to an open oval covered in grass and patches of blueberries. Most of the berries have been eaten by coyotes. He sees their scat in several places. The shadows are long, but there is a place where the sun gets through and the grass sparkles. He hears the Crow River shouldering its way past columns of trees. The Crow runs the length of the woods, then turns south again and flows past St. Michael. If Virgil wanted to, he could ride the Crow all the way to the Mississippi. And then south and beyond to the sea. If he wanted to. He turns his face to the warmth and closes his eyes and searches toward the center of the clearing, tapping his rifle like a blind boy tapping his cane. This is what it feels like for them. Tap, tap. Tap, tap.

"How can anyone stand to be blind?" he asks. The rifle moves side to side. Tap, tap. He has seen blind people in town, with their white canes or with guide dogs. Regina said there was a blind man in one of the classes she took in college and he used a stylus to punch a Braille card. While the professor lectured, the blind man made dots in the card that only he could read. Virgil can't see himself doing that, going blind and learning how to write and read dots on cards. A new way of seeing the world through your fingers. A new language in your fingers feeding your brain. What sort of world would you see that way? No more color. A world of sound and touch and smell and taste. Knocking your head all the time against something sticking out. *Crunch, munch* say his boots as he's walking. If there's a cliff in front of you, you would walk right off it and say *Oh, no!* as you fell. *Crush, crack, crik,* he didn't know the cliff, poor boy. Would it hurt? Maybe it would be over fast. It was quick for the lamb hammered in the head and for the chickens, the quick axe. But of course the chickens had to watch the others and wait their turn. Did they know? Could they understand what they were seeing? Virgil believes all animals know in their hearts that people are waiting to do something bad to them. *Squawk! It's happening to Gertrude and I'm next, I just know it!* From light to dark in a flash. Then someone eats you. Then one day the eater dies and goes to the worm.

A funny system.

If Virgil were God he'd invent something else. Let them eat sunrays and moonbeams.

He takes another step and the ground gives way. For a split second there is only a sense of falling. When he hits the ground, he feels dirt enclosing his ankle. There is another world below. His wounds have come alive, biting into his flesh like teeth. Tears fill his eyes and he shouts, "Cocksuck!"

He stays on his stomach, moaning. The thought that he will never be well enters his mind as it did when he woke in the hospital. Wrapped like a mummy and feeling as if someone had clubbed him with a bat. He was told that he might limp even after he recovered. "Have a hitch in your giddy-up," the doctor said. "And you won't be able to stretch your mouth around a giant bite of chocolate cake or eat corn off the cob three rows at a time or cram double-patty cheeseburgers the way you used to. You will be a nibbler now taking baby bites of life." The teasing doctor smiled and patted Virgil's shoulder and added, "Nah, nah, you'll be all right, son. Give it time."

After a minute the pains ease and he forces himself to stand, dust himself off and look at the hole that tripped him. There is something inside it. A root posing as a fang. No, it is a fang. He picks it up, holds it to the light. He rotates it in his fingers. An inch long. Brown tartar at the base. He measures the tooth over the wound on his forearm. The angry dog treats his forearm like a rag, jerking it, tormenting it, until it breaks off and gets carried away. A huge doggy bone in Husky's teeth.

"Why you turn on me?" Virgil asks. Things turn and you never know why. They never come back and tell you why they drove hundreds into ditches and shot them, showed no mercy. Killing is built into the system. Virgil played with a dog. He chased him with the willow whip. Is that all it took? They had done that before. Virgil had done a lot of things to him, but it was only playing. It wasn't being mean. Not really. Lots of boys are mean. Virgil isn't mean. Is he?

Maybe he is. Was the willow whip the last straw for an old tooth aching, arthritic dog? Is the whip what sent him over the edge? Things turn and good soldiers go bad and out of the blue they kill you. They give no quarter. It's charlie gook. It's never-ending war. At the edge of the grave are mulched leaves mixed with tiny tufts of fur looking like wedged feathers in the chopping block. He scratches around to see if he can find Husky's bones. But there aren't any bones. Just the tufts of fur and the fang.

Maybe coyotes got him. Made him a meal. Maybe they dug him

up and took him home for their pups. And the crows picked the leftovers clean. After thirteen years of walking around eating and barking and herding cows to the barn, there's not a morsel left. A yellow tooth, some wisps of fur. This is what you come to.

The boy shivers to think of what waits for the dead. He pictures Pappy's kidneys and yellow skin, the dark bags under his eyes, the pasty cheekbones, veins in his jaw, deep wrinkles getting deeper, the wattled neck. The spacey old man sitting in the Airstream tired, tired, and one day he won't get up for chores. Just sits in front of the TV and rots. Old people are doing that all over the world. How many of them die each day? Thousands? And how many boys like Vernon in the war? Thirty thousand have died so far. Forget about Christmas.

At the hospital where Pappy goes to have his blood diluted, the rooms have old people lying in bed watching TV. A lot of them sleep with their mouths wide as if they're silently screaming. Some of them drool. Many of them have no teeth and can't be taken seriously. The TV laughs at them. It gives them the news. It holds serious discussions about the war:

They are fighting the forces of violence in every continent. If we abandon the war now, nothing but more and more terror will follow. Terror that will one day fill America's streets.

But thirty thousand and climbing!

Better over there than here.

Bed-people sleep through these remarks. Or they find a game show to watch. They get excited when someone wins. Lots of action and noise is the point. Bright colors and flashing lights. Contestants jump up and down. They want all the prizes. They want the prizes Now.

Pretty soon, Pappy will be there again in an adjustable bed that Virgil can play with. Make Pappy go up and down. The next step for him is the needle and then you lie back and relax while the machine cleans your blood. On TV will be that fellow on *The Price is Right* saying, "*Come on down!*" And someday Pappy will. It will be sooner rather than later and the family will bury him with his son and the other Foggy-dead in the cemetery. Coffin descending and family weeping. And Gramma Nez saying, "*Watch where the fuck you're going, Daddy!*"

If Virgil had been weak the day of the dog. If the dog had pulled him down. Got a hold of his throat—*rip!* Under the ground now. Blind. A million suns wouldn't warm him. No more Virgil walking in the forest, falling in a dogbody grave, finding a fang and fur. It was close. Almost. But

80

the end will come, not now, maybe, or maybe not tomorrow. But one day it *will* come. Live a hundred years, it's nothing.

I hope I die before I get old, sings who in The Who. Does he mean it? When you're young you can say stupid things. *Live fast, love hard, die young,* sings what's his name? Faron Young. *Live fast, love hard.*

Virgil drops the tooth back in the hole. Good riddance. The sun tosses coins over the ground. Jim Foggy mulching patiently in his coffin waits for Jesus to knock on the lid. What will he look like? Will he be thirty-three like Jesus is? Has his ghost gone across the sea to be a guardian angel for Vernon? That's where he should be.

The trees hold hands, ringing him in. *We got you, you little shit.*

There's the rub. Maybe your Dad was waiting but not knowing he was waiting, not knowing anything. Wake him up and he wouldn't know he's been dead these years. It would be like one night's sleep to him and he would want to yell up the stairs—

"Virgil! Vernon! Time for chores!"

Or maybe not that. Maybe never. Forget resurrection. Maybe in ten thousand years he will be plugging a hole in a wall. Maybe that's what you will get too. Plug a hole in an outhouse. Keep the wind from coming through when nature calls. Too much light hurts your eyes. You pull down the bill of your cap. You feel something in your marrow—the fur, the tooth, the dirt. The mummy named Jim boxed in midnight. Your heart flutters. Then pounds so hard it hurts your throat and you're having a heart attack and you want to go *home*. You hobble through the woods. The trees scratching your arms and trying to steal your cap. You swing the gun at three-fingered hands. You cut loose with chopping motions that agitate your wounds. Severed hands twirling in the air.

When you come into the open, you see the road the cornfield the pasture the barn. Milking is over and the cows are out. They are staring vacant-eyed, not moving or eating. Just staring as if wondering where they are. *Who? Do I know you?* You hear the tractor's distant roaring and know that Pappy is piling manure.

Your father tells you to take deep breaths. Calm down. He tells you to be at peace with yourself and get out of your head. "It's not healthy in your head," he says.

The sun is in your face as you walk down the road, singing softly:

". . . *every drop of rain that falls, a flower grows*— " You take your father out of the grave, lift him high where he gets a good view. There is no Santa Claus. There is only— Jesus, Mary, Joseph. The Holy Ghost. And God. The Communion of Saints. The forgiveness of sin.

Walking in the ruts, you see your prayers wrapped in a chain of beads. You see your father fingering his rosary. This bead, *Our Father.* And then, *Hail Mary.* All connected by—*Tap, tap.* Open your eyes. You could have been dead. But you're not. Though every man's death diminishes you, you're still one of the lucky ones, Virgil. Lucky so far.

The War According to V –

Little V,

We went up in a C-130 to jump behind enemy lines. Which is way stupid because there are no enemy lines to jump behind. There is the right way and the Army way which is usually the wrong way. But whatever way it was we took off with a full manifest and crates of ammo and shells and M-79s and claymores and Willy Petes and other shit to blow things up. But as we are trying to climb into the clouds an engine goes POW! and the plane staggers like its drunk. Then after a few seconds of straining, another engine fails if you can believe that. I can feel my asshole puckering. I feel like we are going down. This is it. What are the chances, I mean what are the odds of losing two engines? But once they are in the air these babies can fly on one engine. Or so I am told. And when the plane kept going we thought we would find the DZ and jump no matter what. The pilot is cool and he comes on the intercom saying, Don't worry about a thing. We are near the gulf and if we go down charlie will be right out to pick us up. Funny guy. He is trying to fly us at nine hundred feet which is combat aptitude, but if your main dont open you wont have time to pop the reserve. So pretty hairy Virge. Everything over here will either bore you to death or scare you shitless.

I look out the window and we are barely above the treetops. I see some grinning, wide-eyed monkeys checking us out and dashing over the limbs like crazy. They spend their lives in the trees never coming down to the ground. The monkeys are like the people in this war, every fucking one up the air not knowing where to go or what to do. Driven mad by the noises and smell of death. Think how quiet it must have been before they got invaded by all us and the commies. It would be like our forest out back of the pasture and how when you go in there it is a church and you feel you should whisper. You know what I'm saying Bro? But it is no goddamn church in this Godsaken shitstew. You should have seen the faces of the guys on the plane as it is bouncing around and the two good engines are straining and there are those other two engines with dead props just hanging there totally dead weight. It gives you a sick feeling to see dead engines when you are in the air like that and those propellers are supposed to be turning but instead they throw shadows like dark crosses on the walls inside the plane, shadows moving sideways over fear faces as we turn with the light. I know what pale as a ghost means now. Lots of guys were pale as ghosts. Others were green. No kidding. Actually a sort of bleached lime color. I can laugh about it now and actually it had funny moments even then. I mean there is my buddy Charles Rice cool as can be kicking back reading the porno paperback called Sweets of Sin and here is Melvin Paine saying to me, You watch my back and I watch yours, pull your risers and slip toward me when we jump. Lets come down together and stay low in the grass, keep our heads down till we know what fuck is going on. Melvin is colored like a cinnamon roll, and he's got expressive eyes that roll when he is scared showing lots of white his eyes popping like ping pong balls no kidding. Pretty near funny to see him like that and so I get the giggles, which I get a lot out here being on the edge of hysterical. But my buddies think I just got a strange sense of humor. Haw haw! Yeah, I've blipped my pants a couple of times Virge. So what? Sometimes a parasite giving me the trots like when you eat too many plums or peaches. Other times just pure watery fear like I never known in my twenty young years. When you are that scared is when you know how desperate you are for living. Man you want to survive. Man you want to live to be a hundred and five at least. Man you want to get back home and pick up where you left off. Get a job at the mill. That would be so good right now. A nice Chevy V-8. A pretty girl next to me. Be good, be cool. Dont seem like I am asking much does it in the large scheme of things? I just want to live my life my own way. Not let this war defeat me. Dying now makes my whole life pointless, you know what I mean? Born for cannon fodder, what kind of glory in that? To calm me and Melvin in the midst of this shit going down in this stupid plane, Rice, who never seems to know fear himself, or he is just dam good at hiding it, reads to us from Sweets of Sin, some real nasty stuff about this guy fucking a sexed up mother and daughter duo together at the same time. This guy, I think he was the boyfriend, or maybe her husband, but he is described as twisted around them like a pretzel. Can you imagine? So in the midst of a rattling roaring gasping crippled piece of shit trying to get altitude but dropping inch by inch and Top Smeltzer telling us to stand up, hook up, check your equipment, sound off, stand in the door, red light, and we are waiting for the green light to go and that fucking Rice is hanging with one hand on his static line to steady himself and with me in front of him and Melvin behind him and he is reading out these scenes and we are listening to sucking and fucking, someones sex fantasy going on while the cherries are puking all over their boots and the smell is worse than the barn on diarrhea days when the cows have gotten into clover. So we are all waiting for Sarge to yell Green Light so we can get out of that puking plane. And I hear Rice say he is ready to pop a nut and he is going to beat off on the way down and he bets it will be a first ever orgasmic grunt during a combat jump, a Gunness Book of Records thing. So we start laughing ourselves sick over that stupid idea and the scenes in the book and Rice keeps saying he is going to whack off and Top comes back to see what the hell, what is so fucking funny and Rice hides the book in his shirt and Top said we are dopers and he will fix are dopy asses for us when we got back to base. He was sniffing our breath. Sniffing for the sweet smell of cannabis. He is mad and scared and when you are mad and scared you want to hurt somebody, kill somebody, I learned that fear makes all of us mean, it is fear more than anything that makes you mean because you are mad at yourself of being scared to death so you take it out by being mean, mean, mean. Believe me you do. Well, most guys do. Some guys break down bawling and cant stop shaking, nerves shot to hell they are so scared. Those are the guys who will let you down. You do not want those guys around when things go south.

Then the order came to stand down and we unhooked and sat in the nets and stared at each other unable to believe our luck. They called off the mission. No jump after all. The plane limped back brushing its belly on the trees and we landed and everyone including Top Smeltzer was so relieved that nothing more got done about us being dopers. We took the cattle truck back to base and that night snuck off to Tu Do street and drank and smoked and my girl Candy brought some friends for Paine and Rice and we got detoxified. That is the army. Do not even try to predict what is going to happen. I have not made a combat jump yet and hope I never do.

There it is.

Big V

PS – Let me know when that baby gets born. Do you remember when Cristobell got born? I remember it like yesterday. My first calf. Those were good days when Dad was still alive and it seemed we were going to end up farmers not knowing much more than cows and birthing babies and working the land.

PSS – Ask Ginger why not write. What the fucks with her? Let me know what she says. Take a picture of her Bro and send it will you? Try to

85

get one of her naked, catch her in the shower if you can.

PSSS - Maybe she will pose for you in her birthday suit if she knows it will cheer me up. Maybe if she knows what I am thinking, knows my feelings I mean, she will see that we need to be in touch. We share so much past how can she forget that? How can she neglect me? Some nights is murder thinking of her. A bad night tonight. I am a little high. Wish I could go home. I want to catch the Freedom Bird and fly my bony butt out of here NOW.

PSSSS - Just a note to add that all hell is breaking loose because some stupid ass looy took his company to a village of innocents and wiped out every man, woman, child, dog and chicken in it. It did not just happen. It was 2 years ago but the story has now come out in France and will be full page in America you can bet. Drove them all into ditches and mowed them down. Vicious motherfucker. He gives all of us a bad name. He is not what America is about He is not what it means to be a soldier fighting for the USA. The Army is trying to cover it up, but many reporters know and now and it will be big news, just watch. This thing is why these people will continue to fight so hard. We destroy everything we touch. We mean well but we destroy. Rice says we are like the Romans. They made a desert and called it peace, he says. The hatred for us runs a million miles deep. You can see it in their slanty eyes. REVENGE REVENGE! I hope never faced with some asshole giving me an order to wipe out women and children. I will not do it and I will get sent to the stockade, or maybe shot for disobeying a direct order. Me and Paine and Rice all say that we would rather be court-martialed than follow such an order. I was talking to a Filipino American guy who is here working on an article for Mother Jones magazine and he said our troops are not winning hearts and minds, we are only creating havoc and hatred. His exact words. And he said that the country is blowing up around all these Vietnamese kids and old men and women. Maiming them and killing them truly for nothing. He said we will never win here. We have already lost the war, won many battles but lost the war. The Vietnamese will eventually drive us out, he said because we have a different concept of time than them. We think in terms of Now. They think in terms of tomorrow and tomorrrow and tomorrow. To the Asian mind there is always time. Patience is an Asian virtue, not an American one. They will win he says even if it takes 30 years.

Rolling Thunder

Mr. President, I foresee a perilous voyage, very dangerous.
I have great and grave apprehensions that we can win under these conditions.
(McGeorge Bundy NSA)

But, George, is there another course?
We know it is dangerous and perilous, but
the big question is,
can it be avoided? **(Johnson)**

Mr. President, there is no course that will allow us to cut our losses. If we get bogged
down, our cost might be substantially greater. The pressures to create a larger war
would be inevitable. I think we are in a bad moral position. **(Bundy)**

Tell me then, what other road can I go?
I feel it would be more dangerous to lose this now,
than endanger a great number of troops. **(Johnson)**

We cannot win, Mr. President.
The war will be long and protracted.
The most we can hope for is a messy conclusion. **(Bundy)**

We must take the risk by putting [more] American boys in. **(Nixon)**

Virgil Francis Foggy

After reading Vernon's letter to Ginger, Virgil puts it in his pocket and checks out the sexy way his cousin is leaning on a stanchion, saucy hip curving. The broom she was using idles against her cheek. She is stroking the handle and smirking. Her eyes looking cynical. They look amused, sort of. Nothing in the letter made her flinch. He has seen her this way lots of times. Soft sweet sad one moment, sarcastic scornful world-weary the next. It's the lip-tight smile and mocking eyes that tell you what mood she's in. Her look says she knows things he will never know. She's done things he would never dream of doing. She's far ahead of Virgil in flaming Father Hess's ears in the Confessional.

She winks. "Catch me in the shower?" she says. "How about on the pot? Would that satisfy him to see me peeing and pooping? You guys, it's all you ever think about is what's going on beneath a girl's waist. Not one of you doesn't have his brain in the head of his cock."
And Virgil thinks: *Her mouth is too pretty to say such things.*

"You gonna write him?" he asks.

"I don't think I should," she says. "It wouldn't be good for him . . . or me." She scratches her belly, raising the camisole, raking her abdomen with sharp, pink fingernails. Greedily, Virgil watches, hoping she'll move her hand down, show more skin. "No use stirring things up," she says. "When he comes back he'd expect—"

Virgil waits for her to finish, but she shakes her head. He goes back to sweeping lime along the aisles and into the cow gutters. The parlor is whitewashed from walls to ceiling to floor, white as if decorated for ghosts. The milk inspector is coming and he loves lots of lime. He loves powdery walls that shine.

Ginger makes motions with her broom, "I'm not the only one who's mental, you know. Your brother is mental as me and my dad and your mom. A bunch of couch cases, all of us. Yeah, we belong on this funny farm. For sure. We inherited it from Fergus. So mental he cut his throat. Lots of Foggys were suicides, you know. It's in our blood. You too, Virgil. You're mental too."

"He lets it all hang out in his letters," Virgil says. "He says war has made him a philosopher."

"He always let it hang out," she says giggling. "In some ways he's

88

got nuthin on my dad except he hasn't had as many opportunities. Foggys, you know, are driven by demons, just look at our history, look what Foggys have done. We ain't got a friggin chance, Virge."

"It's not in *my* blood," he tells her. "I believe in God and Jesus and being good. I believe in heaven and hell and sin and—"

"Oh, please," she says. Her eyes rolling.

"Cynic," he says. "You're going to hell."

"You're dumb as dirt," she says. "Your brain powdery as lime."

"Shut up."

"You shut up."

He turns his back to her and continues to sweep. "Cunt," he whispers.

"Cock," she says.

And then she laughs. He turns and laughs too. They both bray like donkeys.

Ginger grabs his broom.

"Don't," he says.

She starts pinching him, smacking his ass. Her broom lies in the aisle. "Like that, like that," she says, whacking him.

"I'll spank *you* if you don't behave," he says, shoving her. "I'll pull your pants down and spank your bare bottom with my bare hand."

"Ooo, you promise?" she says.

They push each other around and he slaps her bottom and squeezes it too and she says he squeezes like a girl. "Like a pussy."

He is excited and has to put his hand in his pocket to make an adjustment. "It's my wounds," he says. "It hurts to use this arm. You shouldn't make me use my arm. The dog bit me to the bone here." He points to the wound. He sees the dog attacking, grabbing the arm. Trying to shake it off. He's glad the dog is dead now.

She settles down and he goes back to liming the gutters and she goes back to sweeping. The gutters look like narrow graves for stillborns. He has seen plenty in his fourteen years, aborted calves lying there cute and perfect in every way. Cute and perfect but stone dead.

"When she left him it might have been a shock to some, but not to me," says Ginger.

"Hmm?"

"I could see it comin a mile. She always said that your first duty is to take care of yourself. To stay alive and not let anyone kill you just because you love them. Love smothers you, she said. She said she couldn't live a smothered life no more. Me and Albert, we smothered her too. Albert more than me, but she eventually took him anyway because he came unglued. Little baby. Little brat. Mama's boy. Never could stand him, you know. He was no competition, not really. I was always Daddy's girl. I competed against my mom. I didn't think of it that way then, but I do now. What a little bitch I was. I'm *bad*, Virgil. They have a name for it. What I am."

"You hear from Albert?"

"Nope. Mom wrote once and said he was learnin how to surf and hang out. I guess I could have gone out there and done that too, but Dad made me promise not to leave him. So I didn't and now I'm stuck with the bastard. We were in love back then. We had a special bond. He said he needed me more than he needed anything on earth and if I wanted to break him I could go live with her and that would be his death. I'm such a sap."

"I wonder if things are better for her."

"She has a new kid. A girl. Too late for me to become a California blond. I've been superseded by a half-sister." Her laugh is shrill. Abruptly she stops. "Let's have a cigarette," she says.

Virgil takes the makings from his pocket and rolls her one.

"Soon as I get out of school," she says, "I'm gone. I'm gonna live in Florida. Peter has been there. He has family there, his dad's brother, and that's where we're goin. He'll get a job in construction. I can do waitress like Regina. Fuck this farm and fuck Minnesota winters and fuck my Dad. He gets crazier by the minute. I mean I really think somethin is happenin to his mind. He's jealous of Peter, you know. You think he's all there, Virge?"

"Those arrows."

"That's what I mean. He drinks way more now and he can't hold it like he used to and he gets so damn mean when he drinks. His eyes scare me when he drinks."

"Me too."

"He told me he's done arrow roulette every birthday since Mom left him. He says he wants fate to decide. I told him we all die soon enough without hurryin it."

"I don't see why he made me do it too," says Virgil. "That's one birthday I won't ever forget."

90

"He was drunk."

"He wants me dead, I can feel it."

"He wants all men dead. He wants to be the only rooster in the coop."

"Hell, I ain't no competition. I don't even want to be."

"They rock and roll, you know what I'm sayin? Even though she's pregnant."

"I got ears."

"They'd wake the dead, those two. He ties her up and blindfolds her, you know."

"How do you know?"

"I got my ways. I see every*thing*, Virge. I've been watchin him since I was this high. You seen things too. Don't tell me you haven't."

The loft. The blowjob.

She brushes hair off her cheek. "Too much, too soon," she says, scratching her belly again. Digging deeper. Her little finger rubbing the button. He wishes she would scratch her crotch. "I saw him hump her from behind one time," Ginger adds.

He leans the broom on his shoulder and covers his ears.

"All right, all right," she says. "Man, you're such a pansy, Virge." She pulls his hands away from his ears. "I'm just talkin facts of life."

"I don't want no facts of life," he says, pushing the broom. White dust settling over his boots—whitewash over everything.

"Who was Cristobell?" Ginger asks.

"Who? Oh her! She was Vernon's first calf."

"Is she still here?"

Virgil looks out the window at the cows standing in the drizzle. South of them, south of the barn, the alfalfa field is deeply green, Minnesota green. As soon as the wind shifts and the fields dry, it will be time to make third crop. It is already late in the season. Which worries him. He needs it to quit raining. He needs to get that last crop of hay into the barn. "No, Cristobell is not out there, that was a long time ago," he says. "She was Vernon's calf. I remember most how jealous I was. I'm not jealous no more. Not where he is. Not with those bastards shootin at him. You think Vernon's a hero?"

"What's a hero?"

Virgil leans his arms on the windowsill, continues staring at the wet herd. He loves them. He loves cows. He loves the farm.

"I vaguely remember," says Ginger. "Vernon havin his own calf. I kinda remember being jealous. I always wanted a pony. Havin a calf was like havin a pony. That's all I envied about you guys—the animals. Now I smell them in my hair and I hate it. Wish I lived in Florida."

"I'll tell you how cold it was the winter Cristobell got born. The heifers on the north end of the barn had frozen cups and we had to use propane to melt the ice. It still happens sometimes if the wind comes hard at that angle. And the cows have to stay in their stanchions day after day. Bad for cows, Ginger. Bad, bad, bad. Breaks down their pasterns, you know, and they start walkin on their joints and their hooves turn into elf shoes and you have to trim them with a hammer and chisel. We put down lots of straw, but they still got sores, and some of them needed help gettin up in the mornin. We would pull on their tails and push their butts up with our shoulders and get them standin. It was tough stuff."

"Cows are mostly nice, I think. Except if they kick you," muses Ginger.

Part of Virgil has gone away. The vision of his father and Vernon and Cristobell. His father so alive! Broad-shouldered and tall. Unconquerable. Virgil sees Vernon home from school and changing for chores. There in the drive is Pappy hoisting a V-8 Chrysler engine into the pickup by himself. He is strong enough to wrestle with God if such a thing were possible. Regina and Gramma Nez are peeling potatoes for dinner. He sees them. And Gramma Nez isn't all saggy skin and gray hair clipped close and her teeth don't slip and her eyes are friendly and she doesn't read the *I Ching*, she reads The New Testament; and Regina isn't chubby, she isn't doubled-chinned. She is slim and her hair gleams and she laughs a lot. "I sure miss em," he whispers. Ginger is leaning alongside him, both their arms on the sill, his eyes shifting toward her as he whispers, "Yeah, I sure miss them times."

And the rain dribbles down the glass. And the cows waver.

"I wish I had good memories like yours," she says. "I wish I was really your sister and lived here when Uncle Jim was alive, and he was my father and you were my real brothers, you and Vernon. That would have been better."

Virgil sees Vernon gathering the best hay, the best clover, the best of everything for Cristobell. Feeding her, keeping her water fresh. Giving her baths, rubbing her down, brushing her until she shined like five-weight oil. These are the images Virgil covets.

92

"Bred her to Abel," he says, "because Abel was listed number one for calf ease. She got special vitamins and minerals and a special kind of sack feed cost ten a hundred. She got a half-pound of protein meal every day. Which should only go to lactating cows. She got to looking like a show cow, it's no lie. I tell you, Ginger, she was more like a pet dog than a cow. She ran to Vernon when he come to her pen and she was always puttin her head under his hand to get petted. They played out there, pushing each other around, and sometimes he would let her run in the pasture and he would try to hang onto her tail and she would whip him off like crack the whip and he'd go tumblin."

He chortles about it again as he had years ago when he saw it, saw Vernon hanging onto the tail and getting tossed and rolling. Why can't things be that way again? Why does everything have to change? Why is life mostly a gyp now? What's God up to? More and more Virgil is having questions for God. What's He let that war go on for? What's He let all those soldiers die for? Why is Pappy sick? Why not Dick? Dick's the one should be dying.

Ginger is grinning. Her front teeth are dull. She needs to brush them better and not smoke so much. But she has a pretty mouth otherwise. He knows plenty of boys who want to kiss her. A long time back in grade school Peter Raven had wanted to kiss her and gave Virgil a nickel and told him to give Ginger a kiss and say it was from him, from Peter Raven in love. When Virgil kissed her and told her it was from Peter Raven, she blushed to her neck and ran off. But later she came by and wanted to hear the whole story. And at the end of it she said, "He better not touch me. I know what he wants. He thinks I'm stupid."

Studying those early memories, Virgil matches them with the frizzy-haired Peter he saw last week with faded circles on the crotch of his jeans, love beads hanging from his neck. And his brother Danny too, same hair, same beads, same faded denim circles on his crotch from rubbing himself too much. The two of them will come again to help with third crop. Probably Ginger and Peter will disappear in the loft during the lulls before another load goes up. Peter does his own kissing now.

He points toward the pasture, at a mostly black cow. "See Sugar there, that's Cristobell's granddaughter."

"That's her granddaughter?"

"Yep. She's the twin of Cristobell, almost. She does eighty pounds a day. Great cow." Then he says. "You know what? Dad was good at it. He

93

handled everything same as Pappy did before he got so sick. I want to be like them. I want to farm strong like them. But I don't know, maybe I'm like Regina. Too nervous. She's a nervous Nelly, don't you think? She's sure getting fat, don't you think?"

"A butterball," says Ginger. Her eyes are tender and it looks as if she wants to kiss him. And she does. She pulls his head over and kisses his mouth and his scar tightens and she says, "You kiss like a board, Virgil."

Dick's voice echoes in the barn as if he's everywhere. "Hey," he says, "you done in here?" He walks through, inspecting what the inspector will inspect. "It looks good," he says. They watch him swing his eyes over the walls and along the gutters. "Yhah, whitewash covers a multitude of sins," he says. And then he says, "Come on, Virgil, we're goin to Lando Lakes."

"What for?"

"Cause I say so."

"To drive you home?"

"Don't look so glum. This is gonna be fun, chum."

"Gonna get drunk," whispers Ginger. "I smell it on his breath already."

She walks down the aisle pigeon-toed, her cuffs swishing. She tries to slide past Dick, but he stops her. His hand holds her neck. His thumb rubs back and forth over her cheek. "I heard that, Miss Smartass."

"Okay," says Ginger.

"Keep your mouth shut."

"I will."

He lets go and she hurries out the door.

"Come on, Virgil, we done enough in here," says Dick.

The boy leans the broom against the wall and walks with uncertain heart toward Dick. Is he really drunk already?

"Are you drinkin, Uncle Dick?"

"Does a bear shit squirrel?"

"Hmm."

"What wrong with you? You're the most contrary kid I know, you know? I'm tryin to be nice to you, Virgil. But see, you don't even know when someone is being nice. I'm sayin to you that today is my treat. We're celebratin."

"You just want me to drive if you get drunk."

"And what's wrong with that?"

94

"I don't have a license."

"Since when did that stop you? You can drive three miles home, can't you? How many times have you driven me home?"

"I don't know."

"Let's go." Dick is full of winks and grins. Virgil smells whiskey, he smells cigarettes.

The War According to V –

Little V,

Another fuck mood today. The Army can suck my cock. You want to know what we soldiers are Virge? Let me tell you the truth. We are fodder for Generals to get their stars. You wont see them on the line with us getting shot. No sir, they run around in their bubble choppers and give pep talks about how we are fighting for America's freedom against commies trying to bury us and we are lucky we can kill the bastards here instead of over there. Maybe they are right. But today I do not give a good goddamn. Who is fighting this fucking war? Hoodlums and nutcases and the super patriot and everyone from the wrong side of the tracks that didnt have brains or cash to go to college. I see no fucking presidents sons or senators sons over here. I see mostly the AINT GOT NOTHINGS being blow up. Two men in my squad fried by napalm yesterday. Killed by Friendly Fire. Friendly Fire, Jesus Christ what a term. Two little slouching snotnose ground pounders that mean nothing to nobody. Except to their daddies and mommies who will bury them like heroes and be proud and put their medals on the mantel over the fireplace. But one day it will hit them like a ton of shit. Their boy aint coming back! Just like birds and insects we come and go and life is nasty. Nothings changed since time began except we are more efficent at killing each other. God amighty you should see what napalm does to a human body, how it sticks to you like a burning jelly and eats your flesh right down to the bones. Thats what we do to charlie and sometimes by mistake to ourselves like those unlucky bastards yesterday. In the wrong place at the wrong time. The lucky ones die right away. What kind of mind could have invented that shit anyway? Fuck Dow Chemical sitting in some lab and creating jelly they know is going to kill people miserably. You best not think about it. Here one minute, gone the next. I think I am losing my hearing. My ears constantly ring and I feel like I am inside a barrel straining to hear what others are saying outside.

I keep thinking about those two dead men. Poor slobs. But then like rabbits out of a hat come their replacements, two FNGs eager and scared and I am looking at them and I think of YOU and I am glad you are not here, but I wish you could be somewhere where Dick isnt fucking with you. Sometimes I feel bad about leaving you there alone with him to kick your ass and bully you. Maybe it was Korea that made him a rotten shit, who knows? War turns saints into sinners. Maybe sometimes sinners into saints but that is rare. No one on the line is going to go home and be the person he was when he left. Just like criminals in prison, combat changes you for the worse. You can see them changing, full of hate and fear eating them alive and becoming dopers or alcoholics so they can escape death all around. It is bliss to get high get drunk and get laid. For a while you get out of yourself and feel no fear. But you know what? Thats life everywhere is what I am saying. There is always Nature in the raw wanting to kill you. Someone like Dick wanting to beat you to death. The Dicks of this world are everywhere you turn. They become sergeants and loootenants and captains and generals and all kinds of loudmouth assholes. They are the bullying foremen of the world who will love fucking you in the ass if you let them. Rice tells me that war has made me a potty mouth philosopher. I think he's right. Sort of. Maybe. But I tell you what I could not stand Dick and Mom being like her and Dad all kissy lovey dovey. It just went through me like a knife every time she kissed him I hated her more and more and I always hated him and never trusted him. So how could I have stayed on the farm? The way he treated Aunt Mary made her what she was you know. She was sweet and kind before he ruined her. Just ask anyone who knew her before they got married. A heart of gold they say. It was him. He is the perverted bastard who warped her. And I mean sexual perversions as well as every other kind. I know what I speak. I saw what he did. Don't let him warp you. If he fucks with you to much, get a bat and brain him will you? And guard your asshole! He swings both ways. So stay away from him and artritis dogs with sore teeth. There it is.

Big V.

Rolling Thunder

I am concerned about world opinion, George. **(Johnson)**

If the war is long and protracted . . . then we will suffer because the world's greatest power cannot defeat guerrillas. [Mr. President], every great captain in history was not afraid to make a tactical withdrawal if conditions were unfavorable to him. **(Bundy)**

The enemy cannot even be seen.

He is indigenous to the country.

But Mr. President.

We hope that peace will come swiftly.

Mr. President.

We must be prepared for a long continued conflict.

Mr. President, I foresee a perilous voyage . .

George, I don't think [it] is worth fighting for, and I don't think we can get out.

Virgil Francis Foggy

Minutes after leaving the farm, they are looking at Big Lake, rain drops hitting the water like fat bullets. Slender maples and birch crowding the lake's length. Evergreens everywhere. Boats rocking beside thin docks. The Lando Lakes Tavern sitting within a horseshoe curve of pines. Pickup trucks and cars in the gravel lot out front.

"I'll buy you a double cheeseburger, chips and a Coke," says Dick. "Totally my treat."

They hurry inside out of the rain. Virgil takes his cap off, slaps his knee with it. He sees several farmers he knows. Some of them wave. Some of them nod. The farmers are in uniform, wearing chore jackets, baseball caps and boots. Virgil smells smoky-beer and wet barn-boots creased with manure.

Wearing tight jeans, a loose blouse, beaded necklace Big Al's daughter, Alma, has one foot raised on the shelf behind the bar. She is leaning forward, showing cleavage, a paperback book in her hands. Her bottle blond hair wrapped in a ponytail. She puts the book down. "The Foggys," she says, throwing Virgil a wink and a smile. And he thinks: *Oh, if only . . .*

"I see you brung your chauffeur," says her father to Dick.

"Don't dare drink and drive drunk, Big Al," he answers. "Layin for me."

Dick orders two double cheeseburgers with the works and a pony beer with a shot of whiskey. He buys Virgil an icy Coke. Virgil fingercombs his hair as he stops to read the yellowing headless chicken article on the cork board again. He stares in fascination at the faceless chicken, its neck reaching skyward, its white chest puffed up, one scaly foot tentatively raised to take a step. "An automaton, a machine running on the autonomic nervous system," the scientist had said. "The thing wouldn't know it was alive no more than a tree." The corners of the article are curling and yellowing with age.

Virgil hears the farmers and Big Al gabbing. Case giving the same story Virgil's heard a dozen times, "I'd sell in a minute if some sorry sucker would meet my price. Just get me outta debt. I'm in debt cuz I was dumb enough to trust the gov'ment. They wanted me to expand. You boys know how it goes. Be a good American. That's what Americans do.

More acreage, more cows, more machinery. They were throwin money at me. Acreage and loans up to here is what I got for it. My nose barely above water now. Can't sell what's got no future. Can't stay and pay my bills. I'd shoot the politicians if I could get away with it. What were they thinkin? They *weren't* thinkin, that's the thing. A fine mess. Add to it this fuckin forever war we're fightin."

Tom T raises a warning finger and says, "Never trust a politician and never take a mortgage on your farm. Look at me, I stayed *small*. I'm poor as a church mouse, but I owe nobody nuthin. You fellas fell for their line. Not me." He raises his head. "Virgil!" he calls. "How much is owed on Foggy farm?"

"Nuthin."

"How many cows you milk?"

"Bout forty or so. It depends."

"There's my point," says Tom T. "No debt and the Foggys make it on forty cows. I rest my case."

"I know. I know. I'm a mug," says Case.

Big Al says, "You just got suckered like most round here. Listenin to gov'ment bullshit."

"I know, I know," says Case.

"Expansion and diversification that's the name of the game," says Chief. "Don't listen to Tom T. You don't need to get smaller. You need to get bigger. You've got to become corporated like me."

"Don't do it," says Big Al. He strokes his full beard as if he's petting a cat. "Fool talk. All Chief's money is on paper. The war goes under, he goes with it. Become incorporated and they got the right to snoop in your bisness."

"My paper good as cash," says Chief. "I can cash it in tomorrow if I want."

Gary is talking to Wes, trying to drum up business: "Your woods need thinnin, Wes, and frankly, goddammit, I need a job to get my family through the winter. Dad pays a pittance for all the chores and milkin I do."

"Hard times," says Wes. "Gotta tighten our belts. Don't take God's name in vain, Gary."

Case pounds the table and says, "This fuckin tax on stored cheese and powdered milk, why don't they sell it to the Russians? Or give it away. Why we gotta store the goddamn stuff when so many starvin people in the world? Somethin ain't right, you know what I mean? It's immoral is what it is."

"We're too good, too efficient," says Big Al.

"That's right, Big Al," says Case. "We expand and get more efficient like they tell us to and what happens? We go broke and the corporations move in. All this here from Golden Valley to Saint Cloud is gonna be corporate in ten years. We'll be workin for them . . . or not workin at all, by gawd."

"Fuckin gov'ment."

"Fuckin gov'ment."

"Don't cuss my government, boys. You done it to yourselves," says Larry.

"I'll give you ten a cord, Wes, and do all the work myself."

"You're not lazy, Gary, I'll give you that."

"I'll get two hundred cords and have it done by February. I'm not beggin, Wes. You want me or not?"

"Let me think about it. Be patient, kid. Ten a cord huh?"

"What about twelve?"

Alma Lando leans over the bar and says quietly, "That's farmin, ain't it?"

Dick jerks his head toward the farmers. "That's why I don't quit my day job."

Alma whispers, "Me too. No matter how good or bad things get, my dad told me this place will be okay and it is. Farmers drink when they're flush and drink when they're broke. Any excuse, like the rain today, and they're in here. You want to make a livin in Minnesota? Open a bar."

"Bitchin and moanin," says Dick, winking at Virgil, who tries to look innocent, who tries to put on a face that says he doesn't know what he knows.

"Bitchin and moanin," says Alma. "She turns around and pops two cheeseburgers in the toaster oven. "So how's our Regina?" she asks. "Had that baby yet?"

"Neh, she's fartin round per usual. Draggin ass. Watcha readin there?"

"*Naked Lunch.*"

Dick looks puzzled.

"About this addict. Actually the author himself."

"Oh."

"It's a comedy sort of. A tragedy too. This guy blew his wife's head off."

"No shit?"

"An accident." Alma plays with a curl falling over her ear as she talks. "He, yhah, missed the can of beer on her head. They were playin William Tell."

Dick laughs loudly. "Jesus Christ, that's one way to get rid of her." He leans way over and Virgil hears him whispering in Alma's ear, "Your dad got some shit?"

"How much?" says Alma.

"A dime baggy? And a ride in the saddle later?"

She waves her father over and nods towards Dick.

"Let's go see a man about a horse," says Big Al. He grins at Virgil and claps him on the shoulder. "How's Pappy?"

"Good. He's good."

"Too tough to die," says Big Al. "Too tough to die."

Virgil nods and looks away, looks out the window, looks at a green world peppered with serious rain.

When Dick and Big Al head for the office, Alma leans into Virgil, takes his hand, squeezes it and says, "Lord, I'd love to plank you. Wish you weren't so young."

Virgil feels himself flushing all over. "Wish I was older," he whispers.

She ruffles his hair and tells him, "Soon enough, soon enough."

The War According to V –

Little V,

Melvin Paine wounded. He was poking through elephant grass and a mortar hit far enough off that it not hurt nobody but him. But Paine. A tiny piece of shrapnel hit him in the back of the neck and he rolled into me and I saw this horror in his eyes that froze my blood. He grabbed his neck and held his palm up full of blood and he gave this sound. Like Awwwk. Something like that. It was all seeming serious until I looked and saw this tiny wound, nothing but a scratch. Paine keeps writhing and going Awwwk and thinking he is dying for sure. And I start laughing. And Paine sits up and says, What's so fucking funny Foggy? What's so fucking funny, Foggy? Which made me laugh more. I tell you everything is so goddam unreal out here that you dont know what is what or who you are or why you do the things you do. Finally I control myself and tell him his groans are a little overdone for such a baby wound. I got him smiling and then he started laughing and we all made fun of him and he made fun of himself. Sounds pretty stupid? How we entertain ourselves on this side of the world 10,000 miles from home. Write soon. Letters are what we live for. Tell Ginger to write me if she wants. I write her back if she would write me. Shit, what would I give to be milking cows tonight instead of going out on patrol to check some VC compound we heard rumors about. If we find it we are not to engage them, but call in air strikes. We always look for shit the planes can bomb. For two cents I shoot myself in the toe.

I said it before and I'll say it again. Nothing makes sense in la-la land. The generals sit in their offices like blind Buddhas sending us out on God knows what path to find the enemy in God knows what bloody tree or down what bloody hole. No front or rear to this war. The thing is all round you over there and over there. And there to. We go this way one day, we go that way another day swooping this country in choppers. We see shadows in the trees spitting fire. The shadows pop up here-there-here like bats out of a cave. We go crazy sometimes and show no fire discipline rattling bullets into a jungle that swallows everything including us and the enemy. You get to feeling like your not accomplishing anything except proving to each other that you can put your life on the line for a joke. Rice talked the other day about a book called Heart of Darkness and he said this was it, this war describes it. A place that eats up everything thrown at it. Swallows it and shows no effect. You napalm a section and a month later it is as if you did nothing. Except for the places seeded with Agent Orange, the jungle moves back in and it is all green and close and morbid again and out of it come tongues of fire or mortar rounds at night to keep you awake. You lay sweating and smacking mosquitoes or dueling with scorpions and smelling jungle rot coming from your armpits and you talk about home and cold beer and women and Christmas and you bitch bitch bitch about this war and officers and the government and the bonehead Army. But what can you do? Walk out of here? Swim the gulf. You are stuck man. Nothing to do but lock and load. We are getting our asses wiped by shadows. Do people see it? I will never volunteer again.

V.

Rolling Thunder

We seem bent upon saving the Vietnamese . . .
even if we have to kill them
and demolish their country to do it. I do not intend to remain silent in the face
of what I regard as a policy of madness, which, sooner or later, will envelop my
son and American youth by the millions for years to come. (**Senator George**
McGovern)

[The enemy] is helping the forces of violence in almost every continent.
[The conflict] is part of a wider pattern of aggressive purposes.
We are there because we have a promise to keep.
To dishonor that pledge, to abandon this small and brave nation to its enemies, and to
the terror that must follow would be an unforgivable wrong.
We will not be defeated.
We will not grow tired.
We will not withdraw. (**Johnson**)

Why and how did the United States become involved . . . in the first place?
Four years ago President Johnson sent American combat forces . . .
Now, many believe that . . . decision . . . was wrong.
I among them have been strongly critical of the way the war has been conducted.
But the question is: Now that we are in the war, what is the best way to end it?
(**Nixon**)

I know what the answer is in my own heart. (**Reagan**)

Americans . . . are dying for a world where . . . people may choose [their] own
path to change. We have no territory there, nor do we seek any.

The war is dirty and brutal and difficult.

105

Why must we take this painful road?

Why must this nation hazard its ease, its interest, and its power for the sake of a people so far away?

We fight because we must fight if we are to live in a world where every country can shape its own destiny.
Only in such a world will our own freedom be finally secure.
We must deal with the world as it is, if it is ever to be as we wish.
[It is] war of unparalleled brutality.
Simple farmers are the targets of assassination and kidnapping.
Women and children are strangled in the night because their men are loyal to the government. Helpless villagers are ravaged by sneak attacks.
Large-scale raids are conducted on towns, and terror strikes in the heart of cities.
The confused nature of this conflict cannot mask the fact that it is the new face of an old enemy. **(Johnson)**

Frankly, we haven't been hard-nosed enough. **(Reagan)**

Virgil Francis Foggy

Virgil continues staring out the window at the rain pattering the lake. His heart feels sullen. When the toaster bell rings, Alma takes the burgers out, puts them on paper plates. Adds a bag of potato chips to each.

"Alma, honey, pour me a draft," says Chief.

"Me too," says Case.

They all line up with their mugs and Alma serves them, smiles, shows cleavage.

Virgil sits at the booth near the door, picking at the chips, sipping Coke through a straw.

In fifteen or so minutes Dick and Big Al are back, Big Al isaying, "So, what's up, Virgil?"

He smells marijuana. The rain drums harder on the roof. Virgil stares at the ceiling. "Gotta get the hay in," he says softly.

"Rain," Big Al says, "it stupefies you."

Alma laughs. Her breasts wobbling. She looks at the farmers, smiles thinly at Virgil and says, "*Deja vu* day after day after day."

A distant rumble of thunder. Lightning follows.

Big Al lumbers back to the farmers and sits, pulls out a cigarette, lights it and says, "At the mercy of nature." He makes the sign of the cross in the air. He chuckles.

Dick slides into the booth. Virgil smashes the cheeseburger to fit the scarred opening of his mouth. He feels the scar stretching like a rubber band every time he takes a bite. No one stares at him. They're used to his scars now.

Dick wolfs his food. Virgil imagines the world like a wafer crammed into that long-lipped, horse-toothed mouth. Dick sucks the tips of his fingers. He drains his glass. From deep in his gut he brings forth rolling thunder of his own. Pats his tummy. Wipes his lips on the back of his hand. Then he whines, "Son, we need to talk man to man." His pupils are dilated.

"Yessir."

"Man to man," says Dick. He raises his empty glass, signals Alma.

Virgil hears Herb Thyng saying the bank is foreclosing. "Let them take it," he says, his tone combative. "Let'm try sell it. I'd like to see em

107

try. Forty acres of thistle and glacier rock. Pig rutted. Farming's for the big boys now, the profiteers. Forget you and me. Just fodder chewed up in the name of progress. In the name of some greedy capitalist sonofabitch who's already got his and don't give a fuck about you."

"Love it or leave it," says Larry.

"And go where?"

"The yellow-bellies gone to Canada."

"You know what, Larry?"

"What?"

"Fuck your fuckin patriotism," says Tom T. "Go join the Army."

"Fuck you. I done that once already. Did you?"

"Me and Alma gonna take off if this rain lets up," says Dick. "Be gone twenty, thirty minutes." He pauses. He grins. His dimples look happy. "Look, Virgil, do you know what discrete means?" says Dick, leaning close, smelling boozy, his big, soft hand covering Virgil's hand. "It means you don't make trouble, you keep what's secret secret. What people don't know don't hurt them. Nuthin's ever been truer than that. We all keep secrets. We all tell lies. World can't function without lies." Dick sighs, shakes his head mournfully. "Look, it's no big deal. You get a little older you'll see what I'm sayin." He flashes Virgil a toothy smile. "No big deal. Let me tell you about Alma Lando."

"You told me all this last time," Virgil says.

"You know Alma's an old friend of mine."

"Yeah, you told me."

"Me and that purty thang go way back to the beginnin, long before your mother, long before I was married, long before your Aunt Mary too, long before you were even a vague notion in Jim's eyes. Jesus, get a few drinks in me and my mouth takes on a life of its own."

"Uncle Dick, I told you before, it don't matter to me what you do. It ain't no secret and who cares?" Virgil watches a fly flirt with a drop of beer, its proboscis probing like a tiny straw. Can flies get drunk? Cats do. "Alma was one of the honeysuckle girls when you were my age."

"Younger than you, close enough," Dick says. "Alma . . . well, it's a story. Alma's brother got to her one day, showed her what it was for, and then she got to me. I was nine. No shit, really. We've been best buds for years, Virgil. She's like a sister to me in some ways."

Virgil forces up solemn nods of understanding, agreeing with everything Dick says. He sees Ginger in the barn, the messing around. He hears her saying that he kisses like a board.

"Nuthin between us but old times," says Dick. "If it's wrong, then nature is wrong. You gonna say nature is wrong? I don't think so. But me and Alma did somethin about it, see what I'm sayin?"

"Yessir."

"And who's harmed by it? I'd like you to tell me. Your mother cut me off. What's a man supposed to do? It's not fair, you know. A man with my appetites needs to be taken care of. It hardly seems like anything to us after so many years. Just old friends shakin hands is practically all. Just old pals keepin in touch."

Dick rises, pats the boy's shoulder, goes to the bar and picks up another beer. Brings it back. His eyes are kind. Yes, but there are detonations in them too, detonations in their deep dilated centers.

"You know what the priest said to me when I went to confession after I balled a girl the first time? C'mon, can you guess?"

"No sir."

"He said, How old are you? And I said, 'Nine, Father.' I shocked him. I was told you can't shock a priest, but I shocked that sonofabitch. It was the last time I went to confession. The whole damn business is stupid. But I was gonna tell you. You'll see when you get a little older," says Dick, "that men's ways aren't women's ways. At least not for the most part . . . well, some women are like men when it comes to spreadin it around. Alma is, but most aren't. They would be, see, but most of them don't have the heart for it, the intestinal fortitude. It takes guts to fuck around on your spouse. Most people don't see that, but it's true. Takes lots of guts, like going into battle. You never know what's gonna get you. You can blow your whole life for a piece of ass. Now wouldn't that be stupid? But, dammit, son, a real man can't help hisself, he's got to have her, no ifs or buts. Ask Freud and Darwin, they know. We're programmed. Every hormone in us sayin get in her pants. Most women, on the other hand, focus on love and one man to give them babies. Some don't, thank God, but like I say, most do. Here's the secret, Virgil. Satisfy her in bed whatever you do. You satisfy her in bed, she won't fuck around on you. Less likely anyway. Unless she's nympho," he glances at Alma, "in which case nobody can satisfy her and you might as well get in line."

"Yessir."

"Just make sure she's happy in bed, and half your troubles are over. This is gospel I'm tellin you. Gospel according to Dick." He raises his hand like he's swearing in court. "Truth with a capital T." He drains his glass and burps big again. "Hey, Alma, I guess I'll have a pitcher over here."

Alma waves.

"Got a thirst would drown a cow," Dick says. "That's another thing you don't understand at your age, but you will. Once troubles start you'll understand the need for booze. Have a few drinks and you won't care. Everything's doable, everything's fine." He lights a cigarette, offers one the boy refuses.

"Go on," Dick tells him. "Shit, I know you smoke. You and Ginger both, I know. It's no hair off my balls."

Looking at Dick's slicked-back hair, Virgil sees pink strips of scalp reflecting the lights above. It occurs to him that one day he will probably look like that, half-bald and getting balder. Maybe Dick will be dead by then.

Virgil takes a cigarette, snaps it between his lips. Lights it.

"Look at you, tough guy. John Wayne."

Someone at the table is talking, saying, "It's 1929 again. Those who work the land, they know a Depression when they see one. When do we get our boom, that's what I'd like to know?"

"Farmers never get no boom."

"Inflation rising. Wages stagnant. Jobs ain't out there unless you wanna flip burgers or wash cars."

"Love it or leave it," says Larry.

"Guns and butter my ass."

"Nap time," says Big Al. He rises and goes to his office.

"I wish these fuckers would get out of here, so she can lock up," Dick grumbles. "So you gonna be my man? You gonna sit tight till we get back?"

"Sure."

"Let me tell you again. Let me emphasize. Nuthin is more true than the sayin that *what she don't know won't hurt her.* I believe in that the way I believe that time is your enemy and you won't get out of this world alive." He squeezes the boy's hand again. "Look here, son, you want to hurt your mother? Go ahead, you tell her what you know. You tell her and then you take the consequences for what it does to her. You want to kill your mother? You want to make her have a miscarriage? Don't let me stop you. You see what I'm sayin?"

"I ain't gonna tell," says Virgil. "I understand."

"Good man. You're a trooper like your brother."

Virgil extracts his hand and pushes the half-eaten burger away. He finishes the cigarette and eats the ice in his glass. He can feel Dick's foot on top of his own, a steady pressure on his toes. "Man to man," he says, raising his glass. "Drink up, seal our bargain." He salutes Virgil and he says, "To *life*. To life and love and sexy women and all the nooky you can handle. Keep your dobber up, my boy."

Virgil takes a sip. The beer is bitter. Pappy has had him drink wine since he was a little kid, just a couple of ounces for his blood. "I like wine better," he says.

"Beer quenches your thirst," says Dick. He drinks deeply. Sighs. Says, "Ain't life grand sometimes? Gettin his ashes hauled makes a man . . . optimistic."

"Well, it's always bad," says one of the farmers at the distant table. "But we'll go on, we'll make it. We won't be defeated. Back in fifty-nine, that's when we thought the end had come. Ain't come yet. What the hell."

"I've had cowshit on my shoes since I could walk," interrupts another. "Now I'm fifty-five years old. What else do I know?"

"We'll make it. Half of farmin is patience."

"Might be a glut of milk, but corn and wheat is up. With this war, we'll be in demand once the surplus goes down. Soldiers gotta eat. They're talkin bout a million soldiers over there, you know. A million mouths to feed."

"I heard they were drawin em down. Gonna have half of em home by Christmas."

"Don't believe it."

"Milkcows have gotta go. Need to get Packerland busy. Ship em out to Packerland. Too many of em. Too much milk and cheese."

"Hogs and beef cattle, that's the ticket."

"Wait a minute, Larry, beefer prices is always spotty. Milkcows is steady income."

"Like a roller-coaster is steady."

"What you say, Wes, twelve a cord? That's my highest goddamn offer."

"Quit saying goddamn, Gary."

Dick is shaking his head. The look on his face says he knows the ways of the world. "I've heard this same shit since I first came in here with

111

Pappy over thirty years ago. Same bullshit exactly. Never catch me chewin my cud twice. Never catch me being a fuckin farmer."

Virgil thinks about how much farmers have to know to keep a farm running. How they have to be veterinarians and heavy equipment operators and mechanics and electricians and carpenters and welders and burners and able to take scrap from the scrap pile and invent a part to use for some piece of machinery that's broken, how they've got to know the land they farm, how to rotate the crops and fertilize them just the right amount so they won't burn up, how they've got to know when to harvest and how to store hay and silage so they don't spontaneously combust. And they need to know where to sell and what price to hold out for and how to do their taxes and how to bargain at auctions and not feel too bad about some farmer who went under because he was too sick to tend his land or milk his cows or God knows what, it's all on his shoulders, sink or swim in his hands, do or die, he's all alone to blame or praise depending on his skill, depending on his luck.

"Pappy's a good farmer," offers Virgil.

Dick agrees. "Pappy can outfarm any man in the county. We never missed a meal when I was growing up. Your dad was a good farmer too. I give credit where credit is due. Nobody smarter than those two. But you know what? Your dad is dead, and Pappy ain't long for this world. Workin hisself to death."

"Vernon might be back before then and take over."

"Vernon? Fuck Vernon. You and Vernon. Farm's gonna bring both you down. All you'll get is an early grave. No, I'm not gonna let that happen. What we're gonna do when Pappy dies is sell the farm. Buy a house on a lake. A boat. We'll fish and cruise. And I'll stay on at Chevrolet. You can get a job at the slaughterhouse. They always need workers and the pay is good and you don't need an education."

"I ain't go no heart for killin cows."

Dick leans forward, eyes shrewd. "You'll do what you have to do when the time comes. Ask your brother about that. Ask him what he does when he's ordered to shoot."

"That's different."

"Nope, it's the same thing. You do what you have to do."

A gust of wind buffets the bar. Angry rain slashes the windows.

"Here she comes," says Alma.

They listen to hail, a million tom-toms, drumming the roof.

Lightning dazzles. Thunder rolling.

"Six miles off," says a knowing voice.

Another boom and the lights go out. The interior of the bar looks like six in the morning. "It's time for chores," Virgil tells Dick. "We should get home."

"Relax."

"But it's time to milk."

"Have another," says Dick. He pours himself the last of the pitcher. "Let me try a bottle of pisano," he tells Alma. "You like wine, Virgil, is that what you said? How about a little glass to seal our bargain?"

"We sealed it, Uncle Dick."

Alma cracks a bottle, brings it over with a clean glass. Lights kick on. The compressor chugging, trying to catch up. Neon signs stuttering back to life. Dick gets up and puts money in the jukebox. The voice of Tammy Wynette. She is standing by her man again. Alma indicates the weather and shakes her head at Dick. "Next time," he says. Raising his glass he drinks deep, his Adam's apple bobbing comically. He pours another. Sighing he whispers, "No nookie today. Honeymoon of the hand gets old fast, let me tell you."

"Listen to it, listen to it," someone says. "How can Big Al nap through this?"

"He's old," Alma answers. "Sleeps through anything."

"Jack Daniels and dope," Dick tells her tapping his temple.

Virgil looks at the door, longs for the door.

Later, he drives through heavy rain, headlights probing while Dick mumbles incantations in the back, punctuating his words with lots of fucks and cunts and motherfuckers and sonsabitches trying to fuck him up the ass. The old Cadillac holds the road firmly. In some low spots water flows over the rocker panels and threatens to drown the starter. The creeks and rivers are moving fast. Water tops some of the banks, washes thinly over the street. Waves push against Chippewa Bridge. The boy holds tightly to the wheel. Dick is singing about a *greasy, slimy old slut, the fungus lies between her thighs . . . the pus runs out her butt—*

Lightning flashes again and again, backlighting the cornfield and the barn and the house. Lights are on in the barn. The yardlight in the killing yard sways at the top of the pole. Virgil pulls into the driveway. The car shifts its tail in the mud, then steadying on the gravel as he turns left

113

and forward into the open garage, onto solid cement.

As soon as he turns off the engine, the back door opens and his mother is there with her hair plastered to her head, her angry voice reaching for Dick.

"What the hell you think you're doing!"

"Hello, bay-beee," says Dick.

She shrieks obscenities at him.

He pulls out a baggy. "A little you know what."

"Put that away, you moron!"

Virgil listens as they yell past each other.

"You stupid . . ."

"Cunt!"

"Prick!"

"Listen, listen!"

She stares severely for several seconds while Dick keeps insisting it's all for her. "C'mon, booboo face, tell me you want it. You know you do. Let's celebrate." Again he offers the baggy.

"You son of a—" she says. Her voice trembling with indignation. "Haulin my kid out in this weather when it's time for chores and for what? To get drunk! To get stoned!"

"The pain, baby, had to doff the pain. So lonely." Looking at his chest, he makes jabbing motions at his heart, eyes crossing with the effort.

She looks at Virgil. "Pappy and Gramma Nez are in the barn," she says.

"I'll go help," he says. "I'm sorry, Regina."

"Sorry is as sorry does," she says. "Come on, you!" She jerks on Dick's arm.

"Lay go!" he says. He puts his foot on her belly and she flies backwards, falls *thump* on the concrete. Her mouth wide, she doesn't say anything. And then she looks at her lap. She flips the coat aside and looks harder. A puddle of water is spreading under her.

"Mom!" Virgil yells.

"Virgil, go in the house and call Doc Albers. Tell him to meet me at the hospital, tell him my water broke. Then come back and drive me over there."

"Eh? Whaz happenanend?" says Dick. "I fig it. I fig it, Regina. Where my wazum?" His hand searches the floor and pulls up a bottle of wine he offers.

114

Virgil grabs her under the armpits. Lifts her, maneuvers her. She insists on putting the tarp down before she sits on the front seat. There are still some bloodstains on the seat, scrubbed but faintly visible in spots from when he bled on her lap two months ago. He folds the tarpaulin over the stains. Eases his mother inside.

He sprints into the rain. Lightning flaring in all directions. Cannon fire echoing. More lightning. More cannons. Dashing by the living room window, he spots the glare of the TV, Ginger watching it, her hair drooping like folded wings over her shoulders. Opening the door, he bursts in yelling, "Gin! Off your fat ass! She's havin that goddamn baby. C'mon, Ginger, let's go!"

The War According to V –

Little V,

      We keep our heads down and shoot blindly in the general direction of the enemy while bullets are sizzling and WIAs and KIAs piling up. The captain called in air strikes, napalmed shit out of everything and we hauled ass back to the DZ and the Hueys. Again as in so many these battles I never seen the enemy. I been here four months and I can count on one hand the number of times I actually seen VC we are shooting at. I could not even tell you if I ever shot any these guys. Some guys brag about how many dinks they kill, but there is a lot of big talk, plain macho hogwash posturing. One guy I know bragged how he used his M60 to roll a VC down a hill and it was like rolling a log, he said. He laughed and showed how the dead man rolled and by the time he was done rolling, the dink was chipped beef on toast. Everyone laughed to loud, you know what I mean Virge? To loud. Thats how calluse you get Virge. But that bragger dead now himself. He walked into a grid of bamboo that slammed into his body and made a pincushion of him. Not a pretty sight. What goes round comes round and this I know everyone of us is fucked and getting fucked for moonshine. You, me, Ginger, Mom, Gramma Nez, Pappy, even Dick and especially every hollow eye grunt over here is getting fucked royal. Sent here for WORDS. Sent here to die. We are not words. We are flesh and blood. We want to live as much as those cushy at home and continuing this shit. The politicans talk talk talk and we die die die. The newspaper guys ask us how we doing and they test what we say to see if its patriotic and of course we always say the patriotic thing about stopping commies and shit like that but let me tell you that in private we do not say no such thing. We could give a flying fuck if you are a commie or a capitalist or what system you believe in. To each his own is what we say to a man. Maybe the officers not think that way but the ground-pounders do. And you at home can take that to the bank. Get us out of this mess! We want to go home! I came here stuffed with propaganda and crap about fighting for my country. Fight for my country? Fuck that! I fight for myself and for Paine and Rice, we fight for each other nothing else. There is no body on earth closer to you than your war buddy, no woman, no man, not even you little Bro. Take the flag, take the speeches, take the old men arguing about dominoes falling and if we do not stop them here we will be fighting in our back yards. Shove all that where the sun don't shine. I can not believe what a airhead I was. All us who volunteered shake our heads in wonder at how stupid we were. This is a mean way to waste your life. There it is.

Big V.

Rolling Thunder

How did America get involved in the first place?

. . . [How did] Johnson's war . . . become Nixon's war[?]

The question at issue is not whether Johnson's war becomes Nixon's war.

Many Americans have lost confidence in what their Government has told them about our policy. The American people cannot and should not be asked to support a policy which involves the overriding issues of war and peace unless they know the truth about that policy.

How and why did America get involved in the first place? [When I took office] the war had been going on for 4 years.

31,000 Americans had been killed in action.

No progress had been made at the negotiations.

The war was causing deep division at home and criticism from many of our friends as well as our enemies abroad.

[But] the great question is: How can we win America's peace? **(Nixon)**

Part Two: Stop Questioning America

Virgil Francis Foggy

Virgil puts the letter away with the others in the drawer. A few more days and Vernon should get the news about Regina and the baby. Virgil thinks of himself as getting the hang of how to write letters. Maybe not as good as Vernon's letters, but how could they be? Vernon has war. A life filled with violence. And drinking and sex with bar girls. What has Virgil to compare with all that? Except maybe what Dick does with Alma Lando when he gets the chance. Virgil has given his word to keep Dick's secret, but he sees them all the time in his mind's eye. He sees his mother's husband having sex with a woman Virgil's known all his young life. He knows he's an accomplice. He and Dick and Alma make a threesome. He doesn't want the image in his mind. Though his hand sometimes wants it. But he can't help it anymore than he could help seeing that blowjob Regina gave Dick in the loft.

After many years it's still vivid. Vivid as today. So are the Alma quickies in her office when Big Al is gone. Neither image turned you on, Virgil. It made you want to cut your cock off and throw it away. Rid yourself of its influence. Not have the equipment to behave so sinfully. You asked yourself, *What's wrong with everybody? Especially, what's wrong with Dick?* And you prayed to get old and not care a thing about sexual intercourse, which might make you act like him. Like cows in the field licking each other's vaginas. The last three years you've been in a home so glutted with sex it's a wonder the heat from it hasn't melted the wallpaper. A house of obsession, house of incest, taboos broken. House of violence. Death of innocence.

Gazing out the window of his bedroom, he watches the wind combing the hay. Long-stem timothy flowing like green shades of water. The timothy ready to mow and the alfalfa overdue, but it's been too wet to cut until now. The fields will yield another thousand bales, which will make 10,000 altogether in the barn, enough to get the cows through winter. In another month it will be time to get the picker greased and harvest corn to fill the crib. Disk the stalks into the soil before it snows. Virgil told Pappy not to worry about gathering or planting. No need to hire field hands after the hay's in, Virgil told him. "I'll do the rest myself. I'm born for it. You said so yourself, Pappy."

But can he? There are many days when he's not sure he has the strength to handle anything. Doubt dogs him, but he doesn't let his fear show. He goes forward and works until he's ready to drop. Like a soldier who manages to do his duty day after day, keeping to himself how inadequate he is. Pappy and Gramma Nez always looking to Virgil. For the first time in his life he is the important one. The center of attention, center of the farm. He sees himself as much older than almost fifteen. He thinks it must be how boys his age used to feel when they pioneered the land. No time for the kind of nonsense kids pull these days. All this marching against the war and all the drugs and long hair and stupid talk—MAKE LOVE NOT WAR.

"It didn't seem to me that they were capable of either," was what Ronald Reagan had said. He got a big laugh and lots of applause. Virgil laughed too and agreed the protestors were a sorry-looking lot. If Vernon could have seen them, he wouldn't have liked them either.

Maybe Virgil will write and tell Vernon that the Foggys got to believe what the government tells them. Commies are coming. Why can't Vernon see that? Maybe the old men are right. Maybe Americans will be fighting in their back yards. Virgil wishes he had been one of the pioneers, one of the ancient Foggys who settled the land in 1851 and fought the Indians in 1862 and gave the name Foggy Meadow to the cemetery and then the town itself before some council changed it to Golden Valley at the end of the nineteenth century. That's the era when he should have been alive. Pappy once called him *an old soul*. Virgil knows the modern world is bad for him. He wonders if lots of boys feel out of sync the way he does.

Shedding his farmeralls, he dons jeans, work shirt, WHO cap, gloves, and goes into the hall. Passing Ginger's room he hears her crooning to the baby:

Crash goes a chimney,
Pow goes a hall,

Zowie goes a doorway,
Zam goes a wall.

The baby's face is dark and flat like an Indian's face. She has a fine mess of black hair. The hair makes a pointed V on her forehead chimp style. Her eyes look slightly swollen. Nub of a nose. A squirmy mouth. In all, an ugly specimen of her species. Next to Ginger, an empty milk bottle sits on the table, the nipple flattened.

"She's a feeder," he says.

The baby's mouth wiggles as if she's trying to talk but hasn't found the right chords, only the crying chords. She is wearing a Sioux headband Gramma Nez made for her. It is beaded black and white, the beads zigzagging like lightning to symbolize the night she was born and the initials P and B and F in the middle of her forehead, standing for Pearl Bell Foggy. A funny name, but Virgil likes it.

"You want to hold her?" says Ginger.

He doesn't want to hold the baby. He tells Ginger he's got lots of work to do, got to get the tractor fueled and hook up the haybine and cut that hay. If the weather holds, they'll be putting up bales in two days.

"Peter and Danny are going to help again," he says. "It'll be just us. Pappy can't help no more."

"I know," says Ginger. She looks down, hiding her pleasure at hearing the name *Peter*. "I'll give a hand," she adds. "I'll drive the tractor and you guys load."

"That works," he says.

Pearl Bell's mouth is still working on a word. Virgil starts to say that she looks like a monkey, but that's what Dick and Ginger call him all the time. "Looks like a fish," he says. "That's how a fish's mouth goes." He makes a gulpy mouth.

"She does not, you idiot," says Ginger. She lifts the baby and pats her back. Burps her.

"Sounds like her dad," says Virgil.

"No way," says Ginger. "Here, hold her."

He backs off.

"Why don't you want to hold her?"

"I got work to do. I'm a busy man. Too busy for babies and shit."

"You're the man," she mocks. "Macho farmer man."

"Who's runnin things?" he says. "You runnin things, Gin?"

"I'm takin care of the babby."

"Well then we all got our jobs, ain't we?"

She frowns, doesn't answer, puts the baby on her lap, adjusts the headband.

"That reminds me of somethin," he tells her. "I seen a hippie t'other day. Not a wannabe. The one I seen was real. I forgot to tell you about her. I seen her in town and she was wearing blue everything and moccasins and she had straw hair and she said, 'Far out.' She was what a real hippie is, not like Peter and Danny and other phony protestors I could name marchin around like a bunch of clowns. She was sellin a book to get money for drugs. That's what a real hippie does."

"Peter's no wannabe," Ginger replies. "He's cool. You wish you could be cool like him. He wants to start a commune where everyone works together."

"Yhah, yhah and sex is free. That's what he wants. A commune for commies. Vernon's fightin against that shit, don't you know. I'll tell you what, Pete's no hippie. Him nor Danny, neither. They're just horn dogs preachin free-love so they can get laid."

"You'd know all about that," she says. "What's a hippie, anyway? Can you define it?"

He opens his mouth, but doesn't know what to say. Then he says, "It's a hip philosophy."

"Where'd you get that shit? Who told you that?"

"A guy on TV sittin like Buddha on a pillow, talkin hip philosophy."

"So what's it mean?"

"What do you mean what's it mean?"

"Philosophy. What's philosophy?"

"It means philosophy," says Virgil, "and if you're too stupid to know what it means, I ain't got time to waste standin here tellin you. It ain't my fault you don't read. I'll tell you this, though, Peter don't got philosophy. He dresses like he has, but he's as fake as margarine butter."

"Is not."

"You won't find me fallin for that bullshit, wearin my hair in curls and talkin like a fool, all that super love-in bullshit. I mean like wow! I mean like groovy. Far out. Bitchin, man. Psychedelic." Virgil rolls his eyes. "Jesus, don't it just make me barf to think these are people Vernon is fightin for."

"Oh, shut up! That war is a big fat lie. All those dead guys have died for what? The survivors gone crazy cuz they know the war's a big fat

122

blooper."

"You don't know shit!'"

"You don't know shit yourself!"

He stands there trying to think of a reply that will fry her. He looks from picture to picture on the wall, all her charcoal and pencil work, the naked girls with cute tits and no hands, no feet. Very vulnerable. And sexy. They're all thin and light. They're all hazy. A slight breeze would blow them away. They look like Ginger in various ways.

"Shut up," she says. "Don't say it."

"You shut up, toots."

"I'll tell him you think he's a girl."

"I don't care what you tell him. I ain't scared of him, nor Danny dipshit neither."

"Danny kicked your ass," she says smiling.

"Yeah? Well but you don't know what I did to him. I got him back."

She raises her eyebrows. Waits.

"Maybe I'll tell you sometime."

Ginger laughs. He tells her to go pound mud. Before she can say anything else, he leaves. Hobbling downstairs careful of the pain in his shriveled hamstring. He looks in the kitchen and sees Regina sitting at the table, coffee in front of her, cigarette burning in the ashtray, smoke vacillating. One finger strokes the back of the Holstein butter dish. Dark rings encircle her eyes. She looks bloated, her neck and shoulders fatter than ever. Mouth twisted bitterly. Virgil hears her whisper, "Who gives a shit?" A copy of *Finnegans Wake* is open in front of her. Even if she doesn't understand it, she is reading it all the way through. She's not far from the end. She shakes her head at the page and looks toward the kitchen window, the sampler hanging a tad cocked. Her finger continues to pet the ceramic cow. "Don't let anything so fill you with sorrow that you forget the joy—" she says, her voice pitifully small.

"Vernon says if you write him, he'll write you back," Virgil tells her.

Her head jerks toward him, her eyes narrowing with what looks to be hate. She's an advertisement for how *not* to look after giving birth. She stuffs her face with chocolates. She drinks Pepsi Cola. She smokes like a dope fiend. She can't stand the baby. Nor anyone else. Most the time all she does is read her book and whine over how obscure every sentence is.

123

She says it's exactly like life itself, an obscene joke. "Death will be a relief," she keeps repeating.

"Vernie better be careful over there," she says. "I don't need a hero, I need a son to come back and take care of this fuckin farm."

"I'm takin care of it, Regina," he says. "It's goin good. We got a good crop of hay out there. If I get it in on time it'll be high protein and the cows will milk like monsters."

"Farm's fallin apart," she mutters. "Pappy gettin weaker and more ditzy day by day. Dick's useless as tits on a steer. We got two old people on their last legs and a crippled boy and a drunk. This place is sinkin. We're all sinkin. We're goin to die in poverty and good riddance."

"I'm a full time farmer now. I'll—"

"Shut up with that! That's all I hear from you! As if being a farmer is such a grand life. Like you're a hero or somethin. Only idiots are farmers, Virgil. God give em dust in their heads instead of brains. Wish I'd never come here. Wish I'd stayed in college and made somethin of myself besides a baby-factory. Which is all I am. I can't even read this stupid book. I don't know what the fuck it's sayin. Because I quit school. You want to quit school and be a moron all your life, go ahead. I don't give a good goddamn. I don't care. Slaved all my life for you kids and what do I get? Look at me. Just look what's happened to me. I used to be . . . I used to—"

"Somebody's got to take up the slack," he says, trying to sound manly. "Pappy says I'm a born farmer. I like it, I really do, and I didn't like school. It was a waste of time. Mostly got D's anyway. There's nuthin school has to teach me about farmin." His weak ham trembles. He shifts his weight, leans a shoulder against the doorjamb.

She points the cigarette at him and he remembers that Dick is always doing the same thing. Everyone shooting everyone else and his parents want to shoot him too. Maybe he wants to shoot them as well. Maybe it would be a better world if they were all gone. Cull out the evil ones, like you cull out useless cows you're sending to market. Maybe those who killed Sharon Tate thought they were ridding the world of evil. Maybe like in the war. What is truth anyhow? Gramma Nez says everything is true.

Regina jabs a finger at him. "I don't care what you or anybody else does, just leave me alone with your stupid teenage bullshit. Kids. God almighty, why did I ever have any kids? Jesus Christ, what gets into us, what makes us do it?" She snarls at the page in front of her. "Look at these stupid words in this stupid book." Her finger runs along the lines and she says: "A hundred cares, a tithe of troubles and is there one who understands me?" She raises hot eyes to Virgil. She grabs the teaspoon in front of her, holds it up. "You don't get away from me I'll stab you."

"With a spoon?" he says, grinning.

The spoon quivers in her hand. She lowers her head. She breaks into sobs.

"Sonofabitchin fucked up bitch!" Dick had called her the other night, threatening to kick her tail if she didn't lay off him. And she called him a first-class bastard and told him to keep away from her. "My mouth isn't your personal sewer! Keep that thing in your pocket!" she yelled.

"Regina?" Virgil says. "Mom?" He tries to express in his tone that he wants to help her.

"I can't help it," she says. "A woman can't help what she feels. Go away, will you? I don't like you today. Will you just get out of my sight?"

Her shoulders shake. The spoon in her hand looks like a silver horn.

Virgil spins on his heel. He tells himself not to let her ruin another day. It's a fine morning. Aaron strutting on top of the coop keeping watch on his wives, all of them scratching and pecking, teaching their peeps how to be adults. *Over here*, they cluck to the babies. *Scratch this dirt. There's a bug. Eat the bug.* Rachel eyeballs Virgil between the slats of her pen. She baas and he baas back. She wants him to pet her, give her a treat, but he hasn't got time for that. Moses is leaning his head against a fence post, baby peeps scurrying between his legs. One stops and pecks his hoof.

"Wake up, Moses!" Virgil tells him. "Gonna get you, Moses."

Moses shakes his ears and saunters away. Stands at the cages, converses with the rabbits. They sniff his mouth. The willow tree is full of whips. The killing yard looks innocent. Virgil likes it today. He heads to the machine shed to get the Allis-Chalmers 180. Climbing aboard, he starts the engine and feels the throbbing power of the diesel running through him and it's as if he and the tractor are one and he's strong again. He drives to the fuel tank and fills up. Then hooks on the haybine and heads to the field. The wind is warm. The sun soothes his back. Whatever could be better than this? He's happy and to hell with all that gloom in the house, and to hell with the war.

When he gets to the edge of the field he stops, shoves the clutch pedal down and gears in the PTO. Lifts his foot off the clutch and the PTO starts spinning, the blades of the haybine ticking, saying *clickclick* . . . Setting his sights on a tree at the far end of the field, he begins to cut hay in a line as straight as anything Pappy could do.

What is truth? Truth is Virgil can't think of what would be better than being on a tractor, driving a straight line, mowing a ready field, watching the timothy spurt in six-foot rows from the back of the blades. Faint dust rising. Making hay while the sun shines. It is all up to him. Ginger called him the man. She was mocking him, but that's who he is. He is the man keeping the farm from going under. Because of him, the cows will eat this winter. They will let down milk. The Associated Milk Producers will buy that milk and send the farm a check, which will pay the farm bills and buy gas and diesel fuel and pay the mill. All because of Virgil Francis Foggy. Dick's job at Golden Valley Chevrolet doesn't count for the farm. When Regina goes back to the restaurant, her money won't count for the farm either. Only the cows and the milk will count for the farm. They are in it together, the cows and Virgil and Gramma Nez and Pappy. Left to Dick and Regina, there would be no farm, no place for Vernon to come home to except some house on a lake that Dick wants and where Vernon wouldn't be welcome. Virgil thinks of the commandment to honor mother and father, and he wonders how to do that and keep the farm and not hate the two of them waiting like vultures for Pappy to die. Getting ready to sell the future, the last Foggy farming Minnesota land.

"I don't hate her," he says, turning the tractor at the end of the row, lifting the haybine, watching so he doesn't crimp the driveshaft. Then back around and the haybine down and the clicking sound cutting through timothy.

He doesn't hate her most of the time. It's just that she married wrong and she's sick and she weeps every time she hears Pearl Bell crying. She keeps saying that babies have broken her spirit, broken her body, her mind, and she had such great plans for herself once upon a time. Until she started having kids. Big dream future—finish college, get a Ph.D., become a professor. She wanted to be highbrow and have discussions with the learned about literature. She hates it that Virgil doesn't have a bookish aptitude. How could a son of hers turn out so shallow? She has no one to talk to. A whole living room full of books and Virgil won't bother to read even one. "You want to smell like cowshit for the rest of your life?" she often asks. And he says he doesn't mind. "Hey, it's honeysuckle to me." She cried over that remark. Broke down and sobbed and beat her head against the table. She hasn't called him honey or sweetheart since the baby got born.

"Valium," Dick had said. "I'm gettin you some Valium and you're gone off this kick or I'll have to kill you, you bitch."

Virgil can't understand how having a baby could make her so sad. Dick has told him to stay the hell away from love. Love brings tons of baggage. It wears you out. Love is a jail with invisible bars. No one in love is free. Stay away from it. No sir, Virgil is never going to get married and have babies and an ungrateful wife always crying in her beer and blaming him for everything and wanting to stab him with a spoon.

After a few passes, he sees a coyote trot out of the woods. The coyote follows the tractor. Staying a few feet behind the haybine, the coyote bounces up and down on all fours along the windrow's edge. Mice scurry in terror of the tractor's puffing and the click clatter of the blades swishing a hair's breadth above their heads. The mice flee death and find it bouncing gleefully after them.The coyote's teeth clicking. It eats them like birds eat worms, raw and down the hatch, a flick of leathery tail and they're gone. You never know where it's coming from. Vernon has said he is a fatalist. If a bullet has your name on it, there is nothing you can do, he said.

When Virgil climbs down to fix a whine in the rollers, the coyote doesn't run away. It lies on its belly, its head on its paws and watches him pump grease into the nibs and then go back to mowing again. A few rows later, full of mice, the coyote goes home. Virgil thinks it was a female fattening up for the coming cold. Virgil has shot a few coyotes over the years, but he won't shoot her. There has been too much death and near-dying lately. His father. Himself. Pappy. This or that guy in Vernon's platoon. And the weekly body counts on TV on the Friday news looking like lopsided basketball scores. NVA 142 - USA 83

After the timothy is cut and drying in the sun, he heads to the alfalfa field. Beyond it are ten acres of tasseled brome. The field is shaped like a heel-less boot, a distorted sort of Italy with a sea of maples surrounding it. At the toe wandering one day a couple of years ago, with pails for raspberries, Virgil and his mother found a den of broken branches still attached to a tree, hanging twigdown and funneled like a teepee entwined with wild grass. Inside were a dead coyote and four dead pups, all shot where they lay in their own blood. Small bore holes, .22 caliber. Dead as the wood crowning them. Dead as the decaying leaves.

"Why do men do this?" Regina had said. "They don't harm anything. They keep the rats and mice in check. They don't mess with the cows. I've never known a coyote to mess with a cow. Why do this? What kind of man does it take to coldly kill these pups? I can't understand it," she said. "Shooting them in anger or jest or whim, I can't understand the mindset that pumps bullets into wildlife. Men think they're gods just because they have a gun in their hand." She looked at her son, her mouth twisting like it always does when she's mad. "You men," she said. "You goddamn men. You make war on everything. It's maddening. It's why the world is what it is."

The War According to V –

Little V,

As far as those body counts you hear about, they have become the only means of winning this war. Kill enough of them and they will quit is what Johnson said. But Ho said no. Ho said we can kill ten of them for every one of ours and he would still win. I am believing him Bro. What kind of war is it when we fight up and down the same burned out hills and in the same claustrophobe jungles day after day and don't conquer any territory but count it a good day and insist we are winning if we kill more of them than they do of us? But mostly let me tell you Virge you just don't see them and you wonder if they have all gone for some R and R or what and then some sniper picks off somebody or a squad buys the farm in a hail of bullets and five minutes later the Cong are gone, vanished like ghosts in your dreams like they were never there except you know they were. Because they left their blood or your blood behind and you pissed or shit yourself and some guy next to you is having hysterics and wants his Mama and some other guy is gasping and wide eyed and has that deathlook and you can hear air whistling through a hole in his chest. I feel like something in me is dying and leaving a gap big as my heart, a gap filling with hate of everything here and everything at home that got us here. Top Smeltzer says I am a good soldier and we all have these moods and I will adjust because I do not have any other choice but dying and I will not do that because I want to live. But I am not sure, I really am not sure. There it is.

V.

Rolling Thunder

The precipitate withdrawal of American forces . . . would be a disaster.
Ultimately, this would cost more lives.
It would bring more war.
This first defeat in our Nation's history would result in a collapse of confidence
in American leadership . . . throughout the world.

But the question facing us today is: Now that we are in the war, what is the
best way to end it?

The precipitate withdrawal of American forces would be a disaster.
Ultimately, this would cost more lives.
It would—
But the question facing us today is— **(Nixon)**

Politics is supposed to be the second oldest profession.
I have come to realize that it bears a very close resemblance to the first.
(Reagan)

Virgil Francis Foggy

All day, except for lunch at the Airstream, Virgil stays with the mowing and the timothy falls into tidy rows, which he will roll with the rake tomorrow and bale the next. If the weather holds. If the rain coming from the west doesn't come too soon and drown the crop, bleach it into straw. Entire crops are wrecked that way, put up with hardly any protein value at all and it's like the cows are eating sawdust doing no good filling their bellies with wood. Their milk will drop off and they will moan and bawl like the spoiled brats they are. Milk cows are the most spoiled cows on the planet. They expect the best hay and grain possible and won't settle for anything less. The last test on the hay Virgil baled showed that it had eighteen-percent protein. He got it inside the barn by the Fourth of July. And he made sure that everyone knew that Foggy Farm had not the usual twelve or thirteen percent, but eighteen-percent protein hay. That's when Pappy said Virgil Francis was a born farmer. Even Vernon or Jim never put up eighteen percent. Only Virgil and Pappy have done that. "Chip off the old block that's what Virgil is," said Gramma Nez when the test results came in. She gave him one of her White Owl cigars.

He is mowing the last row of the day near sundown, ready to head in for chores, when a bird scrambles from a nest in front of him and tries to get away, legs and stubby wings tumbling like a swimmer paddling frantically. Virgil jumps down and snatches it, a baby sparrow. He climbs back on the tractor and goes to cutting hay again. The bird has a look in its eyes that says - *Wow, where am I? Wow, what's happening?* Virgil slips it under his cap to calm it. He feels it pecking around in his hair, scratching, until it finally nests itself. He finishes off the row and stops the haybine and heads back to the machine shed.

"What you got there?" says Ginger when he takes the bird to her room.

"A sparrow," he says, "for Pearl Bell."

"What's she suppose to do with a sparrow?"

Pearl Bell is sleeping in her crib. He sets the sparrow on her tummy. It wipes its beak over the folds of the blanket. Then sits back checking things out.

"Wild birds don't do well in captivity," Ginger says.

"What should we name it?"

They decide the bird is a girl. They call her Bonnie. Virgil gets one of Gramma Nez's White Owl boxes and puts grass in it. The bird nests in the grass, eyes shiny with expectation. He fingers up dead flies from the windowsill and puts them at her feet. She pecks at a fly. Then ignores it and stares some more.

"Get her some grain," says Ginger. "Some cow feed."

After he puts on his chore jacket he slips the bird into his breast pocket and takes her along. She peeks over the rim of the pocket as he goes to the barn to help milk the cows. When he enters the parlor he can hear the old lady crooning as he has heard her ten-thousand times before:

Hold still, my coo, my honey
And fill my bucket with milk
Don't you be contrary
And I'll give you a gown of silk.

The cows are shifting their tails like metronomes keeping time with the song. One of them swats Gramma Nez in the face and she cusses and sings, "*Don't you be contrary, old bitch, or you'll be beef on my table.*" She bends down and slips on the cups.

Virgil works the other side of the parlor, milking the cows in the opposite row. There is a lot of noise, the milkers sighing and puffing, cows throwing hay around, stanchions rattling, exhaust fans blowing, Gramma Nez singing.

Bonnie stays snug in Virgil's pocket observing.

"It thinks you're its mother," Gramma Nez says when the milking is done and they've taken the De Lavals to the milkhouse to be washed. "That's what birds do. They fix on whoever takes care of them. There's a term for it, but I forget."

"Imprinting," Virgil says.

"That's it, imprinting." She runs a finger over Bonnie's head. "Cute little thing. Sweet little eyes. All babies are cute. That's why we put up with them."

"Pearl Bell looks like a bluegill," he says. "Her mouth is always going like this."

"Stop that," says Gramma Nez, but she is chuckling. "Just you remember a fish is the symbol of Jesus. Pearl Bell's an angelfish from the Lord."

"Regina don't like her."

"She'll get over it. She was the same way with you and your

brother."

"She won't bathe her. She says she might drown her if she bathes her."

"Nonsense. Regina isn't herself yet. She'll come round. Meantime it's good for Ginger to know what it's really like havin a baby to care for. Maybe she won't want to have a baby of her own too soon. Maybe she'll stop sneakin off in the woods with that bastard. I don't care for him. Never have. Nor his father, that Wild Bill. He's a devil. I don't like none of them Ravens."

"Me neither."

Gramma Nez fills the sink with soapy suds as Virgil takes the milkers apart. She washes. He rinses and hangs the parts up to dry.

"Did I ever tell you about the devil's bird?" she says.

"The jaybird one?"

"Yes, the jaybird."

Virgil nods. "The jaybird sold his soul for some corn on the cob and has to take feathers to hell for the devil to burn."

"And sometimes baby sparrows fall out of their nest—"

"—on a Friday," interrupts Virgil, "and if that happens the flames of hell get extra hot and it makes the devil so happy that when Monday comes he lets the jaybird go free till another Friday comes. Then the jaybird has to gather more feathers and baby sparrows."

"So this is Friday and you probably saved that little thing from the jaybird."

"Yeah?"

"No doubt about it. I suppose I've taught you all I know," says Gramma Nez. She plays with Bonnie's beak opening wide as if to eat the old lady's finger.

"Where'd you learn all them stories?"

"I had a grandmother," she says. "Who had a grandmother, who had a grandmother. Who knows where it all begins? But the stories keep me tied to them all the way back to Eve."

"And now I know them too."

"You better feed this bird."

He goes to the trough and gets powdered grain and lifts it in his palm to Bonnie's beak. She pecks, raises her head and looks at Virgil with approval.

"She's eatin," he says.

"You done good today, son. You mowed the hay and saved a life."

The drying wind blows all night and the sun comes up hot first thing in the morning. At noon Virgil tests the hay with his fingers and finds it ready to turn. He hooks the rake to the Allis-Chalmers B and turns the rows slowly, not wanting to shatter the leaves.

By Sunday the weather is partly cloudy eighty degrees of Indian Summer. But rain is in the forecast. So as soon as chores are done, Virgil hurries with the 180 and the New Holland baler and starts cranking out forty-pound bales. Ginger drives the B, pulling the wagon behind it. The Raven boys throw bales on the wagon and stack them. Far-off west, clouds are building. If Virgil can keep everyone working hard, the entire crop will be safe in the barn by evening.

Everything runs smoothly till they knock off for lunch on the patio. Virgil eats fast, climbs back on the 180 and starts baling again. Ginger, Peter and Danny sit lazily in the shade and watch him. He points at the sky and mouths the word "Rain." They smile and wave. He sees Gramma Nez and Pappy going to the barn. Pappy has told him to stay with the baling and not worry about chores. Peter and Ginger have their heads close together, his hand on her knee. Danny is looking away grinning about something.

Who was it said Danny ain't your friend?

Vernon said it. But that's okay because Virgil is not really Danny's friend either. Though he acts like he is. The two boys get along most of the time. Virgil still wants to whip him in a fight, though. Maybe if he ever whips Danny, Virgil will tell him about peeing in the mud hole when they were kids.

They had put on gloves and fought on the patio, with Dick as referee. Virgil had first tried a round with Peter because Dick insisted on it and told him not to be a baby when Virgil said he was too tired. Peter had tired him out so badly he coud scarcely breathe. Then it was Danny's turn and Virgil could barely lift his arms. Always something making the matches go Danny's way. But that day Virgil got revenge. After they beat him up, he left the two brothers to spar and went to the garden and dug a hole and filled it with water and took a mud bath to sooth his bumps and bruises. His hands smoothed the sides of the hole and made it a slick, warm place full of chocolate water. He went under the water as far as he could, just keeping his nose up for air. It was peaceful.

And then Danny pushed Virgil's head under.

"Mudboy! Mudboy!" he yelled.

When Virgil came up for air, he kept his cool. Cleaned out his eyes and looked at Danny. Smiled at Danny. Nodding at Danny. "Danny," he said, "you should try it, it's smooth as shit and warm and bitchin. It's like being in a fish hole, man. You feel like a secret fish in here."

"I caught you."

"You did, you caught me, Danny."

Danny stared. Finally he said, "Let me try it, Virgil."

"You want to feel what it's like?"

"Uh-huh."

"I don't know, man."

That's when Virgil peed in the water and said, "You ought to make your own hole."

"I want yours," Danny said.

So Virgil got out, and Danny slid into muddy water and secret pee.

The tines turn and the hay rises on the tines to the corkscrew whirling toward the piston, jamming the hay cajoonk-cajoonk! Rectangles tied with twine, the bales fall off the back in a line that stretches to the road.

He searches the field to see if anyone is working yet. The B and the empty trailer are still parked next to the barn. When he comes round the end of the timothy and heads for the alfalfa, he sees that Peter and Ginger are no longer in the shade near the Airstream. Peter's car is gone. Danny is standing under the oak shaking the dew off his lily. Virgil looks at the sky. Tall puffs looming. Things may go okay if he can just keep baling.

Danny hops on the B and brings out the wagon. He climbs on the tractor hitch and shouts, "It's just you and me. Those fuckers run off."

"What for?"

"What for? Don't be stupid."

"Are they comin back?"

"Who knows?"

He looks around and so does Virgil. There are hundreds of bales in the fields. It isn't likely that just the two of them can load so many in time to beat the rain.

"Ain't gonna happen, Virge. It's no go," says Danny.

Virgil tells him yes it will. "It will go if we push it."

The engine roars, the baler eats hay, the bales fall. Virgil keeping one desperate eye on the approaching clouds. He hates Ginger now. He hopes she gets in trouble. He will make sure that she does.

The War According to V –

Little V,

    I got your last letter late by about two months since you wrote it and I want to tell you not be so bothered about finding Huskys grave, little V. Do not feel sorry for that son of a bitch. I hope the coyotes did feed him to their young. I am glad Pappy took him to the woods and shot him after what he did to you. I would have put the hatchet in his head if I had been there that day. Not feel bad okay? No heartbreak. Not your fault what happen. You were just playing with the old bastard like always. Your heart was in the right place, but his was not. His heart was out to kill you. Your heart was not out to hurt him at all. You got a Heart better than most Virge and what every man needs as he grows up is a lot of Heart. I see the ones that do not have enough and how they fall to pieces out here. You wont fall apart because you got HEART. Which makes me think of my own heart and how I have been losing it lately, sounding like a whiner and a quitter sometimes when I write you. But today my mind is clear, no booze, no pot, no smell of napalm or gunpowder or blood or death. It is a fine clear day with a soft south breeze and I can smell the ocean which is about ten clicks away and I am thinking maybe this war is not so much an obscenity as a necessity and I am doing the right thing by being here fighting for my country.

    Sometimes I feel like a weathervane shifting in the wind. You probably dont know what to make of me. Am I for or against the war, huh? I guess I have to be for it. If you see it in perspective of world events and the future of the world, you have to be for it. Right? This morning Top and Cap were talking to us and reminding us of what is at stake. The American way is at stake. Freedom and Democracy. Sometimes I forget how much is at stake and I go off the deep end and just want out, just want to go home and forget this place exist. But they both made the point of how the enemy wants nothing more than to destroy our country our freedom. They want to destroy us. They cannot defeat us. Only we can defeat us. No one can destroy America but America. We are going to keep fighting and we are going to win even if we have to drop the Bomb on them. The future of humans is at stake. There can be no withdrawal. My country first and to hell with the rest. There it is. Do I sound like a foaming at the mouth fucking rightwing patriot? Geez Louise!

                                          Big V.

Rolling Thunder

Those within the United States that feel that the struggle could be ended more rapidly with less loss of life, that the terror and the destruction would be less if we took a different course . . . they should make their views known. I don't think they are less patriotic because they feel that. In fact . . . they would be less patriotic if they didn't state their views. **(Sen. Robert Kennedy)**

But when that dissent takes the form of actions that actually aid the enemy . This is going beyond the dissent . . . provided in our . . . system. **(Reagan)**

I think that there were mistakes that were made.
If a million civilians have been killed, I would regard it as a mistake.
I don't think Governor Reagan [is saying] that we never made a mistake.
(Robert Kennedy)

[The American government is] spending 20 billion dollars a year destroying the country. **(Interviewer to Reagan)**
You're wrong in your figures again - it's about 25 billion.
Oh, splendid, 25 billion dollars . . .
I challenge your history.
Sir?
I challenge your history again.

Virgil Frances Foggy

West of the hayfield, trees look like steeples painted black, a thousand churches vying for attention. Storm pushing in. Hay weather ending. Threatening to ruin what Virgil has baled. Whiskbrooms of rain sweep across the land a mile or two away, thunder grumbling behind wall-to-wall clouds. Maybe there are bales lying in the fields over there, men rushing to get them in. Virgil doesn't feel good. Virgil feels feverish, depressed, hopeless, clumsy. He is trying hard, but things aren't working out so good. He wants to believe, but he can't. He needs someone to give him a pep talk.

The B putts in low gear. Now and then, either Virgil or Danny hops on it to correct the steering. Virgil is on the wagon stacking, while Danny knees the bales up. Both boys are panting. Virgil's muscles and old wounds ache. Throat burns. Nose leaks. Hay dust making him sneeze.

At the end of a row Danny jumps on the tractor, horseshoes it and jumps off, hustling after more bales. In front of the house is the empty driveway and the open garage, Pappy's pickup parked on one side of the garage, the Cadillac next to it. Virgil is pretty sure he knows where Ginger and Peter have gone—the lover's lane with its old mattress beneath the giant fir deep in the woods beside the Crow. Virgil feels like killing Peter. It's not jealousy, its . . .

Maybe it's jealousy. Ginger in Peter's arms. Sprawling on the mattress beneath the pointed fir. Or maybe in the back seat of Peter's car, his '56 Chevy. KQRS on the radio playing "Go to the Mirror Boy."

See me, feel me, touch me, heal me.

Virgil can see for miles and miles. He can see the storm rolling and the chaos it will cause. He can see bad things coming for him and for Ginger and Vernon and everyone else. The war coming, the war here, the war gnawing at his withering hamstring. The pain makes part of him want to leave this field of battle, find shelter, and to hell with the hay.

"Hey!" says Danny, "wake up, will yah! Earth to Virgil!"

Virgil grabs the bale Danny has in his hands.

"Shit I'm tired," says Danny. He is puffing. Sweat rolling down his face. "I'm killing Peter, the bastard. I'm gonna piss in his gas tank."

"It's a bitchin car. Wish it was mine."

"I'm gonna fuck it up, that'll teach him."

Virgil would look good driving Peter's classic '56 Chevy through

Elk River, past the drive-in and past school, cruising, smoking and listening to KQRS Classic Rock on the radio. He shifts into second. Backs off the accelerator and listens to the mufflers beckoning the girls.

Lights are on inside the Airstream. Pappy and Gramma Nez are done for the day, kicking back, watching TV in their snug, separate, get-away spaces. Safe from the trouble coming when Dick realizes his daughter is missing. Regina has been out to the field asking about Ginger and Peter.

"They were goin for a drive and be right back," was what Danny told her.

And she said, "Idiots! God help her! Dick will kill her and your brother too." She pressed her mouth in a line so hard it deleted her lips. She doesn't know what to do with that Ginger. She doesn't know what to do with Dick either. Nothing is the way she meant it to be.

"Rain's gonna soak the hay," Virgil told her, hearing the whine in his voice, the weakness, the failure.

He saw in her eyes that she couldn't care less about some hay and some rain. "Do the best you can. I'll keep Ginger to myself as long as I can," she told him and walked away. Wind tugging at her clothes and hair. A dumpy, worn-out figure, she reached the edge of the field, turned toward the house, taking baby steps like she didn't want to get there. He felt sorry for her then. He forgave her for threatening to stab him with the spoon.

Drops of rain spatter the field.

"Here it comes," he says. "Here comes trouble."

Danny throws a bale at Virgil's feet and says, "Ain't gonna make it, man. I'm feelin drops already."

"Me too. That brother of yours, we needed him! We'd be done now."

"He's a flake," says Danny. "He never thinks ahead. He never thinks of no one but Peter. Mister Cool Breeze, too cool to care. I'm gonna piss in his tank."

"Ginger's a flake too," Virgil says. "They're made for each other."

"Little Miss Flower Power and Mr. Psychedelic," says Danny scornfully. "Everything's groovy."

Another bale slides up. Virgil slams the hay hook into it. He notes the peace sign tattooed on Danny's forearm, a circle with a cross upside down, wings broken. The anti-Christ.

But is it true? Is an upside down broken cross really the sign of the anti-Christ, or has somebody made that up? Virgil imagines the straw-haired girl in blue he saw in town one day. Her floating eyes. "Far out," she had said. He sees the two of them smoking weed. The two of them touching thighs. She and Virgil are in Peter's '56 Chevy heading for Florida. No, not Florida. California is happening. The serious roar of the engine.

And then what? Does he really want her? She's a stranger. He only saw her once in his life. Why can't he get over her?

"You know," says Danny, "I can't say I'd mind Ginger dropping her petals on me. Peter's a lucky prick."

"Ginger's stupid," Virgil says. "Flowers are for phonies and there's nuthin groovy about her. She's nuts. Peace and love my ass. I tell her to take a look round and show me peace and love. It ain't the way the world's made, except in her head when she's high. Nuthin lives if somethin else don't die. Even this hay was once alive. See what I mean? I mowed it and it died. It has to die if the cows are gonna live."

Danny nods. "Cows gotta eat," he says.

"God made it that way. You gonna argue with God?"

Danny takes his cap off, wipes his face. "I'm gonna tell on Peter. The fuckin jerkoff. Smokin dope right this minute, I bet. And dopy Ginger too, bet you anything. I'll bet you anything those two are—"

"I know. I know," Virgil says.

"Warm and fuzzy," says Danny. He masturbates his finger and laughs and says, "Mr. Soulmate wouldn't mind some of that." He does a pelvic thrust. "Ginger's a fuckin fox, man, no doubt about it. What a sweet ass. If it weren't for Peter, I'd—" He catches another bale, hoists it aboard. "But those fuckers, man, fuck them! Swear to God I'm pissin in his gas tank!"

Virgil doesn't want him talking about Ginger. Think it but don't say it. Virgil can talk about her, but no one else should. He likes Danny a little better for sticking around, but that doesn't give him permission to say things about Ginger. Part of Virgil thinks he should put the hay hook in Danny's head. He starts to say something like - Don't talk about my sister. Then he remembers that he needs Danny. Needing someone is depressing. So is love. Virgil thinks he loves Ginger. He thinks that's what's gone wrong. Everything is wrong with that kind of love. It's disgusting but he can't help it. The tractor idles along. The bales go up. The jealousy thing hits him hard. Her two-timing him with that pig Peter Raven.

"I'm pooped," Danny says, riding on the wagon, letting it carry him to another bale.

"I could get the front-end loader and pick bales with it and you could stack them," Virgil says.

"That would take forever," whines Danny. His arm sweeps the field as if seeing miles of despair. He goes for another bale, grabs the twines, hauls it over, lifts with his arms and one knee. Virgil hooks it, stacks it. The stack is low, only three bales high. He doesn't have the strength to curl the bales and throw them overhead like he used to. Intermittent raindrops continue to patter the field.

"Shit," he says, pointing at the clouds percolating.

"What'll we do?" says Danny.

The B continues to chug at walk-rate.

They finish the row. Then take the load to the barn. Virgil plugs in the elevator. The crossbars clatter upward, steel slapping steel, catching bales and carrying them to the loft. They rise like boxes on an assembly line and fall into the dark hole at the top. There is no effort to stack them. They drop on one another and roll and land wherever they will. A steady pitter-patter of rain is falling now.

"I know you're there," Virgil says, his eyes beyond the pasture, where the steeple trees reach.

"What?" says Danny.

Virgil shakes his head. Looking at the last field, the alfalfa, at least a hundred and fifty bales.

Danny follows Virgil's gaze. "By the time you get to them, it'll be pouring buckets and they'll be too wet. You don't want to put up wet hay, do you, Virge? You want to burn down your barn?"

"If we hurry they won't be that wet. I'll stack them outside under the eave and cover them with a tarp."

"Give it up," says Danny. "We done all right, we got most of it."

Virgil tosses the last bale on the elevator, watches it rise and vanish. Turns the elevator off. "It's not rainin so bad," he says. "This is nuthin, come on."

"Forget it."

"Come on, Danny, this is nuthin."

"Shit, man, I'm tired. That fuckin brother of mine, I'll piss in his tank, I swear. I'll fuck up his car."

"Will you help me if Pappy pays you a bonus? Twenty buck bonus, how's that sound?"

"I'm fuckin pooped, Virge!"

"I'll load, you can stack."

"Oh yhah, you betcha. You can't hardly walk, let alone tote bales."

"I'll use the front-end loader. Come on, Danny. Don't quit on me now, man. Twenty bucks more, okay? Shit, that's like twenty bucks an hour, man."

Danny sighs. He leans against the trailer. Looks west toward the last lines of bales. "Ah shit," he says. "All right, what the fuck."

While Danny drives the wagon back, Virgil fires up the old Massey Harris and raises the bucket, working the hydraulics to make sure there aren't any leaks.

In the field, he lowers the bucket and scoops the bales one at a time, careful not to gouge the earth with the loader's teeth. He brings the bales to Danny. It is slow work, having to gear forward and reverse, forward and reverse, clutch in, clutch out, work the hydraulic levers, coax the bale into the bucket, race to the wagon. Drop the bale. Go for another. Rain not letting up for a second. Not a heavy rain, though, not yet soaking into the bales. The surface of everything is shiny.

Minutes pass. The boys almost have a load. Two more loads and they'll be done.

Then Dick comes stomping out to the field. He climbs on the tractor hitch, shouting, "Where's Ginger!"

Virgil hollers over the engine. "I don't know, I ain't seen her since lunch!"

Dick goes over to the wagon and asks Danny the same question and Danny shrugs.

"That fuckin brother of yours!" yells Dick.

The dark bales stretch like tiny freight cars in the field. Virgil catches a burst of rain on his back. Races another bale to Danny. Dick looks around. Then starts back toward the house, hands on hips, head bouncy with anger. He is telling some invisible presence how furious he is, what bad things he's going to do.

Danny points to Dick and says, "Why the fuck don't he help?"

"He hates farmin," Virgil says. His shirt is soaked now. Water seeping under the seat. Jeans sticky. Again he works the levers and plucks a bale from the ground and heads for the wagon.

Dick comes back. He walks in front of the B and grabs bales and starts throwing them angrily at Danny.

"Stack em high!" Dick orders. "Get em higher!"

He pinches the double twines together and hauls a bale in each hand, throws them up one-armed, weightless as basketballs. Virgil shuts down the Massey Harris and climbs to the top of the load to help Danny. Danny has made stair steps of the bales. He climbs up one, then throws the bale to Virgil.

After a short time, the interlocked hay goes far over their heads. The load hangs in the air swaying ominously. Dick tells the boys to stretch their bodies over the load. They hug it with hands and feet. Dick jumps on the B and creeps in first gear to the barn. Twice the load almost tumbles and they shout and Dick laughs. When they get to the barn, they unload as fast as the elevator can handle the bales. When the last one falls into the loft, Virgil cuts the electric motor and jumps on the hay wagon. But Dick is unhooking it.

"That's it," he says. "Fuck the rest."

"But Uncle Dick!"

"I said let em rot!"

"There's only—"

"Drive Danny home. Then get your ass back here. I'm gonna make a few calls and find your goddamn sister."

Virgil's lips tremble. "Ain't my goddamn sister," he mutters. "Fuck her." Virgil is exhausted and it won't take much to make him cry. He looks toward the final field, those last bales glistening. What an accomplishment it would be to get them in. Who cares about the rain? Rain won't hurt you. It'll hurt the bales, not you.

"How about you take him home?" he asks. "I'll finish the field."

Streaks of rain dive through the tractor headlamps beaming toward the barnyard. Cows crowding each other near the fence, their phosphorescent eyes full of wonder.

Dick says, "Don't fuck with me tonight, boy. I will take your bony ass apart, you fuck with me tonight. And you two better not be lyin. You better not know where they are. I find out you're lyin, I'll tear you some new assholes. You get me? You comprendo?"

Virgil laughs. He feels slightly hysterical.

Dick raises a warning finger. "Don't," he says. "Don't you fuckin try to kid me! I'll punch your lights out. No mood for jokin. You jokin me? You want to joke with me? Huh?"

"No sir."

"I didn't think so." Dick pivots and heads to the house.

"We ain't lyin!" yells Danny. "We don't know where them shits is!"

"Shh," Virgil says. "Don't provoke him."

"Fuck him! I ain't afraid of him. Tear me a new asshole. He fucks with me, I'll tear *him* a new asshole!"

"Danny, you dumb bastard!" Virgil says. "You wanna get us in trouble? Don't goad him."

Dick has paused on the patio, screendoor held open. He is watching. He is smiling a devilish smile.

Danny looks at Virgil. "You gotta a problem?" he says. "What's your problem, man?"

"I'm tired, man."

"Me too, man, way sick and tired. Sick of the smell of you and your fuckin uncle and your fuckin farm. Gimmee my money and take me home. Fuck this haying shit. Fuck it and fuck your slut sister too! Take me home!" He glares at Virgil. "Are you cryin? Are those tears? Jesus, Virgil! What a pussy!"

"It's rain on my face. It's raining, you asshole!"

The War According to V –

Little V,

It's raining again. A dead man smells the same as a dead dog after two days, did you know that? We welcome the rain at first because it knocked down the B.O. My god we stink! Skunks got nothing on a man in the bush who hasn't bathed in a week. They bring in the water trucks now and then and we get naked and open the spouts and clean up best we can. Otherwise we mostly bathe out of our helmets.

I hear rain pounding the tin roof hard above my head right now. They are trying to get me but nope. Not yet anyway. Most days I do not believe I die over here. But today I have my doubts. I think the weather making me feel this way. Gloomy and cloudy and gray and raining for days. The goddamn monsoons, they say. The dank smell of the water puddling around my feet is disgusting. Or maybe its just me I smell. Reminds me of Dick's feet. Har, har. Either you are burning in the sun or drowning in rain warm as piss. Have you got the hay in yet little V? The corn is next I guess. Then the harvest will be over and you have to prepare the machinery for a long winter nap. I think about the cold air coming down from Canada and drying up the corn and making the leaves and stalks brittle and then here comes Virgil on the picker shucking cobs. I would give my left nut to be doing it with you this year. Me and you harvesting the corn. My left nut. I swear to God I would.

Big V.

Rolling Thunder

I have explored every possible private avenue that might lead to a settlement.
The obstacle is the other side's absolute refusal to show the least willingness to
join us in seeking a just peace.
The American people are entitled to know the truth . . . where the lives of our
young men are involved. **(Nixon)**

The obstacle is the other side's absolute refusal to—
The obstacle is—
*The obstacle—***(Nixon)**

The mad dog of the east! **(Reagan)**

Virgil Francis Foggy

After you drop Danny off, you drive home in the rain, not wanting to get there, not wanting to be part of the drama. Dick will be drinking. Your mother too. They will get mean and blame each other and after she passes out, he might come after you, his palms drumming on your eardrums. You're going deaf on account of him. You must try your best to avoid a beating. Any sign of it and you will run to the Airstream, the safety of Pappy and Gramma Nez. And all the hours will go by and the bales left in the field will get soaked through and weigh heavy as concrete, heavy as the dead.

"Get out of my life," you whisper. "Someday I kill you. For sure, you gook."

Parking in the garage, you sit a long while, your head down, eyes inward. You feel the burn of twine on your fingers. You feel your hamstring trembling. You hear rain beating on the garage roof. You almost got the hay in, almost. If you're fifty bales short next spring and have to buy hay, who is to blame? Not you.

Dick's fault. Dick and Danny. Peter. Ginger. Hate them, hate them.

You get out of the car, go into the house and move as quietly as your bad leg will allow. Going upstairs to your room, you strip off your wet clothes and put on your bathrobe. You take Bonnie from the box and feed her. She curls her dry feet round your finger and pecks at bread mixed with crushed corn in your palm. Downstairs, you hear their voices raised but can't make out what they're saying. You hear a lot of fucking this and fucking that going the rounds. Rain clicks like fingernails on the window panes. You remember the baby and look in Ginger's room and the baby isn't there. You look in all the bedrooms and the bathroom. No Pearl Bell. You go downstairs to see if she is with Regina, you peep round the corner and see Dick and your mother at the table, cigarettes and a jug of wine in front of them. Smoke hanging everywhere. *Finnegans Wake* open-winged and pushed to the side. Holstein butter dish calm in the midst of a blue haze and him and her, their thick voices stirring the air.

But no Pearl Bell.

"Just like her slutty mother," Dick is saying. "Made a carbon copy of herself, a whore. Left a copy behind to spite me and give me ulcers.

This is what she would do all right, run off like this. Shack up with some pimply hippie. She's not really my daughter, you know. No way."

"Truss a man blam a woman," Regina replies. "She never run off. When? She never—"

Their voices compete.

"Don't tell me—"

"I know some shit—"

"Shit for brains!"

"You meg me sick, you bassard!"

"Shut up, for I knock your—"

"You meg me sick."

"You drove me to it, you know. You're why we're here."

"You said your love for me drove you to it! Hah!"

"It was that too."

"And I believed you, like damn fool."

"Shut up. You seduced me, Regina, not me you. Never made a move if—"

"Shouldna led you touch me. You meg me—"

"My poor, dumb brother.

"You meg me—"

"You were easy, baby."

"You fuckin fucky."

"If Jim had known how easy."

"Shud the fuckin up."

"One touch, you cream your pants. Remember this table? The first time? They could've walked in any second, but we couldn't stop. Remember that? Remember how hot we used to be? Hiding in closets and outhouses, in the cornfield, behind bushes, in the loft anytime anywhere, gotta have it." Dick laughs.

"Hate you. Hate you! All you know is—"

The wall phone rings. "Hold that thought," says Dick. He grabs the phone. "Hello . . . Who? . . . Herm?" he says. "Yhah, Herm what's up?"

You slip into the kitchen and ask your mother where Pearl Bell might be.

"What you mean, where's Pearl Bell?"

"She's not in Ginger's room, Regina."

"Jesu Chist! What the!"

She jumps up, knocking her chair over. She sways as she stands

149

with one hand on the table. When she walks across the floor, her feet flop as if her shoes are too large. She stumbles. Her butt shifts in her skirt like fish in a net. "Pearl Bell!" she calls. "Pearl!"

Dick says a few words and hangs up. She is climbing the stairs on all fours, still calling.

"I had Ma come get her!" Dick shouts. "She's with them, you drunken cunt."

You slide along the wall toward the doorway, trying your best to be invisible.

She comes back, leans her hip against the stove. "Oh," she says. She stares at the floor. Blinks like someone trying to tune in. "Who was that?" she says.

Herman White. He says Ginger is in his basement in Mary Jane's room. She's afraid to come home."

"Thank God, thank God she safe. Oh, God, thank God." She puts her hands over her face, blubbers.

"She's drunk!" yells Dick. "Daughter's drunk!"

"Drunk? Jesu Chist! Oh, Jesu. What she doin to her life? What she—"

"Kill Peter Raven," interrupts Dick. His voice matter-of-fact.

"The dirty sonsa," Regina says. "I knew! I could tell lookin! Hippie crotch danglin down his pants. Tight jeans show that . . . that coocumber! Nasty thing."

"Oh? You noticed, did you?" says Dick.

She stumbles sideways to the table, picks up the fallen chair and sits carefully, as if she's unsure the chair will hold. Though there is already a cigarette burning in the ashtray, she lights another. Blows smoke, turns over *Finnegans Wake* and says, *"I go back to you, my cold mad father—"*

"Shut your hole!" says Dick. "Jesus, my daughter's raped and listen to this."

"Carry me along, taddy, like you done through the toy fair!" reads Regina. Her smile, her voice perverse, she digs a finger through the air like digging into his ribs.

Dick grabs the book, flings it.

"Improvin my mind!" she says.

"What mind?" he says. He hovers over her, his fist poised. She lifts her glass, salutes him and drinks. Licks the rim. Notices you by the entrance. "Goddamn you goddamn kids!" she screams. "Work to the bone and this is what I get!" She picks up a butter knife on the table. Jabs it at you. Laughter fills your mouth, but you're not dumb enough to let it out.

Noiselessly you creep away, go upstairs. Put on pajamas and get into bed. Your stomach growls. You're very hungry, but you don't dare go get something to eat. Just stay where you are, unless Dick's feet pound up the stairs. If that happens, you go out the window, down the tree.

Bonnie scratches inside her box. Reaching over the side of the bed, you find her, put her on your chest. She nestles her head under your chin. She makes chittering sounds that calm you and make you love her.

"You and me, we gotta stay out of this one," you tell her.

Tree limbs scratch, rattle against the side of the house. Rain pounds the roof as if it's furious. Water sheeting on the panes, blurring everything. Who knows what will happen? He'll get Ginger. And there is nothing you can do about it. She's in for it, brought it on herself. How could she be so stupid?

Picture the dark wet lumps of hay in the field. Green sponges now. You will cut the twines tomorrow and break the bales apart. Let them bleach and turn to straw to use for bedding. You cuddle Bonnie. Keeping her warm under your chin, her sharp, little claws her soft wings embracing your neck.

The War According to V –

Little V,

It be a funny war. Not Ha Ha funny but WHAT THE FUCK IS GOING ON funny. The mud sucking our boots is madding. Some guys actually disappear in the mud in parts like quicksand they die and never get found. This is totally true. I would hate to die like that wouldnt you? We go on search and destroy and set ambushes and try to make contact but charlie says Fuck you. Dont you know it raining fool? He hardly ever comes out of his tunnels to play with us except when conditions are on his side and he can hit and get away. Frustrating very. We get booby traps and mines killing and wounding us more than we get honest bullets from a stand and deliver rifle. We get women and kids wired with explosives blowing themselves up just so they can blow us up too. Who would even think of such a thing as wiring up your kid or turning yourself into a bomb? You think Mom and Dick are strange. But at least they wouldnt martyr you for some lost cause. There is a dose for you little V. There it is. Got to giddy up got to go.

Big V.

Rolling Thunder

Numbers have dehumanized us.
Over breakfast coffee we read of 40,000 American dead . . .
Instead of vomiting, we reach for the toast. **(Dalton Trumbo)**

. . . if we lose that war . . . history will record
with the greatest astonishment
that those who had the most to lose
did the least to prevent its happening.
(Reagan)

Virgil Francis Foggy

The silence unnerves Virgil. No drumming of Dick's big feet on the way to the bathroom, no radio playing downstairs, no coffee smells. Even Aaron is silent, like he knows not to call attention to himself. Virgil sees rain falling steadily, but softer now, no threat in it like last night's deluge. Bonnie is perched on the headboard, eyes alert. She stretches one wing then the other, balancing on one foot.

"Mornin," Virgil says.

She dips her head hello. Cocks an eye at the baby sleeping and says - *Look who's here, Daddy.*

"What's that?" Virgil says. "What's going on?" The baby's mouth opens as if about to cry.

"Don't," he whispers. "Oh don't."

Her mouth keeps working. It says, "Eyyy." He sticks his finger in her mouth and she starts sucking.

"Remember this table?" he remembers Dick saying. The images and words floating by. Him and her and closets, cornfields, cars, outhouses, bushes, the loft.

Looking at the clock Virgil realizes he has overslept and Gramma Nez must have put Pearl Bell in bed with him before going to the barn. He listens and listens, but there is nothing other than the sound of rain ticking on the glass. Asleep or dead? Maybe they killed each other. It doesn't seem a far-fetched idea. He beat her. She stuck a knife in him. He choked her to death before he died. Something like that would be fine.

Virgil once found Dick passed out under the kitchen table. The ash-line of a cigarette near his hand. The cigarette had scarred the linoleum. Nothing would scrub the scar out and it's still there after all these years. That's how people burn houses down. Burn your house down, it might free you. It might let you start over.

He whispers his morning prayers. Asks his dead father and God to forgive him his evil thoughts. But how easy life might be if certain people were . . . were gone. Poof. Goodbye, don't bother to write. Don't bother to send a Christmas card. What if? What then?

Pearl Bell's gums working on his finger feel good. The calves suck harder and you need to give them all four fingers. Sometimes they suck so hard, their tongues feel raspy as a file. And they will butt you sometimes because the milk isn't coming out. You wean them from the teat that way. You let them follow your fingers into a bucket of milk. One or two tries they get the message. This bucket is Mommy.

"The first time? It was this table," is what Dick said. "You remember how hot we used to be?" is what he said.

After a few minutes, Pearl Bell quits sucking and falls asleep and Virgil goes to the bathroom to clean up. He gets dressed. He bundles the baby. She's loose, shifty as a sack of flour. Her head flops. He puts her head on his shoulder and holds it with his palm. Tucks Bonnie into his shirt pocket. Downstairs he sees Dick sprawled asleep at the table. The jug is empty. There is a bottle of Jack Daniels on its side. A pyramid of cigarettes piled in the ashtray. *Finnegans Wake* still on the floor. Dishes unwashed in the sink. The sampler faint in the faint light through the window.

NEVER LET ANYTHING SO FILL YOU WITH SORROW

In the living room, the shades are down, but he can see Ginger curled in the big chair, her feet tucked sideways, head resting on the wing of the chair. Arms folded. One eye plummish.

"You asleep?" he whispers.

A slight shake of her head says no.

"What happened?"

There is a pause before she points at her eye.

"He beat you."

She nods.

"Didn't Mom do anything?"

Ginger points across the room toward the sofa. His mother there folded in the same position as Ginger, knees drawn up, head down. The shadows are deep, but he can see that she, too, has a plum-colored shiner.

"Boy, you did it this time," he whispers.

"Umm."

He stands in the gloom, not knowing what else to say. In the palm of his hand, he feels the baby passing gas. He says in her ear, "Is that your opinion of all this shit?" Her mouth searches for a nipple on his neck.

"What'll I do with Pearl Bell?" he asks. "She's hungry."

"Bring her here," says his mother. She sits up.

Virgil hands her the baby. Up close he sees both of her eyes are bruised, but only the left one is swollen shut. There are slap marks on her cheek. Her blouse is ripped. One breast is partially bare.

"You remember how hot we used to be?" Dick had said.

"She's hungry," Virgil repeats.

"My milk's dried up," says his mother. She clears her throat. Coughs. "Too much alcohol," she says. "It slows your heart and your lungs fill with fluid. People die of heart disease if they drink too much."

"Should I warm a bottle?" says Virgil.

"I'll make her a bottle," she says. "You go on now. Go help with chores. Eat lunch with them. Stay till I come get you." She pauses. Then says kindly, "Maybe you better stay the night."

"Yes, ma'am." Virgil is relieved to hear her telling him to stay away. Ashamed also that he can't do anything for them, that they will have to cope with an angry, hungover, scary Dick Foggy.

He brushes fingers over Ginger's hair. She pats his hand.

Putting on his chore jacket and cap, Virgil goes into the rain and walks carefully past the slippery killing yard. The windmill is a swift, noisy blur *tick-slip-tick-slip*. Yellow willow leaves flop in the wind like puppets. Black Moses stands statuesque beneath the tree. Moses the picture of peace. Feels good, his body posture says, showered clean by the rain, no flies or boys with willow whips bothering him. All the other animals, the chickens, the sheep, the rabbits, are inside their shelters. They will want breakfast in bed on a day like this.

Virgil opens the barn door, walks into exhalations of cow. The noises comfort him, speak to him of home and security. The bulktank grinds. The compressor pumps. Pappy splashes milk into the funnel. The cows' heads move side to side. They spread rumors - *Did you hear about last night?*

Going to the cooler, Virgil gets an egg and taps a hole in each end, sucks the egg dry. Pappy hands him a cup of milk.

"Gin got home."

"I seen," says Pappy.

"Mom's feedin Pearl Bell."

"Good," says Pappy.

"Dick is—"

"I seen," says Pappy.

A thousand silver bristles poke from the old man's jaws. Lines

156

crisscross the width of his forehead. Dry lines encircle his eyes. Virgil cannot imagine himself ever being so old and worn.

"I'm havin lunch with you guys today. Mom said so."

Pappy nods. He points toward the milk parlor. "Help Gramma," he says.

Virgil puts the glass in the sink and goes down the aisle patting each cow on the rump. He grabs a milker and puts it next to Martha whose udders are bursting. He washes her teats with Blu-Shield. He slips the inflations on. They suck, they hiss. He massages her udders and the milk starts flowing. He can hear milk filling the can. Across the aisle, Gramma Nez sings to another cow,

"*Hold still, my coo, my honey.*"

Virgil rubs the base of Martha's tail, watching her head droop with pleasure. He sings: "*Mar – thaaa . . . Martha is a very precious girr-rel; oh, Mar – tha, Martha is a very precious girr-rel . . .*"

"*Hold still, my coo, my honey . . .*"

"*Mar – tha, Martha is a very precious . . .*"

Outside, the rain is letting up, becoming intermittent drops on the windows. The clouds are pulling apart. The wind blows harder, presses in waves pressing on the barn, creating a sense of pressure on Virgil's ears.

"*Mar – tha, Martha is . . .*"

"*. . . my coo, my honey . . .*"

He gazes out the window at the house, the blinds drawn, the screendoor shivering. The trees leaning as if surrendering. Soggy dead leaves cling to the roof. Leaves breaking off here and there whirling. If he could only make the house disappear. Wave a wand and there it goes. But at least he's got the whole day ahead and they're not in it. No Dick to deal with. Do what you can to be safe. Survival of the fittest: nature's law.

"Remember this table? The first time? It was you. How hot we . . ."

"Hold still, my coo, my honey and fill my bucket with milk . . ."

The table.

Leaning her over the table. Doing her like a dog.

Him, her, the table. How young were they?

"If Jim had known how easy you were."

We had a farm in Minnesota. Strange things happened there.

The War According to V –

Little V,

    First confirmed kill, your big brother is Expert Sharpshooter a mankiller. I am saying that after many moons here I actually know without a doubt I killed a human being. He had his moment in the sun and now this place knows him no more. I saw the poor bastard fall. Got him at 200 yards with an open sight M-16 for which everyone was going LIKE WOW YOU SHOULD BE A SNIPER. In the blood I told them. From that distance he whirled like a little boy pretending to die and I thought of watching you when you were playing war outside and acting shot and dying heroically. He was just such a tiny fellow Virge. They are all wiry little fellows, wiry boys for the most part, even though they actually might be 30 or 40 years old, who knows? Harmless-looking fellows that will blow your head off without batting an eye. I got him in the neck. They teach you to aim for the biggest part of the body. So you aim for the chest if you aim at all but I blew a neat hole through his neck instead. I have to admit it was exciting to see it and know I had done it. ME. It was honest and true the way killing should be. Powerful like the finger of God I reached out and zapped him. Jesus what a feeling. Remember how I used to get in fistfights at school? How getting hit always made me crackers? I wanted to kill whoever hit me, whoever insulted me, I want to pound them to dust. You remember me and Joe Carpenter? I won because I would not quit. Because I kept getting up. He blacked both my eyes, both of them near swelling shut. But I keep coming. I just keeeep coming and I wore him out and then I knocked him out with a kick to the jaw when he was on his knees. Killing charlie was like the feeling I had when Joe can not get up and I raised my rifle in triumph and Top call me Dead Eye. He calls me Dead Eye now and says I should RE-UP because the Army needs men like me. But I was going to say, never fight fair Virge, fuck that fair stuff it will get you kill. And those who tell you to fight fair, fuck them too. Fight to win. Whatever it takes.

    I feel like a scratchy record kicking back. I think maybe I am in shock maybe, but one thing to pull the trigger and feel your rifle recoil and spit out a round that maybe smacks some leaves before it gets swallowed by the forest. It is quite another to kill someone for real no doubt about it. It was so vivid, so TOO REAL. More real than TV or war movies at the

Humphrey. Shooting a gook is not the same as punching Joe Carpenter. He carries a scar on his jaw and maybe one on his brain but he aint dead. This little Vietnamese boy is definetly dead. I walked up to him, stood over him up close and personal. His eyes foggy. Most definetly dead yes. And I got to thinking this could be you Vernon. I got sick to my stomach. He may be scar tissue on my brain now. Maybe every time I look in the mirror I think of him. That little bundle. That little man. But maybe not. Maybe I get used to it. Fuck yes. Airborne, Airborne all the way, run all night and run all day. Top says I am born for this shit. Says I am a natural and I should make the Army my career. Fuck him. But I don't know. Maybe I should. You have a talent for machinery. Maybe I have a talent for this. Not killing men I mean. I mean maybe I am a born soldier. 200 yards. Jesus what a shot. So another note just to let you know that I have emptied clips into many dark woods but never knew if my bullets met human flesh until yesterday. Well, I am no conscious objector. I kill a man Virge. Slaughter him. But it could have been me. It might yet. There he is.

Big V.

Rolling Thunder

The defense of freedom is everybody's business not just America's business. **(Nixon)**

Our primary mission . . . is to enable [the people of Vietnam] to assume the full responsibility for their security. And now we have begun to see the results of this long overdue change in American policy. We are finally bringing American men home. **(Nixon)**

[The war] has been unfair here in this country and has discriminated against those who are poor and those in the lower economic groups . . .
I think that it's most unfortunate. **(R. Kennedy)**

I believe the highest aspiration of man should be individual freedom and development of the—of the individual . . . there is a sacredness to individual rights . . . this has been very stimulating . . . weigh everything in the line of government . . . everything . . . **(Reagan)**

Virgil Francis Foggy

"From Vernon?" Dick asks.

"Yep." Virgil folds the letter, puts it in his pocket. Closes the mailbox and hands the other two envelopes to Dick, who looks at them and grumbles about America choking on advertisements. He and Virgil walk up the driveway as Virgil says, "Vern killed a man, Uncle Dick. A cong. A charlie. He saw him fall. It's called a confirmed kill. His first one. Got him at two-hundred yards with an open-sight."

"Uh-huh," says Dick. "That's the idea, ain't it? It's what you join for. I killed plenty in Korea. Eighteen years old, but I was all man. They didn't give me a Bronze Star with Cluster for doing K.P., you know. I got war stories I could tell you, boy. Two-hundred yards, ey? It's in the blood, you see what I'm sayin. We're all good shots. Steady eyes, steady hands. Foggys and war go way back."

Virgil has seen the Bronze Star with Cluster. Heard the stories over and over, Dick practically winning the war single-handed, saving his platoon, saving this guy and that guy, coming back at twenty in 1953, decorated and tattooed *Semper Fi*. He's heard his uncle use that phrase a thousand times. The irony of it not lost on Virgil, young as he is.

"Nothing is the same after you been to war. Everything is anti-climax after you've been in combat. Even pussy," Dick says. "Even pussy ain't the same. Vernon will find out that there is nuthin as grand as war. If you survive. If you ain't crippled or somethin."

"He might re-up, he says."

"He should. That's what I should of done. Should of stayed in. I'd be a sergeant major by now. Or maybe gone to OCS and become a officer. Maybe I'd be a colonel by now, have a brigade of my own over there. Life wouldn't be so goddamn complicated and *bo*ring. Farms and kids and an obese wife and a sick old man. And sellin Chevy parts for a livin. Jesus fuckin Christ, who would have predicted it? Everyday, go to work. Eat lunch at Lando Lakes, that goddamn dive full of farmers smellin like cowshit. Pitcher of beer and a hamburger, and the same old bullshitters talkin the same old bullshit every fuckin day. Every motherfuckin day. Come home, eat dinner, watch some stupid TV. Go to bed. Get your ashes hauled if she's in the mood. Which she usually ain't. Get up and go to work again. Days all mushed together and you don't know what you did yesterday or the day before or . . . fuck Jesus, it's a wonder most men don't blow their brains out. No wonder we can't wait for another war. And another and another. At least under fire you feel alive. This ain't livin, you see what I'm sayin? But you'll find out. You'll see. Life's goin by like a rocket, but you don't feel it yet. You'll see. Maybe this war will last long enough to let you in. Maybe you'll get to actually live large before you die. Instead of dyin inch by inch the way most men do in this candy-ass world." His eyes are puzzled, mystified, angry, disillusioned. He looks toward the fields as if there might be a way out of his predicament. He stops in front of the corncrib, where the wind is obstructed, but they can hear it, the wind, whispering through the crib's wooden slats, whispering like a warning.

Virgil gazes across the pasture, toward the bleaching cornstalks green husks drying, leaves rusting. The machine-shed door is open. Inside is the cornpicker greased and ready, its pointed prows waiting to float between the corn rows, sniffing for corncobs. A touch of frost is needed. It doesn't seem long ago when it was spring, the earth disked and harrowed and black and swirling. Pappy in the field with the seeder making rows as straight as plumb lines. He couldn't do it now. Old Pappy. Old, feeble Pappy.

Time. Dick is right about time going by like a rocket. Young or not, Virgil knows it, feels it despite what Dick thinks.

Dick lights a cigarette, drags deep. Exhales a thin stream. His eyes have a remote look. As if seeing not the life in front of him, but the might have been if he had stayed in the Marines. He sighs. Picks tobacco off his tongue. Spits. Looks toward the house, the garage. The car. "I want that car washed," he says. "I want you to wax it."

"Yessir."

The lower half of the Caddie looks like it's been finger-painted by a two-year-old psychopath, long, muddy swirls running the length of the rocker panels.

"But not today," adds Dick. "We got things to do, me and you." He looks at his knuckles. The middle knuckle is as blue as Regina's bloated eyelid.

"Mom said I should have lunch with Pappy and Gramma Nez," Virgil tells him. "I should stay with them, Mom said."

"Do I give a fuck what your mother says? No, I do not give a fuck. Fuck her and your sister too. Little cunts, little bitches. Never trust

162

a woman, Virge. Women will get you in trouble. It's their mission in life, though they won't admit it. Merciless pair of cunts. They won't even be merciful to one another. Betray one another at the drop of a shoe. And they know that about each other too. Sisterhood, my ass. In their hearts women really hate each other. C'mon, we're goin to town."

"I left Bonnie there." Desperately, Virgil points to the silver-shadowed moment parked beneath the trees, the Airstream trailer. His sanctuary. "I ain't fed her yet today," he babbles. "Ain't fed Bonnie."

Dick cocks a skeptical eyebrow. Even to Virgil, the excuse sounds lame. There is anxiety in his voice, but he can't help it. He doesn't want to go with his uncle. Doesn't want to be part of whatever his uncle is up to.

"Gramma will take care of Bonnie. You come with me," Dick says firmly.

He puts his hand on the back of Virgil's neck and guides him toward the garage, the car. As they cross the driveway, Virgil watches the house for signs of rescue, hoping his mother will come out and say something to stop him. The screendoor bumps against the jam. Its hydraulic piston hanging like a skeletal arm.

Dick drives to Lando Lakes. He and Virgil sit at the bar. Alma makes the boy a cheeseburger. Loads the plate with potato chips. Gives him a glass of iced Coke.

Dick doesn't eat. He drinks Wild Turkey chased with beer. He talks to Alma. Alma fingers her yellow hair, tugs at it, a habit whenever she's listening. Dick is in form, his long mouth motoring. He sounds like a politician, voice full of rattling sabers. Virgil and Alma nod agreement to everything he says. He's going to put his foot up Peter Raven's ass. He's going to tear him a new asshole. Give him a makeover. A man who is a man can't let an insult to his family go unanswered like that. What Peter pecker did is an insult, a personal insult. A flagrant display of disrespect.

"Hit me again, Alma."

"Got you covered, Dick."

Dick says, "If you're gonna take a man's daughter out and get her drunk and bang her when she's senseless, someone's gotta make you pay. Someone's gotta put your ass in a sling. Someone's gotta beat you so bad you shit your pants. Make you wish you never fucked with his property. It's territory. Every man has his territory to defend. Am I right?"

Yes he is.

"You watch my back," he says to Virgil, swinging a glaring,

bloodshot eye on him. "Make sure that punk Danny don't take a bat to my head. You clean his clock if he tries to. You see what I'm sayin? I'm sayin you punch him out. You do what you have to do. You savvy? You *comprendo?* Are you a Foggy or not?"

"Yessir, but—"

"But me no buts."

His stomach turns. He can't finish the hamburger. His scars feel tight and raw. He looks longingly toward the door. If somehow he could vanish. That house with his mother and Ginger nursing their battered eyes. The baby squalling as if she hates being alive. He wants to be rid of all that and these moments with Dick.

"Your sister's no fuckin virgin," says Dick, sighing, shaking his head as if he just heard the news.

"Yessir."

"Ask them in the cemetery. It don't come back. Steal a cherry, it's gone john. That punk's gonna pay, you wait and see. And if she's pregnant, I'm gettin her an abortion. No little bastards runnin round my fuckin house."

Virgil nods and nods and tries to look outraged, but he really doesn't care about Ginger's cherry. There are worse problems everywhere. He doesn't blame Peter. She got in the car with him to go do what she knew would happen. They left the bales in the field. Went off and did it.

It.

And Virgil is supposed to fight Danny now? Danny stayed and helped. Without Danny it would have been two hundred bales rotting in the rain. Virgil doesn't think he can punch Danny, not for a slut like Ginger. Unless Danny punches first. Maybe then. But he doesn't want to. Not today. Can't we do this tomorrow? He doesn't feel very good. Like maybe he's coming down with something. He wants to go somewhere quiet and forget about virgins. She gave it up to an idiot, a lowbrow hippie fake. Or maybe she lost it long ago. Probably so. There it is, Vernon would say.

An hour passes and Dick gets drunk, he gets mean. His voice is hoarse. Bloodshot eyes fill with sorrow as he asks Alma if she knows what it takes to be a good father. Alma says a father has to protect his kids.

"There it is," sighs Dick. His shoulders slump as if the weight of fatherhood is too much for him. He looks at Virgil and points to Alma. "This is a wise woman. This is Socrates with a rack Venus would envy. You hear what she's sayin? It's genetical is what she's sayin." Alma tugs at her hair, nodding slowly, looking wise, her eyes full of hard-won knowledge. She knows men in bars, has watched them for years and years.

Their split personalities.

Three men come in, all of them wearing baseball caps and jeans and workshirts. Boots edged with crusted manure. As they walk by Virgil, he smells barn. His boots are caked just like theirs. His clothes emitting the same odors. They sit at the other end of the bar. They talk farm.

Two men in dark suits and ties are sitting at a table eating lunch, sharing a pitcher of beer. The other tables and booths are empty. Big Lake can be seen out the back window. The wind rippling the water. The docked boats creaking and wobbling.

Dick stands up, goes to the jukebox, puts in a quarter, punches buttons, Hank Snow's "Down the Trail of Achin Hearts." Change is piling up on the bar.

You told me I was your darlin...

Virgil slips some of the change into his pocket.

Dick returns, lays an arm over the boy's shoulders and says, "I ask Dick Foggy why he's so *not* able of enjoyin life, why he's so goddamn melancholy? I mean, a guy like me should enjoy life, but he can't. Why not? Anything I do, I don't care what it is—can't enjoy it. I think I seen too much in my time. You see what I'm sayin? I seen too much war. Your brother will come back havin seen too much war. You understand the course of things, Virge? You understand what we're up to?"

"No, sir."

"Course you don't. Just a boy. But someday you'll know. You'll remember this day and me and here we are, me and you with this disgustin job on our hands, and you'll remember us like this and you'll understand that Dick Foggy was a heavy-hearted, peace-loving man forced to get . . . to get mean. Somethin broke in me last night when I saw her. The day you understand is the day it happens to you, your daughter betrays you like that. Fragrant betrayal, no remorse. She loves him, she says. Like love excuses any*thing*." He tosses Turkey down his throat and bangs the glass and the men at the bar look at him.

"Loves him, my ass!" seethes Dick. "I'll rip his face off and she can mount it on her wall."

Nod nod nod. Steal change. Agree with everything no matter how stupid it sounds.

Dick's voice lowers, gets secretive. "By my age all men are melancholics doing their best to hide it with a smile and a wave. That's no bullshit, that's a fact. Ask those tit-handling farmers there. Why you think they're in here drinkin when there's so much work to do? Seen too much, done too much and what for? For nuthin. For six feet of earth piled on your head. Think of all those Foggys in the cemetery all the way back to Fergus in 1863. Jesus Christ, that's a long time dead."

He puts his finger under Virgil's chin, raises it, looks at him like a hypnotist. His lips snake back and forth, showing his tongue and the edges of his teeth, and Virgil is thinking he's about to be bitten or kissed.

"Are you my man, Virgil? What you say? Can I count on you?"

"I guess."

"I'm proud of you, how you worked your ass off to get that hay out of the rain. See, that's what a man does. He gives his all. That's what I'm doin, I'm givin my all for your sister, our little femme fatale. You see what I'm sayin?"

"What's a femme fatale?"

"Fatal female. A femme who is fatal to men. Watch out for em, son." He caresses Virgil's cheek. "You are *my* boy, you know. I know Jim is your dad and I can't take his place, but you are my boy now. Jim is like Ginger's broken cherry, gone forever. Let's face facts: he's lost. Not comin back. No one knows the way back home. Even fuckin Houdini, who could get out of anything, chained up in steel boxes and shit, even he couldn't find the way back. I feel bad about it, but what can I do? Dead and gone. I'm the only brother left. I took your mother on as my responsibility, like the Bible says you should. Although there's another verse that says you shouldn't, that it's incest to uncover her naked body. So I don't know. That's a fucked up book. Mama made me read the thing cover to cover when I was younger than you and all I learned were contradictions. But you, I tell you, you are my son. I've been a responsible man. Duty-bound brother to Jim. It's in my blood. I get it from Pappy. I go to work and do my job. I take care of my obligations. I bring home the bacon, you see what I'm sayin? My first wife, what did she do? She pissed on my head, showed no respect. She was a femme fatale. Women are fatal to me. I don't beat women, son, they beat me. Women beat Dick Foggy. But fuck them and fuck her. I got over her. Let her go. Let her have Albert. I never was sure he was mine anyway. He looks nuthin like me. Femme fatale like her, who knows? A man can't ever be sure one hundred percent, you see what

166

I'm sayin? Take Pearl Bell, how would I know? No way to know. It's the curse of being male. You never can be absolute about anything that has to do with a woman's pussy."

He signals Alma serving the men at the other end of the bar. He throws a twenty down. It's easy for Virgil to cheat him. He looks away and another dollar slips into Virgil's pocket.

"The anvil is on me," Dick says, his voice raspy full of phlegm so much it makes him cough. He says it again, "The anvil is on me." He nods abruptly—one, two, three—as if hammering his words in with his forehead, as if he knows he's told Truth with a capital T. Masculinity. It's an anvil you carry. It's an anvil called femme fatale.

"Sad. Sad," he says, his voice watery. Does he want to cry? Virgil would give all the money in his pocket to see it.

"Melancholy heart for what she did, for what I must now do for the Foggy honor, the honor of family. The anvil, son. Always the anvil, you see what I'm sayin? Even when I'm drunk I feel the anvil. Can't get away. Even when I'm pretendin I'm happy, laughin, you know, listenin to a joke and I laugh, but the anvil is there like gravity I'm sayin there it is. Hey, what's a good joke? Tell me a good joke, Virge. Get me outta this mood."

"I don't know no jokes."

"Course you do. Ever boy knows jokes."

"Not me."

"C'mon, just one."

He tries to think of a joke. Tries to remember the one he saw in October's *Farm Journal.*

"There's this farmer doing his taxes and he puts down his cows as dependents." Virgil opens his mouth to laugh. The point of the joke is missed.

"What?" says Dick. "What's funny about that?"

Virgil tries another: "This girl says to this guy, she says, Darling, whisper those three little words that will make me walk on air. And the guy says, Go hang yourself."

Dick throws his head back and laughs and says, "Good one, good one."

This Dick wants cooperation. This Dick wants moral support. This Dick wants excitement and trouble. This Dick wants war.

"You're a funny kid," he says. "Sometimes I think you're not all there, you see what I'm sayin?"

167

"Where's there?"

"There is where you're always about a yard wide of what's what. You worry your mother, you know. What if we lose the farm and you without an education? Where will you be then? You'll have to work at Packerland or join the Army."

"*You* didn't finish school."

Dick smirks proudly. "True enough, but your Dad did. He went to college."

"But he didn't finish."

"True too. But you know what your mother worries about? Why don't you have friends? It's not normal at your age to be such a loner. Messes up your mind, livin inside your own head, don't you know? Loners, you know, blow shit up with dynamite and gun down strangers because voices tell them to."

"Danny's my friend."

"Danny? That fuck. Fuck him, he's not your friend. How much did Pappy pay him for buckin hay?"

"Sixty bucks. Gave him a bonus."

"He's sixty bucks worth of friend." Dick waves his hand in dismissal.

"Forget about it, I never had friends neither. But girls. The girls always liked Dickey boy. Shit, they still like me, right, Alma?"

She turns around, smiles, nods. "Right, Dick," she says.

"No brag, just fact." He jerks a thumb towards Alma. "She still wants me even after all these years. It's in the measurements, son. Women try to bullshit us by sayin it's what you do with it that counts, but truth is a matter of measurements. We're no fools, we know better. Man, the things I could tell you about women. Which I will someday. When you're ready." He stops himself, closes his eyes. Shakes his head. "No, you're too young. You got the equipment, but not the attitude. You'll get there, you'll see. You got my blood. You'll get attitude. We'll be swappin poon tunes pretty soon. Every man has his season. But look here, back in the fifties, I was like Elvis to them. I had the sideburns, the pompadour. I had the hot look, right, Alma?"

Alma smiles and wiggles her eyebrows.

"I was very cool back then after the war when I was a hero struttin my stuff."

Virgil looks at Dick's hair slicked strategically to cover his bald spot. Imagines him with an Elvis wave. Maybe the eyes *are* Elvis, maybe the smirky Elvis mouth.

"But *that* was then and *this* is now," Dick continues. "Even a good fuck don't cheer me up no more," says Dick. "Nuthin cheers me up no more. I don't know what's wrong. It's like a disease. What did they call it? Black bile. Worse than V.D. Black bile. Maybe I'll shoot myself. I think about it. I really do."

Virgil brightens at the prospect of Dick shooting himself.

"A sense that nuthin lasts, nuthin matters," says Dick. His lower lip glistens in the light. "Jesus, I'm gettin nicely shitface now. No caring, no conscience. That's what boose does for you. You gonna drive me, right? You know where Mr. Cunt-eater lives, right?"

Virgil steals more change. Feels it lumping in his pocket. He's bad. The mirror behind the bar, all the glasses and bottles and the men reflected there, the back of Alma's head, her long hair in a ponytail. Side by side, Virgil sees himself and his uncle. Their high foreheads, ears half hidden in hair. The same jaw, same aggressive chin. At least Virgil's eyes are his mother's Italian rounds.

"The entire world could blow up tomorrow and what would it matter?" says Dick. "In the large scheme of things, no matter. The universe don't care. Billions and billions. You ever think like that? Hmmm? What goes on in there? Anything?" He taps Virgil's head. "Not much, I bet. Your mother says you're no philosopher. Not deep like her, she says. She's a thinker. She should have a degree, except she let Jim have his way. Horny holes will do it to you every time."

"There's black holes in space that swallow everything," Virgil tells him.

Dick scratches his neck. He squeezes an ingrown hair there, squeezes and scratches. "I'm a black hole," he says. "The trouble is, I'm not livin the life I meant to live. I'm oot of sync with who I want to be. Got off the wrong foot and never got in strep after I leff the service. What's wrong with my tongue?" He grabs Virgil's arm. "Lissen, you tell Vern to stray in and do his time and retire in twenty years with a pension. Smarter any us if he does that, even smarter your father. Smartass college boy. He never finish, you know. Dumb sonbitch, he could had it all. Right from the start. Gets married and does farmin instead. But not me. Not ole Dickey boy. Not gonna keep me down on the farm. Jim's the one. Nobody never love Dick. Nobody cept your mother once upon a time, but I kick her ass lass night and each time I do that I loose her some more. Who's fault that? Peter and your sister. What would Jim have done? What's Jim know about any this shit? He got out, the lucky bassard. But here's the thing—she's heavy load. Breaks balls. Too mush baggage for me to carry on these shoulders, broad as they are. How I spose to truss her? You tell me."

"Another?" says Alma.

"Why not? Sure, one more, we gotta go. We got bisness."

"Want another Coke, Virge?" says Alma patting his hand, squeezing it, showing him cleavage. What would they feel like? Cow udders?

"No thanks." He gets up, heads for the GENTS.

Forty years of diluted piss and Pine Sol. Hard water rust stains. The two men in suits are standing side by side. One man is holding the flush handle and watching his stream. Virgil slips inside a stall, closes the door, opens his fly. Pisses quietly against the side of the bowl.

"Yhah, you think my life so swell," a voice says. "I thought so too, but not after that, no sir."

"After what, Ed?"

"The condom, Carl. The condom."

"Condom?"

"I found a rubber, a condom, in the trash. White tissues crumpled with it full of dried you know what. Like white flowers. White petals on the grass.

"On the grass?"

"The dog being bad. He overturned the can. The thing wasn't mine, man. Never use them. So I snatched it quick and pushed it in the garbage, pushed it down before she could see. She didn't notice. She was bent over preoccupied with picking up wads of Kleenix and cussing that goddamn dog. A man should know enough to flush a condom down the toilet."

"Jesus, Ed, what you saying?"

Virgil hears the urinals flushing and words get garbled. He hears the men washing their hands and he thinks there must be an epidemic of cheating going on. Femme fatales all over the place.

"I didn't know what to do. I still don't know what to do. Tell me what to do, Carl."

"I'd get my fuckin gun, Ed, or a baseball bat or something and

170

take care of some *body*. Catch em at it. Catch em *inflagrante*. No court in the land will convict you, Ed."

"I don't want to kill her, Carl. It would break my heart to kill her. She's so goddamn . . . I could kill her if she was ugly, but she's so goddamn beautiful. I'd have to kill myself if I kill her. Those gorgeous legs. Ass firm as apples."

"Kill him then, whoever he is. Whom do you suspect?"

"I don't know. I don't know. Could be you, could be Wild Bill. Could be a total stranger."

"You know it ain't me, Ed, you know that, don't you? Wild Bill, though, I'd keep my eye on him. He's a lady-killer. Even his wife knows that. I'll tell you, I seen him looking up your wife's skirt when she was kicking back and crossing her legs. I have to say, it looked like she meant to. Like she was flashing him. You were in the kitchen mixing drinks. She didn't do it when you were there."

"I'm to blame. Part to blame, anyway. I done her wrong and she knows it, Carl. All this traveling, selling fertilizer. A man gets lonely. But even if it is part my fault, I can't stand to think of someone touching her. The two of them soaking. A notion that makes me crazy. I'll kill somebody, Carl."

The door opens and their voices fade. Music drifts in. Janine Sherry singing—

I've got a tangled miiind . . . and a brooo-ken haart . . .

Virgil washes his hands and heads back to the bar.

"Virgil, what you think?" says Dick.

"Boot what?"

"You gettin any lately?"

"Any what?"

"It's not your fault, you know," says Dick. "That dog fugged you up. But . . . but the good news is you got a look now. A more interestin face. So there. Some good comes of it. You don't look cute no more. Nothin worse for a guy than lookin *cute*."

The door opens. Bells tinkle. The wind is a moaning pipe. The two men, Ed and Carl, go outside, heads leaning close, discussing death and infidelity. Door slams. Music ends. Janine Sherry slips back to her slot.

171

The War According to V–

Hidee, hidee, hidee ho,
Hidee, hidee, hidee hay.
That's the Airborne Boogie,
It's a crazy song.
All the way, all the way
Blood and guts,
Blood and guts,
Kill a man!
Kill a man!

Little V,

      That's what we sang in Jump School as we doubletimed six miles every morning. Maybe I told you this already? Maybe like Pappy I repeat myself. Have I told you how we sweat pigs over here? We pour our lard over the ground and everyone smells like those farmers who sleep with their cows, shitty and muddy and like acid that eats nails. Some of these guys need to wipe their ass. But you get used to it and finally no big deal, just like getting used to the smell of a farm, the barn with the gutters full and the cows swishing shit soaked tails in your face. A man raised on a farm can make serious war and get used to anything little V. The guys call me Deadeye after I dropped that dink. The Captain wants to make me a sniper now. Put me up in some tree so I can pick off charlies at 200 yards. If I ever see one again that is. Can you see me as a sniper? Snipers are sneaky. Bad guys do sniper stuff, right? Things I hear these days make me think we might not be such good guys after all. I question, I question authority specialy. There are guys here who argue with officers now. No one wants to go out on patrol and draw fire so some fucker in a jet can be given new coordinates to bomb. In some outfits they go on patrol and just hang in the woods for a couple of days and come back and lie about where they been. And the officer in charge wont do a thing about it because he knows his men will frag him. It happens more than you care to know. Not here tho, not in my company. Airborne Elite all the way. We got discipline. We would no way kill our officers. Those punk outfits like the 11th Brigade pull shit like that. It worries me to hear such shit. But maybe they are only rumors? I do not personally know anyone who has done it. But I got to admit things have changed since I been here. Even though they say we win all the battles it does not feel like it. It takes the Gungho out of you. People are falling apart. We are getting a defeated attitude. I run hot and cold. So does Rice and Paine. You probably know that from my letters, huh? But I do my best to fight it. But it is hard to know that people back home are marching against us and calling us names and then this guy Calley wipes out every man, woman and child at a place called My Lai. 350 of them. Jesus they even killed the pigs and dogs and chickens. Pure evil. There is a shitload of pure evil here. How much evil I seen. Hidee-ho, there it is. Jesus, look at my wavy writing. Some days my hands shake like an old man. Have I told you this before? Some days I hardly know my own name.

V.

Rolling Thunder

If the level of infiltration or our casualties increase while we are trying to scale down the fighting, it will be the result of a conscious decision by the enemy.

We really only have two choices open to us if we want to end this war.

I can order an immediate . . . withdrawal of all Americans . . . without regard to the effects of that action.

Or we can persist in our search for a just peace . . . through implementation of our plan - a plan in which we will withdraw all of our forces . . . on a schedule in accordance with our program.

I have chosen this second course.

It is not the easy way.

It is the right way. **(Nixon)**

Our current policy can lead only to disastrous defeat. **(Bundy)**

If it takes a bloodbath
Let's get it over with! **(Reagan)**

Virgil Francis Foggy

Virgil parks at the curb. Peter's muddy Chevy is in the driveway, nose against the garage door. The rain and the wind have flattened the grass. Tufts stand up here and there where the crabgrass grows. The house has an L-shaped porch, no chairs, no table. A WELCOME mat hangs lip-over on the last step. The screendoor droops in a way that keeps it partially open just like the screendoor at home. On the roof the TV antenna has folded its spines pointing east. Up and down the street, it is the only house with a broken antenna, but every yard is littered with debris, leaves and twigs and small branches and newspapers scurrying. Virgil leans on the Cadillac, while Dick goes to the door and pounds with the side of his fist. He waits a moment. Bangs again.

"They're not home?" says Virgil.

Dick frowns at him. "I heard a noise in there." He pounds the door and shouts, "Peter Raven!"

A muffled voice says, "Who you?"

"You know goddamn well who I am! I want to talk to you, muthafucka!"

The muffled voice says, "Go away."

"Where's your old man? Where's Wild Bill? Let me talk to that sonofabitch!"

"He ain't here. I'll call the cops, Mr. Foggy."

Dick is breathing fast. "Dirty son of a—" he shouts. He rips off the weathered screendoor and throws it on the lawn. "Open up, you sonofabitch!" he says. "I'll bust you, motherfucker! I'll rip your fuckin snotnose face off!"

"I'm callin the cops!"

Dick slams his shoulder against the door. Backs up and slams again. A crack runs down the center, but the lock doesn't give.

"I'm callin the cops!" cries Peter. "I'm callin em!"

Dick kicks the door, cussing all the while and calling Peter a coward, a rapist, a miserable excuse of a man, a bastard, a cocksucker, an ass-licker who takes it up the ass.

"Sirens!" Peter shouts.

Dick steps back. Listens. The sirens are far away but closing. "Coward! All you Ravens are cowards," he says.

175

Virgil's knees feel weak. His hands are shaking. He sags on the fender. Palms sweaty, mouth dry. The sirens come closer. Dick's hands are on his hips. He is puffing, making gargoyle faces. The wind whips Virgil's cap off, tugs at his clothes. The wind warns of autumn ending and winter roads, black ice on bridges. He chases his cap, catches it, crams it tightly on and grips the curved bill. The grass is yellow. Tree leaves whorling into his face. He jerks north toward the road that leads home. His hands shake. His hands shake. His knees.

"Shouldn't we go, sir?" he asks. "The cops comin."

Dick's laugh is a wired, hysterical squeal. He whips his head left-right birdlike. He looks satisfied. Like it's all part of his plan. He sits on the steps, a king in khaki, a man of the world. He cups a match, lights a cigarette.

Virgil's teeth chatter, he raises his collar to cover his ears.

The police pull up in two cars, red and blue lights flashing. Sirens turn off abruptly. They get out and one of them stands by Virgil. Two others stay by the cars, their hands resting on their holstered guns. Officer Salter walks toward Dick. Virgil is thinking that Dick will lunge at him and the others will jump in and take Dick down. It will be a hell of a fight. Maybe to the death. The old war hero will make them pay. Virgil's heart is beating so fast it makes him pant. Upper lip trembling. He hopes no one asks him a question. He won't be able to talk. He sees Dick dead. Sees the funeral, the mourners gathered round the grave and Father Hess quoting Bible passages. Regina Perpetua weeping. Badluck Lady has lost two husbands. She's femme fatale. Don't go near her! Virgil will cry for Dick. He will make a show of grief. He went down fighting. That's what Foggys do.

"What's going on, Dick?" Salter looks at the battered screen on the grass. Nudges it with his toe.

Dick shakes his head. He smirks. "Just wanna talk to him, Salty. We got bisness, him and me."

"What business, Dick?"

"What bisness, Salty? Bisness like syphilitic motherfucker fuckin my daughter."

"Are you drunk, Dick?"

"Bisness like that, Salty. This anal-tongue cornholer," he jabs a thumb over his shoulder, "took her to the boonies and got her high and raped her. I want him charged with rape, Salty. I want you arrest him right now." Dick's torso is swaying slightly. He hadn't seemed so drunk a moment ago, but he seems very drunk now. His long mouth moves like melting plastic as he puffs the cigarette, puffs and blows like a flamed-out dragon.

"Does she say he raped her?"

"She don't haff to say it."

"I didn't rape her," says Peter, his voice coming through the door. "That's a goddamn lie, Officer Salter. She knows what she's doing. You ask around, you'll see. Everyone knows Ginger."

Peter's only seventeen, Dick. What's Ginger?"

"Too damn young!" He slams the side of his fist against the house. Lots of neighbors are out on their porches and lawns. Hugging themselves against the wind and watching. Hoping for action.

"Calm down, Dick. Let's don't let it get out of hand. I'll take this up with Wild Bill. We'll get this straightened out. Something will get done, I promise."

Salty calls out to Peter, "Peter?"

"Yessir."

"You okay?"

"Yessir, Officer Salter. He broke the screen off, you see that? He was gonna kill me."

"Lyin sack of shit," says Dick. "If I was gonna kill him, I'd brought a gun and he'd be dead now."

"He was! He was gonna kill me!"

"Fuck you! I was gonna teach him a lesson. I might put him in hospital, but I wasn't here to kill him." Dick's crooked grin is cruel. His eyes look cruelly happy. Dick is enjoying himself.

"You have to arrest him, Officer Salter."

Salty looks at the other officers. They understand the situation. The one next to Virgil smiles and shakes his head like he's seen it all before.

Salty says, "So, got a snootful, hey, rascal?"

"Does a bear shit squirrel in the woods?"

Salty chuckles. "If I take you home will you promise to let me handle this with Bill Raven? Will you promise not to come back here and make trouble?"

"Promise, my ass," says Dick. "Tell that sissy motherfucker to come out here and face me like a man. He can fuck like a man, why can't he fight like a man?"

Salty motions the other officers forward with his head. "Let's go, Dick," he says smiling gently.

"Go where?"

"Where you can sleep it off and not hurt yourself or anyone else. In the light of sober, you'll see things different. C'mon, old boy."

Dick's eyes challenge Salty.

Now it comes. Now he'll do it, now he'll charge, thinks Virgil.

But to his disappointment, Dick stands up, flips his cigarette into the wind, turns around and offers his wrists. Salty waves the cuffs off, takes his arm, leads him down the walk, shaking his arm and saying,

"You're such a rascal."

Dick looks glad to be a rascal.

"This Jim's son?" Salty says, stopping in front of Virgil.

"He's *my* son," says Dick.

"What's your name, son?" says Salty. "I should know, but I forgot."

"Virgil."

"Virgil. Yes, Virgil and Vernon. Vernon is Jim's kid, right? He's in the Army. He's in Vietnam."

"Right," says Dick.

"C'mon, Virgil, you can ride with us," says Salty. And he says, "We need more brave boys like you and your brother in this war. Are you proud of your brother?"

"They made him a sniper," says Virgil.

"A sniper, huh? He must be awful good to be a sniper."

"He gets em at three hundred yards. He's killed dozens."

Salty whistles. Then he says, "I bet you can hardly wait to join up, huh? Get in on the action. We need war to keep America lean and mean. We were gettin too soft since Korea. Your generation doesn't know how lucky it is to get another war. To test your mettle, I mean. Make you into men what deserve this country."

Salty opens the passenger door for Dick, guides him in. Virgil gets in the back. One of the officers drives the Cadillac. Salty eases the squad car away from the curb. He and Dick talk about hunting season, some places up north where the hunting should be good. They talk about a four-point buck Salty got up at Thunder Lake last year. Dick tops it with a six-pointer brought down with a 30.06 at a hundred yards on a dead run through the pasture. The deer making for the woods.

"In your own pasture?" Salty says. "How about that. I go hundreds of miles for four points and you stay home and bag six. You always been good," Salty says. "I remember one time when we were kids, you and me and Jim and Wild Bill, when we were in the woods hunting and that chicken hawk swooped over and you . . . "

Virgil glances at the houses, the wind-battered trees, people staring at the cop car, glad it isn't them inside it. Glad somebody's in trouble, though. Another criminal off the street. Support the badge. Cops doing their job, keeping the streets of Anoka clean. I SUPPORT MY LOCAL POLICE. Hooray for the cops. The cops are tops. AMERICA LOVE IT OR LEAVE IT. Plenty are leaving. Going to Canada. Virgil wishes he could go too. Him and Vernon. Start over. There has to be something better somewhere.

There is a billboard, old and faded, in a vacant lot full of battered weeds and soggy trash. The top half of the billboard has blown over. The bottom half shows a woman's lips exposing grimacing teeth.

TENSE NERVOUS HEADACHES?
ANACIN FAST PAIN RELIEF
HEADACHE – NEURALGIA – NEURITIS
ANACIN ANACIN ANACIN

Virgil has a headache. He rubs his temples. The car turns at the corner and heads east, Salty still talking about how Dick shot the chicken hawk out of the sky with a .22 and it fell in the trees somewhere and they never found it. Looking back, Virgil sees the other half of the billboard, a pair of pain-filled eyes staring at the world upside down. Round, brown Italian type eyes. He remembers something his mother said a number of times. She said she could have been a model, could have been on billboards and in magazines. There were agencies trying to sign her up when she was in college. She was photogenic, everyone told her. She had a very photogenic face. The camera loved her flawless skin. Those are times she can't forget. She should have stayed in school and gotten her degree and gone on to graduate school, done some modeling on the side. Who knows where it might have led? People said she looked like the Italian version of Suzy Parker back then. Cover of *Vogue*. Cover of *McCall's*. $100,000 a year for those high cheekbones and violet eyes.

179

Once upon a time Regina Perpetua had no limits. Now look at her. But she hadn't planned on meeting Jim Foggy in class, taking the same required course that she was. Jim might have been in college to study agriculture, but he was no dope when it came to literature. He understood poetry well and that captivated her. A farm boy, but more than just a dirt-head farmer. He had cool hair and curved eyes, a long, luscious mouth. Those shoulders! What girl could resist? Virgil loved hearing the story, loved the idea of his father coming off the farm and being college smart. Something Virgil himself could never be. He's never read anything but comic books and whatever he was forced to read in class, Romeo and Juliet once, and "The Death of Ivan Ilych," who died of a pain in his side, which scared Virgil badly when he had a pain in his side for a couple of days and thought it was cancer. He closes his eyes, quotes No man is an Island. He's not so dumb, a boy who can do that and has heard of John Donne, *I Ching*, the *Bhagavad-Gita* and Bible things. How can a boy like that be dumb? Regina said that love ruled in her day. *LOVE*. She thinks women don't love in the overwhelming way her generation did. She came to the farm with Jim to meet Pappy and Gramma Nez and fell for them and the country life. And then she and Jim got married, she pregnant with Vernon at the time, and no more college in her future.

Sad now. Depressed often. Three kids, poochy tummy, balloon hips, saggy breasts. Must feel it all the time. The could have been. The what was. The what if. Regina Perpetua with her two black eyes. And Himself in the front seat talking to his old pal. Dick Foggy: a man carrying anvils.

Virgil looks at a spot just behind Dick's ear. A bullet there and he wouldn't feel a thing. Not one second of suffering. No more wondering when. No more waking up and wondering if today is the day. And if not today, what about tomorrow? It's going to happen. Melancholy Dick would be shut of all that. Ready or not. He would be rid of himself, rid of pain to come. You would be doing him a favor, Virgil.

As if Virgil's eyes are burning holes, Dick swings round and says, "How you doin there, boy?"

"Okay."

"Comfy?"

"Yhah."

"You know whad you gotta do?"

"No sir."

"You gotta take care of that steer. Can you do that?"

"Moses?"

"We can't carry him through winter. The freezer's low. You needa shoot him and skin him for Herman White. I talked to him bout it. Herman will pick up and package him. Can you hannal it? Are you the man?"

"Yessir."

"This kid's born farmer," Dick says to Salty.

"We need more like him. More red, white and blue," says Salty. "Too many of these dirty little shits don't know the first thing of honest work, running all over this country causing trouble, making illegal babies and VD and marching against their own country. Treason in the air. I'm sayin you can smell treason when they're around. Traitors to their country. The way I see it, you're either for your country or against it. If you're against it, fuck you. Put them on a farm and put them to work. Idle hands are the devil's workshop. That's the way I see it."

The car pulls into the station and circles round back. They get out and Salty leads Dick inside. Dick sways. He stumbles. Salty says, "Whoa, Joe, what you drinkin."

"Boilermakers," says Dick.

An officer fingerprints Dick and has him empty his pockets and count the money in his wallet. He turns in some keys, a nickel and a penny, a jackknife, a tiny four-leaf clover in urethane, a comb, a book of matches, a pack of gum, pack of Marlborough.

"You can keep these," the officer says, handing him the cigarettes, matches and comb.

An inventory is taken and Dick signs the envelope and the officer seals it. Virgil steps up and starts to empty his pockets.

"Not you," says Salty, laughing.

The other officer laughs too.

Dick laughs. "Call your ma," he says. "Have Pappy run her in and get the car. She can bail me tomorrow, right, Salty?"

"Right, Dick."

He and Dick walk down the hall, past a series of steel doors with six-inch vertical bars at the top. The walls are concrete, painted grayish blue. The boy goes back outside, out to the parking lot, out to the street. Sun at forty degrees. He doesn't want to call his mother. He doesn't want to go home just yet. He walks past the jail, the Bank of Minnesota, the record store. Advertisements for Fifth Dimension's "Age of Aquarius" and Simon and Garfunkel's "The Boxer" pasted to the window. Giant musical notes, like a flock of birds draped over the glass, hanging there— black on silver. An icon portrait of Simon and Garfunkel surrounded by clefts and treble clefts, whole notes and quarter notes, tall guy with bushy hair, a short guy with brown hair hanging over his ears, eyes looking for distance. Millionaires. The short guy is supposed to be the brains of the outfit.

I am just a poor boy—lie la lie la lie. . .

"Why didn't he fight?" Virgil wonders.

This is the Dick who says he gets into fights in bars, knocks guys down, knocks out cops if they interfere. Makes them eat their guns, he says, and shit toy pistols.

This is the man who could have been a heavyweight contender, he says.

This is the man nobody wants to fuck with, he says. War hero. Bronze Star with Cluster.

This is Dick Foggy, baddest man in town, meaner than a junkyard dog, he says.

But it was like he had it all worked out. It was like he was playing a part, growling, cussing, threatening, ripping screens off, pounding the door, slamming shoulders into wood, cracking it. The satisfying sound of plywood splitting. But then the door not giving. Peter inside so scared he's sobbing. "I'm calling the police!" But it was like Dick just wanted to put on a show, scare Peter. And then the cops would come and arrest him, getting him off the hook of having to be this man nobody wants to fuck with. Lock him up because he's drunk and might hurt himself or poor Peter Raven. Strolled away buddy-pals, he and Officer Salter, like they were going for a drink. Salty this and Dick that. Rascal. The chicken hawk, that was some shot on the wing, how'd you do it? Steady eye. A contender's reflexes. The look on Dick's face had been so . . . so calculating. Analytical and smarmy. Dithering between that and the bloodshot eyes, tough sneer, the slight bobble in his head, so they would know he had been drinking. Men who drink but don't hurt others are forgiven. Tolerated. People smile at them. People wink. Well, we know some things about him. We could tell you if we would, but we are sworn to secrecy. Deep down, though, he's a good guy, a prince.

Mildly, he went along with Salty. *Mildly.* He let them take his stuff and seal it and lead him by the arm to a blue-door cell. Lock him up. Sleep it off, Dick. Go home tomorrow. Everything all right by sunrise. Might have to pay for that screen. Might be a fine to pay.

"Don't seem right," Virgil says to the notes in the window. *No more falsehoods or derisions.* Golden visions da-da-da. Revelations, liberation. *Ah-quar-eee-us, Aquarius.* Peace and love and understanding. No more war, dum-de-dum-dum. *Lie la lie la* lie . . .

Hands in pockets, he leaves the display and goes with the flow. His mind on musical notes slammed together like feathers twisting.

Musical notes hung on sun-glinting glass: blackbirds can look like that.

"Geez, Louise! Hah-hah!" He fishes in his jacket for the little tablet and pencil used as a chore list and writes down his inspiration. At the corner, he crosses with the light.

Feeling groovy . . .

Virgil went to the check-in counter, but no one was there. Up and down the hall there was no one. He walked in the direction that Salty took Dick. Looked through the bars at the top of each door and found Dick in the third cell on the left. There were bunk beds in the cell. Dick was sitting on the bottom bunk. One dull bulb in a wire cage hung from the ceiling. There was a toilet and a sink. The rest was grayish-blue walls and grayish-blue floor and grayish-blue blanket on the bed.

Dick was masturbating. You could see part of his penis, the head leaping out of his hand. Dick breathing hard through his mouth. At first it didn't seem possible that you were seeing what you were seeing. How can a man who has just been arrested for drunk and disorderly be sitting in his cell masturbating? You knew if it were you in the cell, the last thing you would care about would be jacking off. You remembered hearing your mother tell Dick one time, when they were fighting, that he, like all men, had his brain in his cock. Same thing Ginger said once. Only she said the head of the cock.

Dick groaned. His breath seethed. He adjusted himself, turning a little to his left and scooting his butt to the edge of the bunk. His knees spread apart as he jerked his penis upward. Freed it of his fly, whacked away, making a slapping sound.

Thick and slick and boiling. The shock of its size made you jealous and also made you shudder. You backed away. The word humongous was in your mouth. You leaned weakly against the wall. Thought of your own unimpressive penis, how small by comparison, how white and frightened and pitiful it was. In manhood you might have a monster like that, though. You giggled out loud, slammed a hand over your mouth and whispered,

"Oh wow, oh wow."

"Who's there?" said Dick.

"It's me," you said. "Where are you, Uncle Dick?"

"Over here."

You retraced your steps and saw Dick standing at the door now, looking through the slot. The bar shadows cleaving his face. "Why aren't you home?" he said. "Where's your mother?"

"I'm going right now." You saw Dick's shoulder vibrating. He was still jacking off while talking to you. You went up on your toes to confirm your suspicions and sure enough, the hand was pumping. Slower than before—Dick pacing himself.

"Don't come up on me, man," he said.

"I guess I'll go."

"Tell your mother to come get me in the morning. Salty will let me go when she comes, okay?"

"Yessir."

"We had that bastard shakin in his boots."

"Peter? Oh, he was scared."

"Probably shit his pants."

"Probably."

"He didn't know whether to shit or go blind."

"He was scared all right."

"The word will get around. Studs not wantin to fuck her now. They know what I'll do."

"Yeah."

"Kick some young-stud asses, that's what."

The shoulder was trembling, trembling. Dick showing lots of teeth. You wanted to see what his face did when he climaxed.

"Go on now," said Dick. "See you tomorrow."

You hustled down the hall and went out to the parking lot, where everything was just as before. Just normal comings and goings, people and cars. Blue sky, popcorn clouds that meant no harm. The sun making long shadows. The wind still mad about something. And you wanted to tell people: *There's a man in a cell there jacking off.* It seemed insane. Virgil, you kept breaking into laughter. Maybe you were hysterical. Mildly maybe?

Virgil goes to the Cadillac, takes the spare keys from the

magnetized tin hidden beneath the front bumper. He starts the car and eases forward.

Heading for home, driving slowly, he thinks about Dick, "Crazy sonofabitch honeymooning himself right in front of me. Didn't even stop, not for one second, whap, whap, whap, crazy sonofa. What does he think, I'm so stupid I don't know what he's doing? He thinks I'm stupid. He calls me a stupid bastard, but he's the stupid bastard. I wouldn't do that in no cell where people can walk by and see me. Penis big round as my wrist, Jesus! A man would be proud to have one like that, geez. No wonder women fall all over him."

When he reaches the gravel turn-off and sees the lights of the farm ahead, the silhouetted buildings in black, the black woods west, he remembers what Dick told him to do.

Murder Moses.

The War According to V–

Little V,

You know what I miss? I miss the Minnesota woods more than I thought possible. The woods here are like nothing you seen. The way the trees grow, they often cover each other in layers going up and up like umbrellas overlapping and when you're in deep you cant see the sun. No shit Virge no lie no sun. It is the twilight zone and things trip you, vines and things. Sometimes a dead guy all folded in the ground has been there for ages sealed like a mummy in mud so he don't even look like a man but rather like roots of a tree. You get a ghostly light at dawn like the mornings when the sun isn't quite up and you climb into the loft to throw bales down for the cows. I envy you doing that. In that light in the loft that gives you the creeps but it can be peaceful to. Like you are walking in a ghost world where everything is settled and your worries are over. It depends on your mood and the time of day and the weather and the light. In this armpit it is hot as hell and humid like Minnesota July and it is as if you are moving through heavy mist that make you cough and you can not get enough air or drink enough water to quench your thirst. It might be raining but if you are hacking through undergrowth and thick enough trees the rain might not reach you and you slog along and get crotch rot and foot rot and leeches parasiting you and hardly no sleep even back at base because VC or NVA is sending mortars all night to keep you company and some guys go wonkers. Especially the cherries who haven't had a chance to get use to things. You can hear them moaning. Some of them cry like babies. I think some of them even die of fright. Not a mark on them and so pale like the belly of a carp, maybe twenty years old and totally dead, I seen it, a couple times I seen it. Two days ago a Huey took off loaded with warriors and as we watched it whip over the trees it suddenly exploded killing everyone, everyone coming down in pieces an arm here a leg there a torso on its own looking like homebase for a ball field. The rumor is it was hit by an M-20 Rocket Launcher. The M-20 is our weapon we invented it, but the gooks use anything of ours they can find. We get killed with our own M-14s and M-16s and M-79 Grenade Launchers and so on, all our own inventions made to KILL THEM, which they steal and turn on us. We do the same. There is a guy in my platoon who has an AK-47 what the dinks use, you can always tell when its him shooting. It is a different sound, a mechanical clacking sound versus the swift burr of the M-16. Everybody wants the AK because they are more reliable than ours, which can overheat and jam if you keep it on automatic too long, the powder in the bullets does not burn clean enough so you never know if the dam thing is going to choke on you. I hear we are up 35,000 dead now. Some say 40,000. What is true? Do you know? Is it possible for the mind to process such figures? A lot of men dead for so small a country. Upside down surreal world, Charles Rice calls this place. I would give ten years of my life to get the fuck out of here right this second. Hell, I would give my left nut and my fungus toes to. Bargain with me, I'm a pushover. I am even thinking of re-uping for OCS that is how desperate I am. It would get me out of this shithole, this Godless timeless land that swallows everything, especially human beings. Let me tell you about those missing in action. All those MIAs will never be found, the jungle eats them, the mud absorbs their bones. Total vanishing. Like never born. Dont you dare go in the service for your country or fall for all that bullshit patriotism the schools and the old men teach you. I will kill you if you do. Stay on the farm and be useful and make things grow and take care of Pappy and Gramma Nez and the cows. They need you. Keep your world small in good order, what we call keeping things STRAC. Nothing but chaos outside those borders little V. Maybe you know that already? I am in a pessimist mood today so sorry. Happens more and more lately. Rumor has a big battle coming soon. Boo koo badass NVA marching down the Ho Chi Minh to take us on. I do not want anything to do with it but there it is.

V.

Rolling Thunder

We have faced other crises in our history and have become stronger by rejecting the easy way out.

Our greatness as a nation has been our capacity to do what had to be done when we knew our course was right.

Honest and patriotic Americans have reached different conclusions as to how peace should be achieved.

If a vocal minority, however fervent its cause, prevails over reason and the will of the majority, this Nation has no future as a free society. **(Nixon)**

But it's so extremely important within our own country that we have a dialogue . . . the decisions that we make have an effect on your lives . . . where you see that we make mistakes . . . you must continue to criticize . . . examine the facts. Plato once said that all things are to be questioned - all things are to be examined and brought into question . . . **(R. Kennedy)**

Freedom . . . slipping from our grasp . . . **(Reagan)**

Virgil Francis Foggy

Forest thick enough to keep out rain. The giant fir tree in lover's lane keeps out rain. Which is why the old mattress underneath has lasted so long. It lies on a cushion of fir needles. Trees layered like umbrellas shutting out the sun. He sees them. Umbrella trees. The ghost world of sleep. Upside down surreal. *Surreal* - what does that mean? Virgil enters the living room. Gets the dictionary. The living room smells of bacon, coffee, diaper. It smells of cigarette butts piled in ashtrays. The television flickers, a commercial for Crest, a carefree girl with fleshy mouth and lovely teeth. Breath mint-fresh. A cute boy puts his arms around her, looks into her face. He kisses her, their mouths sucking. Sexy Crest has done it again. Girl like her will kiss you with the insides of her lips. Her tongue will touch yours. And the surreal war and death goes on and on.

Regina and Ginger puff on cigarettes. The air is hazy. Pearl Bell is in her cradle on the floor sneezing and spastically shaking her fists. The sun sixty degrees east. Virgil looks up the word **surreal**: *bizarre; fantastic; grotesque. To portray the unconscious mind as manifested in dreams; irrational, noncontextual arrangement of material.*

"What are you doin?" asks his mother.

"Lookin up a word."

"He's lookin up a word," she says. "He's using the dictionary."

"Vernon wrote it in his letter."

"Vernon wrote you again?"

"Hmm."

"I got two short notes in the past six months and you've gotten what?"

"Dunno."

"And I'm Vernon's mother." She gives Ginger a look that says Vernon abuses his mother.

Virgil reads the definition again. *Noncontextual arrangement of material.*

"What word?" she asks.

"Surreal."

"Surreal," says Ginger. "That's the word for you all right."

His mother says, "It won't teach you anything about farmin." Is she taunting him? She thinks a moment and says, "Salvador Dali. *The*

Persistence of Memory. Grab that book there, sweetheart, the one that says *Twenty Centuries of Art."* She points to the top shelf. A book fatter than the Bible.

He hands it to her. She searches through pages. Shows him a painting of melting watches hanging from barren trees and cliffs. "It's symbolic," she says, tapping the picture. "It's reality above or beyond what we think of as reality. Subconsciously we know this is what time is doing. We hear it ticking when we hear the beating of our heart. But basically it's—"

"Time is melting," interjects Virgil.

"In a way, yes," she says. "It's metaphorical."

"Everything in the picture is dead," says Virgil.

"Time melts everything . . . everything dies eventually. You, me, the universe." Worry lines furrow her brow. "According to Dali. But he's just a man, what does he know? Maybe time melts, and this painting is a metaphor for that, but God doesn't melt. God is timeless."

The painting looks more like a cartoon than a statement on time. Virgil looks at his wristwatch. The second hand moving, a faint ticking sound, like a muffled cricket. One more second *gone.*

And so is that one.

And that one too.

And—

"What did Vernon say?" asks Regina.

Virgil pulls the letter out and reads about the umbrella trees, the rain, the light, the upside-down world that Charles Rice calls surreal.

When he finishes, she says, "Foggy Farm."

Swollen eyes, black feather hair, ball-tip nose, petite mouth, a gap-toothed grin, like a carved pumpkin with fat shoulders and saggy breasts.

What would Dali do with her?

You were easy, baby. If only Jim had known how easy.

How do you paint *easy*? Is *she* your mother? Is *he* your—

"So what happened yesterday?" says Ginger. "Give us the poop."

He describes Dick, the scene at Peter's house, the cops. He stares through the haze as he tries to remember.

"What're you thinkin?" Regina says.

"Moses," he says.

"Finish your story, sweetheart," she says.

Virgil is *sweetheart* now. She won't be wanting to stab him with a spoon or a butterknife.

"Dick and you. What else did you do?" she says.

"Not much. They put him in jail."

"He's such an idiot."

"If he had a brain he'd be dangerous," says Ginger.

Beneath the shelves are cabinets crammed with antique dinnerware once used by Pappy's mother's mother. Old albums filled with photographs of ancestors, antique vases and tablecloths and quilts. A stack of RCA records in brittle sleeves. There is a box of toys once used by Virgil's father and uncle, toy pistols and spinning tops, a rubber knife, a fire engine, a sailor doll, with its ears chewed off by Dick (very oral little boy, Gramma Nez has said) and a sack of marbles Jim won in a tournament, and a camouflaged tank with treads missing, and plastic soldiers in combat poses, some having lost an arm or a leg. Victims of Dick's powerful teeth? There is more. Virgil has had it explained to him by Gramma Nez. She knows the name of every person in the album. She knows their heritage. When she dies, the doors to the past will close if he doesn't remember what she's told him. He's heard his mother say that you never really forget anything. "Is that true?" he says.

"What?"

He doesn't answer.

"Hello?" she says. "Hello. Earth to Virgil."

So many of the pictures in the albums are of men in uniform. Most with medals on their chests. All of the men have stern faces. The Civil War, The Spanish-American War, World War I, World War II, the Korean War. Dick is there, looking tired and dangerous. Virgil knows none of the women in the pictures, alike in dowdy dresses and hair pulled back. Looking careworn. Defeated. Withdrawn. They have settled for less than what they had hoped for. The kids who pop up making faces, frowning or grinning are strange. He doesn't like them. Gramma Nez can say their names, but the names won't stick in Virgil's mind. Those kids are like the women: boring. He definitely remembers the warrior names. He knows their medals. He knows that the great uncle named Seth Foggy won a Silver Star in World War II. He also won a Purple Heart. And then died of alcoholism in 1954 at the age of 34.

"Where are you?" says Regina.

"Dick tried to bust down Peter's door and get at him, but the cops."

"You already said that," says Ginger.

"But I haven't told you . . ."

"Told us what?"

"Dick. He wants you come get him, Regina. He said Salty will let him go when you get there."

She points to her eyes and says, "How am I supposed to go get him? I can't see six feet. Tell Pappy to pick him up after dialysis tomorrow. Tell him there's no hurry." Her voice is steely. "He made his bed, let him lie in it. Be good for him to stew." She is in the recliner—black leather matching her hair, matching her swollen eyes. On television an emcee is holding off a lady who has come-on-down and is trying to demonstrate her love for him.

"I'll tell Pappy to take his time," Virgil says.

"Blinds me, then wants me to drive all the way to Anoka to get him out."

"Why did you marry him?" asks Ginger abruptly. A strand of hair curves around one nostril and dangles over her lips. Stray filaments shiver with her breath. She's wearing a terrycloth robe, fringe of pistachio nightgown showing her legs are folded sideways, toenails looking like burning embers on the brown couch.

Pearl Bell fusses and Regina rocks the cradle. Pearl Bell jerks her fists, pow! pow! Then settles them (a pair of dimpled stones) on her chest. She sucks doggedly at her pacifier.

"Why do you ask me that?" Regina asks. Her smile is cautious.

"You told Gramma Nez before you married him you weren't sure about it."

"I wasn't."

"Why marry him if you're not sure? Why open that door if you don't gotta?"

"I open doors, dear. I've always plunged into uncharted territory. I've always taken chances."

"It's your nature."

"Yes. I should'a been born a man. I'm full of adventure. Well, I used to be."

"Did you love him?"

"Of course I loved him. Still do. He's very good to me most of the time. If he would just quit drinkin. It's the drinkin that does him. He can be kind and thoughtful and sweet, you know."

"Hmm," says Ginger doubtfully. "He'll drink himself to death like Foggys do."

"Not all of them," says Regina. "You want to know the truth about marriage?" says Regina. "Truth is most women aren't sure about marriage ever. In fact, most will tell you later that subconsciously they knew they were doin the wrong thing, but they thought (they hoped, I should say) it would work out. They think their love will grow mutually huge, that's what they think. Some couples do it. Most others are foolin themselves. But let's face somethin else here, I had more than Regina Perpetua to think about."

"Like what?"

"What? You and Virgil and Vernon, of course. I love you with all my heart and you needed a mother *and* a father. A family. We all need family. What do you have if you don't have family?"

"Family is overrated." Ginger's tone is wintergreen: "And a favor to us, you're sayin? Jesus, Regina."

"It seemed like the right thing to do at the time, honey."

"So you sacrificed yourself? That's how you see it?"

"I wouldn't put it that way. Don't be mad. Why are you so mad at me? What have I done but try to provide a home for you and your brothers?"

"They're not my brothers." Ginger curlicues her hair. "I should have gone with my mom," she says.

"Oh, really?"

"She wanted me. I just didn't want her. Dad had turned me against her. She was the enemy."

"Do you still think so?"

"She was a tramp. He couldn't keep her out of the bars. She—"

"I don't know if I believe that. I believed it once. I guess I wanted it to be true. But I don't know. She was such a . . . such a sweet woman. And even . . . innocent at heart, I think."

"The way she dressed. Those skirts. She didn't dress innocent."

"The style."

"Askin for it."

"Oh? Is that what your jeans clinging to your butt are all about, honey? Are you asking for it? Do you ever take a hard look in the mirror and ask yourself."

"Do you?"

"I'm thirty-nine. I've got gray hairs already. See these lines on my forehead? See? My forehead used to be smooth as Pearl Bell's bottom. Gravity gettin me. *Tempest fugit.*" The lines across her forehead rise like wings at the corners.

"So what? Who cares?" says Ginger.

"Who cares?" Her swollen eyes swim side to side. Leaking tears, but she's not crying. "You can afford to say *so what, who cares*, you're only seventeen."

"I'm not afraid of gettin old. You make it such a disaster."

"It *is* a disaster. We'll see, honey. We'll see if you change your tune when you're pushin forty like me."

"If I live that long." Ginger brushes her hair back. Her shiner looks polished. She keeps wiping it cautiously with a tissue. "I've always had this feelin my life will be short like my other grandma's," she says.

In a whisper Regina repeats what everyone already knows, "She died in a mental hospital. Mental illness runs through that side of the family."

"That don't mean it will happen to you."

"It's in the blood," says Ginger. "I'm doomed."

Creaking cradle. Another second of time flies by. And that one too. Regina Perpetua stabs her cigarette out in the ashtray as she says, "Jim said the same thing. He had a feelin his life would be short. And he was right. Be careful, Ginger. Look out for self-fulfillin prophecies."

"I'm just sayin I won't live to get old. I'm sayin I'm gonna grab all I can right now."

Regina shakes her head. "We're both screwed up this mornin. But we have a right to be. But let's be kind to each other, Ginger. I didn't give you that black eye and you didn't give me mine. Just you think of this, the two of us together couldn't handle him. What will happen if we let him divide us?"

"He divided me and Mom. It was easy."

"Everybody was against her, honey, but who knows the truth? Everyone has a version." Her foot rocks the cradle. Baby's head jiggling, jiggling.

Invisible Virgil clears his throat. Both women look at him, their eyes saying, *What are you still doing here?*

"Sweetheart, why don't you go get somethin to eat?" says his mother. "Make yourself a sandwich."

Shuffling out, he feels the gritty world of women on his soles.

"Go on, honey," says his mother. "Go fix somethin."

Turning around he asks her if she likes the baby now.

She says, "I love the baby! She's a darlin. I love her with all my heart." Her mouth trembles. "How could I not love such a baby? I wasn't myself for a while. I was sick, darlin."

"You wanted to stab me with a spoon." Virgil chuckles.

"I'm much better now. I might not look better, but I am. My heart was bleeding. I can't explain it." She rubs a thumb over Pearl Bell's cheek, adjusts her headband so it rides lower on her forehead. Everything about her says *papoose*.

"She carries like a sack of flour," says Virgil.

Ginger is filing a nail. Both of them like to file their nails. Watch TV and file their nails. Polish them glossy pink or glossy red or glossy orange. Busy, delicate fingers. Devil's workshop idle hands. Gramma Nez knitting at night confounds devils. The clicking needles, the wool jerking in the basket, the string magically turning into a baby cap or vest or sweater or booties. Twenty years from now someone says—*Gramma Nez made you this. Isn't it cute? And this and this and this. They're heirlooms.* What will happen when the old lady is gone? Who will knit? When does a woman lose interest in her nails? Who will open the cabinet and explain the past?

"Did she feed Bonnie?" Virgil asks.

They look at each other.

"Gramma Nez. I left her there," he says.

"She flew away, honey, she flew off. I'm sorry."

"Flew away?"

"Her wings work," says Ginger.

"You mean she's gone?"

"Fish gotta swim, birds gotta fly. It's the law of life," says Ginger.

"Shut up," he says.

His mother says, "Did you think she was going to stay in your pocket forever, sweetheart? Be happy for Bonnie. She's free. Havin a good time. She's livin the way God meant her to live."

"Don't be sad," says Ginger. "It's a good thing."

"It's gettin cold out there! She'll freeze! She'll starve! She don't know the world!"

"Now, now, honey, don't take on. It's nature's way."

He wants to say *fuck nature*, but he doesn't. He walks out of the room biting his fist. He lays his forehead on the cool kitchen counter and breathes slowly.

He hears Ginger saying, "Did you see his face? I think he's gonna cry."

"Poor kid, he loved that little bird. He's got a way with animals. Animals and machinery, there's his niche in life. He's right, you know, this farm is what he was born for. Thank God he can do *something*."

On TV, the local news announcer says, "Twenty-year-old Corporal James L. Wilson, who graduated from Elk River High School in 1967 was killed in action near the Cambodian border on September 30, 1969. He was posthumously awarded the Bronze Star for bravery. The citation reads: *Despite painful leg wounds, Sergeant Wilson kept loading and firing until he ran out of ammunition and his position was overrun by North Vietnamese Regulars.* Principal Bergman has ordered the flags at school to be lowered to half-mast. Services will be announced when Sergeant Wilson's remains arrive." Virgil wonders if Wilson really ran out of ammo or did his weapon jam like Vernon said so many do? How many have died because of that?

Regina says, "Thank God it isn't Vernon. Did you know the Wilson boy, Gin?"

"No, thank God."

"His poor mother."

"Poor him!"

"You notice how different he is, Gin?"

"Virgil?"

"He *is* different. It's not my imagination. He's changed. He never used to be . . . I don't know . . . never used to be sentimental . . . about birds or anything. And I've never in my life seen him look up a word in the dictionary, have you? *Surreal.* Of all words. I tell you, that's not the Virgil we know and love. Even his face has changed. It's not just that nasty scar. It's something to do with his eyes."

"He knows No Man is an Island by heart. He quoted it for me."

"Me too. Isn't that bizarre?"

"He's always . . . he's always . . . drifting, you know. He's never quite here."

"It's much worse than before. There's no there there."

"Husky slowed him down."

"Near-death experience. I suppose that's part of what's wrong. He came back with inward eyes. He came back quiet, not playful anymore, not like our Virgil used to be. It's like his childhood ended in a flash. I liked him playful. I miss his goofin off." She pauses. The cradle creaks. The announcer announces the weather. Temperatures dropping to just above freezing tonight.

"Let's watch *General Hospital*," says Ginger.

The War According to V –

Yo V,

I get to go to Japan R & R a week because I been on the line for so long and my commander wants to give me a break. He is a good guy. I like him today. Guess what? I made E-4 and I'm told E-5 in a war zone is just round the corner, so maybe this is where God wants me to be after all. Doing pretty well I think. Be a Sergeant soon enough. Me a non-commission officer. Think of that. The turnover is so great here that if you got any leadership abilities at all, you get promoted and you wont have to wait the required number of months you would back in the States. Rice is up for it too. But not Paine. Paine is a follower, not a leader. Maybe I will re-up I don't know. I been thinking heavy about it. I guess I have to do something with my life right? I guess so. Farming doesn't seem all that great a career move no more. Corporations and congress are trying to get rid of family farms and doing a good job of it. But the hell with politics and shit. No defeatism in this letter Bro. What the hell I'm celebrating. Spec E-4. I got a pay raise. I am good for today and for at least five minutes I feel happy. I turned down the sniper thing by the way. I am sticking with my squad. I don't want to be out there all alone tied to a tree and picking those little bastards off like turkeys. That stuff feels real shitty to me. Dad once said there has never been a Foggy in war who acted like a weasel. So forget that sniper stuff. Not for me. Snipers are weasels.

Big V.

Rolling Thunder

Once upon a time our . . . goal in war - and can anyone doubt that we are at war? - was victory. (Sen. Barry Goldwater)

I believe the war . . . is illegal, immoral, politically unjustifiable and economically motivated. (Interviewer Anna Ford)

I respect your idealism.
I share your concern for peace.
I want peace as much as you do.
I have chosen a plan for peace.
I believe it will succeed. (Nixon)

I know what the answer is in my own heart . . .
the demonstrations are prolonging the war. (Reagan)

Virgil Francis Foggy

Chilly night. October. Look at the shadowed eaves. TV antenna clutching the chimney. Trees reaching for the house. No Bonnie. Look at the killing yard. Follow the windmill's pyramid up to its whirling daisy. No Bonnie. Inky trees by the river fracturing a bruised sky. No Bonnie. Over the Airstream's window is a pasted luminescence of television, like a minature moon inside the trailer. Human shadows on the glass. They lost her, those old fools. Hear the theme music for *Bonanza*. They don't care. The bonanza brothers and Pa can fix any trouble in town. Little Joe. Hoss. Adam. But forget Bonnie. No one can fix her. She's done for.

"Bonnie!" Virgil calls. "Bonnie!" He hopes they hear him calling and feel bad for losing his bird.

He goes down the driveway and crosses the road. Down the embankment. Sits on the edge of the Crow listening to the water smoothing its banks. Does all water really flow to the sea? It's what his mother said. Can the Crow contain all the tears for Corporal James L. Wilson and all the dead and wounded and missing young men, tens of thousands? KIA. MIA. WIA. Was it worth it, Wilson? Well, if you have to go, go as a true patriot dying for your country. Your shrine will be on the mantel. Until one day another generation comes along and everything on the mantel will go in the cabinet to make room for new heroes.

A bird darts in front of Virgil and fades.

Bonnie?

James L. Wilson?

Better him than Vernon.

A needle in a haystack. He knows he won't find her unless she comes to him. She's not used to the outdoors, not used to frost in the low spots, not used to getting her own food. Bugs digging in for winter, the earth in a coma. Nothing for birds to eat but stray seeds. What does Bonnie know about dealing with all that?

Virgil rises. Goes back across the road, towards the barn. Some of the cows in the pasture moan. Soon they will have to stay in the barn to keep from freezing. His eyes wait for Bonnie to pivot out of the night and land on his shoulder. Moses saunters to the water tank saying—*Yup, yup, fish gotta swim, birds gotta fly*. Noisily he drinks. Looks around. Stands and stares and—It's good he doesn't know what's coming.

Virgil goes in the house up to his room. He opens the Hindu book his grandmother gave him. Skips around. Reads:

Hang on me
as hangs a row of pearls upon its string.
I am the fresh taste of the water; I am
the silver of the moon, the gold of the sun

Gist of the story: Warriors entering a city and killing every living thing. It's okay to kill every living thing if God says so. The *Gita* is a lot about war and killing and passion. God fights on the side of his favorite warrior, telling him to kill his enemies, even if they're family.

Fight and slay with a good conscience and a good will.
Only the body is slain. The soul survives.
He who shall say, 'Lo, I have slain a man!'
He who shall think, 'Lo, I am slain! Those both
know naught. Life cannot slay. Life is not slain.
End and Beginning are dreams.
Birthless and deathless and changeless remains the spirit forever.
Death has not touched it at all, dead though the house of it seems.

They will bury James L. Wilson, in any case. *Life cannot slay. Life is not slain.* It is just and right to kill one's relatives in war. This is your war, Virgil. Slay with a good conscience and a good will. Only the body is slain. The soul survives. Turn out the light, close your eyes and hear a voice saying—*You must change your life.*

Something ticks on the window. You look and there she is: feathers.

"Bonnie!" you say. "Good girl!" You open the window and she hops in, shivers her wings. "Where you been?" you ask.

Checking things out, she says. *Virgil, it's cold out there.*

"I know. I was scared you'd freeze to death. Are you hungry?"

I could eat you! she says.

You fish in the box for the lid and fill it with cow's feed. "Twelve percent protein," you tell her. She sits on your finger and talks with her mouth full, tells you about her adventures, how she dashed here and there and one time got chased by a chicken hawk! And then meeting this good-looking cock at the park in front of the library, but he might have been too old for her, she's not sure. "Wait for spring," you tell her. "And don't build your nest in the hayfield like your mother."

Daddy, you didn't raise no pecking fool, she says. You put her in the box

201

and set it on the bedside table, hear her flipping her food at the cardboard walls. Folding your hands together, you give thanks to God for bringing your bird back. Twigs tap on the glass as if answering you in code: "Finger bone percussion," says your father. You sit up and look and yep, it's him. His white-waxy figure walks through the room, goes to the gun rack, runs a finger over the .22, studies the knife hanging sheathed and nailed to the wall and he says, "The first Foggy cut his throat with this. It's called a Story Knife, two inches shorter than the fifteen-inch Bowie. When the Indians massacred the settlers at New Ulm, Fergus felt partly to blame. In 1862 [he runs his finger slowly over the length of the blade] from Sauk Valley to the Iowa border, they killed them with the hatchets and knives your ancestor Fergus honed on his wheel. He couldn't get over it. That and one of his sons died. But how could he know what those varmints were up to? It's when you know and don't do anything, that's when it's wrong. He walks to the dresser. He looks at Christ suffering on the cross. " Poor Jesus," he says. "All those boys in Nam are Jesus."

He points at the pictures stuck to the mirror: Vernon and you with Cristobell and anonymous cows, and Husky grinning in the background. Vernon, Virgil and himself loading bales. The three of you with the first deer Vernon ever shot. He is holding antlers forked at the tips, like fingers saying *victory*. Gramma Nez in the kitchen with jars of peas in each hand, canning equipment on the stove, a slice of sampler peeking behind her:

NEVER LET ANYTHING SO
THAT YOU FORGET THE

Pappy in a straw Stetson on the Massey Harris 44. Shirtsleeves rolled over his massive forearms. Aggressive chin a boxer would envy. Shaded eyes full of . . . what? What a man!

"They're called Massey Ferguson now," says your father, touching the picture of the tractor. "Ferguson bought Harris out. Those were the days," he says. "I wish we lived there again. Time ticks," he tells you. "Like melting watches draped over cliffs and trees. This is what I've come from sulfur to tell you, my son."

Moving to the table, he looks at the bird and smiles and says, "Be bold and brave and resolute. Don't let Uncle Dick scare you shitless. Don't be a coward. Foggys are brave, not a drop of coward in your Foggy blood." He bends his head. It stretches like a jellyfish. You raise the Hindu testament.

"It says in this book Gramma give me that in some cases it is right to kill a relative. It says that death is an illusion. It says, Life cannot slay. Life is not slain. End and beginning are dreams, it says."

"True," he answers, walking past the crucifix to the gun rack once more, where he pats the stock of the .22.

"He's family, Daddy."

"End and beginning are dreams," he insists. His figure wavering.

Translucent undulations slide over the bed like foggy shadows. He kisses you coldly. Then exchanges molecules with the window.

You stare out the window. The moon a comma in the sky. Below are mowed fields, fragile cornstalks, trees going to sleep. Twigs are playing finger bone percussion. "I'm gonna kill him," you say. "That's what Dad's tellin me to do."

The War According to V –

Little V,

Unofficially I was told I passed the exam for OCS. Maybe so. If I did, I dont know how I feel about it. I swing this way that way almost daily, AC, DC going where the wind blows. But it would get me out of here in mid March, but it also means I stay in the Army for another four years at least. I put in two already, enough to know I am totally disillusioned. Not with my country, but with the Army brass, the ones who send you into harms way. Pour on the steel they say. Pour on the steel. But the NVA is saying pour on the steel to. The little guys get caught in the middle of the big guys egos. I think Jumping Jim Gavin of the 82d Airborne had the right idea. Fight this as a defense war. Form rings round the cities. Create enclaves. And let NVA expend themselves trying to get inside you. This out in the jungle shit getting nobody nowhere but dead or wounded. Lots of dead and wounded in our company. So many I lost count. Do not go after them Gavin said, let them come after you. I ought to go to OCS and get my tired ass out fast. Stop off in Hawaii and get some rest. I can get a few weeks there on leave. But then again let fate take its course I tell myself. It going to anyway, you know what I mean? I let you know what happens. You know what? I wish our people were as polite and civilized as the Japs are. It was a great place to R & R. I learned to like warm saki and geishas scrubbing me raw in steamy baths. And I slept and ate and drank and bathed and got myself laid every day. It was grand. Such pleasures make you want to live a long time when life is fun. I definitely increase my chances of that if I become an officer. I should do it. Something tells me to go for it and dont look back. And you know what Top said to me? He said living, breathing, patriotic men like you are better than gold. He was drunk and leaning on me and I thought he might kiss me. I blushed to my heels. But on the other hand, it made me feel good to know he thought of me like that. I am patriotic lil Bro. I mean in my heart of hearts I am. I just think this war is a big mistake. My buddies might be dying for a mistake that is what I think. But what do I know? Got to trust the President that he is doing what must be done. Us over here are like that song dust in the wind. Who wrote that? You know?

V.

Rolling Thunder

I want to end the war to save the lives of those brave young men.
I want to end it in a way which will increase the chance that their younger brothers
and their sons will not have to fight in some future Vietnam someplace in the world.
(Nixon)

Once upon a time we were proud of our strength, our military power. Now we seem
ashamed of it. Once upon a time the rest of the world looked to us for leadership.
(Goldwater)

> *Parking strips . . .*
> *Pave the whole country . . .*
> *Home by Christmas.* **(Reagan)**

Virgil Francis Foggy

When Virgil enters the barn, Bonnie on his shoulder, Gramma Nez says, "There she is! I thought I lost her! I was that worried, you little ferlie. How did you find her, son?"

Virgil explains how she tapped on the window, how she was shivering.

"Ferrying souls were you?" says Gramma Nez. "Is that what you were doin, collecting souls and ferrying them in your mouth?"

He asks if a soul is small enough to fit in a bird's mouth.

"No bigger than a drop of dew," says Gramma Nez.

"A drop of dew," he echoes. He very much likes the idea of Bonnie ferrying dew-drop souls.

After chores, he takes her back to his room and leaves her there and takes the .22 from the rack and checks to see that a shell is in the chamber. He goes reluctantly to the killing yard, where he has tied Moses to the windmill. Pappy leaves the milkhouse and Virgil tells him what Regina said about getting Dick out of jail. The old man's face darkens. He shows a fist, all bonewhite knuckled now. Thin shoulders like plow shears. "Let'm rot."

"Mom can't see good enough, or she'd go," Virgil says. "She said it's no hurry, though."

"A man hits his wife like that, his daughter like that. With his fists like that, he's no." Pappy doesn't finish. He glancess up and says, "How can this man be my son?" He walks toward the machine shed muttering.

Virgil watches Moses chewing cud, waiting to be let loose, so he can pasture with the herd. Very little pasture is left now. Virgil will need to take hay out in the wagon to keep the cows fed through the day.
He hooks his fingers through the links in the fence and takes deep breaths. The loaded rifle leans beside him nose to the wire. Everything dies, it's nothing new, billions and billions. The infinite can never be filled, not even when billions become trillions. No number can fill it. Earth is basically a graveyard. Virgil too, eventually dust in the wind. His mother and Dick and Ginger and Vernon. Gramma Nez and Pappy soon.

"I don't feel right," he says to Moses. "My mind is . . . very tired. I'm always tired these days, Moses."

The eastern sky is full of long, thin clouds, their edges shot with

206

sun. The slow windmill scrapes and clangs and asks for oil *tick . . . slip . . . tick . . . slip.* Moses blinks. He has girly lashes, lazy eyes. His mouth moves in a figure eight.

Watcha doin, Virgil? he says.

"Waitin on Gramma Nez to bring the tub," you say. "Pappy's bringin the chainfall."

Ain't you gonna feed me? he asks *Lemme go I wanna go pasture.*

"You're always eatin. You can wait."

Where's your willow whip? You gonna spank me? You gonna ride me, you gonna snap my tail? Whatcha gonna do with that stick? Want me to flap my ears like wooden clappers? Want me to say yup, yup. Want to get the dog and you guys chase me? Where's that dog anyway? I ain't seen him for ages.

Moses looks toward the rabbit pens, the corncrib, the machine shed, the chicken coop, the barn. No dog never and never.

"He's hidin, he's waitin to ambush you," you say.

Moses shakes his head. *Yup, I figured,* he says. Sleepy-eyed and unconcerned he looks nowhere special. His mind drifts. He can't hold his mind on anything. He doesn't know if he got the answer to that stick. You pick it up, come through the gate and stop at the bottom of the windmill. You need more air, but your lungs won't expand. Every time you swallow, you feel a lump in your throat. There's a heart pain in the middle of your chest. Moses stares at the stick as it moves within an inch of his head.

"I'm here," says Gramma Nez. "Pappy's comin with the chainfall."

You pull the trigger and all four legs fold under him instantly. The sound like a bag of wheat hitting the dirt. Green shit blowing from his ass. Chin on the ground. Eyes open and already blurred.

Pappy stands on the chopping block and shackles the chainfall to the crossbar twelve feet up. Gramma Nez and you shift the steer to its side. You bind the hind ankles with rope. You hook the rope to the chainfall. As you spin the rattling chain, the steer is dragged around, pulled off the ground upside down. Pappy cuts the throat and the blood runs into the galvanized tub.

When the blood becomes a trickle, Pappy guts the steer, setting aside its liver, kidneys and heart. He takes out the tongue and washes it with the hose. You crack the brain-pan and remove the brain. The eatables are wrapped in waxed paper. You get the 180 and the manure spreader. Pitch the leftovers inside. You will take the spreader to the field kept aside for next year's corn. You will run the guts through the spreader's blades and feed morsels of Moses to the soil.

Gramma Nez and you working together take two hours to skin the steer. The hide will go to the tanning factory. The bones will be made into bonemeal. Pappy will *not* eat the eyes. Unlike lamb eyes, steer eyes have too much fiber. You bring the Massey Harris over and put the tines of the loader under the steer. You chainsaw the front hooves. You wrap the carcass in damp cheesecloth. Roll it into the loader bucket. At nine o'clock Knackerman Herman is there with his truck. He takes away what remains of Moses.

Pappy gets a bottle of Jack Daniels and three glasses. He pours shots and hands them around.

"To life," he says, raising his glass.

You click glasses. You drink to life. Whiskey makes you nauseous. You may shame yourself.

"You did a man's job today," says Pappy.

"Poor Moses," you say.

"It would be poor Moses if we shipped him and he had to wait in line smellin blood in a slaughterhouse and be part of that disgrace. They got a place in Kansas that kills twenty-six thousand a day. Think of that. That's what bovine hell is."

"The system," says Gramma Nez, her voice raspy but fierce. She lights a cigar and puffs smoke that looks thick as cotton. "Americans don't know what they're eatin."

"You gave him a good death, son," Pappy continues. "Any of us should be so lucky to have it over and not even know it happened."

You think of Dick in the cop car, how you could have shot him behind the ear if you had had a gun, and he would have never known it happened. A kindness to him, actually. Pappy heads back to the trailer. He will shower now and go to the Outpatient for what he calls *dilution*. Gramma Nez walks to the main house looking like an ambling chimney. She will have coffee with your mother, while you take the guts to the field and shred them and later plow them into the soil.

On your way with the spreader, you see Ginger disappearing into the woods. You know where she's going. You want to follow her and watch, but you need to get the sides on the wagons, box them for corn. Get the picker out and test it, make sure it works and that you haven't missed any grease cocks. You need to run the picker and oil the chains, crossbars and cleats, let some of the rust get polished off. That slow-leak on the B needs patching. Brakes on the Massey Harris need new shoes, the left one squeals. And the heat gauge is busted and needs replacing. All three tractors need their oil changed to winter weight. A hydraulic hose on the loader is leaking again. Need a new shear bar for the bailer, but that can wait. Its gearbox throws oil. That can wait too.

When you park the 180, you lay your head on the steering wheel, close your eyes and breathe slowly. The amount of work you have to do makes you feel exhausted already. Yesterday wore you out. You had been getting some strength back, getting to feel some of the old energy, until yesterday and Dick and all that stupid nonsense.

Look toward the woods. The rifle beside you. You could go where lovers go. There at a bend round a diving boulder runs the Crow. She'll be there, she and Peter Raven on the mattress beneath the giant fir tree. You could go too. Shoot them or just watch what they do. You could, Virgil, you could.

It is after lunch before Pappy and Dick get home. Pappy pulls the pickup into the garage next to the Cadillac, gets out and slams the door. Dick gets out and slams his door too. They look at each other. The old man turns away and heads for the Airstream. Angry-eyed he goes inside the trailer. Slams the door so hard the windows rattle.

Dick standing in the driveway mouths, "Fuck you too, old man."

Through the screen your mother says, "Wild Bill on the phone wants to talk to you."

"Oh? Well, I want to talk to him!"

You wait until Dick is inside. Creep to the door and listen to him cursing Wild Bill, threatening him, saying he'll kill him and Peter too if Peter ever touches Ginger again. There is a long pause. Then Dick tells Wild Bill to come on if he's man enough, if his balls are big enough. The bells ring when he bangs the receiver down.

You try to run. The hitch in your leg slows you, forces you to limp like a tired old elf. The garden is rusty with shades of brown and yellow, with fading swaths of green touched by the sun. Toe the place where you dug a hole, made a mudbath after Danny and Peter beat you in boxing. And you pissed in the mudbath and Danny got in and never knew. You're like a civet cat, you use piss for defense. You bend down, look for slugs to kill. It is too cold for slug sweat. The garden, like the trees and the cornfield, crackles dryly. At the other end of the garden, stands your father.

"Wild Bill's mad at Dick," you say, sniggering.

"I heard," he says.

"Maybe he'll kill him."

"That would be good."

"But if he doesn't, I will. The book says it's okay, it is written. It is a self-controlled deed, the book says. Did you read it? Did I read it to you? It said we've got to cut free from everything. No desire. Curb the heart. Because desire is the source of pain, it says."

His gaze roots through your eyes. "No killing in anger," he replies.

"Is revenge anger?"

"Justice. That's what you're after."

"Vernon and them, they kill for revenge mostly is what he says."

Both of you look toward the woods. Maybe the place to start is with her and him. The bleached straw in the field is their fault.

"Bale it," he says. "Good bedding for the cows."

"If it's still dry tomorrow I will. And then I'll get the corn in. Fill the crib with corn. Be ready for winter. I like autumn best. I like to reap what we sow, don't you? Autumn is best. I like it cool." You can see sky within his rising body. You start toward the woods, turn around and look for your father, who isn't there. You were going to say, you were going to tell him. Do you know what? Wild Bill wouldn't be more than a jelly sandwich for Dick. You think you'll wait till you see how that turns out, if it turns out at all. Dick sounded like he meant it, but maybe it was bluster. But then again, maybe Wild Bill will bring a gun and kill Dick for you.

Got to get that tire on the B patched. Definitely put the picker through its paces. What's happening in the woods? You know where she goes. She goes to the Crow, the chokecherries and the boulder and the fir. They go under the boughs. Where she spreads her legs wide as they'll go. Commits sin. You turn toward the woods. Turn to the tractor. Turn to the garden. Turn to the machine shed. The sun watches you waver as you dream of midnight standing beside his bed with a hatchet in your hand. Himself washed in moonlight. The covers are around his chest, one arm out, hand on belly. Breath soft, breath innocent. Hatchet rising, blade gleaming. You focus on the pulsing carotid thread of life.

Axe falls—*chop!*

That night Virgil and Bonnie staring out the window see Ginger sneaking away with a shotgun in hand. The hour is late. The barrel of the rifle reflects moonbeams. Virgil follows Ginger. Catches her at the point where the river bends west. She is making her way along the familiar path. She stops at the edge of the lovers' site. The half-moon hangs over the trees. Fog hangs over the water. The breeze is cold on Virgil's face. The stones in the middle of the clearing surround ashes of old fires. There are bent beer cans, Styrofoam cups, old bottles, an ancient cooler that everyone uses.

Watch her dip beneath the fir awning. In a second she is out and hurrying away. When her footsteps have faded, you go under the boughs and find the shotgun hidden beneath the mattress. What is she up to?

The War According to V –

Little V,

Just a short note to let you know I'm still alive but very near NOT. It was a close call. The closest call since I been here. Rice and I pulled through. Paine didn't. It started nine days ago when some of our guys got wiped out on LP duty. It was the second time it happened at that particular post but the first time for us. The Loootenant said we were going to root out the slanty eye bastards. We were undermanned but went anyway. We are supposed to have 185 men in our company, but we were down to less than half that number. Troops rotating out, going on leave, getting wounded, getting seriously dead, not being replaced. Where is the man power now? Gone to Canada? When is Nixon going to call up the Nation Guard and Reserves? That is what we are asking.

We went to get those bastards who killed our guys at the listening post. I was carrying the radio because our RTO was in the hospital with bleeding ulcers. The radio weighs 26 pounds, a thick heavy sucker to haul around along with all your other gear. My platoon searched an area about six clicks west of the old LP where we were sure the bastards were hiding. We thought we were being sneaky but they must have known what route we would take because they wired the place with mines and all went off at once. God knows how many blew shit out of us. I was amazing lucky Virge. The guy behind me had his head blown off. I MEAN OFF! I was hit hard and knocked to the ground and knocked the wind out of me, but the shrapnel tore into my radio instead of my back. If I hadn't been carrying it would have tore out my spine. I did get a hell of a lump as big as a peach on my left wing and some other cuts and bruises and my ears and nose was bleeding from concussion. Every body was wounded in one way or another, but half of us still alive and able to return fire and keep the dinks off. I saw Paine a few yards away thrashing around with no legs and I froze. It never happen to me before but I could not get my body to move. My mind was ordering me to go help Paine but my body said no and the body rules. There was firing and explosions and screams, shit flying everywhere and I was pressing my belly into the mud and trying to hide behind blades of grass my arms and legs quivering out of control and there is Paine screaming and I can see his legs on the grass cut off at the knees and it looked like you could go get them and maybe sew them back on. I must have laid there for only a minute or two but it seemed like hours. When my body came back to me I was still shaking but I had some control. So I crawled to him and tried to wrap his thighs in tourniquets. My hands were shaking so bad. I was so full of fear I could not think and I panicked and bullets flying and grenades throwing more shit into the air and guys screaming and cussing and trying to set up a perimeter and using dead bodies as barriers. It was chaos of the most chaotic kind. I wanted to crawl on all fours into the jungle and hide. Poor Paine was yelling and blood foaming mouth so I knew he must have taken one in the belly as well. His big terrified eyes rolling round and he told me he was in trouble this time and he said, Save me Vernie, don't let me die! I told him he had a million dollar wound and would be going home. He grinned at that, he wanted to believe me. Never forget it if I live to be a hundred and five. He bled to death Virge. Right there in my arms his life bled out and there was nothing I did right. I was telling him I was not going to let him die, but he went ahead and did it anyway. Reinforcements came. Only about ten minutes had passed if you can believe it. It was Rice with his squad who rescued us and together we drove the dinks back and called in Medevac for a dustoff. Rice put me on the chopper with Paine and I held his head in my lap and cried all the way. I could not quit no matter how hard I tried. When we touched down there was nothing left but to zip him in a body bag, him with his blood smeared Bible in the pocket over his heart. Lot of good it did him. Poor bastard, he loved life, he wanted so much to live and was so terrify of dying. But he joined up to test himself like a lot of guys do, what the hell are they thinking? He went out and did his job scared as he was and for me that is what courage is. What does he get for it? A Purple Heart and free burial back home. He was like a brother to me. You go out one morning and walk into an ambush and before noon your brother in arms is dead. The eternity of it is what kills me Virge. Paine is never, never, never coming back. We who buy it over here buy it for good. We are gone gooses and all you folks get of us is a flag-draped shell of what we were. And we get nothing. And let me ask you this, what the fuck is this foreign fucking country to us Virge? Can someone answer me that? Who really cares enough to die for it? Would those who sent us to this hellish place, those telling us we are fighting and dying for freedom, would they die for it themselves over here like this? NO FUCKING WAY!

They put me in the hospital for four days and give me painkillers and tranquilizers and wrapped up my wounds. Next to me was a guy who had no face. A piece of shrapnel had caught him at just the right angle and sliced his face clean off but he was alive somehow and could even grunt if you asked him a question. There were guys with no arms and no legs and blind as bats. There were guys paralyzed from the waist down and others paralyzed from the neck down. All those guys were stabalized and shipped out to our hospital in Germany. Face it their lives are fucked forever. There are over 150,000 wounded so far in this war I'm told. 150,000. I am all right now except that painkillers do nothing for the pain in your head, the ringing in your ears, the smell of guts and shit and gunpowder and this rotten world that does such things to human beings. Do something for that pain if you can. The Loootenant says I get a Bronze Star or a Silver Star and a Purple Heart. What the hell for? The last thing I care about right now is any of that bullshit that some of these dumb heroes come over here to die for. What a crock. Send your medals home to mommy and daddy so they can be proud. Anything dumber than that? There it is.

What is left of V.

Rolling Thunder

The effect of all the public, private, and secret negotiations which have been undertaken . . . since this administration came into office . . . can be summed up in one sentence: No progress. **(Nixon)**

This is the way civilizations begin to die. **(Nixon)**

Virgil Francis Foggy

High in a live oak Virgil Foggy rewinds what he sees on television. He hears the mines going off. Sees the soldiers cut down. Hears them shrieking, cussing, crying. Sees Vernon knocked forward, the radio strapped to his back saving him. Sees Melvin Paine's stumps and the bloody foam flowing from his mouth. Paine's bloody grin because he's going home. Paine's soul rising. He's out of it now, out of the boredom and terror, leaving behind a dead zone in Vernon's heart.

Far below Virgil sits Ginger Foggy waiting to ambush the brothers Raven who raped her. Through a V in the trees, he sees the Crow River sunning itself. Miles and miles past the trees, the river snakes south and skirts the city and the school and back yards and businesses, McDonald's and First Minnesota Bank and the Hubert Humphrey Theater and the pickle factory and the jail and the Court House and a dozen bars and—

Miles and miles downriver in southern Minnesota, near the Illinois border, the Crow joins the Mississippi. The Mississippi flows past people looking back from miles and miles all the way to the Gulf of Mexico. At eye level, Virgil sees tree canopies. Green islands. He sees a lazy God viewing everything. God yawns, closes his eyes.

Look at your watch. It is late for the Ravens. Are they coming?

Look at Ginger. Ginger sits on the rock at the edge of the clearing, the Crow on her right, the monstrous fir on her left, the live oak and Virgil on a limb behind her. Her eyes are fixed on the path down which the brothers will come to bang her again.

Or so they believe . . . is what she told you when she said rape, ambush, rape.

You are Mr. Nervous today. Though out of harm's way you are frightened. You've seen bloody deaths on TV countless times, lots of blood and body parts. How can Vernon stand the war? How did he get so brave? You are not brave. Your fear overwhelms you, paralyzes you. Paine didn't let his fear stop him. But your fear, Virgil Foggy, your fear stops you from killing your stepfather Dick. Mr. Dick Stormy Fists. Brave Paine could do it. Your brother Vernon could do it. Chicken Virgil could never do what Vernon has done. Nor what Ginger is doing. Waiting with mad heart and a twelve-gauge shotgun. You can see death as clear as the rippled leaves in front of your face. Those legs blown over there and the

216

rest of Paine in Vernon's arms. Paine screaming for Vernon to save him. Vernon's hands shaking so badly he can't get the tourniquets on. Vernon is a warrior with wounds inside. Everyone says he will come back with a wounded mind. And Dick is a stepfather who hates stepsons and breaks their eardrums with the palms of his hands. And Ginger is sitting by the Crow, waiting to kill the Ravens who fucked her yesterday. What does that make her? Ginger is a warrior too.

Virgil believed Ginger when she said she would get away with it. Probably she will. And maybe her example will point the way. Maybe the example showing him it can be done as easily here as over there, where God has changed the sixth commandment to *You shall kill*. Virgil had tried hard to do it. Dick was on his way to work and Virgil (had him in his sights) panned him as he walked from the house to the garage. Tracked him all the way to the road, his head between the V and the bead. Virgil had giggled and the rifle shook. It would have been easy. Pop him. Cap him like the wise guys say. He wouldn't have felt a thing. *I didn't know the gun was loaded*. Rifle went off. You were going out to bale straw. Taking the rifle along to shoot coyotes. When you set it on the tractor. *Boom!* Who's to say no? Who calls you a liar? Who can prove it?

Easy death, yes. Everywhere death waiting in the wings. Fall in the river. Jump from a tree. Cut your throat because you can't live with what you've done. Get your legs blown off in a war. Every car, every bus, every train a means of ending it. Jump from the Mississippi Bridge and drown. Your own belt or baling twine around your neck tied to a closet hook. Your mother's Valium. The rat poison in the tool shed. It would take a minute, maybe two. And like Paine you're out of the chaos, out of the mess.

Lean your face against the rough bark. Stare at the spot where the brother-ballers will meet death. The twelve-gauge with its choke will make a mess, all that buckshot concentrated. You want to see and touch and taste and smell what Vernon has seen and touched and tasted and smelled. Get all your senses into it and then you might know. Blood no tourniquet can stop. Oozy flesh. Last cough. Breath exhaled. The taste of gunpowder. Bits and pieces of Paine in the mud. Putrid blood and Moses' organs disked into the soil. So easily dead. So goddamn easy with sleepy God yawning in the wings. *Just another day,* he says.

The live oak has corrugations that make you think of a frozen brain. Its hardness reminds you of Dick's teeth cracking acorns. His teeth

217

can take the caps off of beer bottles. The bullet would have cracked his head like an acorn or a bottle. But Virgil's finger froze. Holy signs all over Dick, signs from Krisna saying *kill a man no sin kill a man no sin*: the arching eyebrows, the hair wedge on his forehead, boozy eyes, vampire canines, evil dimples like craters in his cheeks.

Yet he survives and Melvin Paine is dead in a stupid war. Legs blown off. What did that feel like? The bark corrugations dig into your ass now. You're up a tree, Virgil. But your pain is nothing compared to what happened to Vernon. What if the radio hadn't been strapped to his back? What if he had been in Paine's position? Gone to Krishna. Gone to whatever gods may be.

Then at last, Danny Raven shows up. Curious catlike slinking—he can't keep away. He's got to have her. He slinks tree to tree. Look at that bastard, his shirt red as communism. Winking red, the color of *stop!* Burns by the river, background for ferns. Autumn leaves and branches seared in shafts of sun. Bright Danny Raven. Horny teen flashing through the undergrowth, popping up at the mouth of the path. Burning for her, for Ginger, for her sweet, spankable ass. A flame of love is Danny.

"Hey, baby," he says, pimping cool, "whas up?" He has a ponytail flowingfrom the back of his head. Half of his face shines in a sunbeam. He is light, he is dark. Beaded moccasins. Danny is dressed for war.

"Where's your brother?" she says. "I told both of you to come. I want both your dicks."

"Ain't happenin, baby." He chuckles. "Peter's on his way to Frisco. Went off this mornin. Nobody knows but me." He looks behind him. "Guess it's just us," he says. His ponytail is thick, healthy, clean. Artificially streaked with lemon highlights. His forehead shines like he wiped it with Coppertone. His eyes are never still. His lips smile shyly. He keeps fisting his ponytail, jerking his head like he's reining in a horse.

"You got jeans on," he says. "I like girls in jeans. I've had my eye on you, Gin," eyes worshipping her, he laughs gently, repeats himself— he's had his eyes on her. "You dug me yesterday. You sure looked like you dug me yesterday. Your face said you dug me, Gin."

"My face told you that?"

Danny is thinking hard, trying not to blow it. He clears his throat. Puts passion in his voice. "Your eyes are twin pools of Venus reflecting midnight stars in a cloudless sky."

"They are?" Ginger giggles.

"You have very expressive eyes, Gin."

"I do?"

"Yeah, your eyes are windows of the soul clear as polished glass. They show that you've got a pure soul like angels have." He thinks a moment, says, "The soul is the windows of the eyes!"

"Did you get that from a book?"

"No, I made it up," says Danny. "Seeing you here like this, looking like some sexy Tinkerbell sitting on that rock. All you need is a pair of transparent wings and a green bikini. You see what I'm sayin? You inspire me, you make me poetic. I know how much you love poetry. I saw what you wrote Peter. He give it me. He don't deserve you. He was showin off that he's so hot a girl writes him poetry. All you need is Tink's wings and the picture is complete. Is that poetic? I want you to know I'm no dork dude, Ginger. You write Peter poetry, but he ain't worth your time. I bet he never wrote back, did he? Me, if you write *me* poetry, I'll write back. I'm sensitive, once you get to know me. There's no tellin what I can do if it's what you want. I'm artistic, just ask my mom."

"Uh-huh, you were sensitive yesterday," says Ginger.

"Well, Peter said you would like it with two guys, but I wasn't so sure, but he said he'd prove it. Peter's got this theory that guys are made by nature to rape girls, and girls are made to get raped, they secretly want it. We did what comes natural. That's what Peter said."

"Uh-huh. Even though I kept sayin no, I guess you done me a favor, ey?"

"Never crossed my mind that we were gangbangin or anything like that. I was makin looove. Could you tell the difference between me and him? Mine was looove."

"Danny's love wand," says Ginger. She looks at the fir where she's hidden the shotgun. She glances at the path behind her. She looks up at you as if she can see you hiding among the leaves. Her eyes ovals. Ice ovals.

Danny picks up stones and throws one in the water. He throws another and another, *plip, plip*. "I don't spose you can love me the way you love Peter yet. Takes time, I know, but since he ain't here and he's my brother and it's as close as you can get to home, you might as well give us a chance, Gin. And maybe in time, I'll make you forget him. He's a selfish sonofabitch. Just ask my mom. No one at home likes Peter much."

"I thought we were in love. I thought our love-making was . . . was love."

"Not him," Danny says. "Peter said you were ready anytime and that's what he liked about you. You're a fine piece of ass, he said. I bet most girls don't mind hearin that. A fine piece of ass. What you say? I'm lookin at you and dyin here."

"Why not, Danny?" she says. "You're here, I'm here. I do wish Peter came because I . . . I had a nice surprise for him. But maybe some other time."

Danny comes closer. Lump in pocket he fingers. "Yesterday I almost didn't join in, but when I saw you liked it so much, I said, If she likes it so much, it's okay, and besides you love her, you always loved her, so it's okay. Love has no borders. What you think of that, Gin?"

"But, Danny, I kept sayin no. I kept tryin to make you stop. You held me down."

Danny waves *no-way*. "Peter said you'd do that because girls are trained to struggle. He said you'd say no, but to watch your face and I would see the moment when no turns to yes. It happened like he said. He knows you that much, anyway. All a sudden your face went Jesus-God give it to me! You know you did, Gin."

"If you say so."

"You musta had fifty orgasms."

"Fifty?" Ginger chuckles.

"Don't get me wrong. I'm not blamin you or sayin you're bad because you like sex. I'm cool with that. I want girls to like it and go for it. I think they got a right to get it and not be condemned for . . . God knows you're what I always wanted, Gin. You're so pretty and—and the stars in your eyes are, umm, I don't know what—but like you've got the sweetest ass in the world. I see blue soul in your eyes, like your eyes have been polished with Windex. How's that?"

"Good for you, Danny. Very romantic," she says. "Romantic Windex."

"Oh boy, oh boy." He reaches out with trembling hands, touches her cheek. He puts his other trembling hand on her breast. "Jesus, so fine," he says. His voice is trembling, his ponytail trembling too. Everything about him giddy. "I wish we could record this and watch ourselves on television."

"Sure, yeah, a porn flick. We can do that next. We can set it up."

"It would be so *real*, baby. Over and over watchin ourselves, wouldn't that be too *real*."

Heaven's vantage: you observing this strange boy touching this strange girl's breasts. The boy turns away as if hiding blushes, like the Cowardly Lion in *Oz* turning away with *Shucks, folks, I'm speechless*. Danny kisses the fingers that touched her breasts. He stands sideways looking at the ground. "I said to Peter that you was it for me. Said I wanted you all to myself, and he said okay because he was going to San Francisco and live free in Golden Gate Park and march against the war. He can have that protest shit. I want you. It'll be me and you for the rest of our lives."

"For the rest of your life," she corrects.

He raises his arms toward the sky and shouts, "Thank you, Lord! Thank you, Jesus! Danny's in looove! Danny's in looove!"

Ginger's legs stiffen. Her feet stay solid on the ground as if she's put down roots. Danny keeps his arms spread out, keeps thanking God and repeating Danny's in love. Every inch of her *adored*. Ginger Divinity, angel on earth. Danny's in love!

He whirls and thrusts both hands in the air and says like a preacher, "Amen! You was diggin me most! Yes, Lord! Somethin in your eyes, the way you looked at me! And then . . . and then that kiss like I never had in my life. Whew, sucked my soul away, Gin. I was ready to die on the spot with a smile on my face. Your beauty would be the last thing I seen before I seen God."

"You talk an awful lot."

"God, I love you so much!" he says.

He comes to her, catches her by the shoulders and smashes his mouth on hers. Tries to suck her lips off. When he pulls back he is frowning and he tells her, "Do it like yesterday." He kisses her again. Takes her hand, leads it to his crotch.

She pushes him away. Gently. Palm up like a stop sign.

"What's wrong?"

"Let me think," she says. She puts her hand over her mouth. Wipes her lips.

"Does my breath stink?" he says.

"Smells like smoke," she says.

"You got any gum? What you want me to do, Gin? Name it, I'll do it."

"Anything?"

"Anything at all, you name it."

"Take your clothes off," says Ginger. "I want you naked. Caveman Danny runnin naked through the woods. Then grab me by the hair and pull me under the tree."

"Oh Jesus," he says. He wipes his hand over his brow. "Oh, wow, I never dreamed." He hesitates. Then unbuckles his belt. "You naked too, Gin, c'mon. Let's Adam and Eve!"

"You first, Danny. I want to admire your body. You got nice muscles."

"For a kid, they're pretty good, ain't they?" He throws his shirt aside and flexes his arms and chest. "All them bales of hay I've humped. I'm a hay-humping fool, Gin."

He kicks off his moccasins, drops his pants and skivvies at the same time. He has an erection. Its eye weaves as if surveying the area, checking things out.

"Dance for me, Danny," she coaxes.

He hulas his hips. His voice filling in where the music should be: "Boom ta-ta *boom*, ta-ta *boom*. You now! You now! Take it off, baby, take it all off!" He continues to dance and go boom ta-ta boom as his hands urge Ginger to strip.

You have never known this Danny Raven. He of the foul mouth and girls are good for nothing but fucking. You never knew he could look so foolish, happy and retarded at the same time. Never knew he could wax poetic and strip himself for love, his penis stretching from its hairy nest like a heron's beak—God, he's funny! You cram knuckles into your mouth to keep from howling. He's just too comical. How could anyone shoot such a loony tune?

Danny runs round the clearing. Then dashes up the path and you see glimpses of him winking here-there-here. Sounds of him tearing through the trees. He's hooting, he's whooping— "Danny's in looove! Danny's in looove!"

Ginger walks calmly to the fir, diving under, reappearing with the shotgun.

"Danny's in looove! Danny's in loooooooove!" The announcement ricochets.

She raises the shotgun and fires in his direction—*blam! blam!* The recoil knocks Ginger on her butt. Birds burst in all directions. The report of the rifle stuns you. You had not remembered how loud the twelve-gauge could be. She rubs her shoulder and says, "Ow! Shit! Son of a bitch!" She

222

is sitting in a gray haze of ashen gunpowder. As a minute ticks by, the two of you stare in the direction of Danny's last cry: Danny's-in-loooove. The birds quit making evasive maneuvers. They settle back, look at each other. *What the hell was that? Why are humans so noisy?*

Your eyes search for Danny, but there is nothing to see. Ginger gets up and dusts her bottom. She breaks the shotgun and pulls out the casings, walks to the river and throws them in. She stares into the water gurgling round the boulder in the middle, stepping stones leading to it. This is where you dive when you go swimming in the Crow. You wouldn't be surprised to see her strip and jump in. Clean off the death of Danny. But instead she turns, goes back to the rock and sits down. She brushes something from her eyes, jerks her head once, twice: *no, no.* Seconds later, she stands up and leaves, shotgun in hand, back to the path, back through the woods, back to the farm.

Climbing down, you trot in the direction Danny took. There is no blood, no body. Danny has vanished. Blown into the water, perhaps? Has the river carried Danny in love far away? Or is he still running? The echo of the shotgun urging him on? Run, Danny, run!

You chuckle and say, "He's out there naked. Geez."

When you get back to the clearing, you gather his clothes, search the pockets, take his cigarettes and matches, a twenty dollar bill, a pair of dice, a school picture of Ginger and a folded piece of paper held together by a paperclip. You find a baby toad with a laid-back attitude in one of the pockets. Your finger runs over the toad's head. You turn it over, pet its belly and put it to sleep. Set it on the rock where it can get some sun. You stuff the shirt and skivvies and moccasins in the crotch of the pants and button it and toss the bundle in the river. The bundle rides with the current a moment, looking half-a-boy before it rolls. Before it sinks. Sitting on the rock next to the toad, you picture Danny being silly. Penis slapping his hairy belly as he dances and flaps his arms, dancing for his lady-love. His mouth squawking voodoo—Danny's in love!

"Are you still in love, Danny?" you ask.

You unfold the paper and read a poem written by Ginger for Peter.

> *The day is here again, my love,*
> *And time is standing still.*
> *Just a few short hours, never counted,*

But deeply felt, until I am with you.
Minute by minute – passing by –
A lifetime, my love.

   It's Wednesday, such joy, such pain,
As we walk together slowly in the rain,
Side by side, not touching yet, not speaking,
Saying nothing – yet saying so much!
Together, alone, we look at the river –
We plan – we dream – we love.

   Oh yes, how we love – our bodies
So close, a feeling of wanting to crawl
Inside each other forever,
Never to part, always one, always one.
So pure, so simple, so painful is love.

   No worries, just time passing.
The day so beautiful (gray and cloudy)
The sky so blue (it's raining)
The sun so hot (cold and wet)
The birds coming to us to eat the seeds
From my hand – so trusting (so wet)
So innocent (so cold) – so beautiful (so hungry).

   How wonderful the day has been
   It's Wednesday again and I'm alone with HIM.

The War According to V –

Little V,

Be back in my company tomorrow stiff and sore but otherwise okay. Be glad to see Rice again. He saved my life. I owe him. He should get the Silver Star if anyone does, not me, although the LT and Cap and Top wrote me up for it. Look Bro I do not know how much of what happened Mom should know. I leave that to you to tell her or not. A dangerous world Virge, but I have a feeling to survive this war. If I was meant to die don't you think I would have died with Paine and the others? I feel like I have a charmed life. How else could I have survived? Not much longer for counting the days till I re-up and go on leave. Rice and I are doing Hawaii first. I am going to live it up. Then onto Ft. Benning, Georgia and OCS. I will coast as an officer and call it quits when my hitch ends and I can get my ass back to Foggy Farm our piece of eath, the peaceful cows. Sounds like paradise Bro. And you and Ginger and I will run things and maybe just hunker down for the rest of our lives and simplify. Cows and the land. You and me and the machinery and the cows and the fields of hay and tall corn and the weather driving us crazy like it always does. Paradise.

Big V.

Rolling Thunder

I want to end it so that the energy and dedication of you, our young people, now too often directed into bitter hatred against those responsible for the war, can be turned to the great challenges of peace, a better life for all Americans, a better life for all people on this earth.

Let us be united for peace.

Let us also be united against defeat.

Let us understand: [The enemy] cannot defeat or humiliate the United States. Only Americans can do that. **(Nixon)**

We haven't been hard-nosed enough . . . **(Reagan)**

I"m not going to be the first American president to lose a war. **(Nixon)**

Virgil Francis Foggy

Open the door. See her once more that day: phone in hand, giving directions to someone and saying, "Hurry, he's dy*ing*!" She looks at Virgil and shouts, "Where you been? Did you know your father's been arrested?"

"My father?"

"Wild Bill is dead! He's been arrested and Pappy's had a heart attack. An ambulance is coming!"

Wild Bill dead? Dick Foggy arrested? And Pappy's had a heart attack? In the space between Danny and Ginger and the shotgun and a laidback toad and a love poem are a few more equivalents of . . . of *what's going on?*

Wobbly-kneed he goes to the table and plops in a chair. "I was in the woods," he tells her. "Hunting."

"Where's your rifle?"

"It's." He looks at his hands. "I left it on the tractor. I was going to hook the picker and go test a load." He runs a hand over the Holstein butter dish, petting its porcelain ear with his thumb, and he thinks of Moses not feeling a thing the moment the bullet entered his head. Did Wild Bill die that fast?

"Wild Bill's dead?"

"Someone smashed his skull and threw him in the river. They think Dick did it. The two of them got in a fight at Lando Lakes. So Dick told Wild Bill to meet him at the bridge and that's the last anyone seen him alive. They found him floatin past the pickle factory. Now Salty's taken Dick in for questioning. And it gave Pappy a heart attack when he heard the news. This family is cursed." She is squeaky-voiced, halfway crying, pulling her hair. "What's happened to us? What have we done? Why is God pickin on us? It's always some*thing*!"

The phone is still in her hand. It starts beeping. She looks at it as if it's gone crazy. She hangs up and says, "He's in the barn."

He follows her to the barn. Ginger and Gramma Nez are there, Gramma Nez kneeling beside Pappy, caressing his cheek with her thumb. His eyes are puzzled. What am I doing down here? It's a mistake. The fellow next farm over, Old Johansen with the cancer. Hims who you're after.

Ginger stands on the other side of Pappy, hand over mouth,

blubbering.

Looking over the Dutch door, Minna and Big Mama wanting to know what's up. Cows behind them in the yard crowding forward asking questions. *Whowhatwherewhy?*

They want to see a human die.

"Poor Pappy!" weeps Ginger.

"Stop that," hisses Gramma Nez. "You'll scare him." She looks over her shoulder at Regina. "Ambulance?"

"On the way."

Gramma Nez takes Pappy's hand, the big veins rolling under her thumb. "It'll be okay, lamb," she tells him. "Don't worry. They're comin, lamb. They're comin."

"Sweetheart, don't you know me?" Regina asks, bending close to Pappy.

"Hush," says Gramma Nez. "Course he knows you."

Pappy's eyes roll. When his mouth moves, a foreign language comes out, "Awwa, awwa." He is sweating and his skin is more yellow now.

"Yes, lamb," says Gramma Nez.

Regina turns away, palms squeezing her temples. "Dear God, please!" she says. "I can't take no more!"

"Regina!" snaps Gramma Nez. "There'll be time for that shit later. Right now I need your strength."

"You got it, Ma. I'm sorry." She puts on a brave face. "I'm here for you."

"Where's the baby?"

"The baby?"

"Pearl Bell, your daughter."

"In Virgil's room. I put her in there, so I could take a nap." She looks at Virgil. "Virgil, go get your sister. Bring her here so Pappy can see her."

"I want to stay with Pappy."

"Go get her, I said."

Virgil whispers in her ear, "But what if he dies while I'm gone?"

"He's not gonna die. Do as you're told."

Virgil squeezes Pappy's knee. "Right back, Pappy."

As soon as he opens the front door, he hears what sounds like a cat yowling. He runs upstairs, finds Pearl Bell in the cradle in his room, her mouth wide, face flushed, fists flailing. Bonnie cowers on top of the closet door, her head jerking.

"Shush, shush," Virgil soothes. "Bubber here. Bubber got you, woo-woo." He dips a hand under her head and sits her up. He can smell a mess in her diaper. "Did Woo-woo do ickypoo?" Her head bobs and she smiles. He puts her on the bed, unwraps her blanket, unpins her diaper. She throws her legs and arms around, like riding a pony, urging it on. The stench makes Virgil gag.

"Pee-you, Woo-woo!" he says. "Woo-woo stinks!"

She's happy to stink.

Virgil wants to get his mother or Ginger, but he knows that would be folly. His mother would send him back with a slap and an order to change Pearl Bell's diaper right this minute.

So he holds his breath and jumps in and does what needs doing. He wipes her butt with the folded dirty diaper and trots to the bathroom with it, rinses it in the toilet and drops it in the diaper pail. Gets a clean diaper and talcum and a washcloth and washes her, powders her, cinches her in.

When he's done she doesn't look any worse for wear. Her eyes flirt with him.

"Okay, you are kinda cute," he says. He is about to wrap her in the blanket, but it smells like pee, so he uses his robe instead.

By the time he gets outside, the ambulance is there. He runs with the baby, the sleeves of his robe flapping up and down as if waving. He gets to the door just as they carry Pappy through on a stretcher. The same door through which unproductive cows go to Packerland. The men carry the old man across the killing yard and out of the gate. Virgil walks beside the stretcher. Pappy stares at him oyster-eyed.

"Look, it's Pearl Bell, Pappy," Virgil tells him, opening the robe and hoisting her face beside his own. "See how she can hold her head up now? She can see you, Pappy. She's lookin at you, Pappy."

The eyes stay on Virgil all the way to the ambulance. The eyes try to find him as the stretcher slips inside. Virgil tries to get in too. But only Gramma Nez is allowed to ride.

Virgil takes the baby back to the house. Their mother is sitting in the recliner sobbing into her hands. Ginger is hugging herself and saying, "Poor Pappy, poor Pappy." Her eyes are dry now, but she looks devastated. It's been a hard day for Ginger all around.

"It's over so soon," cries Regina. "Your life goes by and it's almost like it never happened. Pappy's not that old is he? What's sixty-four?"

"He's sixty-six," corrects Ginger.

"Sixty-six? I don't want that old man to die. He's been like a father to me." She blubbers into a growing wad of tissues.

"They think it's a stroke, not a heart attack," says Ginger. "Kidney disease can cause strokes."

"I know, I know," says Regina. "But a stroke can be just as bad. He might live and have to go into a nursing home if we can't take care of him. Strokes can make you incontinent. He'd be like a baby messin the bed. Can you imagine that? Can you see us changin diapers on our Pappy?"

"Gramma Nez won't let that bother her," says Ginger. Her tone is cold now.

Virgil's mother looks at him. "My poor kid," she says. "Runnin this farm is gonna be more and more up to you. It's too much to have on your little shoulders. I wish Vernon was here."

"My shoulders ain't so little."

"Maybe we should sell it. If Pappy goes in a nursing home, we'll have to. We can't afford a nursing home. We can't afford anything."

"Over my dead body," Virgil says. As soon as he says it, he realizes how Regina Perpetua-like it sounds, the cliché, the bravado when she's in her cups, booze making her tough. Virgil has no idea if he can really do everything alone—milk the cows twice a day and all the chores and get the corn in and keep the machinery running and take care of the crises that are sure to come—something always breaking down, some cow getting sick, some unborn calf getting stuck. "Maybe if just Ginger could help with the milkin till Gramma Nez comes back. If she can just wash the milkers, that would be a big help. I can handle the rest."

"I wish Vernon was here."

"So do I."

"That stupid army. I want him home."

"I can help," says Ginger. "I know how to wash the milkers." Ginger dazzles him with an affectionate smile. And Virgil thinks, *No wonder Danny wants her that bad.* But he doesn't want to think about Danny. No doubt he snuck home somehow.

"*Hold still, my coo, my honey,*" Ginger sings.

"Yes, that's it," Virgil tells her. "You have to do that for each one. Then they won't miss Gramma Nez and they'll let down their milk. Cows are creatures of habit, just like people. They need routine. Rub their tails at the base of their spines. It calms them. They feel secure."

His mother blows her nose and tries to smile, her eyes blinking back tears. "Speaking of milk, honey," she says. "Let's warm a bottle and feed that baby." They all pause to look at Pearl Bell. "Look at her in your arms," says Regina. "Isn't she happy, isn't she being good? I think she likes the sound of your voice, honey. Her eyes rivet on you every time you talk."

They go into the kitchen and Ginger warms a bottle and gives it to Virgil and, for the first time, he feeds the baby. She sucks and stares, taking him in like he's better than ice cream.

"Lusty dame," he tells her. "Look at her suck."

"You like her, sweetheart?"

"She's all right."

"She likes you."

"She'll do."

Her body fits the crook in his elbow. She pushes the bottle away and he inhales her milky breath. He thinks of the poem in his pocket, the line where Ginger and Peter side by side, not speaking: *Saying nothing – yet saying so much.*

"Boy, I'm gettin sappy," he says. "This kid is addictive."

"Babies will do that to you," says his mother. Her eyes continue to drizzle tears. But she smiles bravely. She keeps blowing her nose and glancing at the phone on the wall. The three of them sit in silence while the baby drains the bottle.

When the phone rings, Virgil is sure it's Gramma Nez telling them Pappy is dead.

Regina lifts the receiver. She listens. She says, "Uh-huh" several times. Then with a satisfied voice she cuts in—"Dick, shut up a minute. Do you know your father's had a heart attack and is in ICU?"

There is a pause. Her mouth puckers, gets small, smaller, pinching hard. "It's too late for tears," she tells him coldly. "When he heard what you did, he dropped like a rock. You'll have to live with that, Dick Foggy if you can."

Then she says, "Oh, I've just got to quit this cryin, my sinuses are swollen, it's givin me such a sore throat!"

The voice on the other side gets harsh.

"Well, don't yell at me!" says she. "Do you see what your behavior can do to others? Do you see, Dick? I hope you see! If this doesn't open your eyes, what will? So selfish. No one in the world but Dick Foggy."

Then - "Yes, uh-huh, yes, Lawyer Menton. I will, I'll get him. I'll call him, but I'd be lyin to you if I said you're not in trouble. You are the only one who knows if you killed him or not. I can't believe you would do such a thing to us, but who knows? When you go berserk . . . Look, what you did to me and your daughter. Do you think you can treat people like that forever and they're still gonna love you? What you've done, you've done to yourself. You made your own bed, Dick Foggy."

She bows her head and listens and wipes tears from an endless reservoir and says, "Dick, Dick, Dick."

When she hangs up she says, "He swears on his brother's grave that he didn't kill Bill Raven. But nobody believes him. He says he went to the bridge, then cooled off and thought better of it and went driving around and ended up at Minnehaha Creek feeding the birds. He was drivin home when they arrested him. Trouble is, the marks of Bill's fists are on his face and his knuckles are bruised and lots of customers saw them fightin in the bar. Your father's in real trouble this time. He's not going to be able to smooch his way out of this one, Salty or no Salty. He should have gone back to work. Then he'd have an alibi. That's what happens when you get boozed up and get in a fight."

"Wild Turkey," Virgil adds vindictively.

"Was he drinkin boilermakers?"

"I dunno, but most the time when I'm with him he does."

"Well, there you are. Just askin for it. It's hard to feel sorry for him. A man like that. God, what a day . . . what a day."

"Are we gonna eat?" Virgil asks.

"Eat? Who can eat at a time like this?"

Virgil feels no guilt about Dick, about being relieved and happy and hoping that he did kill Wild Bill and they can prove it and put him away. But that conversation in the bathroom at Lando Lakes between Ed and Carl has him wondering. Wild Bill maybe fucking Ed's wife and Carl saying he would kill the man that did it and no jury would convict him. Virgil wonders if he knows something. Does he know the killer of Wild Bill Raven?

"Talk to Ed who has lunch at Lando Lakes" is something Virgil could say to the cops. And describe him: "Medium tall, grayish sideburns, brown hair combed like Hitler's, dark rings under his eyes, big nostrils, nose like an Arab. He wore a gray suit and maroon tie. And talk to Carl, his friend."

"I got Dick's life in my hands," Virgil whispers to the baby. She jerks his finger, tries to gum a bite. Little cannibal.

Little V,

      The heat! It bakes you. It can literaly boil your brains. One guy marching in the sun all day carrying a M-60 collapsed. He had convulsions. His blood burst through his nose and he went down like a sack of turds. We poured water on him and fanned him and such, but it was wasted energy. He was a goner. We couldn't get his temperature down in time. He was a big guy tough as nails, but big or small, one way or another this place gets you. If it isn't the dinks its the weather, it's either trying to drown you or bake you like a loaf of bread. Add to that the insects, ants big as June bugs! Mosquitoes big as hummingbirds, poisonous snakes, creepy crawly things everywhere, the swamps, the jungle saunas, the mountains where you freeze at night, the hills where the trees are nothing but burnt sticks and miles of dead vegitation and it is no wonder we all go around half-crazed and psycho and ready to kill any thing that moves. No sane man could live in these conditions Virge. I think these peasants with their inscrutable eyes are as burned out as we are. We are all trying to fight off madness. We are trying to fight off the enviroment and the savagery that comes with it trying to take over. Some guys are beyond barbaric. They cut off ears and hang them round their necks until the ears stink. One asshole cut off a dinks dick. I better never get that low. If I do I want someone to shoot me. The dinks don't respect the dead either. They show no mercy to the living or the dead. I seen some mutilations that they've done a tiger couldnt match. Not just done to our guys, but they do it to each other for God knows what reasons and to villagers who help us. We go back later and find them skinned alive or impaled or their mouths staked open and fire ants crawling inside or. Well, you get the picture little Bro. If there is anything on earth designed to bring out the worst in you is war. Think of this, we are the only species who make war who kill and maim each other and call it <u>heroic.</u> We will wipe out whole villages, whole cities, whole countries, kill them all and give ourselves medals for it. Every race will kill every other race without a second thought and then for the slightest insult they will kill their own. I mean, what the fuck? Who came up with this system? What are the rules? We make them up as we go. Soldiers are insane Virgil, every fucking one of us. Everybody knows it but so what? We go to that hellhole in our hearts and out comes the psychopath.

It happens every time we get in a firefight, the guys go nuts and God help any dink captured alive. I wonder if I am going to come back worth anything you can call human. I doubt it.

V.

Rolling Thunder

The enemy in the past two weeks has stepped up his guerrilla actions.

I concluded that increased enemy activity . . . endangered the lives of Americans.

To protect our men . . . and to guarantee the continued success of our withdrawal . . . I have concluded that the time has come for action. **(Nixon)**

. . . home by Christmas. **(Reagan)**

A majority of the American people, a majority of you listening to me, are for withdrawal of our forces. The action I have taken tonight is indispensable for the continuing success of the continuing success of that withdrawal program.

A majority of the American people want to end this war rather than to have it drag on interminably. The action I have taken tonight will serve that purpose. **(Nixon)**

Virgil Francis Foggy

October crisp. The Allis-Chalmers 180 roaring. Bonnie riding his shoulder, the picker and wagon bouncing and rattling behind them as they head to the cornfield. At the first row, he lines up the equipment, engages the PTO, eases it in. Noisily, the picker comes alive. Its sprockets and links squawking like deranged geese. He puts the tractor in gear and moves along the first row, keeping the guides and cutting-bar in line with the brittle stalks. Assembly-line steel fingers gather the stalks and fold them into the separator. The naked yellow cobs jiggle as they rise along the picker's slap bars before plunging over into the wagon he's towing. The stripped stalks and long leaves fall through the whirling blades spreading confetti behind the picker.

He completes one row and part of another before the picker breaks down. He has to throw the corn off the conveyor into the wagon and sweep the mangled stems and chopped leaves and husks aside. There is a sheared link in the conveyor chain. He gets the wrench and loosens the tension, pries out the broken link and replaces it with one of the extras in the picker's toolbox. Then he tightens the tension bolts until his hand slides snuggly under the crossbars.

It is already 9:20. It takes him until 10:30 to harvest one load.

He unhooks the wagon, pulls the picker away, and walks over the stubble back to the yard to get the B. He drives it out and picks up the loaded wagon. The elevator is already positioned over the hole in the top of the corncrib. Backing the wagon to the conveyor belt, he plugs in the electric motor and gets everything clanging, a sound in the air like untuned bells. He runs the driveshaft extension from the PTO to the wagon rollers. Puts it in gear and the rollers turn and the corn starts falling from the wagon, rising up the elevator, falling into the yellow pile at the bottom of the crib.

11:15.

"Only one load," he tells Bonnie. "Four hours already. I'm never gonna get done."

Lousy picker we got, she says. *Hunk of junk.*

"It's old," he answers. But then he remembers he is older than the picker. Older than the tractor too. Maybe the wagon is older, but he is old nonetheless.

Your joints feel feverish. How old are you? At least fifty. There is a continuous old man's lightness in your head. If you look left or right quickly, you get dizzy. You wish you could climb in the loft and take a nap. You need to think of some way to hitch the wagon and the picker and everything else more quickly to the tractor. The hardest part is simply hooking things up by yourself. The careful backing into position, trying to get the holes in line, so you can drop the pin through the hitch in the wagon and the tractor's hitch at the same time. Everything is a matter of inches. Off just a quarter of an inch and the pin won't go. The air is cold, but you are sweaty inside your clothes. Sometimes you have chills. Perhaps you are getting sick. Or maybe you are already sick. Your brother says all soldiers are sick: *Soldiers are insane Virgil, every fucking one of us.*

Bonnie flies away. Lands in the killing yard among some chickens. *Cousins.*

She starts imitating them scratching the dirt. The black feral cat sees her, slinks like an evil rumor from under the milkhouse. The chickens alert Bonnie. She leaps into the air as cat-claws slap her tail. Bonnie darts straight to you and tucks herself inside your pocket.

- *That was a close one*, she says.

"You stay put," you tell her. "Stay away from cats!" You point a finger at the ferlie. "You lucky I left my rifle upstairs!"

Aw, screw you! the cat yells back. He blows feathers from his mouth, licks his chops, slaps a chicken aside and saunters with bow-legged arrogance back under the milkhouse. You climb on the tractor, drive back to the field. The woods blaze like patchwork rainbows beneath the cold sun. The rains will come and knock down the leaves and the snow will fall and cover the leaves and bury the fields and the leaves will rot. The river will turn to ice so hard you can drive a tractor over it. The short days will take forever to get longer and it will feel like spring may never come. And you will be fifteen going on fifty. Unless the arrow gets you. You will shoot it yourself this time. You are prepared and won't need Dick or anyone to do it. If it comes down and kills you, then you are done for this round and maybe you'll come back as a blackbird. If it doesn't kill you, you will live at least another year. Or so Dick says.

"Dick might go to prison," you tell Bonnie.

Just don't fess up, she says. *You got the power now, Daddy. You got that bastard's life in your hands.*

And you say, "He better not fuck with me no more. He fucks with me, I'll never tell who really killed Wild Bill and they'll execute him for it."

No matter what, I wouldn't tell, says Bonnie, jerking her head no, no.

"Maybe I won't. We'll see. I ain't in no hurry. Just got to get crop in and beat the snow. It's what's important today. But, I almost shot him. Did I tell you?"

If you could have seen it as a sacrifice, a ritual—Abraham and Isaac in reverse—if you could have done that, your Uncle Dick would have died and your life would be different. You might still be haunted, but in a different way, haunted like a soldier instead of a coward. "Do this and you cannot commit a sin. Duty well done fulfills desire," says the *Bhagavad-Gita.* You were ready to believe anything. And you did believe. You just couldn't perform.

The War According to V –

Little V,

      We came out of the bush and went to town on three day pass. The whole thing a blur of bars called Velvet Voice and Blue Note and Flaming Flamingo and you think you were in some southern town like Fayetteville, N. C. You buy me drink soldier boy, gimme cigrette, gimme what in that pocket, what you name? You buy me drink, yes? Bar to bar we go, all of them filled with women with calculating eyes. Lots of smoke and booze perfume and me and Rice sitting at this table or some other table and talking the rankest bullshit about how our buddies have died as heroes. Killed by people who are cookie cutter copies of the girls and ARVNs in every bar. Who is the enemy? What do they think? What do they believe? What god or gods do they pray to? Someone warned us to know our enemy. Well, we don't know him. Or her. This yellow-skinned, black-haired girl standing naked in front of me her naked belly eye-level as she takes my hand and brushes the back of it over her bush. Is she the enemy? I want to go to Saigon and see Candy but there's no way. I do not miss her like I used to tho. Last time I seen her she felt distant. I think she is fucking around. Hell I know it. But this girl in this bar with her bush so silky, the hairs so black and long, I woke up in her arms in the back room and don't remember doing her the night before. So she says to give her 2000 P and she will take care of me one more time bang bang. 15 bucks so what the hell. Even though I feel pretty lousy when its over thinking how fast everything is and you come and you go and this cookie cutter whore goes to another table and takes another grunt by the hand and rubs the back of his fingers over her bush.

V.

Rolling Thunder

Confronted with this situation, we have three options.
First, we can do nothing.
Well, the ultimate result of that course of action is clear.
Unless we indulge in wishful thinking. (**Nixon**)

The hypocrisy of America, the stupidity and lies creeping out of Washington and the need for compassion and understanding between people if life is to survive on this planet.
(**President Thieu**)

You have to electrify people with bold decisions.
Let's go blow the hell out of them! (**Nixon**)

Virgil Francis Foggy

When Dick gets home he hugs Virgil and says, *"My boy,* good to see you." He is teeth, dimples, bristly beard and stinky feet. The look on his face is friendly-father typecasting. He says he admires Virgil and wants him to know it. He puts him in a headlock, knuckle burns his hair and calls him a farming fool. And says, "I don't think even Vernon could do what you done."

The family sits around the table eating roast beef, mashed potatoes and gravy and peas. Lots of buttered bread. Lots of milk. Dick wolfs his food, talking with his cheeks bulging, telling them that he's turned over a new leaf. He's going to take on overtime at work and he's going to let Regina redecorate the house, starting with the living room—new carpeting and paint and get rid of those guns in the cabinet, put them away and get a new TV with a bigger screen. Close in the bookshelves with etched glass. That'll look nice.

"We're going to make this place smart and cozy, a sanctuary from the rotten world, which I seen all I want to see of," he says. His hand caresses her forearm. Regina looks in love again. *What a fine man,* her eyes are saying. Her lips look like wet pimentos. Her eyes have healed, faded to faint shadows of hurt when she smiles.

"Absence makes the heart grow fonder," he tells her.

He slides out of his chair. Goes down on his knees between her legs, his head in her lap, his hands embracing her hips. She strokes his hair, a melting look, a smile. "I want to paint it robin-egg blue," she says. "And a Rembrandt print on the wall, a *Mona Lisa* if we can."

"Anything my baby wants," he says. "I'm here to make her happy. Lovin her is my mission."

"You missed me," she says. Tongue flicking.

Virgil leaves the table. He makes one more round of the barn. Checks on the cows. Gives them more hay. Then, exhausted, he goes to bed.

In the dark he listens to Dick's voice rising through the vents, promising. He's going to treat her like gold. He's not going to drink anymore, just a couple now and then to celebrate Christmas and New Year's and important occasions like that. But not every night anymore, for sure. Overindulgence leads to depression. It distorts your thinking. Jail

242

was good for him. It dried him out. She's the center of his world now. Oh, baby, baby, I missed you so. Ice clicks in their glasses. They drink and kiss and she says, "I missed you, Dickie."

"Oh, baby, I missed *you*."

"We do have good times, don't we? I mean, it isn't all turmoil."

"We've always known how to have a good time. We've packed up some great memories for our old age."

"Why do you suppose we drink so much, honey?"

"It relaxes us. It's how we relax."

"We just won't drink so much anymore, okay?"

"Whatever you say, baby. I'll stop right this minute, just let me finish this one. No use wastin good whiskey."

"I'll tell you why we drink, honey."

"You tell me, baby."

"Because we're scared."

"I ain't scared."

"Scared of losing each other. Scared of gettin old like Pappy and Inez. Scared of comin to the end and realizing we never lived. That's what I'm sayin. I'm sayin everyone who drinks is scared. Life is scary. God help us, life is scary."

"I'll protect you. Just keep on lovin me and everything turn out fine."

"Oh, Dick, I do."

"And you forgive me?"

"I'll always forgive you."

"You're too good. You keep forgivin me and I'm no damn good. What more could a man ask?"

Their glasses click.

"If I could stop lovin you, I would have stopped by now."

"I'm unbearable. You're too good, baby."

"We have to stick it out. Otherwise our whole life together is a pointless lie."

Click.

"You're too much, baby."

"Love has to overcome. If it doesn't, it isn't love."

"I'm feelin it, baby. One more, we better quit."

"Come here. Come to Mama."

Asks Bonnie - *What's it all about Daddy?*

"They're horny," you say.

Jim appears. He hangs around like ground fog, a haze. Listening to sex through the wall. Then he says, "See what I mean? He stole my life. He's in there fucking my wife. He's in there committing incest." Jim drifts to the gun rack. Fingers the triggers. "He's going to get away with killing Wild Bill, you know. The evidence is thin. It's circumstantial. Hard to know if a jury would convict him. Maybe he's going to be nice now. Maybe what happened scared the devil out of him. Maybe he *has* turned over a new life, who knows? If he has, maybe we don't have to kill him." Bonnie flutters her wings, stretches her neck like Aaron ready to crow. Jim's smile is lucent. "This has become a house of hope," he says. "He stares out the window, his face blending with the glass. "Funny how one man's mood can have so much power over others," he says. His face shines like crystal. His eyes are the color of stainless steel. He is black and white TV.

Indian summer continues and Virgil beats the snow by three days. Three days and too many breakdowns, but he finally gets the crib filled and the machinery winterized and put away in the shed. He even gets time to work the field with the disk, slicing stalks until only papery fragments litter the soil.

Gramma Nez comes home and helps with the chores. With her in the barn singing, everything feels routine. Except Pappy is still in the hospital. He has some speech back, though. And the doctor says he is going to live awhile longer it seems. Says Pappy is a tough old bird. His right side will be weak but not completely paralyzed. If he goes to physical therapy and does what they tell him, he'll get a lot of strength back. There is nothing they can do about his eye. It is permanently blind.

"All things considered," says Gramma Nez, "it wasn't a bad apoplexy to have. Praise God and Vishnu, may he keep dreaming the world. We could be burying Pappy now—that's the thing." Her eyes are moist. She lights a White Owl and blows furious smoke and says, "We must somehow put ourselves in harmony with the universe. We must make it easier on ourselves to die. We're gettin old, you know. Readiness is everything."

Two weeks later, Virgil takes a load of corn to the mill and stops at the hospital on the way back. He goes up to room 203. Pappy is praying, one hand extended toward the ceiling, one side of his mouth moving, whispering to God. His blind eye doesn't see Virgil enter. He sniffs the

244

air and turns his head. Crosses himself and says in a slurry tone, "Vir-gil." Hooks his finger at him."

"Hi yeh, Pappy, how yeh doing?"

Pappy's left eyelid winks. His scrawny neck is roped in tendons. His wrists are all bone and thin skin.

"So, when you bustin out?"

Pappy shakes his head.

"Don't worry about a thing, Pappy. I got everything under control. Cows are milkin heavy. Minna's showin now." Virgil pooches his belly out and strokes it.

"Take . . . care . . . Minna . . . besss . . . coo."

"I will, Pappy, don't worry. She'll do a hundred pounds a day, you'll see."

Pappy's smile is crooked. His broken eye is slightly lower than the other, a cock-eyed look. The corner of his mouth drools.

"Does your eye hurt, Pappy?"

"Nuh."

"Is it really blind?" Virgil waves his hand in front of the blind eye.

"I . . . got . . . nuther," says Pappy. One side of his mouth arches in a smile.

"Better than none, huh, Pappy?"

"S'okay." His good eye glitters. "Thish way . . . I . . . on-ly see . . . half of . . . Gram-ma."

Virgil laughs. "The stroke made you funny, Pappy."

"Stuff . . . they put . . . in me. Woooo." He fiddles the fingers of his good hand.

Sitting on the bed, Virgil pats his grandfather's knee and tells him about going to the mill and how the pickup is loaded with sacks of feed testing at ten percent protein, which isn't as good as he would like, but not bad, especially considering how high the protein in the hay is. He talks about picking the corn and how he got the whole crop in. He tells Pappy that the old John Deere picker has had it. That clanging clattery old bucket of bolts is held together with chewing gum and baling wire and prayers. A New Holland picker in *Hoard's Dairyman* that's the one they need. A picker like that and they would have the harvest done in two days. He tells Pappy about disking the fields and winterizing the machinery and how the leaves have turned color already. The hardwoods look like they're wearing party hats. Pappy has got to get out of the hospital, so he can see the woods

245

before rain and snow knock the leaves down.

Pappy runs his thumb over his grandson's hand. Touches the scars on his arm. Points to the scars with trembling fingers. Raises one shaking eyebrow.

"They're a little tight," Virgil tells him. "They look worse than they feel. I get stronger every day, Pappy. Look at my muscle." Pappy lifts a crooked grin. Clear spit runs under his chin, pooling in the divot of his throat.

"Rock hard," continues Virgil. "Next year this time, I won't know those dog bites. You and me will do the corn together next year. Maybe we can get that New Holland. Minna's comin fresh in March or early April. And then Friendly not far behind and Big Mama and Buttercup. They'll shoot our production way up, Pappy. I got a feelin we'll set a record next year. And you know what?"

"Hmm?"

"I can artificially inseminate cows good as you now. I got Julie to settle first time round and I think Clare has took too and I'm watchin the heifers close. I give them two doses of semen, one each day, back to back, up the left fallopian tube and then up the right. It's worked good so far. I got the touch."

Virgil keeps talking and squeezing Pappy's hand and telling him whatever comes to mind. It is awhile before he hears the old man's heavy breathing and realizes he's sleeping.

The War According to V –

Little V,

Well, almost bought the farm again kid. Lots of happenings. The gods of war have suddenly noticed me and they say Hey, we need to fuck wit him. We aint fucked wit him enough.Yup yup I got wound number 2, a graze along the right side of my head that opened a seam. I felt it sizzling through my hair, but I didn't equate it with a bullet at first. It felt like white heat, like a swipe of lightning. It took forty stitches to close. Jesus it give me a monster headache like I never had in my life and I was temporarily blind in my right eye. The whole side of my face swelled like a balloon. I looked a mess. I still have a black eye. Not swollen any but it looks splashed with tar. So I have two Purple Hearts now, think of that. I do not want a third. Third time is the charm they say. You asked about my getting the Bronze or Silver Star. I still dont know if I get either. In any case my papers may have gotten lost in the bureacracy. Top says I should have had those medals by now.

More later. Saddling up, me and my black eye. Got to go. Go where? There.

V.

Rolling Thunder

Our . . . choice is to go to the heart of the trouble.

That means cleaning out occupied territories and sanctuaries which serve as bases for attacks.

Faced with these options, this is the decision I have made.

Attacks are being launched this week to clean out major enemy sanctuaries on the border.

      . . .

This is not an invasion [of Cambodia]

Our purpose is not to occupy the areas.

Once enemy forces are driven out of these sanctuaries . . . we will withdraw.

Any government that chooses to use these actions as a pretext for harming relations with the United States will be doing so on its own responsibility and on its own initiative, and we will draw the appropriate conclusions. **(Nixon)**

We're in the quicksand up to our necks,
and I just don't know what the hell to do about it.
(Sen. Richard Russell)

It really gives me the shakes! **(Sen. Adali Stevenson)**

Part Three: Peace without Conquest

Virgil Francis Foggy

Her hair is freshly dyed black with blondish streaks. She looks cheap. Trampish. What has she done to herself and why? She's going out. She's read *A Farewell to Arms* and she's going to Mary Kowit's Book Club again. Virgil glances at Dick drinking beer as fast as he can. He is the old Dick again, the unturned leaf. His eyes follow her prancing stilettos, her ass and thighs still too wide in a pair of tight black jeans. She and Dick have been discussing the club members coming around so often, sitting in the house day after day eating and drinking and influencing her. Their ideas changing her in who knows what ways?

And she says, "We read, we talk. I'm learnin a lot."

"Learnin what? I bet I know what."

"I've read stuff you never heard of. "

"I want you here. You're not a teenager. You're not Ginger going off gab-assing with the girls."

"Don't ruin this, Dick. Leave me alone. Let me have at least one thing in life to look forward to."

"Am I standin in your way? Have I put my foot down?"

"Every single time we have to go through this."

"To hell with it. Do what you want. I don't care. Really, I don't care."

There is a superior twist in her mouth. "Tell me somethin, Dick, what did Shakespeare name his son?"

"What? Who gives a flyin fuck. What a stupid—"

"He named his son Hamnet. Now see, I never knew that, but now I understand why he wrote a play called *Hamlet*. Also, did you know that Hamlet means weak hams? Did you know that the story comes from actual history about a prince named Amleth who lived in the ninth century? Did you know that, Dick? It's history!"

He sneers, gets up. Gets another.

While she says, "See that's the difference between you and me. I don't ever want to stop learning. You don't care if your brain atrophies."

"Stuff," says Dick. "Weak hams. Jesus, what a bunch of—"

"All this arguing ain't good for Pappy," says Gramma Nez.

Pappy sits like a shrunken gnome letting her cut up his meat. His cheeks are paper pale now. He doesn't drool, but his hands won't keep still. His ears look too big for his head. His head is sinking into the hole between his bony shoulders.

"Relax, lamb. Say omm," she says.

"Omm."

"You can hardly wait for the trial," says Dick. "Can't wait to see me in prison."

"You're paranoid," says Regina.

"Omm."

"I got a right to be paranoid. Don't anyone understand the position I'm in? They're tryin to frame me. They want to put me away for the rest of my life! Hey, I'm talkin here!"

"Calm down, Dick. Henry says there's no way. He says there's no evidence."

"What you smilin about?" Dick says to Virgil.

"Nuttin."

"Omm."

"Why is Menton going to your book club?" Dick asks Regina.

"He already belonged before I joined. He's a smart man. A *lawyer*. You need him."

"Like I need horns on my head. I seen looks he gives you. "

"Puleeze," says she. "He's sixty years old!"

"He don't look that old."

"Clean living," says Regina spitefully.

"I don't see why this thing has to be at night," says Dick. "I don't like you going out at night."

"Because Mary Kowit works all day," she says. "Everyone works days. The only time they can come is at night. It wouldn't hurt *you* to come. You might learn somethin good. Instead of sittin here picklin your brain with booze."

Dick snorts. He looks at Gramma Nez. "You hear that, Mama? She just called me stupid. Get me another beer, Gin."

"No she didn't. You're in the mood for a fight tonight, buster. I wish you would think of Pappy. He don't need upsets. We'll go home and your wife can go to her club and you can fight with yourself all you want."

She mutters something else Virgil can't quite hear.

"What a supportive family!" Dick is saying, his tone whiny. "No one cares what I feel. No one cares what happens to me."

"Did you kill Wild Bill?"

"I'll kick the ass of anyone who says I did!"

"That's not an answer."

"My own family won't even believe me. Not even my ma. Why don't you do the holograms and see."

"Hexagrams."

"Whatever. They suppose to tell you the truth, right?"

"Say yes or no, Dick."

"No! I didn't kill that bastard. I should have, but I didn't."

"Then stop worryin about it. God and truth are on your side."

"God ain't on *my* side."

"Omm."

"Pappy, will you shut up!"

"Don't you dare talk to him like that!"

Dick holds his head and says, "I'm sorry, all right? I'm sorry, Pappy."

Pappy is falling asleep. Eyes closed. One side of his mouth hanging.

"And you're not goin to that goddamn club," says Dick to Regina.

"Like hell I'm not," she fires back.

He raises his fist.

"You hit her, I'll kill you!" Virgil shouts. He throws his chair back and stands up.

Dick stares at him amazed. Then grins.

Virgil runs from the table.

"Now look what you done, you asshole!" says Regina.

The War According to V –

Little V,

Jesus am tired of how terror comes sudden as a bat out of hell. We had set up camp, put up our tents and posted guard and everything was quiet. Or as they say in the movies, To Quiet. It was nearly dark and I was sitting outside with my squad and we were all like nervous cats in a room full of rocking chairs, feeling on edge and trying to see through the bush because you know they there. You get an instinct about these things after you been here awhile. We were very alert. I had put my rifle down to light a cigarette when I heard the pings of grenade handles and I took off. I had split so fast I left my rifle leaning against my tent and it's a lucky thing I moved quick as I did because one of the grenades went off right where I had been standing and blew my tent to tatters. I am running through elephant grass and I have my K Bar in hand and I drop in the grass like I been killed. But I keep my knife ready, though God knows what that will do against a rifle. Bullets and shit flying everywhere and I thought for sure charlie was going to show up and put a few rounds in me. The fight lasted maybe two or three minutes but it seemed like three hours. Then they pulled out and we were left with three dead and four wounded. Choppers came and take us out.

I wrote you about the bullet that grazed my head? Sure I did, but my memory has been a little unreliable lately so maybe not. Maybe it is the wound or maybe the pressure of war, but I get lot of headaches and my memory quits on me. The other day I could not remember the combination for my locker. I have been using that combination for over a year but I could not remember it to save my life. Until next morning when I woke the numbers came back to me. Where were those numbers hiding? Not a clue. One day I could not remember Paines first name. My dead buddys first name, for Christ sake. It took an hour to recall it but finally it popped into my mind. Lots of memory problems I am having but I wont bore them on you little Bro. I remember after my head wound started to heal feeling the stitches drying up pulling tight and thinking a 64th of an inch more was the difference between life and death, you see what I say? And if I had stood a fraction of a second longer in front of my tent I would have been blown to pieces. If the elephant grass hadn't been there to hide me I would have been mowed down like a dog. Who or what decides these things? Not just here but where you are to. Everywhere an inch here an inch there. I never thought about it so much before, but I sure think about it now. So close. Close to being Nothing. Nothing is everywhere coming for me. What is Vernon Joseph Foggy? Answer. NOTHING. All those killed over here, what are they now? NOTHING. Not even bones in some cases. Blown to atoms. I guess it dont matter because when you are gone you are gone. Thinking where is God and does the soul get blown to molecules to? Feels like it must evaporate. I sound like an athiest. So exhausted I got to sleep little Bro. I wish I was home.

Me and Rice were just now talking about when we leave for Hawaii for a little vacation in March and how great it is going to be. Then it will be on to Georgia and Fort Benning and more training. I will come out of it a 2d LT with a gold bar on my collar. Next time you see me a gold bar is what I will be wearing. How about that? Can you believe it? Funny world when a boot like me can get to be an officer leader of men in the United States Army. I guess it is a great country we live in Virge. I guess so. After training I will be transferred to Fort Ord, Calif, where I will spend six months working with recruits. That gives me a year before they can rotate me back to Nam if they want to, but if my luck holds, the war will be over by then and I can go to college at University of Minnesota on their dime after I prove myself by making 1st LT. Boy will I be glad to be out of this shit.

I got to tell you something that happened the other day. It is as bizarre as war itself Virge. We were on patrol and we had dug in on a hill to watch for traffic below and a very strange thing happens. I go off by myself down the other side of the hill to recon. A couple hundred yards away I find this great little fishing spot about the size of the one where the Crow branches off and feeds Chippawa Cove. A stream flowing in from one side and running out the other and keeping the water moving slow. Not clear water, it was brown but no scum. And Virge there is this guy sitting on the grass and he is fishing. Honest, he is fishing Virge. A bamboo fishing pole in his hands and his sandals off and pants rolled and he is soaking his feet in the water and smoking a pipe. I can see his rifle beside him. It was some ancient thing with a bolt action, must have been from WWI. But him, the kid on the bank, guess who he made me think of. Yep I thought of you but I also thought Huck Finn. It was one of the few books I really liked in school. This little dink he was Huck Finn in a distant territory just kicking back enjoying lifes little pleasures. I snuck up within twenty yards and put him in my sights. I had him dead if I wanted. And there he is all relax and content with his lot and no idea. You have to shoot these guys because if not they may come back and shoot you or your buddies. The rules. We been told to kill, kill, kill til they run out of bodies. Its a war of body counts not territory. You win if you got more bodies to count at the end of the day. I knew little Huckleberry had to go. And I meant to kill him. But then by God the little fellow caught a fish. His bamboo pole was bending over and he was running down the bank trying to keep the fish from breaking his line. The fish jumped out of the water, all sleek big as a full-grown muskie. I was watching this kid struggle and I got so caught up when the fish jumped I forgot who he was and who I was and I stood up and yelled, Don't let him get slack, snap your line! Work him! Work him! Tire him out, he will come if you work him! And little Huck look at me with eyes popping and he drop the pole and zip into the bush. He disappeared like magic, like he was a mirage of my mind. I thought about tracking him, but I didnt really feel up to it and Jesus you know I do not really want to kill him. No bloodlust in me that day. I threw his rifle into the pond but left his sandals in case he came back for them, and I went up the hill. I met Rice on the way. He said he thought he heard me yelling. I said it was those noisy macaques. I didn't want to get into it. Only you get to know what happen. Funny moment in the middle of a war. There it is.

Big V.

Rolling Thunder

*A majority of the American people want to keep the casualties of our brave men . . .
at an absolute minimum.*

The action I take is essential if we are to accomplish that goal.

*We take this action not for the purpose of expanding the war . . . but for the
purpose of ending the war.* (**Nixon**)

The more I think about it
the more I think
we're . . . into
another Korea.
(**Johnson**)

What's the rest of the world going to think?
Most we need to do is pray with it for a little while. (**Bundy**)

255

Virgil Francis Foggy

Under the porch light you read the first letter and see yourself going upstairs and getting a rifle, coming back down and blasting Dick at the dinner table. Vernon might not kill Huckleberry Finn, but you would kill Dick Foggy in a heartbeat. You tuck the letter back in your pocket and go through the yard and climb the windmill. You sit on top in the cold dry air. Above is a crescent moon. A slender cloud crawls beneath the moon. Below on the earth are islands of snow everywhere except the road and the driveway.

"Better quit treatin her like that," you say. Your father hangs upside down from the windmill rudder. He looks like whipped sugar. And he says, "He's never gonna change, Virgil. I could have told you that. There's no way to deal with a man like Dick Foggy except get rid of him once and for all. Make it look like an accident. It's easy enough to do. Invite him to go hunting. He loves hunting. What's more natural than the two of you going hunting? You think you see a deer moving behind some trees and you fire and it turns out to be your Uncle Dick. Who's to say you killed him on purpose? Nobody. You're a kid. No one will suspect you. Not like they suspect him of murdering Wild Bill. We know Ed did it, but everyone else believes Dick did it. I am telling you they will be relieved he's dead. They'll close the case and things will get back to normal. Won't be all this arguing in the newspapers and around town, people taking sides. You'll be doing the town a favor. And you'll be saving your family from more grief. Save your family from grief, son."

Now your father's hair is spun glass. You reach out to touch his hair. A spear of it breaks in your hand. "I'll do it, Dad. I mean it this time. The hunting accident idea is good. If I can work it that way I will." Your hand breaks off another spear of hair. The rudder shifts and he falls like a transparent arrow.

Dick's birthday is coming up and the day for arrow roulette to see if God wants him to live another year. Dick has said you can shoot the arrow. You know how to make an arrow hit a spot now. How to make it come straight down where you want it. Through Dick's clavicle into his heart It seems a good plan. Ginger will back you up on how Dick initiated the game, how the two of you had been doing it in secret every birthday. People would see God's justice in it. Dick killed by his own folly.

Out the door wobble Pappy and Gramma Nez heading toward the trailer. They stop and gaze at the sickle moon. How many more will they live to see? How many more will you? Or Vernon? They go inside the Airstream. Lights come on, the television flickers. Pappy will sleep in the recliner. Gramma Nez will cover him with the quilt. She will sit beside him watching some show or reading *The Book of Changes*. Which she says she likes better than the Bible or the *Bhagava Gita* now.

The house door bangs and your mother storms out, heading for the car. Dick follows her. He says, "Yhah! You think I'm stupid!"

"You are!"

"I know what you're up to. You're puttin the horns on me."

"Think what you want, I don't care."

"Look at the way you're dressed. Mary dressed like that. I know what ass-pants mean. Who you dressin for? Sure as hell not me. Is his prick as big as his nose?"

"You're so disgust*ing!*"

"It's Menton isn't it! You think I'm gonna trust you? I know you, baby. I know what you're capable of. You go down easy, baby. You're natural position is on your knees."

"You too, baby!"

"Is it Danny Raven? You like young stuff, huh?"

She stops, turns, looks astonished. "What? What?"

"I saw that little prick hangin round. I saw him." He points toward the Crow. "He was lookin at the house. He was expectin someone to come meet him. I asked him what's he doing there and he ran like a rabbit. But I know what he's doin there. I know what he's after."

"You are one sick fuck, Dick Foggy. Do you know how old Danny is?"

"Age don't mean nuthin and you know it! Henry Menton is sixty, but I can tell you got the hots for him. I know when you got the hots. If anyone knows, I know."

"*Sick! Sick!*"

"And you don't care how old they are. Look how you dressed. Where'd you get that vest? Where you get those spikes? I got your number."

She laughs scornfully. "Danny Raven, my God, I've heard it all now. If he was there waitin for someone, do you think it would be me? My teenage lover? I'm going to sneak out and meet him at the river. We're going to ball in the snow. Don't you think he might be there because of

Ginger? I think she's more his wet-dream than me."

"That Peter Raven boy, that sonofabitch, he—"

"One brother, now the other. Why not? They look a lot alike."

"I'll kill her. I told her I'd kill her."

"Dick, you can't keep her from it. You can't be everywhere at the same time. You can't prevent this sort of thing. It's useless. If anyone should know that, it's you. I mean, look at us. Who could have stopped us? Tell me. And yet it was a far worse thing than what she might be doin. God forgive us."

"You really think she's—"

"I said *might*, not *is*. I really don't see . . . well, but who the hell knows? Who knows anybody?"

"Bastard, I'll—"

"Love finds a way."

"You don't love me no more, I can tell."

You cover your ears and don't hear the rest. You watch their hands flail, their heads jerk. A minute later, she turns and her heels peck, peck, peck to the car. Dick stands in the driveway. You uncover your ears and hear him saying—"Now wait a minute!" His tone whimpering, his tactics changing. "Look, baby, I'm sorry. Honey, come on. You know I love you."

The engine starts. Regina backs up. Turns. Starts forward.

"Listen to me! Let's forgive each other, okay? You are forgiven! I forgive you, do you forgive me?"

She guns past him.

"You are forgiven!" he shouts.

She turns onto the main road, guns the engine.

"I'll never forgive you, you bitch!"

You have to somehow get up to your room without Dick seeing you. Climbing down from the windmill, you do a walk-through in the barn and give the cows more hay.

Then you sneak to the kitchen window and peek inside. Ginger is washing the dishes. Dick sits at the table with a bottle of beer. His eyes are narrow, his slippery mouth moving. "I think I'm losin my mind," he says.

"What?"

"What's a man to do with his demons, daughter?"

"Are you askin me?"

"Are you my daughter?"

"You're not the only one who has demons."

"Mine are vicious. Mine rippin me apart."

"So, what else is new?"

"No one knows me. No one cares to know me. You all hate me. I spose I deserve it. I'm pretty hard to live with, I spose."

Ginger glances over her shoulder at him.

"You know, Ginger, you're the only one on earth I ever really loved."

"Yeah, sure."

"It's true. The only one on earth. How can you be so cold?"

"What you expect?"

"You never loved me? Can you say that?"

"Get real."

"You have no idea what it's like to be me. I feel everyone's hatred, yours, Virgil's, even my mother's. If your mother can't love you, who can? No one's ever loved me truly. That's why I'm so bad. Yeah, and maybe I hate me too. I've done terrible things. I've killed men in war."

"Did you kill Bill Raven?"

"No! How many times I got to say it?"

"You're not the only one who hates himself. I don't like me either. I wish I was a better person."

"I bet I die a bitter, unloved old fool. Do you love me? You don't love me."

Ginger doesn't answer.

"See what I mean?"

"I see you feelin sorry for yourself. I do that a lot too. But I remind myself that life could be worse. Always could be worse."

"You sound like my mother. Look, I got reasons to feel sorry for myself. Jesus, my world is fallin apart, daughter. Can't you see I'm sufferin? Can't you see how depressed I am? Maybe I should kill myself. Do you all a favor. Christ, I'm so depressed, so lonely, so . . . so isolated. I should have died in the war. I wish I had died in the war. It's a good way to go. Everyone honors you if you die in the war." He puts his head in his hands and says, "What am I gonna do?" His voice goes up in pitch. "I think maybe I'm havin a nervous breakdown. Too much shit in my head. I get no support from you guys. Fuck, look at my hands. My hands are shaking."

"You told us you were gonna quit drinkin. How long did that promise last? About two days. Your hands shake because you drink so

259

much, Dad."

"I tried to stop. It was drivin me crazy. If I can't drink I can't live. I'm sorry, but it's just that simple. Daughter, you don't know what it's like to be a rotten bastard like me and be married to someone like her. Everyone thinks she's a saint puttin up with me. I look twice as bad by comparison. But I could tell you some things. Boy, could I ever blow her cover."

"I know about her, I know she's not so good," says Ginger.

"You bet your ass." He pauses, drinks, rubs his face awhile. Says, "But on the whole, the best thing ever happened to me."

"Is that Dad talkin, or is that Bud Weiser? One minute you're callin her a bitch and the next she's your angel. Which is it, Papa?"

"A fine woman, Ginger. Had to put up with a lot from—"

"Who hasn't! Am I a fine woman too? I've got a reputation at school for—"

"Shut up."

"You tell me what makes her any better than me, Daddy."

"Ginger, you better shut your mouth before it overloads your ass!"

"Where did I learn my trade? Who taught me, huh?"

Dick stares at her with alarm. "Now look," he says, "we agreed never to bring that up no more. It was a phase, it was madness. You were just as fucked up as me, Gin. You the one crawled into my bed first."

"I was lonely and scared. Mom was gone. I needed assurance, I needed comfort from my Daddy."

"I gave you comfort."

Ginger puts the last dish in the rack. "I guess you did. Yeah, it seemed such a good thing. We were gonna run off and get married in Mexico, hah!"

"There's all kinds of love, you know. If it's love it can't be wrong."

She pulls the plug. She wipes her hands on a towel and leaves the kitchen.

Dick throws the empty bottle at the wall. Dents it.

He grabs another beer, sits, puts his hand over his forehead, shakes his head and says, "I'm dyin." He stares at the doorway as if Hope might walk in and rescue him.

"I need distraction," he says.

You climb the frozen birch and let yourself in through the

window. Quietly, you undress for bed, not bothering to wash up or brush your teeth, very afraid to make any noise that will call Dick's attention.

Faint music filters from Ginger's room.

This magic moment . . . with your lips so close to . . .

You take out Vernon's second letter. Bonnie hops up beside you. She pecks the paper. Your father sits crosslegged on the footboard.

Says, "Foggys, you know, are born for war."

The War According to V –

Little V,

What happening? Sounds like shit going down. Regina wrote but didnt say anything about Uncle Dick latest mess. Am I surprised? Asshole, he did it, he is GUILTY. He going to get his now. About time. Reginas letter was full of Pappys stroke and I guess that was pretty scarey. It made me think that I might not see him again and it hurt to think that. He always sort of scared me when we were little because he was so big and gruff. But as I got older I think to myself he never laid a hand on us, just talked tough to keep us in line. Dick said he use to beat him and our Dad with the belt when they were bad. Dick said he got beat ten times more than our Dad got beat. That is one thing I believe, no problem. Someone out to beat him now. I would if I was there. I would kick his ass off the farm except stupid Regina would go with him. Sometimes I think she has a brain the size of a flea. Stupid women go for the bed games and pay lipservice to what is inside a manheart. Did she think he was going to be Dad all over again? I think she did. She was lonely for Dad and she married Dick as a stand in. That is my theory. Also I think Uncle Dick is more excited to women than Dad was. Dad was a plow horse. Up at five, work all day, get to bed by ten. Dick don't live that way, boozing and whoreing and our mother gets some kind of kick out of that, like she is living a more excited life because he is wild and that makes her wild. I feel like I have chewed this fat before. I know I have. Thoughts loop round my mind, round and round, especially thoughts of those two and their perpetual war.

Speaking of whoreing. The whores around here are not like the ones you find in that movie From Here to Eternity. Those whores had heart. These whores are the kind that will put razorblades in a sheath up their snatch and cut Cock Robin off at the pass. That actually happen to a jarhead in Danang. Didn't cut it off but he dam near bleed to death. And she got away. She is out there doing her bit for the cause. I have swore off whores. I thought they were cute and fun at first, tiny dolls like Candy Chieu Hoi, like fucking a twelve year old who has got her bush and titties prematurely, but after six months of them I am sick to death of it. They are greedy pigs who go for your pockets and will pick you clean as a whistle in two seconds. I got so drunk the other night I passed out and they rolled me. Took every dime and my K Bar to. I suppose I am lucky they didn't cut my balls off with it. These fucking pigs Virge, they look warm and sexy but they are not for real. Something in them hates us totally. You can feel it. You come, you come, G.I. they say, trying to hurry you so they can get out and fuck another sucker. When a woman tells you to come, you cant and half the time all Cock Robin wants to do is go soft and hide his head in shame. That's probably part to do with being Catholic and the guilt. But I dam sure do not believe in that crap no more, nor God neither none of it. What a fucking joke. Take a look at a human body spattered over an acre of land like fertilizer and swarmed with flies and maggots and you learn pretty quick what God thinks of us, how much he cares for us. The thing you do not want to do is bang these bitchs if you are sober. If you are not drunk enough you smell the garlic coming through their pores. They leak garlic and sometimes it can make you want to puke. No perfume can hide it, in fact the combination of the two odors make things worse. What am I talking like this? Sounds like I am turned off women. I guess so. I am turned off women and war and sex and death. A few months over here will burn anyone out. My heart is about the size of Reginas one-track mind. Enough of this shit. Shut up Vernon!

A few more weeks Bro and on to Hawaii, and then to Ft. Benning. Can you see your big Bro as an officer? Neither can I. But Rice and Top say I will be great. They say I got the carisma to be an officer. Men listen to me. Do not ask me why. They do what I order. So maybe I found what I was born for. Top keeps saying I am born for it. Who knows? But he does not know what goes on deep in my brain at night like this when it is quiet and I can really think terrible thoughts and see all the horrid things I done and I know I will never get over them and there are nights I really hate me and everyone here and our stupid government and God most of all. Yeh, but on the other hand if they make me an officer I will stay awhile. Am I a contradiction or what? Well who the hell aint? Bad as the service is, it is one thing I can do without batting an eye. The guys in my squad are glad I am the squad leader. They think I am lucky and that I know what I am doing. I dare not tell them the truth. I could not keep Melvin Paine alive. He haunts me. He comes in the night and stands over there and looks at me like I really let him down. Poor Paine, I miss him a lot. If I had not frozen and clumsy and my hands shaking with those tourniquets he might be alive today. Who knows? Fuck it man. At least it is over for him. There it is.

V.

Rolling Thunder

I would rather be a one-term president and do what I believe . . . than be a two-term president at the cost of seeing . . . this nation accept . . . defeat . . . **(Nixon)**

The main object is
To kill as few people as possible . . .
Americans against terror . . .
[But] I'm not sure we're the country
to do this job. **(Bundy)**

We will not be defeated.
We will not grow tired.
We will not withdraw.
(Johnson)

Virgil Francis Foggy

"Do you hear Dick downstairs carrying on?" says your father. "Three bags of mean."

Dick is playing all the parts in his own play. Bottle after bottle has been thumping into the wall. Very drunk. You know what that means.

Your father is the no-color of ice fog, a cobweb with vague borders.

Ginger's radio is too loud.

"Calling attention to herself," says your father.

"Maybe she wants to," you say.

Another bottle thumps the wall, bangs as it hits the floor, rolls.

"There will be dents all over that wall. Wait till your mother sees them."

"Be quiet, I need to think," you say.

"Too late," says your father. "Here climbs monkey-shine."

You hear Dick's shoes pounding up the stairs. He stumbles. Pauses. He is growling deep in his throat.

Get your gun.

But you are unable to move. Your eyes shift to the gun rack, but your feet refuse to go there.

"No Foggys was ever cowards in the wars. This is your war, Virgil."

"I don't care, I don't care." you whisper.

Dick reaches the top step, hesitates, turns the squealing knob and enters Ginger's room. The radio gets louder.

The door closes.

Then.

"No!"

You sit up, your throat so tight you can't swallow. Again you hear her saying, "No!" The baby starts crying. Dick's voice pleads, "Baby, oh baby, I'm so lonely, baby, I'm dyin. Why can't it be just you and me again? Let's go to Mexico. Let's do it this time." Then he shouts, "Shut up! Shut up, Pearl Bell!"

The baby shrieks. Or is it Ginger shrieking?

You get out of bed. Your hand selects the .22. Injects a shell. You force your unwilling legs to move down the hallway to Ginger's room.

Mouth dry, you're panting.

Throw open her door. See Dick purple-faced bellowing at the shrieking kid—"I said shut up, goddamn you!" He is shaking Ginger's torn panties at the baby. He grabs the crib violently. The baby sounds like a diva hitting high-C. Naked butt hanging out beneath her shirt Ginger is pulling on Dick and yelling, "Leave her alone! Leave her alone, you bully!"

"Leave her alone!" you command. The deepness of your voice surprises you and gives you courage. "I'll blow your brains out!" you say. Thinking—Jesus, I sound like John Wayne.

Dick pulls his face out of the crib. He looks at you and says, "What? Whaaaat?" He straightens to full height, six feet of real man, his neck veins swelling. His eyes devouring you. With each breath he grows larger, filling up the room, blocking out Ginger and Pearl Bell, drowning the room in the sound of his own harsh huffing and puffing. Your upper lip and legs trembling. But the rifle is steady. It is aimed at Dick's heart.

"Put your clothes on and get the baby," you tell Ginger.

Swiftly she does as she's told.

"If you're really serious about shootin a man," says Dick, his rubbery mouth smiing, "don't use a twenty-two, son. It's hard to kill a man with a twenty-two. Don't you know anything? Get your thirty-thirty. Use a lead tip bullet with the hollow head. Go ahead, I'll wait, go get it."

You are shaking your head. You are thinking, *Now what do I do?*

"You're such a stupid little bastard," says Dick. "Standin there dumb as a ten penny nail waitin for the hammer, thinking you have it in you. You're not your brother, boy. He's a man. You're . . . you're nuthin, a punk-ass pussy, skinny little gimping shit-britches. Look at your legs. You're so scared you're gonna pee your pants. Are you gonna cry too? Let me see you cry like you always do. Gimmee that goddamn gun!"

Dick lunges. Grabs the barrel and tries to jerk the rifle away, but you hang on with both hands and fight him. He shoves you backward to the floor. Then twists the barrel as you roll in a circle.

"Let go!" orders Dick.

But you won't let go.

The baby is screeching. Ginger is crying, "Daddy, don't!"

You are at an angle directly between Dick's feet when the rifle fires. It's not much of an explosion, a *pop* like a fingerling firecracker under a can, but Dick does a Moses. Drops in a heap so swift he might be a rock.

Ginger shrieks, "Daddy!" . . . Then: "You killed him, Virge!"

The baby is stunned into silence. Ginger takes a step, slumps against the wall, slides down it as if her spine has turned to water.

"What have you done?" you say to the rifle.

Dick moans and you jump and Ginger and the baby scream together.

There is a small hole under Dick's right eyebrow. Blood trickles from another hole at the top of his forehead, where the bullet came out. Ginger reaches over and pushes his shoulder and he moans. She leaps back, then scrambles with Pearl Bell down the stairs. "Don't run away!" you shout. But she's already gone.

You go into your room. Your fingers find the cross on the wall, the suffering god with his suffering head crowned in thorns, his suffering, wounded body, his bleeding heart bleeding for all your sins. You drop the rifle and fling the cross into the wall. No man is an island, but right now you are. Your legs give out and you fall to the floor. Thoughts race beyond tomorrow and you know whatever dreams you once had, whatever scenarios you might have written for your life, none of them will come true now. Jail. The penitentiary.

Faint light burnishes the faintly yellow floor. Twigs scratching like fingernails at the window. Shadows making a pattern that looks like a net. You hear Dick's buckle scouring the floor. The scraping of his shoes.

"Hep . . ." he rasps. "Hep."

"Hunnn?"

"Hep."

You blink but he won't go away.

"Hep," he says.

"Shh-sure," you say. You help him turn over. You rush to put a pillow under his head. You pat his hand.

He squeezes your hand back. Hot tears flood your eyes. "Oh Dad, oh Dad," you say.

There is noise on the stairs. Gramma Nez arrives. Behind her are Ginger and the baby. Gramma Nez looks from you to Dick.

"He shot hisself," you say.

You look at Ginger and she nods to let you know she understands.

Gramma Nez gets on her knees and says, "Son, can you hear me? An ambulance is comin. Hang on." She tells Ginger to call Regina. "Tell her to meet us at the hospital. Move your ass, girl!"

"Meet us at the hospital," Ginger repeats.

She hands Pearl Bell to you and the baby is all smiles and big-eyed winks. You pull her to you like a life raft. You hug her hard and your tears are dark polka dots on the pink baby blanket. Dick is looking nowhere. There are two holes in his head. It was an accident. Or maybe none of this is true.

The War According to V –

Little V,

The CO gave us thirty days leave instead of two weeks. Damn desent of him. Thirty days to kick back and let the war go. Hawaii is the place for it. Although it is similar in some ways to parts of Nam, it is minus the oppressive heat and billions of insects and crawly things that go bump in the night. Minus the smells of war. It smells nice here Bro. It is balmy almost everyday and when it rains the clouds hardly ever stick around very long and the sun comes out and dries the sand and you can sit in the warmth wiggling your toes in the sand and watching the babes in bikinis strolling by showing off what they have for you if you are man enough. So far Rice and I have not been man enough. We talked about our lack of energy the way we just sit and veg. We feel like we are inside a beautiful but fragile dream and might wake any second back in the war. We try to root our feet in the sand so nothing can drag us away. It is a weird feeling being here. I can not explain it. You fly the Freedom Bird out of a country that has gone crazy and you land in one that is sane but you can not process it. Part of me feels real guilty. Its like why me? What am I doing here when my buddies are still there getting shot at wounded killed? How can that kind of thing be going on when there is so much beauty and peace in places like this? Go figure. Well, that is the point actually, no figuring it out. Rice and I agree there will be time enough to sort things out later. Right now we need to rest and recoop. The war may be thousands of miles away now, but it still comes back around midnight when I wake in a sweat not knowing where I am. It takes some seconds to figure out I am safe at Schofield. And when I finally realize it I am so relieved I want to laugh or cry or scream, become a hysterical peacenik screaming HELL NO I WONT GO. Melvin Paine dont come to me as often since I got here, but he does come now and then and he still wont say a word. He shakes his head and stares same as always and I curl up in a little fist and ask him to forgive me. I keep wishing I could have those minutes on the battlefield over. Give me that day back and I promise better. When I relive it in my head I dont freeze up and I get to Paine fast and get the tourniquets on and save his life and win a medal for it. War teaches you how little your dreams count. Well not a dam thing I can do because Paine is dead and I just have to live with that. I sure hate it though, how it leaves you feeling you failed a test and no chance ever to make things right. That moment of truth is over, forget it, you flunked! Do you know what I mean? It probably sounds insane. It is just that I get in these moods and start thinking things that bring me down. Instead, I should be counting my blessings. Count your blessings kid, things could be a lot worse is what Gramma Nez would say. Count your blessings.

Yeah so for the most part I am doing fine and now you have an address to write to and you can fill me in on what is going on over there on the Mainland. That is what they call where you are. They call it the Mainland. I hope everything is fine and that Dick is not kicking your ass to much and the cows are milking heavy, like they usually do when it is crispy cold and no flies plague them. I hope Pappy is better. I feel like I would know it somehow if he was dead. Tell Mom and Ginger hello and that I will see them sometime in August or September. Sorry I missed your birthday, but we could have a party for you when I get there, a late one and it will be like having two birthdays this year. Are you up for it?

There is a lot worth seeing, but the thing impressed me most so far was the Arizona in Pearl Harbor. All those sailors still inside that metal tomb under the water. Rice had a little joke when we were standing there together looking at the monument. He says to me, Do you know how many dead guys are in that ship? And I said, How many dead? And he said, All of them.

How many dead guys? All of them. I had to laugh a little. Not funny if you dont like dark humor. War is filled with dark humor and it is either you laugh or you cry. I will always remember the bubbles coming up through the water. After all these years that ship is still breathing. The ghosts of the dead are still breathing in their tomb waiting for what Waiting for Resurrection of course. There it is.

Big V.

Rolling Thunder

We have stopped the bombing.
We have cut air operations by over 20 percent.
We have announced withdrawal of over 250,000 men.
We have offered to withdraw all of our men if they will withdraw theirs.
The answer of the enemy has been intransigence at the conference table,
belligerence, massive military aggression . . . and stepped-up attacks . . . designed to
increase American casualties.
This attitude has become intolerable. **(Nixon)**

. . . kill ten of my men for every one I kill of yours
. . . even at those odds
you . . . lose . . .
I win. **(Ho Chi Minh)**

Freedom has never been so close to slipping from our grasp **(Reagan).**

We will not withdraw.
We will not withdraw.
(Johnson)

Virgil Francis Foggy

Every morning Virgil checks Minna and Big Mama and Friendly, their hard, round bellies rewarding him occasionally with the feel of a calf kicking inside. He runs his hand over the tendons at the base of their tails, searching to see if their pins are down. He watches for softening, swelling, loosening of their vulvas, the dance of the hind hooves that will indicate labor. Day after day the three cows burn hay and their girths swell. But there are no signs that gestation is over. He milks the herd, singing *very precious girl* to each, tuning it to the sounds of shuffling hooves and the exhaust fans blowing. The music of the barn is part of its atmosphere, like the smell of hay when he pops the twines, spreads it whispering for the cows, and the creamy odor of warm milk pouring into the cooling tank.

After the cows are milked, Virgil runs the barn cleaner, its motor grinding to move tons of manure. Paddling waves of manure toward the chute, its snout thrusting ten feet past the barn into the freezing air outside. Lumps of steaming manure pile up. The chain, the paddles continuing round the nose gear, the paddles marching back into the trenches, like obedient soldiers. Day after day the same reflex, the endless cycle of chores he does without thinking.

One March morning, he comes in from chores and finds his uncle sitting in front of the TV watching Sesame Street. A huge yellow goose is teaching him the concepts *winter, spring, summer, fall.* "Not this kind of fall," says the bird as it falls on its tail, "but the fall that is full of colorful leaves and Indian Summer weather." Animated leaves blow across the screen. Dick's many wrinkles look like knife wounds. His eyes might as well be pebbles stuck in his face. He doesn't blink as he stares at the bird. In his hand is a cup of coffee. A cigarette between two fingers. Veins curve from his knuckles to his wrist. He has gotten jowly and his hair is flecked with white along the sides. His sideburns are white. Long strings of hair slicked back on top are thinner than ever. Two scars shine on his forehead, two dime-sized dots two inches apart where the bullet went in and where it came out. There are liver pouches beneath his eyes. He hunches like an old man melting into his center. He resembles Pappy sort of.

"So, you're finally home?" Virgil says.

The head turns slowly. Lightless sockets, no heat in his stare, no measuring or caring. "Yeah," he says, his voice deep, but sluggish. He sips coffee. Drags smoke into his lungs. Goes back to watching the yellow bird.

Virgil looks at his mother. She shakes her head, puts her finger to her lips and motions him to come to the kitchen. The two of them lean on the counter.

"Yeah," they hear Dick say again.

"Doctor says he's healed as much as he'll ever heal," she whispers.

"He looks bad. He looks sicker than Pappy."

"Do you know what a lobotomy is?" She is rubbing her forehead, looking like she wants sympathy, as if what's happened to Dick has also happened to her.

Virgil answers, "Lobotomies make you cretin."

"A piece of his brain was seared by the bullet," Regina says. "The bullet cut a path through his frontal lobe. The bullet grazed it, you see?" She zips her finger up her forehead. "Like that. When such a thing happens it changes your personality. It calms you down. If you're a violent person it cures you. Or maybe you're depressed and suicidal. It cures that too. Understand?"

"Sure, the bullet give him a lobotomy."

"He won't be the old dragon we used to know. He's a sort of, umm—"

"A peacenik," Virgil offers, checking him out, the peaceful lump of his uncle's head and shoulders. Smoke lingering over him a peaceful crown as well.

"Not happy, but not unhappy neither," says Regina. "Look at him, you'll see nuthin's buggin him. He's completely indifferent. It's a little unnervin."

The TV shows winter icicles hanging from a roof. The bird compares them with stalactites in a cave. "Look at the resemblance. Isn't it wonderful! You can count on nature to always do it the same way every time, because nature has rules that must be obeyed."

No more predator? No more hands-on-training? No more bellowing? No more size thirteens pounding up the stairs, turning your guts to water? No more Dick on a rampage? Dick defeated?

"Naw."

"Believe it or not." Her voice is soft. Her eyes swimming side to side. A nervous smile playing with her mouth. Virgil knows she's glad this happened. Everyone knows she's having an affair with Lawyer Menton. Now people will understand and feel sorry for her. Feel sorry for Dick too, of course, but not as much as for Regina who will have a useless man in the house.

"Will he be useless?"

"He doesn't have to be. He can work. He can do what you tell him to do. At rehab they made him mop and wax floors and carry out trash. Maybe he'll help you? Just take him to the barn and see what happens?"

"Neh, no way. He'll snap out of it," says Virgil.

"I don't think so," she says.

"Well, if it really is true, there's no way he'll stand trial."

"Salty says they can't try him in his condition."

"Does Gin know about all this?"

"She believes he'll snap out of it."

"Gramma Nez? What does she think?"

"She says it's a mercy he won't torment us or himself anymore. You know her. You reap what you sow and count your blessings, things could be worse and it's all part of Vishnu's dream or some god's inscrutable plan."

"She's never liked him much." Virgil thinks of what Dick said about never having his mother's love. *If your mother can't love you, who can?* What if he woke to that again? What if he woke? "He might someway remember what happened and that would be bad, Regina. He would want revenge."

"Why would he want revenge?" she asks. "Revenge for what?" It occurs to him that his mother still doesn't know the truth about that night and he has let something slip. "He might, I don't know. Who knows what he thinks?"

"The doctor said he won't remember what happened. The brain shuts down on traumas if they're bad enough. He doesn't care how he used to be, so what he is now can't hurt him. We can be grateful for that." Her eyes probe, as if she's looking for a window into his mind.

"If there's something—"

"Like what?"

"It was an accident. He was getting ready to go huntin."

"That's right."

"You said he was gettin the gun ready to hunt in the mornin."

"That's right."

Her eyes click back and forth.

"It's true," Virgil says. "Ask Gin."

"It wasn't a suicide attempt?" she says.

Does she really want the truth? If she knew everything what good would it do her? For years the truth was plain enough. But she couldn't (or wouldn't) see it.

"You should see your face, Virgil. What are you thinkin?" says Regina.

He forms a speech. He opens his mouth.

Her eyes grow large as if she knows you are going to say something bad. And you recall a show you had seen once on television, where a macho man suspected he had cancer and he kept calling it the Big C, his big, bad enemy, and he bragged how he would fight it. Said he was a fighter to the bitter end and he wasn't afraid, not him. When the doctor found out that, yes, the man did have cancer and he truly was going to die, the doctor went into the room to tell him. But when he saw the terror in the tough man's eyes, he couldn't give him the truth. The doctor lied and the man who was dying of cancer, who had six months, grabbed the lie and left the hospital. The grateful love of a lie is necessary the Hindu sage has said. Without our illusions we go crazy. Only the truly enlightened can cope with reality. The rest of us need tricks. We need lobotomies.

She waits for him to tell her. Fear in her eyes. She doesn't want to know. And he knows people are like that in their heart of hearts. He shuts his mouth. He swallows hard.

"Never mind," Virgil says. "It don't matter."

"What don't matter?"

"Nuthin. I better get goin. I got work."

A day later a blizzard hits. It snows non-stop for two days. The wind howls. Snow piles so high against the barn Virgil has to dig a pathway downward to the door. Snow patters the windows like insane bees. The wind makes the house shudder as if something bad is trying to break in. It is late for such a storm. No one remembers one like it so close to April. Gramma Nez says, "Maybe it's an omen."

When the storm blows over, a rolling vapor crosses the land, the wind breathing ice fog freezing eyebrows and nostril hair. Turning cheeks hard and bright. The land shrinking, the trees shriveling, the hungry birds flying in frantic paces from bough to eave to frozen earth. Some die like curling leaves embedded in the snow.

The sparrows that survive line up on the roof of the barn and watch him pile steaming manure outside. Politely they wait until he's done.

Then they land and pick out bits of undigested hayseed and corn. Bonnie on his shoulder watches them. The coming of the birds excites her.

Brothers! Sisters!

She joins them and starts pecking. When they fly off, she flies with them.

"Bonnie!" he yells. "Hey!"

He believes she will return by dark but she doesn't. Around the panes, the wind seeps through, its freezing breath on his face filling him with fear. Hours pass as he watches for the little brown bird. The air smells of leaf mold, old straw, and bird droppings in the sill. Virgil keeps the light burning. Frozen twigs tattoo the panes. The TV drones downstairs. The furnace hums. The bird doesn't come.

Then there's this—what her loss foreshadows, the unthinkable something on which illusion won't work: A phone call comes and the family is told that Vernon Joseph Foggy is dead. On March 28, 1970 he drowned in Oahu, Hawaii. An Army officer has written a letter to explain. The letter should arrive in a few days. Vernon's death was a freak accident, the man on the phone tells Regina, one chance in a million, but there it is.

The War Without V –

3 April 1970

Mrs. Regina Perpetua Foggy
Route #2,
Elk River, Minnesota
My dear Mrs. Foggy,

This letter, in behalf of the Command and fellow United States Army soldiers who knew your son, Vernon Joseph FOGGY, RA 16738852, Specialist E-4, USA, is to extend to you our sincere condolences over his untimely and tragic loss. Additionally, I desire to inform you of the circumstances under which he was lost and to offer my assistance to you should you feel a need for further information or explanation of official procedures.

I know that you want to know more of what happened; therefore, I shall discuss the incident from personal knowledge of it. However, as is required in all cases of accidental death to a serviceman, the death of your son is subject to a thorough official investigation in which all known facts will be determined and reported to the Judge Advocate General, Army Department, Washington 25, D.C.

As you know, your son was part of a small cadre of young soldiers who had been tested to determine their fitness to be trained as officers at the Officers Candidate School (OCS), Fort Benning, Georgia. Your son had already passed all of his tests with flying colors. There was every indication that he was psychologically and physically prepared for OCS. It was only a matter of days before he would have been transferred to Fort Benning to begin his training. To a man, we all believed that Specialist Foggy would become an outstanding officer in the service of the Army and his country.

While here in Oahu, he and a friend whom he had served with in Vietnam were vacationing for thirty days before proceeding to Georgia and OCS. On the day the accident happened, they rented a jeep and started to tour the island of Oahu. As you may know, Oahu is a beautiful place, characterized by its volcanic origin with lush mountainous terrain, magnificent beaches, and rugged shorelines created by lava flows.

Vernon and his friend, Sergeant Charles Leon RICE, RA

195289254, drove to the end of State Highway 90 westward along the coast, then onto a jeep trail continuation of the road for several hundred yards to an isolated spot near the water. They walked down an embankment to a wide lava formation, the edge of which formed a sharp drop of about 15 feet to a small lava shelf near water level. It was a little after four o'clock, 28 March 1970, Honolulu time.

RICE described the incident as follows: Your son decided to take a picture of waves breaking against the steep rocky edges of a small cove adjacent to the spot on which he was standing. The force of the water was driving turbulent surf into the cove and into the mouth of a cave, which was partially submerged at the head of the cove. This would have required him to turn with his back to the sea, as he stood at the edge of the lava formation. A wave hit and sent spray over the two men, causing Vernon's friend to start back, thinking Vernon was coming along. RICE heard another wave hit, turned around and Vernon was gone. He ran to the edge of the formation, where he saw Vernon down on the lava shelf near the water level. RICE said that Vernon's back appeared to have been scratched somewhat in the fall, but he didn't appear seriously injured and he called to RICE. Another wave came in before Vernon could get off the ledge and it washed him into the sea. RICE couldn't find Vernon after that, so he ran back up the hill, drove several miles and notified police, who alerted the rescue organization. A policeman returned with him to aid in the search until rescue teams arrived. Two fishermen with whom Vernon and RICE had spoken earlier, had come over to help. One of them heard a call from the cave. RICE called and Vernon answered. They told him that help was on the way.

RICE started to lower himself on a rope into the water at the mouth of the cave, but he was restrained by the others, who realized that such an effort in those waters was suicidal. Specially trained rescue teams from the police department and the Hawaiian Armed Services Police came with inflatable rafts, line, lights, breathing apparatus, an electronic megaphone, medical supplies, and other equipment. Most of these men are volunteers, highly motivated and very experienced through the frequent need for their assistance in the treacherous waters around the island. They were well organized, operating under the direction of experts. They had an Air Force helicopter on the scene also, in the hope that Vernon could be gotten into deeper water away from shore where the calmer sea would permit a helicopter pick-up. They tried desperately to get assistance to the cave, but the severe turbulence of the water as it smashed into the sides of the cove ruined every attempt.

Vernon evidently had either been washed into the cave by the force of the water or, finding himself unable to cope with the turbulence, he may have taken refuge back into the cave, where the water was calmer. He could not be seen, but he continued to wait for aid, answering calls now and then for several hours. Meanwhile, the rescue parties lowered one member on ropes. They intended to keep him from being dashed against the rocks by the water. This man, a marine sergeant, was caught by the waves and had to be pulled back ashore before he got to the cave entrance. They lowered a life raft with the intention of floating it into the cave, but it was smashed into the rugged wall and punctured. They got metal tanks and tried to float these into the cave, but the waves tore them to pieces. As darkness fell, they lighted the area and continued trying, hoping that as low tide came (around 11:30 P.M.) the waves would be less forceful.

I know it must be difficult for you to realize how the efforts failed under such resourceful direction. I went to see for myself and I felt the same utter despair that these brave men felt. I had thought that a diver might be able to go underwater where it would be more calm and swim into the cave. When I saw the situation, it became obvious that this was not possible. The cove was full of jagged rocks under the surface; the water was not over 12 or 15 feet deep and about 40 feet across at the cliff face, narrowing toward the cave. The force of tons of water in the waves was hard to imagine, but the situation was clear as I watched those waves pounding up and down the cove.

It is not known when Vernon died. The rough waters prevented the recovery for two days as the teams relieved each other with little rest, grief-stricken, but trying their best.

As you may realize, such an event gains wide publicity. I regret that public notice of the incident was beyond our control. It is policy to try to provide the next of kin the courtesy of official notification and to withhold names, addresses or any details until this has been done. If you learned from the news stations on the mainland of the tragic events unfolding, I can only say I sincerely regret the terrible shock it must have caused you. It is terrible enough that a mother must lose her brave son in the way that you lost yours, but the manner of finding out about the loss can be, I believe, almost as devastating when it comes through the media, rather than through a sympathetic phone call or letter. I do believe, however, that the newsmen reported the incident as accurately as they could, always in good taste. I am enclosing clippings of these reports so that you may realize the heartfelt sympathy with which thousands of people here followed the tragic story; there was an editorial for you to read which expressed this well. The news photographs will enable you to see the circumstances more clearly than I have described them.

Vernon's officers and fellow soldiers started a fund for a suitable wreath from his company. The money was wired to me this morning. However, the amount is considerably above that which would be required for flowers or a wreath. Since we are so far away and we do not know your plans, I have been asked to send the enclosed check in the hope that it may help in some way. They also asked me to express their deep sympathy for your loss. The United States Army has lost an outstanding and very brave soldier. Believe me your son was known for his courage in battle and his loyalty to his friends, his unit, the Army and his beloved country. The inexplicable manner of his death is not lost on any of us who have learned of your son's experiences during this past year in Vietnam. We have discussed how he went out on patrol after patrol and saw death and destruction almost daily. But then to be in relative safety at a barracks in Hawaii, only to be drowned in "paradise," so to speak, is an irony almost too poignant and heartbreaking to bear.

You may wish to make further inquiries, so I've given addresses where possible. The Catholic chaplain on base is planning a memorial service. I have asked him to write you after it has been held. The Army's Casualty Assistance Calls Officer nearest your home should be able to provide you with complete technical assistance and aid you in many ways. Should you see the need for further information or desire to contact me, please write and I shall be pleased to respond.

I convey my sincere personal sorrow.

Yours truly,
Angus C. O'Neal,
Captain, United States Army,
Company B, Second Brigade
Schofield Barracks, Oahu, Hawaii

P.S.- I've enclosed a letter found in Vernon's locker. The letter is addressed to Virgil Foggy.

Rolling Thunder

Mr. President:

I realize that it is difficult to communicate meaningfully across the gulf of . . . war.

But precisely because of this gulf, I wanted to take this opportunity to reaffirm in all solemnity my desire to work for a just peace.

I deeply believe that the war . . . has gone on too long and delay in bringing it to an end can benefit no one.

The time has come to move forward at the conference table toward an early resolution of this tragic war.

You will find us forthcoming and open-minded in a common effort to bring the blessings of peace.

Let history record that at this critical juncture both sides turned their face toward peace rather than toward conflict and war.

Sincerely yours,

Richard M. Nixon

[PS] There are powerful reasons I want to end this war.

This week I will have to sign 83 letters to mothers, fathers, wives, and loved ones of men who have given their lives for America.

There is nothing I want more than to see the day come when I do not have to write any of those letters.

Virgil Francis Foggy

The check is for $5,308. The enclosed clippings describe Vernon's hopeless plight inside the cave:

... the savage pounding of the waves and the relentless roaring of the sea, as if it were alive and determined to keep its prey forever.

You learn that hour after hour Vernon had to hold his breath as the water rushed in and submerged the cave. When the water rushed out, *with a sound that was like a sonic boom*, the rescuers could hear Vernon calling to them. There is a side-view sketch of the cave. It looks like a fallen ice cream cone. At the narrow end in back is an ink figure drawing of Vernon slightly smaller than the cave itself.

"How cold it must have been," you say.

"How awful," says Ginger.

"Horrible," says Gramma Nez.

Both of them are weeping, but not Regina, she sits at the table stunned, the letter in her hand. Her eyes staring at Dick, her head shaking as if saying "No, no."

And you're thinking that if you had been there you would have gotten him out. You would have gone down that rope and pulled him out. Or died trying. They might have stopped Rice, but they wouldn't have stopped you, is what you keep thinking. Yes, you would have done it because you love your brother and you know your brother would have done it for you.

It is strange to think that at the moment of his death you were not aware. You should have felt it somewhere in your soul, somehow you should have known. But you didn't. Not a clue.

One of the articles describes Vernon as a fallen soldier on a watery field of battle:

Incredibly, two days later the battling sea was calm and blue and people could see fifteen feet to the bottom. The waves washed languidly in and out of the cave and with their back and forth motions sucked the fallen soldier's body out, spilling it over the edge, where it floated free at last in the calm cove and was easily retrieved. The sea, as the sea always does, had its way with one more brave heart gone out to meet its destiny. One could almost imagine the Valkyries, those collectors of the fallen, reaching down from the sky and taking the young warrior's courageous soul with them home to Valhalla.

"He always said he would live to be a hundred and five," says

282

Ginger. "Twenty years old and he's dead? Is that fair? What's the point of that?"

"A nightmare," murmurs Regina. "I'm havin a nightmare." She sets the letter and the articles and the check down carefully, as if they are fragile. Her finger traces the drawing of the prone figure in the cave.

Dick sits next to her impassively.

Gramma Nez says, "I don't understand how God could let this happen. I've remembered Vernie in my prayers everyday since he left. I've burned a candle and incense for him every week. I give Father Hess donations to say masses to protect him. The *Ching* guaranteed me he would survive. All the gods were on his side."

Pappy looks confused. His head comes off his chest where he has been studying a button, fingering it. His voice sounds timid. "My boys is dead?" he says.

A week later, Vernon is buried in a steel coffin in Elk River Cemetery. At the head of the grave, Father Hess talks about God's inscrutable will, but Virgil doesn't listen very long. He walks away, strolling from one headstone to another, reading familiar inscriptions.

SETH FAIRFIELD FOGGY
1844 - 1862
INDIAN FIGHTER

FERGUS FAIRFIELD FOGGY
1812 – 1863
MARTYR OF INDIAN WAR

IGNATIUS SPEARSON FOGGY
1845 - 1864
DIED FOR HONOR IN GREAT CIVIL WAR

JETHRO PYNCHON FOGGY
1840 – 1886
MAY GOD GIVE JET PEACE

MARY BETH FOGGY
1844 – 1864

BELUV MOTHER BURIED WITH BABY BESS

ELOISE JANE FOGGY
1880 – 1900
SHE DIDNT KNOW HOW TO GET OLD

PEGASUS FOGGY
1900 – 1918
PILOT WWI ETERNAL WINGS

SOMER MARVELL FOGGY
1874 – 1955
NEVER LIKED PEOPLE

PERCY FERGUS FOGGY
1920 - 1950
TOO GOOD FOR THIS WORLD

SETH IGNATIUS FOGGY
1920 - 1954
SILVER STAR HERO WW II

Virgil hears the priest telling the mourners they should—
Cast your cares on the Lord
And he will sustain you;
He will never let the righteous fall.
Returning to the crowd, Virgil stands behind his mother. She is a lump of black on a folding chair. Alma Lando provides a wind block on one side of her. Dick is on the other. Next to Dick is old Johansen leaning on canes and chewing his gums and still refusing to let his cancer kill him. His wife Anna is next to him with her parka hood up, face hidden. Virgil stands next to Ginger. He glances at her. She doesn't wear sunglasses like everyone else. She glares at the priest as if Vernon's death is God's fault. Or maybe she is looking at Peter Raven, back from California and on probation. Or Danny kicking his feet and playing pocket pool. The brothers and their mother are shoulder to shoulder. Mrs. Raven keeps wiping her eyes. Some of Vernon's old baseball team, The Elk River Elks, look mystified. Salty the cop stands tall and sad-eyed in the background.

The two men Virgil saw in the bar, Ed and Carl, are there. Ed's wife clutches his arm. She is wearing a pale blue mini-skirt and a fur jacket. Her shapely legs look impervious to the cold. She keeps glancing at Mrs. Raven, who doesn't seem to know that her husband's ex-lover is there. Case, Gary, Tom T, Rick, Herb, Larry, Chief, Big Al and other regulars at Lando Lakes are in black, their serious faces saying, *This is how you should look at a funeral.* A few feet away from the foot of the coffin stands a detail of riflemen in Class-A uniforms. Their spit-shined boots and insignia gleam in the sun. Near them is Jim Foggy's grave.

JAMES JOSEPH FOGGY
1930 – 1966
TIME THAT WAS SO LONG GROWS SHORT

+

At the reception, the beer keg comes out. On the kitchen table are hams, beef, pork, a turkey, numerous casseroles, vegetables, breads, cakes and pies. Coffee, tea, cider, milk.

Plates clatter. The cold graveside has made the mourners hungry. They heap their plates. There is a lot of talk about what a unique boy Vernon was.

"Do you remember the time he . . ."

"And what about when . . ."

"Wasn't he just . . ."

"You'll never believe how that boy could . . ."

"There was this one day he . . ."

"And what an athlete. He could have gone pro."

Weaving in and out of Vernon's life, Virgil wants to interrupt everyone. He wants people to read the letter Captain O'Neal wrote. Read the articles that were in the Hawaiian newspapers. Everyone should know that Vernon was a very brave warrior. They need to understand that he should have died a hero in combat. Not drowned like some rat in a hole. Don't they think God has some explaining to do? Isn't God on their shit list now? And if not, why not? Virgil wants the mourners to quit talking about a boyhood gone. Be angry for the hard, ugly death Vernon endured. Someone should question the purpose of such vicious deaths. Pointless as Sharon Tate's slaughter. She and her unborn baby and her unlucky friends. Where was God then? Where is He in time of real need?

285

In a corner, Alma Lando and Salty talk to Dick, their manner protective. "Fine," he keeps saying. "Fine." He nibbles from a plate his mother prepared for him. He doesn't smile. He has become a good listener. Father Hess sits on the couch with Regina, patting her knee, murmuring of God's mysterious ways. She looks at the priest as if she doesn't know him or what his words mean.

"It was known from the beginning of time that Vernon would die in 1970, he tells her. All dates are known. It is all part of God's cosmic plan. There are no accidents, my dear. Remember, not a sparrow falls but by His decree. God gave His only Son to a cruel death in order to save the world and prepare Paradise for His followers. We cannot know the purpose for Vernon's death, but we can know this: *If anyone would come after me, he must deny himself and take up his cross and follow me. For whoever wants to save his life will lose it, but whoever loses his life for me will find it.*"

"So true, Father," Ed's sexy-in-blue wife murmurs. Ed keeps running his hand in comforting circles over her back. Her nylons shimmer. It's hard to keep your eyes off her legs. Every movement of her mini-skirt draws male gazes.

"Those who follow God will not taste death," the priest continues, saying it boldly for all to hear. "*For the Son of Man is coming in his Father's glory with his angels, and then he will reward each person according to what he or she has done.* Let the words of Matthew comfort you. Do they comfort you?"

"Amen," says Ed's wife in a choking voice. She wipes her eyes. You would think it was her son who died.

Others in the room echo, "Amen. Amen."

Regina says, "It's so painful. It hurts so much."

Gramma Nez says, "In my grief I haven't remembered how God's ways are not always our ways. I hated God. Forgive me, Father, I have blasphemed."

"We must trust in Him!" cries a woman in the back of the room.

"Those who believe in Him shall not perish," says mini-skirt.

Look at Pappy. He is drinking a brandy martini and staring at the books climbing the wall. His eyes are perplexed as if he's wondering where so many books came from. Rounds of "Amen" follow whatever Father Hess says. Like a sorcerer he slashes crosses in the air, his head surrounded by light burning through the window. He looks so holy. So . . . so sanctified.

"This is fuckin awful," seethes Ginger. She takes Virgil by the hand and leads him to the kitchen. The two of them bolt shots of whiskey. The whiskey makes Virgil nauseous. He sips a cup of beer to induce a burp to get the pressure off.

"A chip off the old block," says Case. His callused hand ruffles Virgil's head affectionately. "Your old man dropped boilermakers like that." Even though Case is dressed in his Sunday best, the scent of alfalfa and cow radiates from him.

Gary, Tom T and the others agree that Jim was a boilermaker man.

"He could hold his liquor," one of them says.

They all salute Virgil with another round. "To Jim's son and Vernon's brother!"

"You're the hope of the future, lad," says Case.

Virgil hears old Johansen saying, "God can take me anytime he likes."

"Well, here's how I see it," says Larry. "The way I see it, Jim has company now."

"Havin a good time, him and Vernie," says Chief.

"If you listen hard, you can hear em laughin their asses off," says Tom T.

"I hear them doin a jig," says Gary, cocking his ear.

"I seen em dancin on the coffin," says Tom T.

"I'm ready anytime God wants me," says old Johansen.

Ginger takes a mug of beer and retreats upstairs. Peter follows her. Danny's eyes follow her with longing.

Catching blurred images of his face in the windowpanes, Virgil wonders if the whiskey and beer have gone that quickly to his head. He's never been drunk. Is this how it feels? There's a sense that nothing matters very much. He finds himself sneering at death. He fastens his gaze greedily on a pair of blond legs falling from a blue mini-skirt. No wonder Wild Bill had to have her. Beside him appear a shaggy head and a shaggy beard. He turns when Big Al catches his arm, pulls him aside and whispers like a conspirator, "One of the symptoms of a nervous breakdown is when *you* see two of *you*." He is pointing at the window.

Virgil counts four Virgils in the windowpanes.

"Compound schizophrenia," Big Al Lando says.

"I want Santa Claus," Virgil asks. "I want him to be real."

Lando nods. "Me too," he says.

287

Virgil says, "My gut feels ishy."

"I have just the thing for upset stomachs. Good for heart conditions too." He touches Virgil's chest.

"Here's to gettin the hell out of this bitched up world, lucky him," says Herb Thyng. He raises his glass.

"God can take me anytime he wants," says old Johansen. He is saying it to a light bulb.

"Away, my good man," says Big Al Lando. "Take care of your wife."

Anna is standing stiff as a totem. Her face is a rainbow of lipstick, mascara, eyeshadow, rouge.

"Get a plate, Anna," orders Johansen. "Over there, right there." When she doesn't move, he says, "Jesus, help her."

"Weawy, weawy, weawy," she sighs.

"Me too," he tells her.

Alma Lando says, "Here I'll help her. I'll fix her a plate."

Big Al and Virgil go upstairs to Vernon's room. The bed is made. A stuffed Holstein toy lies on the pillow. Cotton leaks from its belly, where Vernon as a little boy used to bite it. There are pictures of baseball heroes on the walls, Joe DiMaggio, Lou Gerhig, Mickey Mantle, Roger Maris, Bob Lemon, Sandy Kolfax, and his favorite, Harmon Killebrew. There is a bronze-plated batting trophy on the desk, a picture of the team next to it—Vernon and the Elks. Most of Vernon's clothes still hang in the closet. His Minnesota Twins cap hangs from the closet doorknob.

Big Al Lando thumbs pot into a tiny metal pipe. Lights it. He and Virgil smoke and the room softens. Music comes from Ginger's room, the hard-hammering rhythm of "My Generation." Virgil holds the smoke in his lungs.

"To make the moment bearable," says Big Al. He points at the fog around their heads. "This is all we know about death. Bitter it comes to the young man and too late it comes for the old. It is inevitable, but it always seems long time off. "

"I can't never see my own death," says Virgil.

"No one can. If we could, we'd go stark raving mad." He raps his chest with his fist and coughs. "Arrhythmia," he says.

"You don't think Vernon's in heaven or purgatory, do you, Al?"

"Nor in hell neither. He's nowhere. Other than in Virgil Foggy's heart."

"I ain't cried for my brother, Al."

"Some things too deep for tears, Virgil."

"My dad don't come round no more. Did I tell you that?"

"You don't need him."

"Bonnie flew away. Did I tell you that?"

"She has her own life to live."

"Dick don't know I shot him. Did I tell you that?"

Big Al says, "I'm a retired bartender. Nothing surprises me."

Virgil inhales and the world becomes a harmless blur. He is content for the moment to carry Vernon in his heart.

"This must be what Dick feels now. Everything groovy, nuthin to get bummed about, nuthin to get excited or thrilled or scared or . . ." He searches for words. "He's got the best of it. He's got peace without passion. That bullet was a blessing. But why him, though? Why should he get a break like that?"

"Don't envy a dry well," says Big Al.

Virgil hears an angry voice down the hall. It is Ginger's voice. It takes a moment to register, before he propels his flopping feet towards her room. The door is open.

"Whass up?" he says.

She is shouting at Peter, telling him to get the fuck out.

"Cool it, cool it," he keeps saying. His electric hair looks too big for him, like someone glued a bush to his head. On his vest are peace signs and the word *PSYCHEDELIC* in neon green.

"Out! Out!" she insists.

"Come out, Peter," Virgil says. "Don't bugger Ginger."

Peter turns on him. "Shut it! Shut your hole!"

"He's stupid drunk!" says Ginger.

"Am I buggering you, Ginger?" he says. His heavy brow dips in the middle. He is leering at her, trying to make her smile. "Bugger," he says. "Bugger-bugger-bugger up your other-other-other, heh, heh, heh."

"Out, man," Virgil says calmly.

No fear at all.

"You don't get out, I'll have to toss you out myself." He is in control of the situation. Benevolent and kind and with no personal malice, no hatred, no lust, he will commence beating Peter Raven to a pulp.

"You and what army!" says Danny suddenly appearing.

Danny swings. Connects. A smiling Virgil goes over, banging his head on the floor. "No pain," he says, looking at Danny, then at Peter. "Now I got to use your hairy head for a mop."

Peter starts kicking him. Well Danny yells at Ginger, saying to her, "Why'd you do it to me, Gin? All I ever wanted was to love you."

"Love, my ass," says Ginger.

"Yes! Yeah!" cries Danny.

Virgil is hanging onto Peter's ankles, wrapped around them while Peter bends over and continues to pound him.

Peter is halted finally by Big Al, reaching in, catching Peter by the throat. "No, no!" Al says, lifting him off the floor. "Don't you know whose brother is dead around here? Have some couth, motherfucker." He looks over his shoulder at Virgil. "Shall I break his neck?"

"Ask Gin," says Virgil.

"Let him go," she says.

Peter's eyes are bursting. He can't speak. He flails helplessly. Big Al bangs him against the wall, sets him down. Coughing, his hands feeling his way, Peter stumbles downstairs. Danny follows shouting, "Wish he broke your fuckin neck!"

Virgil rubs the back of his head. Fingers a tender lump there. His right eye is throbbing.

"Are you okay?" says Big Al.

"He didn't lay a glove on me. Too fast for him."

"Nevertheless, you have a nice egg on your cheekbone. Take care of our boy, won't you, Gin? I'll see if I can persuade Peter to go home." Big Al puts a hand on Virgil's head as if bestowing a blessing.

"You're Santa Claus," says Virgil.

And the fat man says, "The thing about pot is it gives a man courage he shouldn't have."

"Santa!" shouts Virgil.

Ginger guides Virgil into the bathroom. She washes his face with a wet cloth. Puts a cold compress on his eye and cheek and holds it there while she says, "Bastard thought he was going to pick up where he left off. Are the Ravens the densest people in the world or what? Treats me like his personal slot, like I'm supposed to be, like, all grateful that he wants me at all."

Virgil replies, "We can shoot him. And Danny too. It's okay. It's a favor to them. Peace passes understandin."

"Virgil, you're high."

"Yes, my love."

She laughs. "Well, it's about time," she says.

Leaning heavily on her, she guides him into his room, rolls him onto the bed.

"Time to milk my girls?"

"Not yet, honey."

"Are you my sister?"

"I don't know." She stares at him. "We don't look a thing alike, do we?"

He closes one eye to steady her. "I have large suspicions," he says.

"Me too."

"Your father in his cups said you weren't his kid."

"I know."

"But I might be your father's kid."

"I know."

"I don't know who I am."

"Me neither."

"But Mom is my mom, right?"

"I think so, yes."

"But you can never be sure of your father, that's the thing."

"It's a promiscuous family."

"Did you and Vern ever?"

She wags her head yes.

"I thought so. He hinted in his letters. I never knew a thing."

"You're like Regina, always in your own little world."

"I never imagined it even. I shoulda heard him sneakin. I shoulda seen it in the way you looked."

She smiles. "You don't want to see what's under your nose. Life is easier that way. When you don't know it, you don't have to deal with it."

"Vernon said that about Mom. Dick said it too. Can't hurt you if you don't know. I'm not like her, am I?"

"I'm afraid you are. Not totally. But in some ways, yeah."

Virgil feels miffed. "Bloody hell, I don't want to. I wanna be like Vernon. Vernon is my hero, he's my . . . my . . ."

"Role model?"

"Role model. I'm goin in the Army. I'm to the war and chase charlie gook."

She laughs. "No you're not. I won't allow it," she says.

He cocks his head in order to see her eyes.

"Yhaaah," she says, stretching Minnesota vowels to the breaking point, "It's me. You betcha. You love me a little, little Bro?"

A song from her radio keeps muffled time on the walls—

Tommy, can't you hear me . . .

Virgil feels detached. He feels he's floating. He has felt this way since the news about his brother, but he is even more disconnected now.

Ginger says, "There's all this mystery to our lives. Everybody hidin things." She breathes awhile. Then she says, "I suppose it don't matter."

"I'd like to know who I am," Virgil says, feeling unclaimed.

"Sex," she says softly. "I'm givin it up for Lent."

"Artificially breed a few cows, it turns you right off the whole thing," Virgil tells her.

"To hell with boys," she says.

"To hell with girls."

She laughs raggedly, brushes a hand through Virgil's hair. "You smell like whiskey and pot," she says.

"You smell like beer," he says.

The door opens. Alma stands there smiling.

"Watcha lookin at?" Ginger says. "Don't you have any manners to knock before you enter a room?"

"I was lookin for the bathroom."

"Next door down," Ginger tells her.

"You okay, Virgil?" asks Alma.

"I'm good."

"I wanted to say I'm sorry about Vernon. I'm so sorry, Virgil."

"Me too, Alma."

"If you ever want to talk or . . . or somethin . . ."

"I'll call," he says.

"Promise?"

"Yeah."

Alma vanishes.

Virgil looks at Ginger. She is laughing soundlessly. "She was comin for you, Virgil."

"Naw."

"She's hot for you."

"Alma's way too old for me. She's Dick's girl."

"She told me she thinks you're cute."

"She never said that."

"You are gettin cute," she says. "Scars or no scars."

He looks at the wall, the Story knife hanging there. "Sometimes I get why he cut his throat."

"What?"

"Old Fergus. Why he cut his throat. It was the only way to make up for what he done. Sometimes there's no way to atone."

"He didn't do anything wrong, Virgil. He just sharpened the Indians' knives. He didn't know what they was up to."

"I spose. But still, how could you stand livin with it? Your knives stabbin innocent people. Your blades killing them. It's a point of honor to kill yourself. Japanese kill themselves for honor."

Ginger flounces off the bed. Goes to the door. "You always think too hard," she says.

He sees her with the shotgun in her hands. Danny running naked in the woods.

"You should talk," he says.

"What?"

"Nuthin," he says, "I got cows to milk."

"You act like you're married to those goddamn cows," she says. Her head is wagging, brows curving as if something hurts, mouth crumpled in . . . is it sorrow?

She leaves. A moment later the volume goes up on—*crystal blue persuasion.*

He takes the knife from the wall. Goes to the mirror, holds the blade to his throat like he imagines Fergus did. He still feels high, but not sweetly so.

"You're a fake," he says. "Mr. Coward Virgil." He hangs the knife back on the wall. "Soon enough. Soon enough," he says. "What if I live fifty more years, what's that in the overall scheme? Ask Vernon. Vernon knows."

From the bottom of the stairs Gramma Nez calls, "Virgil! Virgil, you up there?"

"Here!"

"Time for chores."

"Right down!"

He takes his brother's last letter from the stack in the first drawer. It's an old letter, written months ago. Reading the letter, he understands why Vernon didn't mail it.

293

The War According to V –

Little V,

    This last patrol I went on was hairy. We found a big fucking tunnel and I went inside and I felt those walls around me crushing me like I was in my grave. I always hated that feeling, like my lungs are collapsing. But I kept going and I found the place full of rice and dried fish and cans of fresh water and stuff like that. I planted charges and blew it up. Nam is a maze of tunnels and caves. Maybe I told you this? Some are huge and will house a whole company. Some are just storage depots. I think about the little fellow I almost killed at that pond and I bet a dollar he dropped into a hole in the ground. I wonder if he will survive this war. I hope so. How many of them and how many of us will be around next year or the year after that or in twenty or thirty years to talk about what we did in the war? I killed men, women and children Virge. And dogs and cattle and hysterical chickens. The women and children accidently on purpose I killed. I told you once that I thought you could cut the numbers in half on the news reports on TV, but nope. It is generally known that we don't report all of US killed. The Brass believes everyone back home would freak out. Fact is I have seen to many coffins laid out who are US inside getting transported back and they could easily fill a football field every week. And that is just in my tiny corner of the war. No Bro there are thousands of us dying over here. I mean tens of thousands! Best figure we get from those who know is that we are over 46,000 dead Americans now. And there are twice that many thousands who are dead VC and NVA and civilians. A million maybe. Where do they get all these guys? You keep thinking they will run out of fighters but nope. They keep coming and coming like the north has an eternal supply. And in the middle of it are the peasants just trying to make a living one way or another. If civilians wander in our way accidently we kill them because we don't know who they are. No taking chances on who is good guy or bad guy. You just cant tell the difference. Madding it drives you crazy. I feel like my heart is covered with black spots, every spot a dead human I murdered. How did I ever come to this? The boy who cried over dead cows is now a stone killer as indifferent to death as nature itself.

    Okay I confess. This is what will put me in hell. We torched a village and this woman comes running out of a paddy and she is pointing at the fires and screaming something no one understands and then we get it that a baby is in one of the huts. We run to it and knock the fire down but it is to late. The baby is roasted. It looks like a charred turkey with its legs pulled up. We are always suppose to check inside before we fire the huts, but obviously no one did. There was a dead puppy with it. Lots of puppies and babies die over here. Lots of dying of all ages going on and they tell us we are saving the world from communism. But days like yesterday I believe in nothing but survival. Whatever it takes I do it. If it means babies die, then better them babies than me or my buddies. You can guess what I am coming to. We drove the whole village into ditches and killed them all. Then we moved on not feeling a thing, no sadness, nothing. So what if they are dead? We all die someday. You know, this business never going to change. Never going to end. There it is Bro.

V. Forever Foggy

Rolling Thunder

*We live in an age of anarchy . . . small nations . . . find themselves under attack from
within and from without.
We will not be humiliated.*
    We will not be defeated.
    It is not our power but our will and character that is being tested .
    If when the chips are down the world's most powerful nation . . .
acts like a pitiful, helpless giant, the forces of . . .
anarchy will threaten free nations . . .
throughout the world. **(Nixon)**

    You know, it's easy to get into war. It's tougher to get out of it.
    (Johnson)

    I gave my dead dick for John Wayne.
    (Disabled Vet Ron Kovic)

The World According to . . .

The Chinook winds came and spring ended what had seemed an eternal season of ice and snow. Virgil went into the fields. Using the disk, he pulverized corn stubble and dirt clods and a winter's worth of manure. He smoothed the peaty earth into harrowed swirls. Planted corn in straight rows. Aerated the pasture.

With their confinement over, the herd was let out of the barn. Some of them, the younger ones, went nuts and ran like overgrown children back and forth over the grass. They bawled and butted, kicked up their heels. A few of them, as if by magic turned into males, mounted their sisters. The grownups looked on with disapproval at the antics of the young. The old ones kept their dignity and went off in groups to crop sweet new tufts of timothy.

Along the pasture's southern peninsula, the trees lining the Crow were thick with leaves now. In the afternoon the herd gathered in the shade of those leaves. They would sleep, chew cud, stare lazily into space. The rush of the river was soothing. It seemed to be saying:

We'll live forever like this, won't we?

 DUFF BRENNA is the author of nine books, including *The Book of Mamie*, which won the AWP Award for Best Novel; *The Holy Book of the Beard*, named "an underground classic" by *The New York Times*; *Too Cool*, a *New York Times* Noteworthy Book; *The Altar of the Body*, given the Editors Prize Favorite Book of the Year Award, South Florida *Sun-Sentinel*, and also received a San Diego Writers Association Award for Best Novel 2002. He is the recipient of a National Endowment for the Arts award, *Milwaukee Magazine*'s Best Short Story of the Year Award, and a Pushcart Prize Honorable Mention. His work has been translated into six languages. His memoir, *Murdering the Mom*, was published by Wordcraft of Oregon, June 2012.